I0562831

BATTLE FOR THREE REALMS
Clovel Sword Chronicles: Book 2

BY GORDON BREWER

CLOVEL SWORD CHRONICLES SERIES
SHIELD OF SKOOL (BOOK 1)
BATTLE FOR THREE REALMS (BOOK 2)
DOWNFALL OF THE GODS (BOOK 3)
CLOVEL SWORD CHRONICLES: OMNIBUS EDITION

PARANORMAL AND FANTASY
BEOWULF: CURSE OF THE DREYGURS
INFINITE LOOP
THE CURSE OF BLACKBANE

RAY IRISH OCCULT MYSTERY
A SHOT OF IRISH
(Ray Irish Occult Mystery)
DIE IF YOU WANT PRAISE
(Ray Irish Mystery Occult Book 2)
DRINK WITH THE DEVIL AT MIDNIGHT
(Ray Irish Occult Mystery Book 3)

NOVELLAS
CLOVEL SWORD SAGA: Volumes 1 - 2
SKELETONS OF NILGAVA: Clovel Sword Saga 3
DEATH STALKS THE RUNWAY: Ray Irish Mystery Case File #1
DEATH STALKS THE RUNWAY: Ray Irish Mystery Case File #1

BATTLE FOR THREE REALMS
Clovel Sword Chronicles: Book 2

GORDON BREWER

Thorn Bishop Press
2020

Text Copyright © 2019 Shannon G Brewer

All rights reserved. This book or any portion thereof may not be reproduced or used in any manner whatsoever without the express written permission of the author except for the use of brief quotations in a book review or scholarly journal.

This book is a work of fiction. Any references to historical events, people, or real places are used fictitiously. All characters in this book are products of the author's imagination, and any resemblance to actual persons, living or dead, is entirely coincidental.

Second Edition

Thorn Bishop Press

Cover Illustration Art © Dusan Kostic | Dreamstime.com

Cover Illustration Design: https://www.fiverr.com/oliviaprodesign ©Gordon Brewer

ISBN: 1-945590-17-3

ISBN-13: 978-1-945590-17-7

Visit the series website at

www.gordonbrewer.com

Dedication

To my son Teige, who decided I needed to finish writing this story, which I started some 20 years before. A special, and profound thanks to my wife who told me I needed a hobby and who spent long hours helping edit this work.

Contents

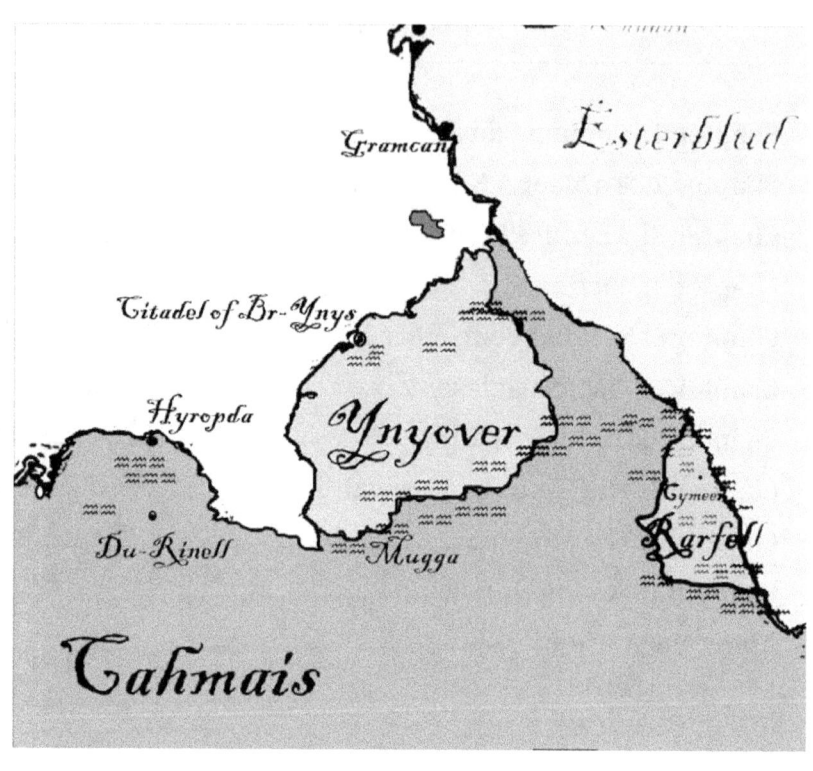

Chapter 1: Coming Storm

Hidden in the foliage that covered the shoreline, a scar-faced man watched the merchant *cuggle* silhouetted on the horizon. His yellow teeth showed when he smiled. He was pleased with the sight of the crew taking up their sails after they dropped anchor. The small ship would remain for the night to make repairs to its storm-damaged sails. The thin man thanked the gods as he looked overhead; his face wrinkled a bit as he calculated the tide and timing of the twin moons which would be rising over Kamin that night. While the timing was not perfect, he figured there would be enough darkness to hide their small boats as they rowed out to the ship. The poor fools on the merchant ship would never understand what happened until knives slit their throats. His master would be pleased, and he licked his lips at the thought of the cargo.

Perhaps enough to pay for better heathmead and females, he thought.

Backing out of sight, he carefully retraced the path to the ossane. The long-necked animal looked up from its meal of blue-green grass, its elongated head showing no fear as it went back to chewing. The man stroked the beast's neck of soft fur while he took the reins, his nose still wrinkled at the smell given off by the animal. But he was a man of the sea, still not comfortable with the mount he climbed upon. After adjusting himself in the stiff saddle made of *erba* leather, his soft whistled tune soon came from his lips. It was the bandit's song. He carefully steered the beast onto the path leading to the village of Casab.

~~~

Securely anchored in the bay, sailors scurried down from the masts of the low-slung ship called *Shackle*. During the long trip from Cahmais, powerful winds along with violent waves tossed the ship until they finally broke away from the continued series of storms. Late in the day, the bearded captain, named Jirla, found a suitable spot where ordered his men to anchor their ship off the island. It was near the coast of Vulthnal which made his short temper even worse. Slightly shorter than many of his men, Jirla enjoyed barking orders at his sailors while he stood with his hands on his hips. Watching over his men from near the cabin of his paying passengers, he wore gray canvas breeches and red wool shirt. While his clothing was the same as his men, he also sported a wide-brimmed blue hat made of highland wool. It was a symbol of authority over the rest who wore simple canvas skull caps. The captain paid no attention to the passengers exiting from out of the cramped confines of their quarters.

Ducking his head to avoid the low doorway, Urith walked to rail followed by his nephew, Oslaf. Similar in size, the two large Esterblud warriors enjoyed the refreshing breeze. They were joined by their companions, Mivraa and Fedelm. Like the men, the women relished their release from the stinking confines of the small cabin. Mivraa, in particular, hated the cramped confinement on the ship. As demigoddess of Haligulf, the female warrior was accustomed to the open sky within the realms of the gods. She felt this self-imposed isolation on the ocean must keenly. Fedelm, on the other hand, hardly noticed the ship's daily activities. Since the loss of her father who was ruthlessly killed at Du-Rinell at the command of the Sacred Overlord, she remained aloof and unusually quiet.

The warmth of the afternoon sun they felt through their clothes was a welcome change from the damp cold which permeated their bodies since their hasty escape from the temperate climate of the southlands.

While on deck, the small group tried to avoid the sailor's activity as the men dashed by them. On the other side of the blue-tinged wood platform, several men worked to restring the clew lines. A few others remained aloft, high on the dark brown mast, pulling up new ropes for the standing rigging. At one point, Oslaf had offered his help. Urith's nephew was an Esterblud and, like his uncle, well versed on sailing the Maflow Sea. The captain looked at him suspiciously before telling him that a land peasant would just get in their way.

Oslaf immediately dropped the subject.

The foursome stayed on deck as long as they could while gazing at the island's shoreline. The sun's last rays created a purple haze that spread over the ship. As they finally turned to head back to their small cabin, they heard the captain barking orders to the cabin boy to light oil lamps at either end of the vessel. The boy scrambled to complete the task before feeling the wrath of his captain's backhand.

Urith walked over to the captain who was yelling orders near the wheelhouse.

"When do you expect we'll make landfall in Damicia?" He asked.

The little captain eyed him, insulted that a mere servant would approach him so brazenly. Dressed in the gray tunics of retainers, Urith along with his nephew tried to maintain the intended facade of being attendants to the women they accompanied.

"We'll be there when we get there!" Jirla stiffly told Urith.

He pushed past the Esterblud, going directly to the women and telling them he expected it would be another three mornings before they reached their destination. He boosted his ship would soon deliver them to the great city along the coast of Eernicia. The women nodded politely while they continued to watch the final glimpse of the sunset. Dressed in fine linens which bore brilliant colors of blue and green, Fedelm and Mivraa strategically maintained their aloofness. Their manner coldly dismissed the captain.

After a long pause, the master of the ship stomped off, his pudgy face revealing his distaste about his arrogant passengers. He cursed at the cabin boy who was standing too close to him. Jirla gave the boy a cuff across the back of his head as he walked by.

Following their narrow escape from Cahmais, the travelers remained vigilant about keeping their identities secret. Caution remained paramount since they were wanted by the Sacred Overlord as well as his ally, King Asgurd of Cahmais.

Fedelm glanced at Mivraa, whose profile adorned many of the temples in Kamin. While the sailors might eye the pretty women's figures, they were notorious for keeping out of the temples. Disguised as Eernicia nobles, the women understood that the men of the ship would expect them to remain aloof.

Urith and Oslaf's green Esterblud tunics, chain mail, and swords along with the fearsome Shield of Skool remained safely concealed inside the cabin. The sailors, like their captain, came from the lands of Vulthnal which meant they were unlikely to know about the travelers. However, if the clothing was discovered, the travelers could expect questions. The crew of the merchant ship was carrying the most hunted people in the Kamin world.

Fedelm heard Urith grunt behind her, and she tapped Mivraa's arm.

"Our servant tells us that it's time to return to our cabin," she told her. Mivraa nodded before turning to give Urith a slight smile. She enjoyed the image of Urith acting her servant. Although the Esterblud seldom acted that way, as a demigoddess, she expected deferential treatment from humans.

When they re-entered their cabin again, Urith stood by the closed door. He listened carefully for footsteps outside to make sure no sailor decided to eavesdrop on their conversations. Since he used the Shield of

Skool to destroy most of the Aberffraw army at Du-Rinell, he maintained an almost paranoid attention to his surroundings. He believed it was his burden to watch over his friends. Since he first met the women in the lands of Ynyover, Urith developed a strong bond with them along with a healthy respect for their capabilities. Mivraa and her demigod powers helped them to overcome several situations which would have killed Urith and his nephew. And Fedelm's hakra visions provided them with insights into the future. As much as it might pain his male pride, both women were far more valuable than he could have imaged before they met.

While he watched his companions find their usual places in the cabin, Urith wondered when Fedelm's visions would return. Her dreams only held restful sleep for her as the ship rolled in the waves. Yet, they relied upon Fedelm to provide them with guidance to reach the next piece of the Skool. Nothing she told them recently gave them hints or clues. And there were others seeking the ancient weapon of the gods. People who nearly killed them before.

Fedelm sat on the hard wooden bunk that served as a bed when they laid out their blankets. She began tearing long strips of cloth from one linen shirt she still carried from her past life in the Citadel. She tried not to remember her time in blissful ignorance in the company of the Sacred Overlord. At the same time, she sought to ignore Oslaf who sat on a small bench across from her. The young man kept looking at woman while he tried to think of something to say. However, the woman remained focused on her work.

"What are you doing?" Oslaf finally asked as the words nearly tripped out of his mouth. Fedelm gave a slight sigh and looked up.

"Getting ready for when we land. You Esterbluds have a great knack for leading us into fights. We will need the extra dressings to cover our wounds." She explained. "I plan on getting herbs and remedies when we land to make sure we have a full bag. You never know what might be coming."

Despite the wit in her tone, there was no humor in her eyes. During her time with the men, Fedelm learned quickly how the sword, ax and spear cut through flesh. Each person within the cabin carried scars from their recent travel. However, some like Fedelm carried their scars on the inside as well. Since leaving her sheltered life in among the *satgerts,* as the priests were called, Fedelm discovered the vicious ways of humans

4

and gods.

Convinced no one was listening into their cabin, Urith moved away from the door to sit next to Mivraa. The two lovers spoke quietly about their trip, talking about anything they could think of while avoiding discussion of the gods or the underworld. While he could not show his affection for the demigoddess outside the cabin, the closeness they felt for each other became quite evident. It was a display that bothered Fedelm, but she really could not understand why. She tried to ignore it while she found things to do. Oslaf forced himself to pay no attention to his uncle and the goddess, trying to tell himself it did not bother him. Instead, he took refuge in fantasies about Fedelm when he caught glances of her green eyes and her slightly freckled face. However, her continued aloofness grew tiresome, and Oslaf felt left out of the group.

Isolated within the little world of their ship, their forced confinement in the cabin for so much long had grated on their nerves at times. Originally, they came together as a group seeking different things in the land of Ynyover. Forced into an alliance by the actions of others, each person became familiar with the habits and peculiarities of their comrades. However, the comfort of that familiarity was juxtaposed with the overlying tension with the enormous burdens thrust upon them.

As Urith listened to his nephew and Fedelm, he leaned back to think about their trip just to reach the ship.

The Skool became the quest for Urith and his friends by the work of the Fates. They found the first piece which attached to his shield. While incomplete, the Skool held the immense power of the gods, capable of destroying whole armies. Urith used the power against the Aberffraw army. As the pieces were discovered, the stories told the Skool would eventually achieve the power to destroy the realms.

Urith felt like he supported the weight of the gods on his large frame. Trained as a warrior for his homeland of Esterblud, Urith carried a reputation as the Clovel Destroyer. He now followed a path far removed from his training. He bore the Shield of Skool on his back.

Yet, the largest burden him was the question of his ultimate objective. Each day, they sought to understand the puzzle left to them. To what ends would this god weapon he carried help the human race? Or was this entire journey nothing but a joke perpetrated by the Fates upon those who inhabited the Kamin world. No seer appeared to know the answer.

They barely escaped capture by the Cahmais king's guards who discovered them in Uugaraa. While their ship traveled to the kingdom of Eernicia, they knew little beyond their planned travel to the village of Ffestini. The plan was to give offerings at the temple in Fedelm's ancestral home in remembrance of her father, Caestias. Consistent with her Eernician spiritual beliefs, Fedelm believed her father's spirit flew among the Sky Realm to help the warriors who filled Haligulf, the Hall of the Slain. Despite her mistreatment at the hands of the priests and the gods they followed, Fedelm continued to believe the Sky Realm gods would guide them to the next piece of the Skool. It would be a fitting commemoration of her father if she provided Urith the means to destroy those who chased them. In particular, she sought revenge against the man who killed her father, Lyncus, the son of King Asgurd.

"Not sure if I can take another night here. I was tempted to swim across to that island," Urith spoke aloud, tired of the quiet in the cabin. He used the Aberffraw language, continuing his activities as a simple peasant as he stretched his massive arms.

"I see you still want to pretend you are from Cahmais," Mivraa teased him, speaking in his native Esterblud. "I think I'll have my servant bring me breakfast in the morning."

She was content to be with him and she enjoyed the warrior's attention. While Mivraa was loath to admit it, she had fallen for the human. She knew the tales of Urith long before she found him in the lands of Ynyover. Over the seasons, she met the spirits of the dead which followed his battles. His reputation as the Clovel Destroyer fit him. However, his good nature, intelligence, and focus upon honor showed through during their time together.

While only a human, Urith proved himself worthy to be her companion. He could even be considered handsome in spite of the long scar that ran across his cheek to his ear, giving him a permanent sneer.

"I'll remember that," His gray eyes twinkled in jest. "Just don't be surprised if you get a bucket of water in bed with it." Mivraa's own hazel eyes flashed a momentary glare, and then she grinned. Few men could survive such a joke with the red-haired woman.

"Anyway, I've spent too much time in this cabin hanging about. We have nothing to do but to try to keep out the water leaking through the quarterdeck above us," Urith told them as he stretched.

Almost as soon as they entered the Maflow Sea, the cuggle encountered sunrise after sunrise of storms and rough seas. At first, they decided the weather was a natural occurrence. However, as the rains continued, Mivraa believed there was something supernatural involved. While she kept it to herself, she felt that her brother god, Uugor, was making his displeasure known. Her unspoken fear was that the boundaries between the realms of humans and the gods was strained to the breaking point. As a warrior goddess, she well understood the intrigues of her half-brother gods. On top of that, she suspected the sea god was looking for Urith and the Skool. Those in the Sky Realm and the underworld wanted the god weapon. Duwdamon, her father, showed great displeasure at her for joining in an alliance with the humans. Mivraa was concerned that she might have gone too far. So she decided she would travel back to the Sky Realm to confer with her father. However, this could only happen when their ship docked. The gateways to the realm of Haligulf existed only from the land at the base of sacred lellowtere trees.

"I need to get on some nice dry soil," the auburn-haired woman sighed as she lay back on the wooden planking of the hull. "Haligulf is home and I don't like leaving the spirits of the warriors to wander the lands seeking their paradise."

She turned to Urith, grabbing his arm. "Not that I can do much about it right now." Mivraa gave an evil grin.

"Anyway, my worthless brother, Wurms, can do the work for once," she said.

During their trip, she made it clear to her giant lover that she despised her stepbrother. Like Mivraa, Wurms could escort the souls of the deserving warriors to Haligulf, although he was quick to avoid any responsibility or the work. He preferred to hide in the shadows of the Sky Realm, spying on the other gods for Duwdamon.

"Well, I hate to break up the fun, but I'm hungry," complained Oslaf. "That cabin boy better come soon."

The others exchanged glances and Urith sighed. They had grown tired of the young warrior's continued grievances about the journey. Urith knew his nephew was feeling left out by his growing closeness with Mivraa. Also, he was aware that Fedelm was not showing him anything beyond friendship which left him visibly frustrated. Urith held sympathy for his nephew's frustration.

Urith stood up, thinking of going to the door again. He too felt much like a caged animal. Then, he heard the familiar footsteps of the cabin boy bringing their food in a small iron pot from the crew's cabin. While they were considered guests of the captain, travelers normally ate the meals with the crew. Using their few remaining koinons, they bribed the captain to have his cabin boy serve them in their cabin. It helped them remain anonymous. Urith watched Oslaf circling around the food, reminding the warrior of greedy bird waiting for scraps.

"Well, it's a start," said Oslaf to the others, his sour mood cleared for the moment. "Hopefully, we can get better food when we get back to land. Soon the Fates will be on our side." He pulled himself up and helped himself before the others came to the small table. As the travelers gathered around, Urith grabbed Oslaf by the shoulder, squeezing hard with his vise-like grip.

"If you continue to complain, I think I'll have the captain drag you behind this boat for a while. That ought to shut you up," Urith told him. While his manner was joking, Urith's hard glance caught his nephew's attention. Oslaf shrugged sourly, resolving to keep his mouth shut for the rest of the night. He could never be sure whether his uncle would actually carry out such threats.

~~~

It was near morning when the twin moons of Kamin dropped from sight, leaving an inky darkness across the water. Three small boats silently approached the cuggle. With only a small thump from the padded bow and edge of the vessels, dark figures dressed in black quickly crawled up the side of the hull and slipped quietly onto the deck. One barefoot man sped across the bridge, climbing up to the quarterdeck. Other raiders scurried across the dark, open parts of the ship taking up positions outside the crew quarters. The barefoot assassin on the bridge peaked over at the helm where he saw a sleeping watchman with his back to him. Two steps later the man in black ensured the watchman never woke again, leaving the body to die silently from a slit throat. Other marauders, dressed in black, entered the crews' quarters while two more entered the cabin of the captain.

Urith awoke to the muffled sounds coming outside the cabin. An uneasy feeling crept over him, and Urith quickly pulled his Clovel Sword from the scabbard. Rising quietly from the bunk under Oslaf, he crept to the door. He put his ear to the wood where he could hear the muffled, weak sound of struggling. Urith slipped out of the door; his padded undergarments appeared gray in the dim light coming from a few oil

8

lanterns strategically placed on the ship's rails. Then, he saw several dark forms entering the crew cabin. He moved out of the shadows from under the quarterdeck.

Urith felt the blows as two men slammed into his back, sending him sprawling down face first on the deck. Urith hung on to his sword, trying to roll away while one of the men grabbed at his legs. The other man stabbed at the giant warrior with a dagger, digging into his side. However, the thin-bladed weapon failed to cut through the padded layers of flax fiber the Esterblud wore. Urith slammed his elbow into the man's head, causing the assassin to roll away. While Urith tried to pull himself away from the man who had his arms locked around his legs, he saw the attacker coming at him again. This time, he swung up his sword into the throat of the man holding the dagger. Blood spurted across Urith while the man groaned and fell aside. The Esterblud slammed his sword pommel into the man holding his legs. As he pulled away, he didn't hear the soft footsteps while he got to his feet. A hard blow to the back of the head sent Urith into a black pool of unconsciousness.

When Urith came out of the blackness, his head throbbed. He was lying face down on the hard deck, near the open hold of the ship. His hands were bound at the wrists behind his back. Urith struggled to look around. He found his nephew lying face down next to him. Oslaf was unconscious and bound as well.

Footsteps came up from behind him, and Urith was pulled to his feet. Two robed figures, their heads covered by their hoods, dragged him along the deck while he scrambled to get his feet under him. They passed by two men who dumped at sailor's body over the side of the ship, mocking the unfortunate man as fish food.

The lamp lights in front of the captain's quarters revealed Fedelm and Mivraa on their knees surrounded by a group of bandits. Relieved they were still alive, Urith grew angry as the bandits roughly tied the woman's hand behind their backs.

A short man with a barrel like a chest stepped out of the captain's cabin door. Urith was forced to his knees, and he glared up at the bandit leader who smiled at him. The man was dressed in a long black tunic with its hood pulled back showing his dark hair. A red sash that wrapped around his waist several times held a single, large Regiussan battle ax.

"You should thank Uugor for your lives," he said in broken Esterblud, his eyes deadly cold. "It seems your women must be of some importance.

That was the intent of your disguises, eh?"

Urith said nothing as he glanced over at Mivraa, who, like Fedelm, wore simple white linen bedclothes. The demigoddess was missing her black shawl which meant the raiders had gotten to her before she could change her appearance or retrieve her spear from within the enchanted cloak. The bandit leader kicked Urith to get his attention. The warrior turned back with a growl. Even in the thin veil of white moonlight that mixed with the yellow lantern light from the quarterdeck, Urith could see the markings of the wavy *S* scar visible on the man's cheek. The bandit leader carried the brand of a sea raider, at some point captured because of his violent life.

Too bad someone didn't kill him before!

"Nothing to say have you? Well, we can beat it out of you, but I don't think I will need to." The short man spoke in Esterblud as he walked over to Fedelm, putting his hand on her head and stroking her golden hair.

"These women wear the delicate garments of wealth. Yet, they lie to me. They tried to tell us that you and the young one are humble peasants, helping them on their travels back to Eernicia." The man stepped behind the women. Urith noticed Fedelm's frightened expression when the leader placed his hand on her shoulder.

"However, my fighters found the Esterblud armor and the symbols and colors of the *Geniht*, King Penhda's personal guard inside your cabin," the bandit leader said. "I've seen those colors before when they invaded our lands here. I personally killed an old savage who came before me in those colors."

When he finished his words, the man savagely struck Mivraa across her face with the back of his hand, knocking her to her side. Urith immediately jumped to his feet, charging at the sea raider leader. He only took a step before the two men behind him slammed their sword pummels into his back. Urith fell hard on the deck of the ship. He looked up to see Mivraa shake her head at him, her eyes telling him to do nothing.

"Thulmare doesn't like those who lie," he told Urith. Then, he slapped Fedelm with a backhand as well. The girl glared back at him; her expression filled with hate. Urith could only watch the abuse of the women while he remained silent.

"You see I've heard a tale of Esterblud rogues wanted by their own King Penhda," Thulmare told them. "Then again, my men and I have heard stories from the skalds about a disfigured Esterblud warrior. It is said you brought dishonor and blasphemy to the holy sites in Cahmais. Normally, we would generally welcome such a person and honor them with a huge banquet." He laughed heartily at his joke, and some of his men joined in. Then he stopped. "It appears you have a great price on your head, large enough to make overlords of my kinsmen and me. The great Thulmare should send you back to this Sacred Overlord called Satres." His men murmured agreement with their bandit chief and his wisdom.

It took all of the Esterblud's self-control to keep from jumping up at the short man. He pulled on the rope binding his wrists in the slim hope he might break free. The action hurt his wrists and helped to steady the rage that surged through him.

"Funny, I've never heard of you, so you and your men are not much of a threat to any overlord," Urith finally spoke up in Esterblud, his voice a deadly low growl. "I've heard tales that the sea lanes along Vulthnal had cowardly sea raiders. If you untie me, I will be happy to remove your head."

The group of men grumbled at his insult, but their leader only smiled, nodding at a man standing behind Urith. The man struck Urith in the back of his head with the handle of his short sword. He went down on his side, shaking his head, but refusing to yell out.

"You have a thick skull," Thulmare observed as he walked over to his prisoner. "It's good for you that I, in my great wisdom, think you have some value. Unlike the worthless crew who now look to the gods as their bodies float in the sea, we will keep you alive. We may return your whole group to those willing to pay. Otherwise, these girls will bring some decent koinon when we sell them as slaves or *dockes* in the port we visit. Men of the ports always enjoy new women." The man squatted down close, playing with a souvenir in his hand. Urith noticed the souvenir in the man's hand was the *Djeed*, the bloodstone amulet given to Urith by his friend, Dughorm. Without the talisman and his Clovel Sword, the Skool Shield was useless.

Before Urith could say anything, the stout bandit chief stood up and walked through his men toward the center of the ship. As strode along, he signaled to his men, and they grabbed the women and Urith. Roughly dragging them over to the edge of the cargo hold, the pirate held them over the darkness below that held the supplies the ship carried. At the edge of the large square hole, the musty odor of the grains wafted up. Two of Thulmare's men dragged the unconscious Olaf to the hatch, throwing him into the darkness below. From the sound of the soft thud, Urith guessed he landed on the bags of *zeam* and *vulgere*, the food stock the ship was carrying.

"Perhaps we will have time to learn more about you and your friends when we arrive at Casab," said Thulmare. "For now, I will let the women keep you company. It would not be wise to let my men have them first. The profit on slaves is reduced after my boys get their turns." The bandits laughed while their leader beamed a great smile. When the bandit leader gave the nod, Urith, Fedelm, and Mivraa were pushed into the darkness below.

~~~

Across the sea within the Citadel of Br-Ynys, the Sacred Overlord was meeting with King Asgurd, the overlord of Cahmais. They sat in the grand banquet hall oblivious to the frantic commotion of servants hustling metal plates of food from the kitchen to the huge table filled with the king's nobles and advisors. Filling out the room was the citadel's eclectic mix of the priests along with their noble families. Coming from across the lands, the satgerts within Br-Ynys provided the central authority on matters of faith and reverence given to the gods. As head of the Citadel, Satres had authority over the temples throughout the lands.

The sounds of wooden plates and full clay mugs striking the wooden table mixed with the loud voices of men who rose to give honors and thanks to their overlords. The two leaders pulled close to toast cups of Aberffraw wine, brought in from Cahmais for the occasion. They were in celebration over their latest agreement.

"I wish upon you a great fortune, my friend," Satres saluted King Asgurd. "Your wisdom and honor will continue to be sung about throughout the lands. May the gods favor your great kingdom!"

"It is well we have come to an agreement that will ensure our mutual needs," the king replied. "I must say I was skeptical at first, but the stories brought to me by my son, Lyncus have swayed my thoughts. We cannot let this weapon of the gods become a tool used by our mutual enemies. The Esterbluds cannot get the Skool."

The old king took a large swig of his wine, waving over a servant for a refill while grabbing another large piece of erba meat. His red face contrasted with his blue garment and his thick neck poked tightly out of the tunic while his gray beard hung down his broad upper chest. The leader of Cahmais had a large belly and an appetite to match. After stuffing his mouth full, he wiped his hand on his tunic, nodding to the nearby servant to fill his cup. Satres sat patiently with his beady eyes scanning the hall, seeking Lyncus, who had yet to arrive.

"I have spies telling me that fool Penhda now claims his favorite warrior, this Urith, is now a traitor to Esterblud," Asgurd told him. "The king of Esterblud turns inside a web of his own creation." The king drew in close to the Sacred Overlord. "No doubt Penhda is waiting on this Urith to return with the Skool. Now, have you and my son come up with a plan to rid us of these Esterbluds and bring the god's weapon to us?"

Satres smelled the foul breath from the old man's rotting teeth, but his thin face remained a mask. He nodded his head as he caught sight of Lyncus pushing through the line of people as he entered the hall. While the king's son no longer had his leg in the crude cast, he still walked with a pronounced limp. Lyncus lost in his first encounter against Urith in Ynyover, and he blamed the man for his handicap. Dressed in a blue robe, the second son of Asgurd appeared upset as he approached.

"Yes, my lord," Satres told Asgurd. "Your son is working quite closely with me on this. As a liaison between our lands, he is unmatched." Satres waved the Aberffraw noble over to the open chair next to the king. "I'm sure he has more to share about our plans."

Lyncus arrived, bowing as he greeted his father, his blonde hair fell over his broad shoulders when he rose. King Asgurd noticed Lyncus' long face as his son scowled at the cup of wine given to him. He took a sip before speaking, calculating that his father was sufficiently drunk and happy in his indulgence.

"My lord, I'm sorry to say I don't have any better news," Lyncus told the king. "The Esterbluds appear to have escaped the port of Uugaraa. They were trapped by the city guards, but they managed to avoid capture after they burned down the food stock warehouse. The latest news from my messenger claims the guards wounded them, and they are still searching the area."

"Are you going there, my son?" asked Asgurd, his eyes staring at a young, brown-haired servant girl who brought them large loaves of split bread.

Lyncus shook his head.

"No, I have reason to believe they left the city on a ship. They cannot remain there, and a ship left on the night tide to Eernicia," he said. "I believe they are going to the port of Damicia. I understand the traitor called Caestia and his daughter came from Eernicia. It is my belief these *wafaoils* must be going to Esterblud through Eernicia."

He looked over to his father as the bearded man's attention remained on the girl. "Yes, that is not good," the distracted king told him. "It would seem you need to catch up with them. This confounded weapon must not get to King Penhda. Yet, our friend, Satres, has good news for you. It comes as part of our agreement."

Lyncus glanced at Satres, who smiled back as he held up his cup slightly.

"Yes, I have excellent news for our young friend," the Sacred Overlord stated. "I've persuaded our *fealharan* friends to join you in our search for the Esterbluds and that docke who claims to be a demigoddess."

The king laughed Mivraa being called a whore, his deep voice carried over the din. He jokingly reminded the Sacred Overlord that he should watch out if the goddess got wind of such disrespect.

"Mivraa might decide to place his head as a trophy on the steps of the Citadel," he told Satres who smiled broadly, offering no apologies.

"Our priests believe the gods of the Sky Realm have even less respect for her," he replied.

Satres glanced over at the quiet Lyncus, realizing he took the news of the fealharan badly. Satres understood the reason. The feared death creepers were specialized assassins and they were not in the young warrior's plans. While they would be a perfect group to take out the small band they were hunting, Sates surprised his young friend with the news. Although the assassins failed to kill Urith during their first encounter, they would have another opportunity. Plus, they took orders from those paying their fees, and the Sacred Overlord made sure this payment came from his treasury. It was a masterstroke designed to capture the Skool, kill the Esterblud, and keep the weapon from ending up in the hands of a filthy king who sat next to him. King Asgurd and Lyncus remained the leaders of the Aberffraw tribe which dominated Cahmais and, by extension, Ynyover. He knew he could not trust Lyncus to return this powerful weapon to Ynyover, despite their nightly intimacy. The death creepers would be Satres' assurance against any treachery by his friend while keeping control of the situation.

"Of course, you will have full authority over these mercenaries, just as your father required," Satres told Lyncus, keeping his voice sympathetic. "The king felt it wise to keep Cahmais from becoming too well known in the foreign lands you will be heading to. I must say that I agree with such a decision."

The son of Asgurd raised his cup to his father, then the Sacred Overlord. "I drink to your wisdom," he said while thinking just the opposite. He knew the fealharans were suggested by Satres. Such a plan was far too devious for his father.

Well, two can play this game.

Lyncus turned to his father.

"My lord, perhaps we should allow Tuncel to join in this important work?" he suggested. "His judgment is second to only yours, and I could use such wise council within the foreign lands of Eernicia. His work there as our envoy to their king could be useful."

The Overlord of Cahmais immediately turned his gaze away from the serving girl to his son. He brightened at the thought of his children working together. While surprising given their differing ambitions, he quickly agreed.

"Lyncus, you make a bold and wise suggestion," the king told him. "Tuncel would be a great value to your work there. I shall have a scroll sent along. Go with my blessing."

Lyncus held his cup aloft and nodded his thanks. He could not miss the change in Satres' expression despite the overlord's attempt to suppress it. It gave him satisfaction to know he was learning the ways of Satres. No doubt he would hear more when they would meet later. He smiled as he wondered what his brother might say if he knew the son of King Asgurd would be busy in bed with Satres while his father kept company with a serving wench. He was aware that his earnest older brother had little stomach for the web of intrigue and deceit needed to achieve power within Cahmais. That was the reason Tuncel went to Eernicia. And now, King Asgurd just delivered his crown to Lyncus without a clue. Lyncus took another sip of the warming wine and shifted his attention to the merriment going on around him.

~~~

The next morning, on the docks just outside of the harbor town of Casab, the sea bandits dragged up their unfortunate prisoners from the hold of the merchant cuggle. Dumped to the deck amid the sound of laughter from the bandit crew, the men whistled at the sight of the two women while cascading crude remarks concerning their fate. Urith struggled to his feet, only to be stomped back down by a man called Vitmus who enjoyed strutting around like his captain. The dark-skinned man was loyal second in command to Thulmare, barking out orders to the rest of the crew. He wore a long shirt of blue, gray canvas pants, and no shoes like many of the raiders. The prisoners noticed that none of the original ship's crew remained. All were killed, and their bodies were thrown overboard before the pirates sailed to the nearby port.

"Keep your face down, you stupid rangifer," Vitmus spit out the words as he stamped his foot on Urith's head to humiliate him. "Thulmare will lead our slaves ashore. He enjoys the crowds of our adopted home."

After the bandit removed his foot, the Esterblud glanced up. It was hard to see his face under the wide-brimmed leather hat he used for protection from the sun. But the warrior recognized the S mark on the man's face, the same mark as his leader. Around his waist was Urith's belt along with the bloodstone talisman hanging from it. Thulmare had given the spoils of the battle to his loyal crony. Urith spate at him, receiving a swift kick in the face for his trouble.

Thulmare walked on deck to view his prisoners. The new captain of the *Shackle* wore the blue wool hat of the dead predecessor. The hat was adorned with the feather of a black *krill* stuck in the band in pure sea raider custom. Hanging from Thulmare's leather waistband was the Clovel Sword, inside its leather scabbard. The short man let the sword scabbard drag on the deck as he walked up to his captives with a wicked gleam in his eye.

"Today you will learn your fate, Esterblud warriors. You will be taken to the cages in the public square for display. Since the Sacred Overlord offers many *koinons* for you, I told my men that we will see who pays more, your king or this man called Satres for your hides," he explained. Thulmare turned, then he stopped.

"By the way, I decided your females will be sold to the slave traders who operate from this port. Pretty young women are their specialty." He walked away.

"Take them," Thulmare commanded his crew.

The bandits swarmed the prisoners, forcing them to their feet. They led the prisoners down the gangplank where a small army of gawking merchants, traders, and other bandits lined the path. The crowd inspected the merchandise whenever a new ship entered the Vulthnal harbor. The Esterblud warriors stood head tall over most of the people, causing gasps from a few who scurried into the shacks nearby. Soon more onlookers came out to witness the spectacle. The crowd noise mixed with a few hawkers who offered pints of heathmead the sailors as they went into the village of Casab. A dumpy looking bearded man wearing a trader tunic stepped next to the female prisoners. He unexpectedly groped their breasts and butts as he made a large offer to Thulmare for their services. Urith smiled when Mivraa head-butted the foul man. A chorus of hoots and laughs swept through the crowd. The man sped away with a bloody nose while the captives were led into a public square where they were presented to a small group of town leaders waiting for them.

"Welcome, Thulmare. Again, you bring us great tribute," said a middle-aged man wearing the purple robes of the *mear* or town leader. The man was perspiring in the chilly morning. Thulmare stepped forward with a few of his men while the town elders backed away, bowing in respect. While the territory of the township was ostensibly under the control of the weak Vulthnal overlord named Barcal, the sea raiders ruled over much of the coastline. Through the use of threats and bribes to local officials, the marauders ran the ports and kept stolen goods flowing into the kingdom.

"Yes, we return to our home with a good haul," Thulmare told his audience. "During our celebration, your merchants will be allowed to make their bids for our merchandise. Put these prisoners in your cages. Keep the two large ones together since they are not for sale. The women will be sold when we find a suitable offer.

The town elders quickly sent over a group of four guards, each armed with short swords and padded leather armor. They marched the prisoners in front of several small iron cages near the public square. Oslaf attempted to kick out as the guards pushed him into the large square cell of banded iron. One of the Casab guards struck him with the flat of his sword, enraging Urith, who barreled into the surprised man. Despite the fact his hands remained tightly bound behind him; he rammed his shoulder into the guard. It took two villagers to help along with the other guards restrain Urith. They pummeled him with sticks and the pommels of their swords. Finally, they pushed the two warriors into the cage. The cage was barely wide enough for one of them, and they could not stand.

As they tried to find a way to sit, the men watched as Mivraa and Fedelm were thrown into separate, smaller cages nearby. The crowd pressed in closer to look at the new trophies of Thulmare. Dirty-faced children stared at them from outside the bars while the people talked about their fate. A man reached into the cage of Fedelm, trying to pull her robe away. He received a savage bite from her for his effort, much to the delight of the crowd. It was an unfortunate world where captured humans were sold to others.

Thulmare and a few of his men pushed their way through the crowd to gloat about their prisoners while the crowd listened to the bloodthirsty tales of the pirates killing the crew. Having reassured himself that his prisoners were trapped, the stout bandit grabbed a nearby woman. Dressed in a long light blue robe and wearing the yellow girdle of a *docke* around her waist, the tall blonde woman laughed lightly as he led her off to the mead hall to be his companion for the night. While such practice was frowned upon by those who ran the temples, as long as the koinons flowed, the people who wore the yellow belt would provide whatever pleasure the money holder wanted.

Vitmus stood nearby, staring at Mivraa with an evil grin under his broad hat. She watched him turn away, heading to the tavern. Mivraa spat in his direction, vowing to remove that foul grin from the human's face. However, her shawl was gone, and even her muscular strength would not move the iron bars that held her. Fortunately, none of the outlaws and those in the town recognized her. While the bandits might fear the gods, they resented any thoughts of the warrior code. Capturing the goddess of Haligulf would be a great prize for these men who would not easily let go of her. Even at the risk of Duwdamon, her father's wrath, the bandits would become a showpiece for their cruelty. Mivraa recognized the Sky God would never come down to save her. Despite their powers, the gods seldom protected their human offspring, considering it unworthy of their position. Unprotected by her powerful family, the woman's best hope was becoming an unrecognized slave like Fedelm. At least, if she were sold to a trader, Mivraa would have an opportunity to escape.

After a while, the crowd quietly dispersed. The villagers had grown bored with the captives who continued to look down, apparently paying little attention to the events outside their cages. As the shadows of a nearby tree moved over the cages of Fedelm and Mivraa, they remained quiet.

"Urith, what are we going to do?" whispered Oslaf, his face perspiring from the discomfort of his position in the cage. "We can't go back to Ynyover; Satres will kill us. They are saying that our king calls us traitors. How can we explain to Penhda?"

"Our king had no choice but to call us rogues after we landed on that beach outside of the Citadel of Br-Ynys. But as we knew already, he sent us on a mission to die or be captured. This Thulmare is quite bright. He's playing both sides to get the best price," Urith quietly spoke, trying to adjust his body to relieve the pressure on his leg muscles which were cramping up.

"I think the Sacred Overlord got the word out among his messengers and *satgerts*. No doubt he put a bounty on our heads after we nearly killed him at Du-Rinell. The bounty on us spread the word quickly," Urith said. "I'm willing to bet that's how the guards back a Cahmais nearly got us. Thulmare knew about us when he saw our tunics and weapons in the cabin. For the moment, we're fortunate that they must keep us alive for the money."

"What about Fedelm and Mivraa?" Oslaf asked.

"I'm not sure," Urith told him. It appears their fate will not be with us. I doubt Penhda will try to outbid Satres. It would be better for him to let us die at the hands of the Sacred Overlord. We are pawns to his plans, whatever they are." He suddenly growled out in anger. "But I'm not playing as a pawn anymore. We have our own path now. We have to survive to return to our home with the Skool in hand. That will be our future." Urith tried to sound convincing at the words, but he was unsure where the Fates were leading them.

Oslaf grew quiet at his uncle's words. There was little comfort in them, but the talking kept their attention away from the cramped confines for the moment. He concentrated on trying to loosen his wrists, still bound behind him by a thin rope. However, it was a fruitless endeavor given the knots tied by pirates.

"The locks on these cages will be too stout for us to break without something to force it and we have no weapons," Urith told him as he looked over the cage again. It appeared no one was watching them now.

"Mivraa, how about you and Fedelm?" He raised his voice slightly. "Can you try the locks on your cage?"

Mivraa shook her head. "No, I can't get my hands free yet, so we're locked tight as well. We will have to think of something else. Do you know where the Skool is?" She asked.

"I think I know," Fedelm spoke up. "I saw men carrying weapons from the cuggles into that shack by the dock. You can see a guard still in front of the building."

Urith looked over where she indicated. "I noticed that little sea bandit has my sword and the one called Vitmus has my talisman," he replied "From the sounds in the mead hall, I'm guessing that those pirates are getting quite drunk. That could be an advantage for us later."

They grew quiet, thinking about their situation. Each person tried to disregard their imprisoned discomfort. They searched for a way to escape. Urith remembered the words of Dughorm, his mentor who died at the hands of Satres. His mind kept coming back to the Djeed talisman.

"The words of the gods, engraved upon the sword, have great influence through vessels of stone."

The old man's words kept popping up into his thoughts, and he focused upon the engravings on his sword to distract himself from the heat of the afternoon and cramps of his muscles caused by his confinement. When his mind struggled to focus, Urith turned his attention to his thoughts about how he would make Thulmare pay. As a Geniht of his king, Urith took his easy capture at the hands of the thugs very personally. To emphasize his need for vengeance, he struck at the cage his head in frustration. The others looked up, and a nearby villager turned his gaze at the noise. Urith growled out a curse in Esterblud to the man who sped up his pace, looking ashamed.

Listening to the loud voices that arose on occasion from inside the mead hall, the prisoners gradually realized the pirated goods from the ship were being sold by the bandits in some type of sale. Since their cage was closer to the building, Fedelm and Mivraa could hear more about the exchanges and bartering. Then, they overheard someone say that the slave girls would be sold off the next morning. When Mivraa relayed that information to the Esterbluds, Urith cursed the sea raiders and spat in the direction of the hall. He watched as a few traders slunk out of the ramshackle mead hall, talking among themselves about their collection of goods they would resell as they went up the coast. The merchants called out to several young boys standing nearby, instructing them to round up extra hands to begin unloading the stores and cargo from the stolen cuggle.

After the sun finally set in the eastern sky, the sounds coming from the nearby tavern started to change. The voices filled the air with laughter, cursing, and general mayhem as the sailors and townspeople enjoyed the full flow of heathmead. The tavern keeper came out of the hall to light two of the oil lanterns on either side of his door. The lamps cast a pale yellow light only a few steps away from the entrance, leaving the nearby prisoners in the shadows of the night. When opened the thick door to re-enter, the captives could fully hear the depraved songs in tribute to the sea raider's god they called Kriell. The song immediately caught Mivraa's interest. The ancient god's name was taboo in the realm of her father, the sky god. It was a name never uttered by humans under pain of death by the kings and their *satgerts*. The sea bandits were using the song as a direct affront to Uugor, her brother, and god of the oceans.

"What are you thinking?" Fedelm recognized the focused expression on Mivraa's face.

"I am listening to the song," Mivraa said. "I know the realms are in upheaval, but those humans are singing praise to an old god cast out to the Great Void. It might be nothing but it's strange they speak of the ancient god like he has returned to help them in their evil ways."

Mivraa wanted to say more, but she returned to release herself from the tied rope. With a grunt of pain, Mivraa finally freed one bloody hand. She heard the door to the mead hall open with several sea raiders falling out into the dirt street. All but one staggered to their feet with drunken laughter and stumbled into the darkness, their voices fading as they moved down the street toward the ship. The solitary figure stumbled back to the doorway, pulling down an oil lamp and he turned toward the prisoner cages. As he got closer, they could see the broad-brimmed hat of Vitmus as he staggered toward them. He stopped at the box holding Urith and Oslaf, thrusting out his large silver mug. It was stolen loot, far too expensive for everyday use in a tavern.

"It is unfortunate you missed our celebration, Esterblud spawn," the pirate said, using their native language with a thick Regiussan accent. "I drink to the koinons you will bring us. Thulmare has sent word to the Sacred Overlord and your king about your capture. So we wait and celebrate."

After taking a melodramatic swig from the jug, he spat the heathmead into the cage, covering the Esterbluds. Laughing as he walked over to the cage holding Fedelm, delighting in her attempt to back away to the far side of the cube.

"Fear not little one, I'll have you later," he told her before he turned to Mivraa. "No, I want this redhead under me first. Solid and well built, our leader believes you will sell for a good price. Not as much as we will get for the little blonde girl, of course, but you are fair and will breed well."

He staggered over to the cage holding the demigoddess, leaning over to peer in at her as he held the lantern close.

"Yes, you look mighty tasty," he told her. "I will have you before you are sold. Perhaps, if you are good to me, I'll outbid the rest to make you my little bed slave."

"You worthless *pitshog*, may the gods turn you into a *cruicad*," growled out Urith. He hoped Mivraa would strike the drunk with some power he did not know about.

The drunken sea raider placed the lantern and his mug on the top of the cage, oblivious to the curse words Urith threw at him. He pulled an elaborate key from a bag hanging from his belt and unlocked the cage, putting the key back in the bag.

"Now, you Esterblud scum, I do this for your entertainment." Vitmus swung open the cage door as he drew the long bladed dagger from his belt.

"Come here slave," he commanded. Mivraa pushed to the back of the cage, appearing terrified of the long, shiny blade. Her hands remained behind her.

"Ok, you make me come inside," he wagged his dagger at her. "This is not what your new master wants. You are very bad. So, I'll make sure you are taught what rough means."

He knelt down and carefully crawled into the cage on his hands and knees, his sinister grin filled with excitement. He kept staring at the terrified woman as he drew close. Then, he saw the iris of the woman's eyes suddenly grow black with fury. Before he could react, Mivraa grabbed the man's wrist holding the dagger, while she kicked out with her foot into his stomach. She kicked him twice in the groin while savagely twisting his wrist. Vitmus yelped in pain, releasing the dagger. Stunned by the attack, he tried to overpower her as she scrambled for the weapon on the floor of the cage. Unfortunately for the bandit, the demigoddess was faster and stronger. She grabbed the dagger handle with one hand, expertly rolled over on top of his back. Using her free hand, she grabbed the man's hair, pushing him face down into the dirt, then she drove the long blade into the back of his neck. The woman felt him convulse beneath her as he died almost instantly.

"That's what deserve, filthy offspring of a *beorh*," said Mivraa as she spat, immediately wishing she killed the man slowly. Pulling out the dagger and wiping the blade on the back of his shirt, she paused long enough to pull the key from his waistband and crawl out of the cube. Pushing his feet back in, she closed the cage. Hurriedly, she opened the other cage doors, releasing the captives.

"Open your hand," Mivraa instructed Urith after she cut the rope from his wrists. The warrior turned around and he held out his hand, and he felt the rough hand of the demigoddess who placed his amulet in his palm. He draped the cold stone around his neck and gave her a quick peck on the cheek. He thought he could see her blush at the gesture.

"It's good thing that I keep you around," he softly joked as she smiled. She offered the dagger to him, but he declined.

"It's your souvenir," he said before turning to the others. "We need to find the Skool and get the Clovel Sword from Thulmare. Let's start with that guarded building first and get our weapons. Then, we get some revenge."

Urith blew out the oil lamp, leaving it on top of the cage and the group moved through the darkness along the path to the docks. As they approached the building where the weapons were stored, they saw the faint outline of someone sitting in the shadows near the corner of the large shack. Urith motioned to the group for them to stop.

"Stay here," he whispered to his comrades before he crossed the road to come up behind the shack.

Urith slid around the corner and froze when he noticed a guard sitting on a barrel which lined up against the wall. The guard's head was nodding down into his chest as he dozed. Urith came next to the man and quickly wrapped his muscular arm around the guard's neck. They fell to the ground where Urith choked the life out of the pirate. The death struggle was brief and quiet.

He pulled the dead man's sword from the body and searched for a coin bag. After he retrieved the leather bag, Urith smiled to himself. There were spark rocks used for starting fires as well as a few coins in the bag. He moved to the front of the shack and waved the others to join him. The door was unlocked, and he entered, finding an oil lamp just inside the door. He used the spark rocks to light the wick. Urith told Oslaf to keep lookout near the door while they searched for their armor and weapons.

Urith's shield was found first by Mivraa, lying under several other shields. Fedelm noticed the woman pause momentarily when she reached for the god weapon. Instead of picking it up, Mivraa pointed Urith to the shield. Fedelm came next to her, handing Mivraa her mystical shawl, which the demigoddess gratefully took before swinging the black cloth around her shoulders. It fell down her back, and Mivraa pulled out her silver spear from its magical recesses. Despite seeing her use the shawl many times during their journey, the magical clothing still impressed Fedelm.

The Esterblud tunics and chain mail were thrown in the corner along with other weapons dumped there by the sea bandits. Urith decided to take the extra time to put on his armor while he considered his plan to retrieve his Clovel Sword. Mivraa pulled on her leggings while Fedelm put on a sword belt. Fedelm kept glancing over at Urith. She recognized the grim hardness in the warrior's face along with his silence. He was not thinking of escape.

After sliding on his tunic over his large shoulder, Urith put his amulet around his neck. He absently felt for his missing sword. He kept the smaller sword he took from the guard, sliding it into his belt. He swung the Shield of Skool over his back and was turning to leave when Mivraa stepped up to hand him his battleax. She said nothing when their eyes locked for a moment. He simply gave her a grinning death sneer from his disfigured face.

"Do you have a plan?" she asked.

"Not really," he confessed. "I've just decided I've had enough of this place and these people. These thugs deserve a particular spot in the underworld with Caruun. I will see they get there."

"Since when do you play like a god?" Fedelm asked. "The Skool said justice when we found it. Are you the god of justice now?"

"I will be on this night," he told her gruffly as he let Oslaf pass by him.

Urith walked back into the darkness and Mivraa followed him. Fedelm pointed Oslaf to his tunic and chainmail, telling him to hurry as she left the building. Fedelm joined the others by the edge of the road. She overheard part of the whispered argument going on between Mivraa and Urith. He appeared intent on destroying the village with the Skool while Mivraa rejected the idea.

"You'll kill everyone for revenge and your sword. You're better than that!"

Oslaf hurriedly joined them. He handed Urith his black battle helmet which his uncle had forgotten in his haste. He also gave his uncle one of the black robes the sea raiders wore when they attacked the cuggle.

"Mivraa's right. We need to find a way away from this place as well. Using this robe might get us in closer," Oslaf told his uncle who looked at the garment.

"You might have something at that," Urith reluctantly agreed as he thought about Thulmare. He glanced over to Mivraa and Fedelm who were whispering.

"Fedelm gave me an idea," Mivraa suddenly said in hushed voice. "You put on the robes and follow us."

Before Urith had a chance to argue, Mivraa set off with Fedelm toward the mead hall. As the Esterbluds pulled the garments over their tunics, they hurried to catch the women. The loud sounds of drunken raiders still rang from the thin walls as they slipped around the back of the mead hall. They followed the rough wooden walls to a corner where Mivraa stopped to explain.

"We cannot wait too long before they discover we have escaped," she told them, staring at Urith in the thin light. "You can't just run in there destroying everyone with that shield. Instead, I'll use my power to lure Thulmare out to us."

Before anyone could say anything, Mivraa whispered a spell as she drew the shawl up to cover her head, then she let it drop back. In an instant, the tall, muscular woman with auburn hair turned into a seductive woman with long blond hair. She appeared to be a younger sister of Fedelm. The dark fabric turned into a yellow girdle of a *docke* which she wrapped around her waist, indicating her availability for the night.

"As I watched this stinking place, I noticed how the women bring their men out through a side door taking them to that building across the alley," she said. "I'll bring Thulmare and the Clovel Sword into this alley."

Mivraa didn't wait for any discussion while she disappeared around the corner, slipping inside the door at the end of the building. Fedelm whispered she was following her.

"Stay out of sight," she told the Esterbluds. "If anything goes wrong, I'll let you know."

Inside, Mivraa made her way through the crowd. She expertly slipped

25

through the arms of a drunken man as he tried to grab her to sit her on his lap. He was too incoherent to follow her as she pushed through a group of men holding their whores. The room was dusky from the feeble light being given off by the little oil lamps and the smoke from the large hearth in the middle of the chamber. The disguised goddess soon spotted Thulmare. The leader of the pirates was sitting off in a corner at a rough-hewn table with the blonde docke he took with him earlier. He held a large mug in one hand and watched over his crew's antics with the smug reassurance of his control over them. Then, he noticed the new beauty stepping toward him. He gave her a smile, appreciating her assertive glance back at him. He licked his lips when she came to the table. The tall blonde girl sitting next to Thulmare rose defensively.

"It looks like we have another to help entertain us tonight my dear," Thulmare told his companion as he slapped her on the butt.

"She is not of this village," the women said spitefully.

"This is true," said Mivraa as she strolled to the table, moving close to her target, ignoring the girl who stared daggers at her. "I've heard of the great leader named Thulmare, and I came from my small village to meet this person."

"Is that so?" he asked thoughtfully. "You are quite adventuresome coming from a small village. Do I know you? You seem familiar somehow."

"No, you would remember me when I'm through with you for the night," Mivraa declared. "I like those who lead. They're worth far more to me than the weak people who follow them."

She gave the man her best smile while licking her lips, hoping he would accept her lies without further interrogation. The bandit leader gave her an appreciative once over with his gaze, pleased with what he saw. The whore next to Thulmare interrupted their mutual gazes.

"She is not worthy of a great leader like you, my lord. Come with me and let me show you things that only Henther can do for you." The woman tugged at the man's arm. He didn't budge. Instead, his grin broadened.

"I should have you fight each other for my attention," he thought aloud, seriously considering the idea for a moment. Suddenly, he rose from his chair.

"I feel generous. Come, I'll take you both with me," he declared loudly, slamming his large silver mug on the table. He grabbed the

26

disguised Mivraa around the waist, steering her to the back door as he slapped her butt. Henther gave them an evil look, but ran up on the other side of the man, joining them. She smiled evilly at the interloper, vowing the smaller woman would receive nothing from Thulmare in the morning.

The trio pushed through the drunken men who still stood while others of his crew were face down on the few tables. Thulmare pushed through the door into the night with his two women. He let the women guide him along the alley.

In the dim light, a sudden movement caught the bandit's attention, but he had no time to react before Urith slammed into his side, tackling him. They fell to the ground with the stout Regiussan able to roll up onto his feet. He tried to pull the Clovel Sword from its scabbard. However, a painful jolt of energy struck his hand when he grasped the sword. Urith took advantage and slammed his shoulder into him again. Both men fell out of the alleyway between the buildings and into the muddy road that ran along the side of the tavern.

The sudden battle caught the rest of group off guard. The docke next to Mivraa tried to scream for help, but the demigoddess backhanded Henther. Mivraa swiftly changed back to her real appearance. While the prostitute stared in amazement at the transformation, Mivraa whipped out her silver spear from her black shawl. She pointed it at the neck of the girl.

"Another scream and you die," Mivraa whispered, her face grim as she pulled the woman close to watch the fight. Oslaf moved forward to help, but Urith told him to stay out of the fight. Fedelm and Mivraa looked around to see if the noise of the battle would bring the bandits from the nearby buildings. Fortunately, there was no movement by the raiders to join the struggle. The fighting could not be heard over the singing and bellowing inside.

"You will die tonight, Esterblud," the pirate said, then he attacked Urith. The Clovel Sword struck the Shield of Skool, sending sparks into the night sky like shooting stars. The intense light blinded Thulmare for a moment, allowing Urith to swing his battle ax. The pirate anticipated the move and was already moving as he countered the blow with the sword. He repositioned himself for another attack on Urith. Thulmare swung the sword again, cutting through Urith's battle ax handle and sending the ax head flying off into the night. The move convinced Urith that his opponent was fast and strong, a skilled fighter.

When Thulmare swung at him again, Urith used the shield to fend off the stroke, sending more sparks into the night. Urith pulled in close to the Regiussan, grabbing the short sword from his belt. He tried to impale the bandit. However, Thulmare countered as he backed up to give himself some distance from the bigger man in front of him. Both men were breathing heavily now, but Urith held on to the vengeance still pouring through him. He attacked again. His short sword swing was parried by the pirate. However, Thulmare didn't see Urith suddenly bring up the Shield of Skool, using the edge to slam into the enemy's jaw. The action sent the bandit flying back. Urith pressed his attack. This time, his sword found its mark as he struck Thulmare in the groin. The sea raider screamed in agony, taking a wild swing at his opponent again. Urith did not give the man another chance when he deflected the Clovel Sword using his shield. In a well-timed move, Urith jabbed the point of his sword into the man's thick neck. Thulmare gasped in disbelief as he fell on his side into the muck. His hands grabbed at his neck, trying to stop the bleeding.

"Die and tell Caruun how unworthy you are," Urith spate on the bandit leader. Thulmare kicked out desperately, croaking out blood before he finally trembled and gasped out a dying breath. The pirate's open eyes stared at the feet of Urith who picked up his Clovel Sword.

"Now, we can leave," he told the others. Grimly satisfied, Urith leaned over to wipe the bloody sword clean using the dead man's robe. Then, he pulled his belted scabbard from the dead man's waist.

"Do you know how to leave?" a deep voice asked from the shadows. A robed man stepped from the gloom of the building next to the mead hall.

Urith spun around with the cat-like quickness of the vicious *baters* that prowled the highlands. Oslaf was nearly on the stranger before his uncle stopped him with a quick growl. Urith recognized the man he had seen earlier that morning as the town leader.

"I'm here to help," said the man desperately looking at Oslaf's sword pointed at his throat.

Urith stepped toward the man, joined by Fedelm and Mivraa, who still held Henther with her spear pointed menacingly at her face. As they approached, the man shifted his feet nervously, his eyes darting across the dark landscape. While he stood as tall as Mivraa, somehow he appeared smaller despite his large pot belly.

28

"Explain yourself," Urith snorted as he stepped in front of the stranger.

"My name is Dacca, and I was the leader of this village before the sea raiders came," he told them. "I've come to thank you and offer you a way out." The man's nervous eyes darted back and forth at the people surrounding him.

"After our treatment here, how about I just burn this place down?" Urith watched with some pleasure as Dacca nearly choked at his words.

"No, you can't do that," he pleaded. "These are decent people. It was the sea raiders who did this to you."

"No, you and your people are just as involved." It was Fedelm who spoke up now. "I watched your people trade with that scum as the sun filled the sky. Not one of this village came to us to offer water or food. You sit on your fat butt and only come out now to collect the spoils of this Clovel Destroyer's victory."

"I agree with Fedelm," Urith said, smiling at her. "But let us hear what this man has to say before we decide his fate." He turned back to the man. "What are you offering?"

"I've heard of the Clovel Destroyer," he said with his gray beard quivering underneath his thick lips. "You are a fair man. Look, I'm your friend. I have ossanes available along with food and drink. Please accept them as our thanks. You are a hero to the village, but we ask that you leave. The pirates will come after us if you stay."

"Enough with the platitudes," Urith growled. "Show us the ossanes and provisions. You will guide us to prove what you say."

"I'm sure I will have a painful death for you if you are lying to us," Oslaf reminded Dacca who nodded, his face paled at the threat.

The party carefully followed the *mear* through winding back streets, past the dark hutches and small buildings. Despite the silent progress, Oslaf felt the presence of others watching them every move as he followed the potbellied man. Mivraa continued pushing her female prisoner along just behind Oslaf. Fedelm walked next to Urith who kept glancing behind them.

"I don't trust him," Fedelm whispered to him. "Dacca has been just as bad as the others. You were right; we should burn this place down." She didn't see his smile in the darkness.

"You are turning into quite a vengeful person," he told her softly. "I agree we cannot trust him, but he may be telling the truth. I suspect he believe that the sea traders will follow after us when we're gone. Then, he has his village back, and the sea raiders leave him alone for a while. Still, the whole thing feels a little too perfect for an escape."

Dacca stopped them at the outskirts of the village. The foul stench given off by the ossanes across the road identified the nearby building as the home of the ossane trader. The sleeping animals stood in the nearby corral and a small light in the window of the building. A larger building was attached to the shack. Dacca stopped, then looked around carefully. He was about to step out to cross the road when Oslaf grabbed his shoulder.

"I think you and I will go check this out together before the others come across," he told Dacca, then turned to the others.

"I'm going across first, and if this person is telling the truth, I'll signal back," he said.

"Alright, but first, what's in the building next to the trader's home?" Urith asked their guide.

"That's where the village stores our hay and seeds for the crops," Dacca told him, nervously wringing his hands. "The ossanes are fed, and I've already had bags filled with food put on the mounts for your journey. We must hurry."

Oslaf pushed the Dacca into the road as the others waited. Urith watched approvingly as his nephew took charge to scout out the danger. His young protégé was growing up. Watching the two men cross the road before entering the building, he felt himself stop breathing for a moment as he thought a trap was about to spring. Nothing moved in the darkness, and the stillness only intensified his unease. Finally, he saw a large figure waved them forward. After a quick scan of the area, the rest of the group crossed the road and entered the shack.

Oslaf greeted his friends. "They have the mounts for us behind, tied up at the gate. I've checked the ossanes, and everything seems as Dacca tells us."

Inside they found the stable keeper, standing at the back of the room. The room had straw covering the floor. The tall man stunk of ossane and soiled clothes. His stench nearly overpowered them as they gathered closer. Urith noticed Dacca remained behind them along with Henther. The ossane trader stuck his head out the door, holding a lantern before him as he carefully peered into the night, then pulled himself back into the room.

"You should leave now," he told them.

Urith grabbed Dacca and pushed him to the back door.

"Yes, we should leave now," Urith agreed grimly. "Since we don't know who may be waiting out there, I'll have our new friend here lead us to the ossanes." Urith's glare forced the stable keeper open the door for them. Urith shoved Dacca through the opening and into the night. As the man fell forward, landing on his knees. Dacca immediately began yelling out his name while he held up his hands, staring into the darkness. The telltale sound of arrows swished through the darkness, striking the man several times. Arrows struck the shack as well, embedding near the open door. Urith and Mivraa watched as Dacca gave a desperate groan before tumbling to his side.

"Just as I thought," Urith told them. "Hand me that lantern!"

He grabbed the lantern from the stable keeper who knelt, begging for his life.

"When you get outside, head for the mounts," Urith yelled as he pulled the terrified man from the floor and pushed him out the back door, ahead of him. Immediately Urith threw the lantern on the wall of the building. The flames shot up the wall to the thatched roof and across to the other building.

The group quickly scattered, the burning building behind them lit their way. Moving as fast as they could to the mounts tied near the gate, Urith glanced back to see the ossane trader yelling into the darkness for help in putting out the fire. Henther sprinted behind the man; her long legs allowing her to catch up with ossane trader after Mivraa released her.

When they got near the animals, yells came from the nearby line of trees. Several would-be assassins, villagers holding bows, had forgotten about the Esterbluds. They were running toward the burning building.

His blood still boiling at the ambush, Oslaf wanted to take after them. However, before he could go after them, he felt the tug on his arm from Mivraa.

"No time for that now," she told him. "We have to get out of here."

Oslaf and Mivraa reached the ossanes first, moving past the beasts which pranced around nervously at the smell of smoke near them. Urith went to the gate where he slid open the wooden bolt while Mivraa unhooked the mounts from the fence. She passed the reins to Oslaf and Fedelm. The pair climbed onto the beasts and galloped through the gate while Mivraa scrambled up on a dark-colored ossane. She held the reins of the last animal for Urith, who ran over and swung himself into the saddle. They followed their comrades into the night. Entering the dark trail away from the cursed village, Urith glanced back, disappointed that the flames remained only in the one building. He briefly wondered if he should have stayed and burned the entire town to the ground after the double cross he just witnessed.

Chapter 2: To Meet A King

In the Sky Realm high above the mortal world, Duwdamon floated between the temples of his realm. Wearing a white and purple robe, he entered the open home of Sky Realm's Sybil, a human spirit once known as Umcal. As the prophet of the gods, Umcal used his visions for the benefit of the Sky Realm. Passing through the arched door, the sky god appeared mildly perturbed at the inconvenience of bringing a new oracle into the realm. He needed steadiness of Umcal and his counsel to guide him now in such troubled times. For all their formidable powers, the gods of the Sky Realm and the underworld lacked the unique human ability of foresight. The situation forced the gods to turn to the souls of great seers who departed from the human life. However, the spirits of the prophets slowly lost their energy over time. After entering the realm of the gods, Umcal, like all the souls who became Sybils, maintained their foresight abilities for only a limited amount of time compared with the near-immortal gods. The spirit of the Sybil might last many human lifetimes, but eventually, their energy was exhausted along with their prophetic visions. Knowing his time was nearly complete within the Sky Realm, Umcal readied himself to pass on to the Great Void.

Duwdamon expected his demigod daughter, Mivraa, to find a worthwhile spirit to replace Umcal. Her last trip to the realm brought a seer. Yet, the sky god distrusted his daughter. She was a woman warrior who sympathized with the humans. It was a weakness he made no attempt at understanding since they were gods, naturally superior and destined to lead the realms. They were worshiped by the people. It seemed unnatural for a deity to concern themselves with the needs of those wretched creatures who prayed to them.

Entering into the vast circular chamber of Umcal's home, he saw his old seer kneeling at the Exyts Spring basin where the healing waters of the gods flowed. The supernatural force flowing from the otherworldly blue of the sky filled the waters coming from the Mythrol peaks. While the waters would heal the mortal body, it held very limited usefulness to their souls. The gods could use this force to maintain their physical bodies' immortality; the waters only gave Umcal limited time to keep his form visible to the sky god. Soon, the spirit energy would pass into the Great Void where all spirits came and went.

"It is good for you to see me off, great one," Umcal said. His old shriveled form bowed low before his master.

"I'm sorry to see you go," Duwdamon said stiffly, trying to show the human spirit some compassion. "Your visions are needed now, more than ever." His long white and gold hair hung long across his robe. It gave the impression of thoughtful wisdom to someone viewing his human form.

"I'm sorry that my soul is being called away," Umcal said half-heartedly, his form growing translucent from the expenditure of his force.

"Do you approve the new Sibyl?" He asked.

"The spirit is a solid choice, my lord. Unique among the humans since his was both a hakra and warrior as well. His visions and common sense are hard qualities to find in people, a true follower of Heptarc."

Duwdamon scowled briefly at the name before he nodded. "As long as he remembers his place among us, I will see what his visions can provide us."

"Yes, my lord," said the former Sibyl, seeing the nearly transparent form walking toward them. "I see him coming now. I will take my leave."

Duwdamon absently nodded as Dughorm walked before the sky god, bowing and looking up, happily enjoying the sense of sight again. His frail body, tortured to death by Satres, now felt renewed in the spirit form, although the form still bore the marks left during his life.

"My lord, I'm both honored and surprised to see me here," said Dughorm. The soul standing in front of the god showed him in his former body, stooped over from age and warfare. He wore a white robe, similar to the gods who inhabited the realm. Dughorm took a deep breath out of his human habit, thinking he wished had his pipe to smoke.

There were disadvantages to being a spirit, he decided.

"Hopefully, you will not give me cause to regret my actions," Duwdamon sniffed. "Although, I must admit that my daughter's retrieval of you from the underworld gave me enjoyment. Inconveniencing Caruun pleases me much of the time." He gave a grim smile as he floated over to the spring, sitting upon the elaborately engraved white stone bench.

Mivraa rescued Dughorm from his descent into the underworld. It was an action Duwdamon intended to discuss when he saw Caruun again.

"Mind you, his action against you for your transgressions over the Skool could be justified," Duwdamon warned as Dughorm stepped closer. "However, I've decided the needs of the Triad outweigh his rights."

"Interesting," replied Dughorm. "How may I help you?"

The god scowled at him. "Your visions, of course," he said. "I need to know what is coming. I can feel the turmoil within the Sky Realm and the underworld but my reach into Caruun's world is limited. I must restore calm among the realms." He paused, staring at his new seer. "You believe there is damage among the gods who make up the Triad. I don't accept such a premise. I know my family."

"What of the humans?" Dughorm asked, surprised to find that Duwdamon could read his thoughts. He understood only Duwdamon's wife had the power to read a human's mind.

"What of them?" Duwdamon raised his eyebrow at him. "You know the people have nothing until they worship me, I mean us. Their lives are only useful for the souls which pass through the realms. Once we settle the problems between the Sky Realm and the underworld, the natural order will be restored. The humans will be satisfied as long as the sun rises, the rains come, and their crops continue to grow. You should realize that most are simple minded things like the rest of the creatures of the realm."

Dughorm said nothing but he let out a sigh as he decided to take a different tack.

"Since I've come to this realm only recently, I can give you only the revelations that I saw before entering this dominion," he told his master carefully. "I'm not sure you will like them."

Duwdamon's blue eyes grew hard. "You will let me decide such things," he said. "I only seek your visions, not your opinions."

"Very well, my lord. The visions are cloudy, but I see much blood in the Kamin lands," he told the god. "The lands of Esterblud and Vulthnal will soon flow with the blood of innocents...."

"Enough, this is known!" Duwdamon cut him off. "I already know about the disasters which have destroyed the human villages and towns. My son told me of the people's wicked trespass against him."

"I understand this, my lord," he said patiently. "However, I was not speaking of your son's alliance with Caruun to inflict suffering upon the human realm. Natural disasters of the gods, I believe."

He watched the god's expression, expecting defense of Uugaraa and his offensive actions. However, Duwdamon revealed nothing. Dughorm continued.

"My images show the blood of humans spilled by beasts from the underworld realm," he told him. "From the gateways, monsters and creatures are coming to snatch up those for their pleasure."

"Are you saying Caruun is sending such beasts into the human realm?" Duwdamon asked as he stood up from the bench. "Do you realize you are accusing the god of the underworld of breaking the pact between gods and humans."

"I accuse no one of anything," stated Dughorm calmly. "I merely give you my visions. The prophecy of human suffering showed nothing about Caruun, only the monsters coming from there. While isolated at first, the attacks are spreading to all of the lands. I've confirmed with Umcal. Your sons and wife know about this as well, if asked. As I recall, there are others within his realm who have no love for humans. Either way, if such attacks continue, the temples will grow empty."

Duwdamon let his form wander through the courtyard, clearly working through the news from his new prophet. The ghost of Dughorm kept his mind clear as he looked across the open floor past the columns that surrounded the courtyard. In the distance, he could make out the highest peaks of the Neewar Mountains. It was an idyllic setting and worthy of his new spirit world.

"I agree there are those among my family who will create havoc in the domain of humans," Duwdamon conceded. "However, this is a small matter. If the underworld is doing this, it is not something we need to concern ourselves too much over. I will speak to Caruun." Dughorm tried to mask his dislike of the god's indifference to the underworld monsters ripping apart humans.

"Perhaps my lord, but there is more I have for you," he told the god. "Just before my death, I saw something that would mean danger to all of the realms." Dughorm hesitated, unsure how to explain his vision.

"Continue then," Duwdamon replied, not happy with the information he was receiving.

Again, the seer took a breath. "It appears an ancient one has come forth from the Great Void."

A bitter laugh erupted from the sky god.

36

"So, from out of nowhere, our new Sybil comes up with a vision about something that is impossible," Duwdamon's mocking laugh echoed across the gardens. "You are either a fool or a liar with your visions. I will not listen to such fables."

Dughorm's spirit face turned red with anger as he moved toward the sky god. "God or not, no one mocks me," he told him. "I'll give it to you straight. The ancient one is a spirit stealer who has returned from the void, using an underworld god's energy and human blood sacrifice. It would be a risk for you and your realm if you chose not to believe me. You can think that over."

The ghost of Dughorm turned away, furious at the contempt Duwdamon showed him. Within an instant, he felt the flash of searing flame strike him, wrapping him in an excruciating torment that went beyond the worst pain he ever experienced as a human.

"No one dares walk away from me without my permission," Duwdamon's voice roared like thunder as he released his godfire whip from around Dughorm. "You forget you are not a god."

Dughorm's form went invisible for a moment before coming back into view. But when he turned, he showed no fear of Duwdamon whose body suddenly grew two sizes to hover over him.

"No, we cannot forget how you keep humans cowering by our powers to control and destroy the world around us," Dughorm shot back. "As a god, you know my past. If you truly read minds, then you know that I have told you the truth. Whether you wish to accept this fact remains on you." He waited for a reaction, expecting more punishment from the god towering over him.

"Do you need any help, my lord?" Umcal asked, his voice came from nowhere. The question caused Duwdamon to pause. There was a bitter tension hanging in the air.

Umcal appeared before them again, his luminous appearance still struggling to take shape. "If you forgive me, I believe I can assist," he stated in a voice nearly as soft as the morning breeze.

"Yes, you can remove this imbecile from my sight," Duwdamon said huffily.

"I'm afraid you must recognize the truth," Umcal said. "I've seen such visions myself; although without the clarity of Dughorm. While my friend lacks the diplomatic skills you want, his spirit remains honest and his dreams are accurate." Duwdamon scowled at the fading shadow as he sat down on the bench again, his mind in turmoil as he considered the news.

"A spirit stealer in the underworld? It cannot be," the sky god said, mostly to himself. "No god would ally with Kriell. The Guardians cannot return." Duwdamon momentarily looked bewildered. His scowl returned as he glanced between Umcal and Dughorm.

"As I recall, Kriell is not ally with anyone," Umcal reminded him. "While I can confirm something has come through the Void, my lord, my insight is too limited to help further. I urge you to ponder the words of Dughorm. Consider that the Fates have suddenly sent a person to find the Skool, something lost for generations." A silence fell over the courtyard.

"Leave me," ordered the sky god. "I must think about this revelation."

Umcal and Dughorm turned away, following the stream of the spring water as it departed through to the front of the temple. Umcal reached down to dip into the healing water, causing his form to become fully visible again.

"Who is Kriell?" asked Dughorm. "I've not heard that name before."

"You wouldn't know about it, for it is a profane name not spoken since the time of Heptarc," Umcal said. "He was one of the Guardians, cast out along with the rest of those terrible gods during the Great Passing." They strolled along the floor to the outer ring of columns where they stopped. Dughorm's spirit was still adjusting to the lack of fleshly rules in the Sky Realm that his human body knew so well in the Kamin world. He mentioned this to Umcal.

"That's because the gods and spirits really are the same energies," Umcal told him. "Just as the gods must follow the natural world of the humans when they are in the Kamin realm, so the spirits of the people can fly like the gods here. As spirits, we no longer have ties to the natural world we once knew so well. Each realm has a limit to those who reside there."

"My energy fails me again so I cannot explain more for the moment. Come back this evening after I rest near the spring water," Umcal told him. "I will tell you more about the past as I know it, for it may be useful in dealing with the gods. In the meantime, seek out the engravings you will find engraved on the temples. The knowledge of the past can be deciphered with work. Listen to the words coming from other gods and spirits within the Sky Realm. They can tell you more if properly motivated." He grew invisible again.

"However, know that they will be reluctant to speak of Kriell. That profane spirit has more than enough reason to return, and the gods of Kamin fear him," Umcal's voice turned into a soft wind, disappearing like a fleeting dream. Dughorm continued his journey as he wondered how much he did not know of this realm and its' occupants.

~~~

Buried deep under the Mythroloy Mountains, Caruun, the underworld god, was sitting upon his black and white throne in the middle of the gigantic beehive cavern. He watched his wife who came to him along with a few of her pet *beorhs*, the remnants of human warriors turned into beasts. The creatures provided the bulwark of terror inside and outside of his realm. Caruun's vulture face revealed nothing in its expression, but his yellow eyes grew angry looking at the beautiful human form of Alrpan. She knew how he despised the appearance of the human form and used her human beauty to mock him. His own hideous features constituted the ideal form of gods in his eyes.

Nearby, Actita, the last remaining Vanth, could sense his father's displeasure. A winged creature with snake-hair, rat face and the beak of a hawk, the Vanth was one of the few beings allowed to leave the underworld. As he watched the interplay between Alrpan and Caruun, Actita knew his father was in a terrible mood. Somehow, Alrpan re-discovered her power to regain her human form. His mother lost her powers when she underestimated the human warrior called Urith and his shield holding the Skool. Her fire spell was cast back, causing the underworld goddess to suffer the searing torment and loss of her power. Alrpan's miraculous recovery could interfere with Caruun's plans. And this recovery was something that none of the creatures understood. While it was well known that Caruun disliked his wife, the Vanth realized something else was creating the distance between them. He had heard the terrible vengeance his father swore upon the humans after the battle at Du-Rinell, but Actita knew the death of his twin sister was only an excuse for his father's vengeance. Caruun, unmoved by thoughts of love or sympathy, could hardly change eons of indifference to the death of his daughter, even by a human.

"Why are you here, Alrpan?" asked the underworld god, not attempting to conceal the contempt in his voice.

"Great one, I come to tell you that your servants have done considerable damage to the human realm," she replied coolly.

"This is interesting since I don't recall ordering such events to occur," said Caruun.

"I believe you must have, my lord," said the goddess steadily. "They would not have left the underworld to do such things without your command."

The underworld god scowled at her, his slow but steady mind appearing to grasp the quiet defiance of his queen. However, something else bothered him about her miraculous recovery. Her human body was still irritatingly desirable and appealing, even to him. But her superior ways annoyed him even more. Her manner, always seemed so self-assured, but now there was an added boldness; he could feel an almost contemptuous demeanor directed toward him. It puzzled him, and he did not like this change. Despite her powers, it was proper that his wife would remain a subservient god to him.

"You return to your old methods of creating problems within the human realm again. Perhaps this is good. You know I don't mind as long as it doesn't come back upon my dominion," he warned.

"Oh, I will make sure of this," the form of Alrpan smiled innocently to Caruun, who missed her eyes flashing red the instant before. "I think you will find great sport from the souls that will be coming. However, it will keep Actita quite busy."

"Sport?" Caruun repeated incredulously. "Since when have you bothered about the spirits of humans and duties of the underworld?"

"Perhaps I have more reason than I used to, my lord. For was it not the humans that did me a great wrong." Alrpan suggested, and the underworld god grunted his agreement.

"What are you planning?" he asked. Caruun stood, then floated down the steps to join his wife.

"Planning my lord?" she asked. "I'm not sure what you mean."

The vulture-like creature now stood towering over Alrpan's small stature. Giving a curt nod, he dismissed the beorhs next to her and watched as they ran away into the shadows. Then, taking her arm, he led her toward the darkened tunnel behind the throne.

"Come now, my wife," he said. "You always have a scheme which you dangle in front of me, assuming I'm too dumb to realize this."

"I'm not sure what you mean," she replied slyly. "However, it appears the chaos you envisioned will soon give you a chance to bring down the Triad. A bold chance to control the Sky Realm."

"What makes you think I would want this to happen?" he asked, stopping to look at her.

She smiled sweetly. "Where there is a weakness, a superior leader can step forward and mold the realms as he might want," she told him.

He smiled at that thought, stepping to the entrance door of their bedchambers. Seldom used by either one, the underworld god took her arm to lead her into the room. He intended to make sure she realized he was still the master. However, she politely but firmly refused his advance, stopping them outside the door.

"I'm sorry my husband, but the memory of our daughter's destruction is too vivid for me," she said. "I cannot."

She turned away from the dumbfounded god, moving quickly down the dark tunnel. Her rejection was a surprise, even if he seldom sought her out. Her rebuff had left him with a rising anger as he cocked his head. First, the humans destroyed his child, not that he could understand such an alien concept as love. But now his wife has changed after her disastrous encounter with those pitiful Esterblud humans. As he thought about this, he decided the people continued to hamper his desires. His anger slowly took the form of resolve as he decided it was time for him to take charge. His intention set, he turned back to the cavernous main hall of his domain and disappeared from sight, leaving a vaporous outline of his form.

The form of Alrpan continued down the dark tunnel into the depths where the beasts and monsters held by the underworld remained captive. The beorhs came running to catch up with their master. The group of creatures followed the winding, twisting tunnel until it opened into another beehive like structure towering above. The walls were filled with outsized holes in the rock and barred with iron bars. It was a prison where the beasts of nightmare were created. Each creature, adding its own incessant chattering, filled the chamber with the thundering echoes.

As the deity entered, the sound suddenly stopped, leaving the reverberation of echoes and a deathly quiet as each beast stared out at their new master, sniffing at the smell of the god hidden inside the illusion of Alrpan. Coming up to a large opening, sealed off with stout iron bars, Alrpan moved close despite warning growls from inside the cage.

"You won't have long before you can seek your revenge," cackled the Guardian to the creature hidden in the dark. "However, we have more of your offspring to create."

Suddenly the body of Alrpan began changing. The rigid, human skeletal structure became soft, and the skin tone darkened to black as the goddess morphed into a dark nebulous blob, much like a misshapen creature from the ocean depths. Soon, the creature had only one recognizable feature to distinguish what it was beyond a large black globule with tentacles. On the back of the creature, was the face of Alrpan as if engraved on the body. The fear in the underworld goddess's face, which once tempted humans could be easily recognized. The human mouth moved as if attempting to speak, but the face disappeared into the slimy discharge oozing from the blob. Sliding into the cage, the actual form of the Guardian called Kriell, the spirit stealer, began wrapping around the fearsome monster. More underworld creatures would come from the god while Caruun continued to focus upon the humans.

~~~

Mivraa rode next to Urith as they traveled along the wide sandy trail leading to Alurican, the nominal capital of Vulthnal. Fedelm kept her mount behind them, listening to the conversation. Oslaf brought up the rear, still in a foul mood since their escape two nights before. His uncle criticized Oslaf for his failure to thoroughly scout the area near the ossane stable. While Urith admitted he should have thought more about the potential of an ambush by the villagers in Casab, Oslaf believed he should have done more that night. He also held that Urith did not acknowledge Oslaf's accomplishments well enough.

Oslaf remained behind them, watching the interplay between Urith and Mivraa. He thought his uncle was too occupied with the demigoddess. He felt crowded out by their close bond. Oslaf noticed when they occasionally stole away in private and he decided they were rutting around like black baters in heat. Not that he cared, he told himself, for he knew the ways of lovers. But he felt like his uncle had a hunger for the wrong person. A demigoddess was not likely to become the wife of a human, no matter how great the hero. Then his thoughts turned, as usual, to Fedelm. The young man hated her indifference to him. Oslaf knew every expression on the attractive girl's face as he watched her every move. At one point, he decided that if he dreamed of her hard enough, his ideas might enter into her visions. But it had not worked. She seemed to pay more attention to his uncle, and he resented that as well.

"Are you going to keep up or should we slow down for you?" Urith sarcastic question pierced through Oslaf's thoughts. He looked up to see his uncle glancing back at him. His ossane had dropped back even further from the rest of the group.

"I'll catch up," he snapped back. "I don't know why you are in such a hurry. I still say we should have gone back to take care of that town. Your shield would have made short work of them."

Urith stopped his mount, speaking when Oslaf rode up. "When I was younger, I might have agreed with you. I'll admit that I thought of doing just that the other night. But the cry for vengeance against everyone in that town is foolhardy and not worthy of a noble warrior. You should know that by now." He glared at the young man.

Oslaf stared back, not letting his uncle intimidate him. "You are wrong," he insisted. "That place was nothing more than a den of thieves. Better to wipe it out and start again."

"Listen, you have been grousing about everything since we left Uugaraa," Urith snarled. "Now, start acting like an Esterblud and take the lead. Maybe your skills as a scout will have improved since last time."

Oslaf dug his heels into his mount and whipped the flanks of the animal with his reins as he shot ahead, his face red with anger. Urith remained quiet, turning to follow the trail. Fedelm and Mivraa came up on either side of him. There was no talk for a while until Fedelm spoke up.

"You aren't going to get through to him if you keep digging your spurs into him," she suggested. "He's too much like you."

"Perhaps," Urith conceded. He watched his nephew finally slow his ossane near the top of a sand mound overlooking the trail ahead. "Then again, he's young and impulsive so he needs guidance."

"He is at a tough time in his life, I believe," said Mivraa. "Perhaps I should talk with him."

43

"No, you are part of the problem," interjected Fedelm. "I've seen him look at you when you are with Urith. He sees your closeness with his uncle and I think he resents it."

"I don't think I'm his problem," Mivraa replied defensively. "He pants after you like a lovesick *wearhs* pup, but you treat him like a servant. He has tried so hard to please you, but you just keep turning him away."

Urith partially listened to the back and forth as he thought about Oslaf. What Fedelm said was true, they were much alike. He was fiercely proud of his brother's son. He remembered that age, wanting to take on the world and be recognized for it. Such was the culture of his tribe. Urith suspected all men sought adventure and respect as a warrior. It was the reason that Esterblud fighters took on a *sakreta*, or trial by fire ordeal. Presenting their trophy to the elders, the warrior was acknowledged as an elite member of the tribe.

Urith remembered when he convinced his elders about the location of the Clovel, a genuinely evil monster used by the Guardians, ancient gods from the Great Void. He was able to hunt down and destroy one of the last of the creatures, coming back to his village as the hero they started to call the Clovel Destroyer. Urith realized he was about the same age Oslaf when he took his trial.

"Both of you are going down the wrong path," Urith interrupted the women. "Oslaf carries the problems you speak of but he needs to control his future soon. While what each of you say has some merit, he must be looking to take his sakreta soon."

"And what does that mean," asked Fedelm. Since she grew up among the priests, she knew little of the Esterblud warrior traditions.

"The best way to translate it for you is to say it is an ordeal and at the same time, a quest," he told her. "A fighter must take such a path alone. I'm not sure when this will happen since that will be up to Oslaf to decide." Urith sighed. "I just know that he feels the need to take charge, and he will decide when he faces his trial and where. All I can do is guide him. I must hope for the best, just as my father did for me."

They went silent while they plodded along the trail. Even Mivraa, who was somewhat familiar with warrior ways, worried about Oslaf. She feared the young man might do something reckless that would lead his uncle into danger. She recognized he had a soft spot for his nephew. She hoped that this urge for the young fighter would stay away until they finished their current journey to find the Skool.

"Hopefully, he'll remember why we travel together," she said.

It was near evening on the third sunset of their travel when they reached the outskirts of Alurican. The bustling, walled city was home to the overlord of Vulthnal. They passed through the open gates, discovering the guards of King Barcal paid little attention to the visitors. Spurring their mount past two white stone towers, they followed the main street. Most of the Kamin world knew Barcal was a weak ruler, unable to completely control Vulthnal. However, the overlord apparently believed he had little to fear from outsiders coming into his home city. Urith noticed no one paid any attention to the warriors on ossanes traveling the streets wearing Esterblud tunics. The city itself appeared nearly unguarded. Few sentries were seen within the stone towers above. Urith guessed loyalties and order were still bought and paid for by this overlord. His past experience in this kingdom taught him that a weak and fragile command meant the sea raiders would remain to pillage and plunder along the coasts. Urith heard stories about people in the king's own council who benefited from trading with the bandits as well. It left the people at the mercy of the wealthiest and powerful.

Traveling through the crowded streets, they found a small stable to sell their mounts and saddles, deciding they would travel on to Eernicia by ship to save time. Iaral, the ossane trader, handed over the koinons, paying a fair price. He was a thin, bald man with a shaggy, brown and gray beard. He wore a brown hooded robe with a worn emblem representing the local merchant guild. Urith asked him about a place to stay and Iaral steered them to the tavern down the block, mentioning the owner was his brother, Ical.

Walking along the stone paved street to the inn, they carried their bedrolls and miscellaneous packs on their shoulders. The crowds milling in the streets forced them to push through at times, but the locals remained uninterested in more foreigner visitors to the city. The various foreign languages along with a dizzying display of colorful robes indicated many tribes called the city home. Traveling along city walls, they noticed the white lathe and plaster buildings gradually gave way to dingy buildings. The farther they walked; the clean streets near the entrance of the city gave way to the stinking piles of garbage in the gutters close to the building fronts along with large potholes in the rutted, muddy path. The street vendors, for the most part, were gone, along with the throngs of customers. As they moved deeper into the city, the travelers found suspicious people carefully watching them from the shadows of the alleys or near doorways of dilapidated buildings. The eyes following them carried a mixture of greed and suspicion.

They found the tavern at the end of the street; its wooden frame held up by the old fortress wall. A row of derelict two-story shops lined the other side of the street, providing cover from the sun for a few men sitting on a bench. They entered the tavern through a low door into the smell of pipe smoke and sour barkmead. Urith frowned, thinking of his dislike for the bitter, cheap drink. Walking past the few wooden tables where two locals eyed the big man, Urith went to the bar and asked for Ical. A large bearded man turned, looking over the collection of strangers suspiciously. He looked nothing like his brother, a fact not lost on the group.

"I'm Ical, what do you want?" He asked foully, placing his hands on the mead stained wood. His face showed pockmark scars along the big cheekbones which were not covered by his long beard.

"Your brother sent us here. Said you had rooms," Urith replied as he observed the locals trying to listen in on the conversation. He pulled out a couple of koinons to show he was serious.

"Aye, I have one above," Ical said as he eyed Urith's hand greedily. He moved from behind the bar. "Follow me."

They followed the tavern keeper up the stairs to the second floor of the building and down a dirty, narrow hallway that turned sharply into a dark open area that smelled worse than the floor below. Mivraa noticed the walls of plaster had large holes and dark stains that appeared to be the result of fights. But she also thought it was a good spot for an ambush by those who would rob guests after they left the rooms. That would explain the locals so interested in their conversation at the bar. She noticed how many stared at the koinons Urith held.

After opening their room, Ical took his down payment from Urith and left them, his heavy boots stomping down the hallways. Inside they found two large beds with thin straw mattresses, so stained it was hard to tell their original color. A broken table with a single chair sat in the corner behind the door which hid the single window. Mivraa went over, trying to open it, but it was sealed shut.

"They don't want anybody skipping out on them," joked Oslaf.

"Or escaping," she replied. "I don't like it."

46

Urith came up next to her and looked out the dingy glass. Overlooking the street, he saw the shadows had grown darker as the sun went down and the men across the street were watching the building.

"I agree with you," he said. "I think our ossane trader sent us here to get his money back. Judging from the thugs below, they might have come up with a little trap for us. It's too bad for them; they don't know us very well." Combined the ragged scar on his cheek, the grin gave Urith a death sneer. "I think we should get some rest for a while. When the time comes, we'll play their little game."

Urith laid his bedroll out on the bed, moving his weapons out of the way. He lay down on the blanket as the others followed along with their blankets and bedrolls. Mivraa sat on the edge of the bed, watching him as he closed his eyes and relaxed. She was again pleasantly surprised by his actions. When it came to danger, he became deadly calm and coldly efficient. It was a trait she greatly admired, especially in a human.

Fedelm sat down on the other bed as she dropped the bag she carried while showing the anxiety she felt. Urith had not explained what they were doing, and she knew something was coming. But she realized Urith would tell her when he considered the time to be right. It frustrated her when he did that as if he expected her to read his mind. Fedelm understood he was used to dealing with experienced fighters who understood what he was thinking. He would just make a joke of it if she asked, so she remained quiet. She decided to look through the bag at her makeshift healing supplies. When Urith grew so quiet, it meant a fight was coming.

Oslaf sit in the chair next to the door. He leaned back in his wooden chair, which creaked at the effort. Letting his head rest on the wall, he listened through the thin walls for anyone coming down the hall.

After darkness fell over the city, Urith took the lead going back inside the tavern. Before they left the room, he told his friends to have their weapons ready. When the group entered the lower level, the small room, now filled with a mixture of people in conversations which suddenly stopped. The Esterblud leader found an open table in the corner where he sat with his back to the wall. Mivraa and Fedelm placed themselves on either side of the table. Oslaf waved over a fat old lady who was near the bar.

"Food and drink for my friends," he told her as he handed her koinon, sitting with his back to the room.

Urith leaned forward and gave his nephew a wink. The prearranged display of gold caught the attention of several men within the room. Urith caught sight of a light-skinned man with a large round face who kept glancing at their table. He recognized the stranger as one of the thugs standing outside earlier. At the table with him were two more who had the backs to him. He guessed they were part of the same group. When Ical came into the room from a door behind the bar, Urith saw the stranger at the table give a nod.

"They're pretty obvious," observed Mivraa softly as she caught a glimpse of what Urith was watching. He nodded while Oslaf leaned forward.

"Will they try here or outside?" he asked.

"It will be here and soon," Urith replied as he noticed a local couple dressed in brown tunics rise from their table and quickly leave the tavern. Their departure left several men standing at the bar who occasionally glanced at the table. Urith knew his enemy outnumbered them, but he believed his group held the advantage.

The fat lady came back holding four mugs of mead, which she put on the greasy table. She was short and round, and most of her stringy white hair covered by a scarf, but a few strands that escaped were plastered to her forehead with sweat. She stared at Mivraa for a moment as though she wanted to say something. Instead, she quickly scurried off. Urith quietly told them not to drink the barkmead and then put the mug to his lips as though he took a drink. He sat the cup back on the sticky table top. Ical sneaked a grin which confirmed Urith's suspicions. Urith's face darkened as he fought to control his rising anger. He wondered how many others walked into this inn, directed there by the ossane trader, only to be attacked and robbed by these cutthroats.

The Clovel Sword would reward them with proper justice, he decided.

Fedelm noticed the fat lady slipping out the back door, covering her head with her shawl while Ical bolted the door behind her. She touched Urith's arm and whispered to him. Mivraa slowly put her hand inside of her black cloak which told Oslaf to get ready. Oslaf watched his uncle's eyes as they followed a man walking to the front door and bolting it closed with a heavy iron latch. The light-skinned man who appeared to lead the bandits stood up along with the others at his table. The group started toward the bar.

Urith stood as well, stumbling as he did, and walked from behind the table as Oslaf followed his lead. "Come, my friend. Let us get more of this mead."

They put their arm around the other's shoulder, each with a mug in the other hand. On their approach to the bar, they could see the occasional glint of silver from weapons hidden under the robber's robes and long cloaks. As they reached the group, several men pulled away from the bar to let them pass. Urith threw his cup in the man's face and whipped out his sword. Oslaf pulled out his long sword nearly as fast.

"Which of you intends to die first?" growled Urith as he waited for them to charge.

There was a pause, and the room was silent as the leader wiped his face with his forearm, pulling his sword with the others. Fear and desperation filled several men at this turn of fortune.

"Urith! Look out," shouted Mivraa.

A dark-skinned man with a heavy beard tossed a large ax toward Urith. He dodged the weapon which slammed into the bar next to him. The action sent the ruffians after the Esterbluds.

Urith blocked the short sword of one bandit, slicing off the man's hand in the process while swinging around to impale his partner. He pulled out his sword from the dying man but received a hard sword blow in the lower back. The strike from the bandit leader sent Oslaf into the bar top. The thug was about to strike again. Urith turned in time to see the bandit leader suddenly stop and fall to his knees, a burst of blood coming from the mouth. Fedelm pulled out her dagger from the man's back; the woman's eyes were wide in shock at her first kill. Urith pushed away from the bar, turning around with a swipe of his Clovel Sword to slice into another thug coming at them. The man fell to the floor, screaming in agony.

Next to the bar, Oslaf fell to the floor when a bandit jumped on his back. He tried to scramble to his feet, but the thug slammed his sword down into Oslaf's back. The blow was unable to cut through the chainmail, but the strike knocked the breath out of him. Powerless to defend himself, he could only twist around, expecting a fatal blow. There was a blur of action as Mivraa impaled the bandit with her silver spear. She pulled Oslaf to his feet as the remaining thugs backed away. At the door was the ruffian who lost his hand. He frantically covered the bloody stump with his tunic, while pleading for them to leave.

49

Urith ripped off his coin bag, throwing it down in front of the men. The koinons jingled across the stone floor.

"You want it, you cowards," he raged. "Then come and get it. I've seen better fighters among our women and children," he spate in disgust. As he expected, three men charged at the Esterbluds. They made short work of them. Urith cut through two men in quick succession before they could counter his sword moves. Blood flowed across the wood floor as Oslaf finished off another. Parrying the man's sword strike, Oslaf finished off the man with a thrust into his opponent's throat. By the time the Esterbluds finished, the last bandit ran into the night.

Mivraa worked her way back to the bar, capturing the tavern keeper as he was trying to escape through the rear entrance. Fedelm joined her and they led Ical in front of Urith. Urith rose after picking up his coin bag from the floor. Icals' face bleached white when he looked at him.

"Your little game is up, tavern keeper. You will play by our tune," Urith said, his gray eyes showing his deadly intent. "We are justified if we kill you now, just for the fun of it." Ical began to beg for his life, but Oslaf slapped him across the back of the head with his fist, allowing his uncle to continue. "However, since you're unarmed, I have decided to be merciful." Urith bent down pulling a bit of cloth from a body to clean his sword.

"You and your worthless brother will leave this city now. My friends and I will hunt you down and place your heads on a pike outside the gates if we see either of you in the morning. Your tavern and your brother's stable will be given away."

Stunned at what he heard, Ical's lips began to tremble. "You cannot do that, the king will not allow this," Ical declared as Mivraa dragged him to the door by his hair. She shoved him out the entrance, sending him tumbling into the dark, stone covered street. An oil lamp on the tavern wall illuminated the area. She placed her spear at his heart.

"You are lucky he was in a good mood," she told the tavern owner. "I would have cut your heart out for the wearhs to scavenge on. If you want to keep your head, you leave now," she advised. Ical hesitated, tears streaming down his face at his public humiliation. Mivraa took a step toward him with her spear, and he screamed in panic before running away. She stood there for a moment, then shouted at the people she saw hidden in the shadows nearby.

"If you didn't hear what happened, this building is to be given to those who help clean out the dead vermin inside." She told them before re-entering the building.

Inside, Urith was standing behind the bar, filling four mugs with mead, which he placed on the bar. He offered the cup to Mivraa, who took it with a grin.

"I don't think the tavern keeper will be returning anytime soon, but you should have killed him," she told him. She saw Oslaf give a mug to Fedelm.

"Perhaps, but I believe his brother would come back with the king's guards," replied Urith. "Killing Ical would give his brother an excuse. They will either flee the city or go to the overlord. I'm betting neither will stand before King Barcal. People must know about these scavengers preying on the city's strangers. I would be surprised the guards would help restore that."

"Should we leave?" asked Fedelm, as she came next to Urith.

"No, I don't think that will stop the guards if they want us. I saw plenty of people watching this building from the shadows. It wouldn't take them long to track us down." Mivraa told them as she walked over to a nearby table that was unbroken and still upright after the fight. She picked up a chair and put it so she could sit down. The others followed her, each pulling up chairs.

"It's a shame we didn't get the food first," Oslaf said, over the growling of his stomach. He smiled at them when he looked around.

"Well, I guess we drink and see what the Fates have in store for us." Urith held up his mug in a toast to his friends. "To my friends, I guess. Either we leave in the morning or we find ourselves inside the dungeon."

Suddenly, they heard the back door of the building creak open, causing everyone at the table to place their hands on their weapons. Carefully peaking inside was the fat maid who served them earlier. Seeing the group of supposed victims alive, the woman gasped and closed the door. Outside they heard her voice calling out. They listened as she talked to neighbors, demanding they come with her. Soon, she came around to the front door. The woman stepped inside with two men dressed in their simple brown robes of tradesmen. The men stopped at the door. She came up to the table, carefully stepping around the bodies and pools of blood.

"I would like to have these men remove those bodies. Is that alright with you?" The group looked at her dumbfounded for a moment before Urith nodded. The two men grabbed a body, dragging it out into the darkness.

"Can we get you something?" the maid asked.

"We never got our food," Oslaf piped up. She nodded and went back to the back door of the tavern, going back into the night. While waiting for the fat woman to return, the tradesmen continued their work removing the bodies. Not long after the last bandit was carried out, a couple of brave locals entered the tavern and began righting the salvageable tables and chairs. The maid entered the rear of the building again, carrying a thick plate filled with erba meat. Behind her, a small girl entered carrying a large loaf of unleavened zeam bread which she placed next to the plate. She immediately took the mugs from Mivraa and Fedelm, taking them to the casks to refill them.

"I'm so sorry I wasn't able to warn you about them," the fat lady explained suddenly. "Ical and his men always watched me around foreigners who came in. I couldn't go against their gang, it would put my family in danger. You see they stole this building from us. You have honored us by your actions. Please accept this meal as our gift to you." Her brown eyes glistened with emotion, and she wrung her big hands in the stained apron she wore.

"Then, you must accept our thanks for your generosity," Urith told her, touched by her emotional plea. "What is your name?"

"I'm Wiga and the little girl there is my granddaughter, Ovila. Our family are merchants who owned the buildings on this street since before Ical arrived. Once his band of thugs came, we lost much of our trade and business. Since my husband died, I have not protection, so I was forced to work for Ical. My son's pleas to the palace went unanswered since we are not wealthy. Some of our neighbors left when more of these bandits stayed here. But those who remain will not let this happen again." She wiped her tears from her face with the filthy apron.

"Then, this tavern is rightfully yours. If the guards come for us, you can tell them what happened," he told her. "We'll take the judgment of the king."

"Don't worry about guards, they are afraid of this area at night," she beamed a smile. "You can eat and drink until you are full for you are safe here." She waved in a few people watching from outside the door.

Soon, they entered the tavern, joining Wiga at a table where she gave them the news. As the travelers began their feast, they noticed the dramatic change inside the room as more men along with women and children came inside.

The next morning, Urith awakened to the sound of Mivraa getting out of the bed and softly walking across the room. She was retrieving her shawl which hung on the chair. He jerked awake with his long Sgian dagger at the ready. She looked back at him and smiled.

"It's alright," she told him. "I'm going to find Wiga and check on things. I'm not convinced that Ical and his brother will give up so easily. You rest." She winked at him, a mannerism she picked up from him during their time together. Urith smiled and fell back into the bed, ignoring the foul stench of the mattress that came through the bedroll lying on it. He would be glad to leave the filthy place soon. Mivraa put the shawl over her shoulders and walked out of the room, closing the creaking door behind her.

Oslaf woke at the sound, turning over to see Fedelm next to him. Typically, he would have enjoyed the sight of her lying so close as he watched her breathing. Now he hated it. He looked at her slightly upturned nose and the freckles on her handsome face, growing unhappy as he watched her breathe. All he could think of was that she showed little interest in him, despite his efforts to gain her favor. Still groggy from the late night and too much heathmead, he struggled to his feet. He did not bother to be quiet, enjoying the thought he might wake her from her peaceful sleep.

"Where is she going?" Oslaf asked Urith.

"She's checking with Wiga for any information about the bandits." His uncle replied, his eyes remained closed.

Oslaf grunted and sat in the rickety chair, leaning it against the wall. He tried to hide the pain of the bruised area where one of the bandits struck him.

"You made a few mistakes last night. We need to continue your training on your sword techniques." Urith sat up, scratching his head wondering if there was a place to bathe given what he slept on. It would have been cleaner to sleep on the floor he decided.

Oslaf gave his uncle a cold look, "What do you mean? We took them easily."

"Only because Mivraa killed the one standing over you," Urith said, his face grim. "Had that been a sharp sword with a skilled warrior, she would have been taking you to Haligulf instead. We will find time for you to practice."

"No!" The young warrior jumped his feet, his face livid. "I'm tired of this. Nothing I do makes you happy." He stomped to the door, throwing it open and walked out. His heavy footsteps shook the wood floor of the room as he went down the hallway.

Fedelm was now awake, trying to grasp what she heard.

"What was that about?" she asked.

"Nothing," Urith replied, standing up as he retrieved his chainmail shirt from the end of the bed. "Might as well head down to see what Mivraa has found out. Maybe find some food."

"Before you do, I should tell you something," she murmured. Her tone caused Urith to stop. He saw her face looking at him, pale and fragile and he pulled up the rickety chair. Sitting in front of woman, he was convinced something was wrong.

Downstairs, Oslaf interrupted Mivraa and Wiga with his muttering as he passed their table. She said nothing as she watched him stomp out of the tavern. Urith came into the room soon afterward. He finished strapping his baudrik belt around his chest.

"Wiga was telling me that our exploits overnight were noticed by others in the city," Mivraa explained. "There has been no sign of the tavern keeper and his thugs. But she thinks that we should leave. Rumors of our fight have already spread. Wiga thinks the guards will be coming soon." She glanced over at the fat lady who nodded her agreement.

"We will need to get passage on the next ship out of here. Can we make it to the harbor?" He asked.

"I was just telling this lady that I could lead you to the harbor," Wiga spoke up. "There are places you can remain hidden until you can board the ship."

"Are you sure you can afford to be seen with us?" Urith asked. "I might scare off your boyfriends." The fat lady blushed slightly as the giant warrior teased her.

"Very well," he said, trying to mask his worries. "Let's gather our group and follow our new scout."

They turned as they heard footsteps coming down the stairs. Fedelm entered the room, awkwardly trying to carry two bedrolls. Both were filled with some of the weapons. Wiga moved to help her.

"I overheard your conversation," Fedelm told them. "We have more things that should be gathered upstairs."

Urith went back upstairs and collected the rest of their blankets and belongings. When he left the tavern, he found Oslaf standing near the street corner. He was pacing back and forth with his head down, his blonde hair in his face.

"Next time, pack your own things," Urith said as he tossed him the bedroll with his chainmail wrapped inside. Oslaf responded with a glare. He said nothing as he took his shield and slung it over his shoulder along with his bedroll and followed the group.

Wiga led the way through the maze of side streets, her plump form moving quickly. She was still in the same dirty blue robe she wore the night before. Despite his usually keen sense of direction, Urith became lost as the fat lady pushed through the early morning crowds. They followed carts being pulled by erba, a strong long-haired type of oxen. She would stop on occasion, waiting for the rest of the group to catch up. After many twists and turns, they finally came to the main square of the city.

On the far side of the plaza from where the group stood was a knoll where the main temple stood in white splendor. Even to a skeptic like Urith, the temple was impressive with its gleaming white columns across the front of the rectangular structure. Wiga hurried across the plaza, heading to the docks they could see further down the stone street. They saw a few people in white robes going up the broad staircase into the temple. When they reach the other side of the courtyard, the group walked along of stone buildings with stained glass windows. As they turned a corner, a line of guards stood in front of them. The Vulthnal Guard held their pikes at the ready; their purple and gold tunics shimmered in the morning sun.

"Stop!" yelled the leader of the men, pulling his sword. He was dressed in the same uniform as his men, his long brown hair falling from his metal, golden helmet. On the top of his helmet was a band of purple plumage.

Urith gave a momentary thought to fight with his hand on the Clovel Sword. But, he glanced back as more guards surrounded them. They were too heavily outnumbered.

"We are going to the docks to get passage," Wiga told the leader. "We meant no harm. Please let us by."

He stepped through his line, looking the group over as he lowered his sword.

"You Esterbluds are wanted," he said firmly. "The king has ordered your capture. You will come with us now."

"And what if we don't?" Oslaf spoke up as he stood next to Urith.

The Vulthnal warrior looked over; his face gave him a grimace. "You seem smarter than that, boy," he said. "My men are well trained, and you wear no armor. You will not last long."

"Since it appears we have little choice, we must follow you to your king," Urith interrupted the conversation. "Lead the way."

The leader nodded to his men who moved into a formation around the travelers before turning to guide them back to the plaza. As he walked along, the Vulthnal fighter came alongside Urith.

"We heard of your fight with the bandits," he told Urith. "It is a pity I could not have been there. Too many areas of this city have the same problems."

"Why is that?" Urith asked him. "Your guard looks fit enough for a few bandits."

The man turned sober. "There are not enough of us to clean up this place for one thing. The lands are filled with refugees coming to the city since the devastation on the Regiussa coast," he said with regret in his voice. "Now those who prey on them come into the city, silently like roaches. There are other considerations, as well."

Urith did not ask about the other considerations as they marched across the plaza to the temple. He noticed the man had not taken their arms, so for the moment, they were not considered a threat to the king.

"King Barcal makes his home within the temple," the Vulthnal told them before he rushed to the top of a long flight of stairs. While the group followed, Urith saw the Vulthnal warrior talking with two satgerts who were standing between the white fluted columns. The priests turned back inside, and he motioned the column of guards and travelers to follow him through the tall white stone corridor. The echoes of boots filled the air as they followed the hallway, bypassing huge statue of

Ecarca seated upon a magnificent throne in the middle of the interior chamber. During their journey on the outside of the hall, they caught glimpses of the gigantic stone image of the god as they passed by the columns. The travelers noticed the impressive stonework throughout the temple, adorned with engraved symbols and messages about the gods.

Even Mivraa was impressed by the work that went into the shrine for half-brother. She sarcastically wondered if he even bothered to come to see such devotion. Sadly, knowing Ecarcas' temperament and callous disregard of those who worshiped him, she doubted he even knew of this temple. The gods seldom bothered to understand the faith which gave the Sky Realm much of its power.

Soon the column of people reached another passage leading to the rear of the building. The passage opened into a large room where dark wooden chairs and tables haphazardly strewn about the space. There was a flurry of activity around a slight man seated at a simple table in the corner. His back to them, they could only see his head, which revealed the man wore his hair cropped short, making his large ears stand out.

The Vulthnal Guard stopped, and their leader went to a short, wiry man dressed in white. The short man in white, holding his hands inside the wide sleeves of his robe, received the news somberly. He turned and whispered in the ear of the seated person who barely nodded. A short while later, the man at the table said something the group could not hear.

"Come over here," the Vulthnal guard waved the closer. The seated man who kept his focus on the papers spread across his table, reading and scribbling notes on the parchments.

"Captain, you have our heroes?" He asked.

"Yes, King Barcal," the Vulthnal Guard told him. "Two Esterbluds warriors and two women from other lands who arrived yesterday. We found them with a local woman heading for the docks."

The overlord said nothing for a moment, continuing to work on his papers. Finally, he spoke. "I suppose that I should be honored to have an Esterblud Geniht in my lands. I'm told you are called the Clovel Destroyer, which gives me pause. I am left wondering why you are here. Why come to my city and play hero?"

"My lord, we were captured at sea by bandits and taken to Casab," said Urith. He glanced around as everyone but Mivraa bowed to the back of the king. "My name is Urith as you seem to know. This is my nephew, Oslaf, and the women are Fedelm and Mythrol. We are just passing through to Eernicia."

The man at the table stopped his work. "That was not an answer to my question." His voice was higher pitch, like that of a young man, not quite past puberty. However, Urith knew there was an underlying menace in the statement.

"My lord, we stopped only for food and sleep," he said. "It is not by choice that we dealt with several bandits who preyed upon the travelers to your city. We were going to leave on the first available ship out." Urith waited for the reaction from the king but received nothing he expected.

"Then, you would leave our fair land?" The king asked. "That would be quite unsociable of you since I have received information that your group are considered heroes in some quarters of our city. Word of your fight has spread into our temple. I would expect you would want to stay. Perhaps you can help clean up our city from such bandits," the king told them from his seat, nodding to an aide who scurried out of the room, passing by them.

"It is a fine city, my lord," Urith agreed pleasantly. "However, as I said we were only passing through. I'm returning to my homeland from an important mission for my overlord."

"Are you telling me a renowned warrior needs women for your critical mission? I find that unusual," Barcal observed. "Besides, unless I'm mistaken, I've heard that King Penhda let it be known you are not welcome back to Esterblud."

"You are correct, and that is what I seek to remedy, my lord. As for the women, Fedelm has recently lost her father," he said. "We are attempting to give him proper homage by escorting her to his home village. He was a man worthy of Haligulf."

"That is an admirable sentiment," agreed the king as he turned his chair to look at the group. Dressed in the elegant white robe of the temple's inhabitants, the face that looked upon them with a mixture of boyish charm and deep reserve. The king's freckled face and brown eyes were alight with interest at the people in front of him. Hanging down from his neck was a heavy medallion of gold and rubies showing two intertwined snakes; the symbol of the Vulthnal kingdom. He laid his thin arm over the chair back,

"Your skills interest me," Barcal told them. "Would you not be interested in fair retribution against those sea bandits who captured you? I dare say you would fit such a mission."

"I would be happy to destroy those who humiliated us in Casab, but I have made a commitment to the gods," replied Urith. He was surprised at the level of information the king heard about them. Urith gathered the king was a devoted guardian of the gods with his residence in the temple. He planned to use this knowledge to his advantage.

"My lord, I would be honored to join your cause," Oslaf suddenly spoke up. "I knew well the stories of our two lands allying together against these bandits in the past. Our skalds have many honorable tales about the alliance between our kingdoms."

The young king looked over at Oslaf who was about his age and smiled.

"Are you not part of this commitment with your uncle?" He asked.

"My uncle is duty bound to return to Esterblud, however, if he would give me leave, I would gladly accept your offer. I follow the Heptarc Code and I would be unable to call myself a warrior if I failed to offer my services." Oslaf forced himself not to turn to Urith for approval. He felt his uncle's eyes staring at him.

"If your uncle agrees, I will accept your generous offer," Barcal replied. "From my reports, you bring skills we could use. No doubt you can help us to ferret out those wretched bandits within my kingdom that my guards cannot seem to remove."

Oslaf bowed deeply, happy at his decision. He refused to notice the dark scowl on Urith's face about this news. Fedelm caught the captain of the Vulthnal Guards go stiff at the criticism of his men.

"My lord, I must certainly defer to Oslaf's wishes," Urith said as he gave his nephew another hard glance. "No doubt your people's needs outweigh any help he would provide our small group. I only ask that he comes with us to complete the journey to Eernicia."

The young king had already turned back to his table, busily writing out a message as he waved his other hand in dismissal. He gave to the messenger beside him who, in turn, handed it to the leader of the Vulthnal Guard. The meeting over, the captain led them out of the temple, using just a couple of his men to escort their new allies. Mivraa frowned as she followed; her thoughts focused on the sudden loss of a needed warrior in their group. Urith was still fuming at the unexpected turn of events and was glad for the long walk.

"I should introduce myself to you. My name is Gerharn," said the leader of the Vulthnal Guard. "Barcal has asked the shipping guild to give your group quick passage to Eernicia as a personal favor to him. You should have no problems leaving this city now, although I would welcome your assistance to our cause."

Urith looked over at the man, who appeared just slightly younger than himself. "I wish I could join you," he told him. "Removing the sea bandits is a worthy goal but my duties remain unfulfilled. I would thank you for keeping an eye on my nephew. He has been known to be rash, as you might be able to tell." Oslaf paid no attention to the conversation as they walked, thinking only of his upcoming adventure.

"I will make sure he is treated fairly," he said. "We have other foreigners who will be joining us." From the tone of Gerharn's voice, Urith could tell it was something he did not approve of. The group paused at the top of the stairs, the sun blinding them. Two white-robed men arrived, escorting Wiga. The woman's face was pale with fear. She gave the group a quick farewell, racing down the steps. It was clear that she was told to return home by someone within the holy place.

"Barcal keeps a close eye on his subjects," Fedelm quietly told Mivraa.

"Mercenaries are notorious for their lack of discipline within large groups. And your king must pay well for them to take on the bandits. Forgive me for saying this, but your king does not strike me as a warrior," said Urith carefully, moving the hefty bedroll over to his other shoulder.

Gerharn motioned for them to follow him as he continued down the stairs. He led them across the plaza, leaving the guards at the temple.

"You are correct about our king," Gerharn told him. "He is young, and his advisors are, let's say, inexperienced as well. I believe that is why he plans and organizes. This will be his first campaign. That seems to be why he seeks your assistance. The Esterbluds are remembered fondly in our lands. The stories are still told about the Clovel Destroyer's battles as an ally to Barcals' father." He glanced over at Urith. "I've seen you before when you and your Esterblud fighters fought off the recurring charges from those warriors lead by the Death Bearers. I was only a young lad when you passed by, but I remember that sneer as you were ordered to escort the young queen away from the battle and back to the city of Alurican. For a moment, I believed you might disobey."

Urith, surprised by this news, remembered that cold afternoon when he lost his uncle, overwhelmed by bandits during an ambush upon the king's men and their supply wagons. He sensed Gerharn was confiding much more than he could rightly expect. It convinced him that Gerharn had doubts about the coming campaign and King Barcal.

"I remember that time well," said Urith, letting the man take the lead again. "I had thoughts as you say. As I recall, the Vulthnal Guard on the moors of Wermana gave us time enough for your queen to get away. It appears I owe you thanks for this. I have no doubt that I leave my nephew to learn great things from you and your men."

The captain took the compliment with a slight grin as the group turned down the street. They followed the road, now bustling with activity, to the docks. The merchants and traders, dressed in their colorful robes and tunics, showed only passing interest in the group before they went back to their business. When they arrived at the wharf, Gerharn led them to a small building near the main pier. Several large ships, along with various small fishing vessels lined either side of the berth.

"That is the Malhair House," Gerharn said, handing Urith a parchment paper with the king's message regarding their passage. The captain turned to Oslaf.

"Contact me when you return," he told him before walking away.

Urith put his bedroll down, telling Mivraa he would return soon. He walked to the small building, almost a copy of every house in the other ports controlled by the shipping guild. Each office housed documents and letters regarding the trade and passengers on the ships. The wealthy guild controlled the shipment among the business routes on the Maflow Sea, and these same looking offices provided their secretive masters with valuable intelligence about the kingdoms as well.

Mivraa and Fedelm drifted over to heavy wood crates stacked near a high wall which was covered with fishnets. They sat next to each other on one of the smelly containers, making small talk about the upcoming trip. Soon, Urith came out of the small building and carefully crossed the paved road, dodging large carts and people carrying items from the ships and warehouses that lined the road. Oslaf followed him as they approached the women.

"We have a boat leaving at the height of the sun and the tide," Urith told them, then turned to Oslaf. "Are you still planning on returning to this kingdom?"

"Yes, I've given my word," he said. "Listen uncle, you have taught me much, and now I think I must strike off on my own. I would like to finish what our people could not finish before."

Urith grunted. "You see this as your sakreta?" He asked

"I do." Oslaf told him with a nod. "It's something I'm ready for."

"I'm not sure of your timing about this." Urith said, then paused. "But I think I understand. Just keep close to Gerharn. He's a good man. With so many mercenaries being rounded up, he is rightly worried and things which can go wrong. I don't want Mivraa coming for your spirit, keep the Fates on your side."

Oslaf smiled at him. "You hold me no grudge?" He asked.

"Well, I've had time to reflect upon this," Urith told him. "The time comes for us all to find your own path. Besides, I have the help of two beautiful women now, so life is good." Urith gave him is sneer grin, but his eyes betrayed the concern he felt. He turned to the women. "I've already used the last of my koinons to get Oslaf a boat back. However, I want us to meet with the satgert of the temple in Damicia. Fedelm told me there were rumors that the priest is not sympathetic to Satres, and he might be able to get word back to our overlord in Esterblud. Perhaps he could arrange a meeting with Penhda."

"Why don't we ask King Barca about this? He wants our services; we could have made a deal with him." Oslaf wondered.

"That is true," Mivraa agreed.

"No, I thought that would be too risky," Urith said. "Besides, I'm not sure why he let us leave. He must know of our value to Satres. He seems interested in glory, but that does not always make a wise king."

"Do you think he'll betray us?" Fedelm asked.

"I'm not sure of his motives which means I want to leave as soon as possible," Urith replied. "If Barcal knows about us, it means others will know as well. Fealharans could be arriving soon looking for us." He turned to Mivraa.

"That's partly the reason why I told the king your name was Mythrol, I wanted to confuse the reports he must have about us," Urith said with a grin.

"And I still owe you for that," she replied as she struck his massive arm. "I like my own name."

"It would not be wise for us to advertise a demigoddess is with us," Urith lowered his voice.

"Alright, we go to the temple. But why do you need me along?" Oslaf asked.

"Because, danger awaits us," Fedelm spoke up finally, giving Oslaf her best condescending look. "You didn't stay around long enough to find out, but my last vision warned me about our journey to my homeland. I saw Dughorm and my father. It seems our enemies are growing in strength and spreading the word about us. Your uncle is worried about weakening our group now."

Oslaf's expression changed at the new, revealing his concern as he watched Urith walking away. He considered her words, feeling he had betrayed his uncle. But he could not escape the feeling of jubilation which filled him at the thought of the upcoming assignment for the foreign king. It could be an opportunity for him to make a name for himself.

"We can discuss this on the ship. Let us get the voyage underway," said Oslaf as he started down the docks with his bedroll and weapons in hand. The rest of the group gathered their items to follow him, ignoring his unconscious mimicry of his uncle.

"I've never heard you offer him a blessing of the gods," Mivraa slowed Urith with a tug on his arm while she watched the giant man struggling not to show his feelings.

"No, I didn't," he said. "I sought the Fates for he might need their help. I fear there will be a greater danger than he thinks in this quest he finds. Remember, I've fought in Vulthnal before. This land is constantly in turmoil. It will be hazardous because he doesn't know the people who live here." Urith unconsciously scratched at his long scar as he remembered the past.

Later that morning the ship carrying the wanted refugees from the Sacred Overlord left Vulthnal's harbor. Oslaf watched the city disappear from his sight as he stood under the bridge, paying little attention to the scurrying of sailors around him. He remained torn. On one hand, he was afraid he would not be able to return. Oslaf nearly considered running back to the docks when he saw the ladder pulled away from the ship and the lines cast off. He could not bring himself to do it. In a way, he felt his uncle was asking for his help. He knew Fedelm's visions were accurate and, if danger waited for them, Oslaf must meet it with his uncle straight on. He joined the group on the bow as they stared out at the blue horizon ahead while the ship slowly plowed through the waves.

The trip went quickly for everyone, but Oslaf pestered the captain about the timing of their landing. Urith had grown to accept Oslaf's determination to strike out on his own, freely handing out advice to the young warrior who patiently took it with an occasional roll of the eyes. Urith told Mivraa that he expected Oslaf to return to Vulthnal when they reached Damicia. He explained that whatever the dangers posed by Oslaf's departure from their group, his nephew's word to the Vulthnal king would be kept. His nephew must strike out on his own.

Fedelm reluctantly agreed as she continued thinking about her visions, but she could give little information beyond what she told Urith before they left the capital of Cahmais. She remained quiet during the journey, seemingly lost in thought much of the time. Her mind remained uneasy with the departure of Oslaf.

Still, Urith looked forward to getting to the city and, he believed, a step closer to returning to home to Esterblud. Urith had not told the others of his resentment at King Penhda for leaving him and his nephew exposed by putting a price on them. Urith wanted nothing more than to confront the king over such treatment of a loyal warrior. He knew the man, who he considered a friend, had great courage. However, he also knew he took the wrong advice from those in his council. However, Urith felt like he must meet his overlord alone, so he would not expose his friends to the dangerous intrigues within Esterblud.

He thought over his original mission to meet with Satres. Any reconciliation between his king and Satres remained just a distant hope. Visions of Fedelm and Dughorm, along with the Fates, sent him after the remains of the Skool. He felt as blind as his dear friend, Dughorm, who died at the hands of the Sacred Overlord. Urith looked over the little group that followed him on this quest as he strolled on the deck. Considering the Skool was something he never wanted, Urith hoped he remained   worthy   of   their   trust.

Chapter 3: Enemies Wait

Just as Urith and his friend left Vulthnal, Lyncus arrived in the land of Eernicia. Dressed in his long blue tunic and light canvas pants, the son of King Asgurd stepped onto the long pier. He walked quickly, paying no attention to the activity inside the large harbor filled with ships. Six hard men dressed in long dark green tunics followed Lyncus as he weaved along the busy dock that led to the walled capital city of Damicia, looming before him.

Lyncus paused to let the feared men in green push past the press of traders and merchants milling about the cobblestone street that was the main street into the city. Two guards at the end of the dock appeared indifferent until they noticed the milling crowd moving aside when they saw the familiar clothes of the fealharans. The brown leather bowl helmets gave the assassins a distinctive, threatening look to match their loathsome reputation throughout the lands. The guard's eyes widened inside the eye slits of their silver helmets when they saw the group come closer.

Taking the lead again, Lyncus confidently marched toward the gate, only to be intercepted by the leader of the guards who appeared out of the nearby shade of a tree. Lyncus scowled at the larger man wearing a silver helmet before giving him a rolled parchment. The Eernician leader gave a suspicious glance at the men with hathrow bows hanging across the shoulders before turning his attention to the document. Quickly scanning the impressive credentials of the Sacred Overlord and the endorsement of the King of Cahmais, the Eernician guard returned the parchment to Lyncus. Protocol satisfied, the captain of the guard ordered his men to stand aside for the son of Asgurd and his group to pass. He watched Lyncus and his group of fealharans walk toward the heart of the city before leaving his men. He went to the nearby stone tower that overlooked the harbor. Inside, he found the first guard he could see and quickly gave the man a series of instructions.

As the two guards outside were talking about the assassins in their city, they saw one of their comrades run from the stone tower, racing up the paved street leading into the city. Stepping out of the tower was their captain who continued watching the messenger until he was out of sight. He did not like the idea of this son of King Asgurd searching for some

Esterblud defilers in his city. Such events would only mean trouble for him and his men.

Lyncus led his group along the wide paved street into the capital of Eernicia. His thoughts focused on getting to the area of the metropolis that held the small community of foreign diplomats, where his brother, Tuncel, was staying. His brother's reports about the city were filled with descriptions about the numerous small enclaves of people from the surrounding lands. Lyncus knew what to expect within the kingdom of King Merkhan. The overlord of Eernicia had a beneficial alliance with the Esterbluds. But Merkhan could not afford the disruption of his trade with Cahmais. It was a situation Lyncus intended to use to his advantage. His first order of business was to locate the Esterbluds. His blatant display of bringing the fealharans into Damicia would send rumors throughout the city. He counted on the fear, along with a reward, to help with the discovery of the Esterbluds. However, his plans for them were only one part of his reason for coming to the city.

Lyncus stopped at the cart of a local merchant peddling his wooden drinking cups and plates. He was given directions to the area of the city where those from Cahmais resided. He turned, leading the group along the street to the white buildings in the distance. After walking for several blocks, Lyncus and his men went into a large square. In front of them, the kings' massive white stone residence stood. The royal house sported long columns around the building, each engraved with tight spiral twists, producing a dramatic, serpentine effect to the visitors. They turned down a side street coming to a brightly painted wooden building at the corner. A picture of a mug hung over the short door of the inn they entered. They entered in a room with a long slab of wood where the bar sat. Fresh straw covered the dirt floor but the stubble could not cover the other persistent odor of stale mead that hung in the air. The group found a sturdy table in the corner where they could watch the door and the two small windows facing the street.

The leader of the fealharans, a man named Pertac, sat next to Lyncus whispering a few words, before going to the bar. The bartender was a thin man, his unshaven face and buck teeth gave him a rodent-like look. Next to him was a large woman who ordered him to serve the fealharan.

"Don't mind him," the large woman said as she tried to comb her straggly hair with her hand. "What can we get for you?"

Pertac ordered food and drinks for the men, and the large woman sent the thin man to fill the mugs. Then, he asked about a place to stay.

"Best place would be here," she said assertively, pulling a large knife to cut meat for their food. "We have a couple of rooms that will do you well."

"How far from the Cahmiama building are we?" Pertac asked.

"Just down the street, it's the only brown building as you head that way." She didn't look up as she shaved elban meat from the bone for their meal. "Are you looking for another foreigner? They would be there if so."

Pertac said nothing, just left the woman to her work and returned to the table. He followed the thin man carrying their drinks. He spoke briefly with Lyncus and the group grew quiet as they began their meal. A short while later, Lyncus left the mead hall while he went down the street to the brown building described by the woman. Lyncus entered the Cahmiama building through a doorway cut of exotic redwood found only in Cahmais, finding an old man sitting at a table inside.

"Does a noble named Tuncel live in this place?" Lyncus spoke in Aberffraw to the scruffy looking man. The man leaned forward in his seat, rubbing his scraggly beard before absent-mindedly adjusting his small red cap, which he had pulled down over his ears.

"Yes, he lives here," he said. "Hasn't left for the king's palace yet, he's on the second floor, on the right at the top." He pointed up the wooden staircase.

"That's ok, I'll meet him on the square," Lyncus lied and left.

He walked back toward the central square, looking for the central Malhair House. King Merkhan, the overlord of the Eernicia land, was not known as a warrior. Instead, he built his kingdom around trade and diplomacy. Because of his relationship with the sea trade guild, a central Malhair House was built near the palace of the king. It was an open secret that shadowy figures within Eernicia worked to provide Merkhan the best information throughout the world from the guilds. Damicia grew very wealthy, becoming the home of the diplomats.

The Malhair House in Damicia, situated in the corner, was a polar opposite of the little buildings in the ports spread throughout Kamin. The sea trade guild spared little expense as making their central headquarters fit within the lavish nearby structures of King Merkhan. A large three-story stone structure, the building mimicked the façade of the multi-columned palace and temples which sat across the square.

Quickly climbing the white stone steps to the massive double doors, Lyncus entered the ornate public chambers. Inside, even he was surprised at the opulence surrounding him. Dark wormwood paneling and striking red painted furnishings contrasted with the slate pilasters that rose to the domed ceiling. A richly adorned map of Kamin showing the major ports covered the open dome interior. Moving across the blue marble floor, Lyncus could hear his leather shoes echo amid the whispers of a few people huddled around the few tables. He came to a shriveled old man, dressed in an immaculate and expensive purple robe, sitting behind an oversized table in the middle of the grand room. Lyncus asked about information concerning the Esterbluds he was tracking.

"I'm not sure I can help you," said the old man carefully. "We don't make it our business to know about such things. However, if you wish to make a donation, perhaps we might check the archives." The man's wrinkled hand casually pointed to a money box with an open slot at the end of the table.

"How much of a donation will this information cost?" He asked.

"Like most things in our life, much depends on how much you give others." The old man sighed as he looked like he just ate bitter root with their continued conversation.

Lyncus gave him a scowl before he put five koinons to the box. "I expect a lot for what I might give," he replied.

Out of nowhere an attendant came to the side of Lyncus. He looked as old as the one at the table and he wore the same type of fine robe.

"Please follow me," the man lifted his arm, directing the warrior to a small alcove across the room. The attendant moved swiftly to the recess, Lyncus hesitated, but quickly caught up.

Entering past a curtain, he found himself in a hallway which ended at a spiral staircase. He followed his escort down a level where they entered another hall that appeared to go on forever. Lyncus was led into a room with a standing desk. Behind the desk was another shriveled man with large eyes, dressed in the same style robe. He looked up from a scroll he held. His eyes were red from reading in the dim light, and his gray hair fell past his shoulders. The two men whispered briefly before the attendant left the room, quietly closing the dark wooden door behind him.

"You are searching for information. I'm the keeper of scrolls. Quite valuable information it appears. Please take a seat and explain how may I assist you?" The ancient one moved from behind the desk and sat in a simple chair with his hands placed on the lap. Lyncus took the chair opposite and laid out his information about the Esterbluds and their female companions. He didn't bother to explain his reasons for asking.

While he listened, the old man nodded with his eyelids closed in thought. After a long silence, he spoke and his eyes remained closed. Lyncus skeptically wondered if it was part of the show, a mystical ability to tell those who donate what they wanted to hear.

"Yes, we know of these people for your good friend Satres has put a mighty death warrant upon them. And we are aware that the Esterblud overlord seeks them with a bounty as well. As you suspected, they have left Cahmais. However, they have not appeared in this city yet. I have reason to believe we should know more about them soon." The old man seemed to be reciting from memory. Lyncus looked around at the hundreds of scrolls of parchment that filled the tiny room. He recognized that the guild selected people who had a nearly unlimited ability to remember details. It was something he had seen once when a troop of performers and skalds came to the castle he was young. He remembered a young boy, no older than himself at the time, read the entire contents of several scrolls brought by a *satgert* from the temple.

"Do you know where they are now?" he asked, startled at the mention of the Sacred Overlord as his good friend. He wondered how much was known about him and the overlord.

"The latest information within the guild states they are in Vulthnal. They met with the king who offered them a place in his upcoming venture. The women are still with them."

"How do you know this?" He asked.

The old man opened his eyes, unsurprised by the question. "We have our ways," he muttered. "Now, do you have any other requests?" It was apparent he would not say any more on the subject.

"Yes, can you notify me when you know more about the Esterbluds?" Lyncus asked.

"Of course, we can provide such information when we find out more," the keeper told him. "I'm assuming you will be staying in the city?"

"The tavern near the Cahmiama building," the warrior nodded.

"Very well, I'll make sure you are notified, Lyncus." He said before he paused. "Of course, we would expect further donations."

Standing, Lyncus nodded, suddenly noticing the attendant that brought him into the room, held an opened door as if on cue. Lyncus left the room, suddenly feeling uneasy about how much the man in the room knew of him. He obviously knew his name and no doubt had information about the fealharans who accompanied him to the tavern. He did not like how much seemed to be known already before he arrived. While this guild would be very useful to him in the future, it could also be a threat.

When he left the building, Lyncus spotted a familiar figure coming up the street toward him. Taking a hard turn, he stepped behind a merchant's cart parked along the street where he paused briefly before he doubled back. He watched the familiar figure as his brother made walked along the main street to the palace. He recognized Tuncel's tall figure striding along with others, his thin frame, and manner so similar to their mother. Lyncus breathed a sigh of relief that he had not been seen as he headed back to the tavern, knowing they would soon meet.

~~~

Coming around the rocky point that marked the entrance to the harbor, the cuggle carrying the travelers from Vulthnal slowly made its way to the dock. While they waited for the lumbering ship to complete the journey, Urith asked Fedelm about the city.

"I've not been here since I was a young child," she replied. "But my father often spoke of his friends here. I seem to recall stories about King Belmar and his friendship with your overlord."

"Yes, that is true," Urith said. "I hope that is remembered when we arrive. After what the bandits kept saying during our capture, I'm unsure of our reception anywhere." He lowered his voice. "If there is a bounty on our head, I suspect more than a few might take an interest in us. Any ideas about where we can stay?"

Mivraa joined the conversation. "I think we would probably fit in near the diplomats' quarter, which is near the palace. I've been here many times. There are places we can find where Esterbluds reside. Foreigners would not be inspected too closely."

"It seems like the best idea," Fedelm agreed. "We might be able to get lost in this city. It worked reasonably well for us in Uugaraa."

"Yes, until we almost got caught," Urith said in jest, his scarred face trying to make a smile. "We'll just be extra careful now."

70

After their ship had docked, they moved with the crowd of merchants and sailors going ashore. The guards paid no attention to them as they passed the gray towers and followed the street to the center of the city. Mivraa led the party, taking them off the main road and along the side streets. They followed the warren of streets, passing a few trader carts and workmen along the way. After several blocks, they came to several nondescript buildings which appeared like the rest on the block. However, on the door, the two warriors spotted the green painted picture of the Esterious, a giant sea serpent. Entering as they stooped to avoid the header above the door, they were struck by the thick smoke rolling out to meet them. A few men hunched down at a table were in deep conversation. The men's conversation stopped when they noticed long green tunics worn by the Esterblud warriors entering.

Urith and Oslaf went to the bar with the women following behind, feeling the stares of the men focused upon the warriors. Urith approached the wood counter where a portly man with red hair slouched. Speaking in his native Esterblud tongue, Urith asked if there was a room available. The man's green eyes widened when he caught sight of Urith's face and accent, but he recovered quickly. He told them that he had a room available for his countrymen. Urith eyed him carefully, thanking him and ordering four heathmeads as the women joined them.

"Where is the Temple of Duwdamon?" Fedelm asked the man.

"Take a right out the door and follow the street to the city square. It's the great temple at the top of the hill," the man said as he nodded toward the door. "However, you won't get in there with these warriors traveling with you."

"Why not?" Urith asked.

"There's been recent talk about Esterblud warriors who are sought by the Sacred Overlord and they have a large price on their heads." The red haired man quietly replied. "If it were me, with such a price on my head, I wouldn't enter the sanctuary of the enemy."

"Would an Esterblud be wise to remain here among his countrymen?" Urith asked.

"No longer than necessary," the tavern owner replied. "With the price I've heard the overlord is offering for your death, soon many others within the city will be here, sniffing about like a *kuon* after a bone. Even some of our countrymen might get ideas." He leaned over, lowering his voice. "My friend, you are well known as the Clovel Destroyer, and you are wearing the colors of the Geniht in public. I cannot risk my tavern or my family should someone come looking for you."

"I appreciate your advice, friend. What is your name?" Urith asked.

"They call me Helite," he said.

Oslaf forced himself to suppress a smile as he realized the man was named after the color of his red hair, so similar to the Bloodstone amulet Urith wore around his neck. Helite noticed Oslaf taking a drink from his mug with a grin and he grinned as well.

"I had a mother with a sense of humor," the tavern keeper turned his attention to Oslaf. "I know of Urith but what is your name?"

"Oslaf," he said, feeling a surge of humiliation that the man had no idea who he was. He was determined that would not happen after he returned to Vulthnal. Oslaf remained quiet, focusing upon his heathmead.

"Helite, can you tell me where an honest ossane trader might be?" Urith asked.

The tavern keeper smiled at this, for it was an old joke among the Esterblud's that no such creature existed in Kamin.

"Well, there is one less crooked than the rest," Helite said. "His stable is on the outskirts of the city. You can find it on the main trail as you travel toward the interior lands. He carries the banner of the Gallaeci above his door, so he is a man far from his homeland."

"That is interesting indeed," Urith replied. "Those traders from Ynyover are a hardy breed. If you hear of anything that might cause you problems, just let me know." Urith put down several koinons on the bar. "That should cover us tonight."

The tavern keeper pushed the coins back. "Pay me when you leave in the morning," he said.

Nodding his thanks, Urith led the way out into the street where he found an alleyway between two buildings and spoke quietly with his friends.

"Fedelm, I know you'll want to make offerings for your father in the temple. Why don't you go with Mivraa? Oslaf and I will find some merchant robes to cover these tunics. Then, we will get ossanes for our trip. It shouldn't take us long. I'll drop Oslaf off at the docks for his ship and then meet you both at the central square near the temple."

Fedelm agreed, pleased with the gesture by Urith, and his understanding of her wishes. Her feelings for him now were dramatically different from when they first met. At that time, she had been entirely willing to send Urith to his death at the hands of Satres.

Fedelm pulled the hood of her cape over her head while Mivraa did the same. Keeping a low profile had become second nature over the time they had been traveling with the Esterbluds. As the women walked away, they followed a few children along the street. Mivraa was quiet; distracted by something she was keeping from the others.

"You seem troubled," said Fedelm. "Would you like to talk about it?"

The women turned the corner onto the main road which led up the hill to the gleaming white temple in the distance. The mid-morning sun lit up the large structure, giving it an aura of grandeur even from so many blocks away. Fedelm glanced over at the demigoddess as they stepped around a merchant's wagon filled with aromatic *starkts* cheese and erba sausage from the highland region.

"Something is bothering me," Mivraa finally admitted. "However, I'm unsure how to speak of it."

Fedelm hooked her arm in with Mivraa's, keeping her tone light. "You can say anything to me. We, women, must have some secrets from the men."

Mivraa expression grew serious. "Yes, this is true. You know I'm very fond of Urith, but I cannot speak about the dream I've had recently. Tell me, have you seen anything in yours visions?"

"Like what?" Fedelm had a gnawing feeling she knew what the goddess was asking, but she kept it buried.

"Any premonitions about me? There is something unsettling in my dreams. It seems something is coming, but I cannot see anything clearly."

"Nothing is clear in my visions either," Fedelm admitted. "That is part of the reason for going to the temple. I need to refresh my spirit among the temples, and hopefully, the spirit of my father will come forth."

"I worry for Urith," Mivraa continued, changing the subject. "Since we met I've learned much about him. His wife and child died, and he believes the gods are at fault." She paused for a moment. "I don't blame him," she confessed.

"I don't know much about him," said Fedelm, not sure where the goddess was going with the conversation. "He saved my life, of course, so I know he's a hero at heart. I've heard of his battles and the Clovel

Sword, but nothing much of his personal life, even Oslaf doesn't speak much about him."

"Yes, he is a hard man to know," Mivraa agreed. "Much of what I learned came from Oslaf. I don't think Urith realizes how much weight he carries. With the power of the Skool, he could do terrible damage, even with only part of the pieces we've collected."

"Are you afraid of him?" Fedelm asked, wondering why Mivraa was confiding her fears. It seemed the demigoddess was worried about all of the troubles Urith had gone through with them.

"No, I'm afraid of his reckless impulsiveness," she said. "His quick temper and need for action might cause the harm. We both know he has no use for the gods, even when they might help, and I'm not sure about what he thinks of the visions. I think he only tolerates our dreams." Mivraa tried to keep it light, but Fedelm sensed she was trying to express something deeper that bothered her.

"He has given consideration to the advice we have given him. I think he trusts you as the god he can count on," said Fedelm.

"This is true, for I believe he and I have a special bond between us," she admitted. "However, if something happens to me, I'm concerned what might happen. Since Oslaf is leaving, it may be up to you to help guide Urith. I worry Urith's temper may cause him to seek a bloody revenge. Remember that vengeance is the word on the Skool we found at Du-Rinell."

"It could be a coincidence," Fedelm thought aloud before she saw the look on the demigod's face. She found it difficult to believe such things were a chance occurrence. "Ok, maybe you're right, but it appears we are in it with him unless you know different from your visions."

"I'm not sure," Mivraa told her. "Who knows what the Fates have in store for me?" She paused. "Or what awaits you, for that matter." Fedelm grew silent.

As they walked to the crowded square, the women pushed through the mix of merchants, tradesmen, and laborers. The heavy traffic caused them to dart among the combination of ossanes and erbas that drove through the streets with their riders and carts.

"So, what can we do?" asked Fedelm as they followed a vehicle carrying wood. "Much of this appears out of our hands, even out of the hands of the gods. It seems the Fates have more control over our destinies now. For all of their powers, the gods don't seem to have our future controlled."

"You might be correct," she replied. "I'm pretty sure the sky gods have no idea where this is going. That's why they tried to kill Urith before. One thing is sure; I have defied my god family because of this quest. That means anything can happen. I'm afraid of what my brothers might do to get the Skool now."

Fedelm stopped them just before they reached the steps leading up to the temple entrance.

"Could it be that you and I are being misguided by those sky gods," Fedelm asked. "I've never understood why your father doesn't just strike Urith with a lightning bolt and settle this. Then I remembered that Unis has the ability of vision and mind control. Could they use the god's Sibyl to confuse us? You know they are a devious lot."

Mivraa considered the woman's words for a bit. "That could be true," she agreed reluctantly. "Do me this favor. No matter what happens, make sure you stay with Urith. I've seen you around him. He has grown to trust you. Can you do that for me?"

Fedelm's face lit up at the suggestion. "There is no need for you to worry about that. It is a promise I can easily keep," she assured her. "Now, let us go into the temple and purge your mind of these troubles. Perhaps we can find our path in there."

Above them, overlooking the city was the Temple of Duwdamon. The women climbed the many steps made of large slabs of white stone. Reaching the top, they passed between great, fluted columns which rose up to an expansive ceiling high above them. Moving through the oversized twin doors, they walked past six Ionic columns, each engraved with different tributes to the Sky Realm. The procession of humans and *satgerts* stopped before the gilded statue of Duwdamon; his chest draped in a tunic with the colors of the Eernician overlord. Fedelm thought it was an outrage that an overlord would do this, in essence telling the world that the mightiest sky god oversaw Eernicia. She mentioned it to Mivraa who paid little attention, lost in thought. As the two women lined up with the column of worshippers, they could see a few crude tables lining one side of the room between the columns. On each table lay assorted items, offerings of the gods to be purchased. The scent of herbs and foods filled the air, mixing with the incense smoke coming from the smoldering twigs held by some of the devout. Both women noticed the tables were doing a slow business. Fedelm went to one of the tables to retrieve a small sprig of flowers as an offer to the god, Duwdamon. She would remember her father's sacrifice for his friends. When she returned, she noticed that Mivraa was staring at the statue, obviously uncomfortable at the cold stone image of her father. Fedelm knew of some of the stories about the demigoddess and the troubles in the Sky Realm. She told Mivraa she did not need to stay with her, but Mivraa insisted she would be alright.

When the women were leaving the temple, a tall man walked behind them, remaining nearby. His gaze was focused upon Fedelm. Mivraa noticed him first, watching him in the corner of her eye. He was dressed in the robes of the temple *satgerts*. However, the red trim of the cape made Mivraa immediately suspicious. It was the color of the Sacred Overlord.

"Fedelm, is that you?" A voice called out.

She turned as the tall man stepped forward to greet her with a broad smile on his face. Mivraa put her hand under her shawl, glancing around quickly for any other people approaching, but only the man walked toward them.

"Don't you remember me? I'm Imenal," he said. "Our families were friends at the Citadel of Br-Ynys. We used to play on the ramparts along the top of the fort."

Fedelm blinked a few times as she tried to recall this blonde, green-eyed stranger. Suddenly she remembered a shy little boy who her classmates bullied and teased when out of sight of their *satgert* instructors. The person in front of her was a tall, good-looking man who bore the confidence of his position. She was immediately taken by his sparkling eyes.

"But of course, Imenal," she told him. "It has been so many seasons since you left. What have you been doing?"

"My family and I came here at the request of the Sacred Overlord. I'm the *yolma* of this temple and others in Eernicia."

"I'm impressed," said Fedelm, suddenly careful at the mention of Satres. "It takes great knowledge to becoming the leader of such a impressive temple at your age. Let me introduce you to my friend, ah, Mythrol."

76

"Um, pleased to meet you," the *yolma* told her as he curiously noted Mivraa's hand in her shawl. "Come; let me show you around the temple. I think you will be impressed."

"We need to meet our friends," Mivraa interjected quickly.

Fedelm missed the cue as she looked at the tall man. "I think we have a little bit of time," she told her.

"Come it's only a short distance," said Imenal, his smile broadened again as he focused on the blonde woman. "I won't delay you for very long. We have much to catch up on."

He led them through a set of doors and along a dull corridor which followed just inside of the massive outer walls. He asked about Fedelm's family, expressing great sorrow upon hearing of her father's death. Imenal replied that he understood her loss, as shortly before he had been appointed *yolma*, his own father had passed to the gods. He explained to Mivraa that their fathers had been lifelong friends having grown up together in Eernicia, so the connection between their families went back a long time.

They took a short passage coming to a line of doors on the side of the temple complex. Imenal told them the doors led to rooms where the *satgerts* and their servants performed their duties. He opened the first door, indicating they should enter. Inside, they found a small room which held several chairs and a wooden table. Along one wall of cut stone, there was a small window, with shelves on either side. On the shelves were old parchments which gave off a musty smell that hung in the air.

"It's a quiet place for us to talk. I thought we should discuss the next matter in private," he explained, offering them chairs as he sat behind the table. "We will not be overheard by those that spend their time in the corridors of the temple."

While intrigued to know more about the young man, Fedelm looked at him suspiciously with Mivraa again moving her hand inside her black shawl. Fedelm carefully sat across from her old acquaintance while goddess chose to stand behind her.

"Rest easy, Mivraa. I have no cause to do you or Fedelm harm," Imenal said. "Since you are a great warrior goddess, and I'm not a skilled fighter, you have the full advantage over me."

Mivraa stepped to the door, listening for the expected footsteps while Fedelm stood, grabbing for her dagger. She would not be taken as quickly as the pirates captured her before.

"There will be nothing to hear because only I know your secret here, Mivraa. Please believe me that I will do nothing to bring harm to either of you," said Imenal before turning to Fedelm. "I brought you here so we will not be overheard. You are in terrible danger."

"You are telling us something we already know. We found out the price on our heads in Vulthnal," Fedelm told the man before she joined Mivraa at the door, listening.

Imenal looked confused. "I'm not sure what you are talking about," he told them. "I am speaking about the fact that Fedelm and her friends are branded as *wafaoil* by the Sacred Overlord. I'm the only one in the temple that knows this. Not even King Merkhan has heard this news yet. However, it will be difficult to stop the news from spreading. The overlord has many spies within the temples."

Fedelm was surprised at the news. She and her friends were denounced as defilers who should be killed immediately by anyone. Those who killed a wafaoil would be given great honor by the Sacred Overlord. "It was lucky that the sea bandits were interested in the koinons we could bring them. I didn't really think about the reach of Satres," Fedelm said, growing bitter as she spoke. "I should have expected it since I've defied Satres and his *sconce*, Alrpan."

Imenal appeared shocked when Fedelm called out one of the gods with such foul language. It was not the woman he remembered.

She turned away from the door. "So why are you telling us this?" Fedelm asked. "You are putting yourself and your position in jeopardy."

He looked at her thoughtfully. "My father asked me to keep watch over your family, as a favor to him. I'm merely extending my duties as *satgert*."

"I'm glad to hear this, but you are bound to Satres, just as I was," Fedelm observed.

"No, I'm bound to the Sacred Overlord of Ynyover." His face grew dark. "Satres is just a vain man who happens to wear the robes. I'm bound to my obligation to serve the gods. Since I came to Eernicia, I've learned about the Sacred Overlord from those who deal with his diplomats and advisors. His deviousness and crookedness are well known here. Even the guild has reservations about his strong alliance with the Cahmais king, and they will take koinons from anyone. There are strong hints about a war coming between Esterblud and Cahmais." He looked at them, but both women remained silent.

"Besides, I remember your family and I highly doubt you and your father could be *wafaoils*," Imenal continued. "And you now have the demigoddess of Haligulf with you. Oh, how I envied you when I heard that Mivraa was rumored to be with you." He stared at the goddess who remained focused on the sounds coming from the other side of the thick door. "I know that Mivraa would not side with defilers of the temples. I'm sure the sky gods protect the humans from such people."

He paused as he watched Fedelm lightly bite on her lip. It was a mannerism he recalled so many seasons ago. She was still as beautiful as the morning he left Ynyover. For her part, Fedelm thought back to the tidal wave sent by one of the sky gods when they arrived at Cahmais. Surely the surge of destruction wiping out the village was not the protection the humans wanted. She decided to say nothing.

"Now that you know about us, what's next?" Mivraa interrupted the silence.

"I don't understand why you came here or what you intend to do once you leave," he confided to them. "I'm only warning you about the danger you face. It is unsafe for you to enter the temples with Mivraa. Those who see her image on the walls of temples will surely recognize her as I did. Also I don't believe you can trust many people at this time. The *satgerts* within the temples or the advisors to the overlords would be happy to destroy you to please Satres. I would suggest you trust no one and leave this city as soon as you can."

"Why should we leave?" Fedelm asked. "We can get lost easier inside a city than as foreigners traveling in the backcountry."

"Not here," he told her emphatically. "The guild knows all that passes within this metropolis. Such information is bound to get to those that wish you harm or want the bounty that is apparently on your heads. I would suggest Ffestini would be a good spot to travel since many will be traveling there." He turned to look at an elaborate sundial that sat on the edge of the small window and rose from the chair. "Unfortunately, my other duties call, which includes a meeting with King Merkhan. Let me take you to the entrance."

The group walked back through the passage they took earlier until they came to the doors leading out of the temple. Imenal stopped and turned to Fedelm.

"I carry little authority outside of the temple, but if you need my assistance, I will try to help." He smiled at her. "I remember someone used to call you 'little Kiki'?"

Fedelm smiled, nodding as she reminisced about the name her father used to call her.

"Good, you can send a note to me using that name; just remember to have someone else deliver your message to a temple priest. No matter where you are the temples will get messages to me. It helps to have this post in the heart of Eernicia." He left unsaid that they would need to be careful since the messages would be looked at by those people aligned with Satres. Fedelm thanked him for his help and left the temple, entering the bright sunlight. Fedelm walked along as she relived her past memories of childhood with Imenal. Mivraa, for her part, was looking around the large plaza for Urith, hoping he was able to get them transportation out of the city. The warning from Imenal left her unsettled. She could almost feel eyes staring at her while the walked down the steps.

~~~

Not far away, Urith and Oslaf slowly followed several carts, attempting to sidestep the many erba droppings that filled the road leading down to the harbor. They were dressed in brown robes over their green tunics and heading to the docks. Their meeting with the ossane trader got them their animals and saddles for the trip out of Damicia. Urith traded the last of their captured weapons they carried away from the sea bandits. It left them with just their own weapons and a few koinons to complete their journey. Urith left the captured weapons as a down payment on the animals, expecting to return the next morning.

During their journey through the backstreets, Oslaf made another impassioned plea for his return to Vulthnal. He pointed out that nothing had happened since they arrived. With a sigh, Urith turned them back to the dock, telling him that he would see him off. He gave Oslaf some of his last koinons for his trip back to Vulthnal as well. Oslaf tried to refuse, but his uncle insisted, claiming he would need it to pay for his meals on the cuggle back.

When they reached the dock, they both watched the hectic activity as traders and sailors loaded and unloaded the cuggles in the harbor. They stopped at a small shack with the symbol of the Malhair House above its door. Inside, they found an unfriendly clerk whose eyes lit up when Urith pulled his bag of koinons. While the man complained about the weather and the lack of space on the next ship out, Urith slowly kept adding koinon after koinon to the pile. Finally the clerk agreed Oslaf could sail on the ship leaving later that morning. After sliding the gold coins into his desk, he sent them away, telling Oslaf to go to a cuggle at the end of the pier.

As the Esterbluds walked from the shack, Urith shook his head.

"I would be happy to remove the guilds and their leeches if an overlord asked me," he said with a growl. Oslaf agreed with a laugh. Unexpectedly, Urith clasped his nephew's forearm with a solid shake.

"I will leave you here," he told him. "After you complete your *sakreta*, come join us. We should be in Ffestini. If not, I'll leave word where you can find me. I would like to have us go back together to face our overlord together, whatever may come," he told Oslaf.

His nephew nodded, giving him a surprised grin, "You can rely on it!" He said.

Oslaf walked away, keeping his mind focused on his trip and mindful not to look back at his uncle. He knew the difficult path he took was required and he did not want to appear weak at this moment. Oslaf reminded himself that his sakreta was something Urith had already done at his age, and the thought gave him comfort.

Urith watched his nephew walking away, trying to keep his concerns buried deep. His doubts about Oslaf's readiness for this venture were mixed with his pride at his mentor. After his nephew tall figure disappeared in the crowd, he turned and slowly began walking back into the city. Urith hoped his nephew learned enough from him.

Coming toward the palace square, Urith noticed he trailed behind a small line of foreigner dignitaries. Their striking robes emblazoned with colorful trim, symbolic of their homelands. With an air of superiority which befits their rank, two diplomats strolled along the road. Their status was signified by purple stoles which draped their shoulders and was held in place by a brooch of gold. Followed by their attendants, who listened with apparent admiration, the diplomats engaged in a discussion about the beautiful weather. Urith overheard parts of the trifling conversation, and he observed the tall, slender man leading the group wore the colors of his enemy, the Cahmais. He briefly wondered how the man would react if he looked back to see a Geniht warrior of Esterblud following him. Seasons of warfare between the Cahmais and Esterblud left both sides with an enmity for one another. While there was a peace treaty between the lands, the people continued to look for ways to keep the hate alive. Urith felt an irony in being close enough to destroy a long-standing enemy while being unable to strike him. His sole purpose now was to complete the Skool, not to start a war between his kingdom and Cahmais.

Urith turned his path away from the Aberffraw group. Moving across the chaotic street traffic, he saw Fedelm and Mivraa as they stood on the open courtyard. They slowly walked toward a line of merchant carts parked along the side of the street. Behind the parked vehicles, a long row of wattle and daub plaster merchant buildings with blue slate roofs shouted their contrast against the grand palace in the middle of the square. Realizing the women had not seen him yet, Urith altered his path to meet them, hastening his pace.

With his focus on the women, Urith nearly missed a flash of a silver blade as a man expectantly closed on him. He reacted, striking the fealharan with his massive fist. His punch caught the man in the jaw, knocking his head back, exposing his golden hair when the green hood flew back. The Esterblud grabbed the man's hand which held a long dagger. Wrenching the man's wrist hard, Urith slammed his fist into the man's nose, breaking it with a crunching sound. Blood immediately gushed down the enemy's face as he fell to the ground. Urith pulled his Clovel Sword but he didn't see another assassin drawing back his bow string.

Fedelm noticed the commotion and she saw the fealharan with the bow. She screamed out Urith, who tried to dive to the ground. But he moved too late and the arrow pierced his back just above his shoulder blade. The archer was notching another arrow when Mivraa, sprinting toward the man, threw her silver spear. Her weapon skewered the assassin against the cart, sending his brown bowl helmet tumbling into the air. The fealharan weakly pulled at the spear before dying in his standing position. Fedelm noticed the look of disbelief engrained upon the dead assassin's face.

Mivraa took a quick turn, outrunning Fedelm in the race to the wounded Esterblud. Urith was scrambling to his feet with his Clovel sword in hand. Another arrow came from behind him, striking Urith hard, but it ricocheted off his shield which was hanging from his back. At the same time, another arrow hit him from the side, but it failed to penetrate his chainmail undershirt. However, the impact of the arrow winded him, nearly knocking him off his feet. Somehow he kept his balance, focused on getting to the relative safety behind the merchant carts. Mivraa caught up with him, grabbing his tunic and pulling the warrior with her behind the carts.

As the rain of arrows came in from the four other fealharan assassins, Fedelm ran behind Mivraa trying to catch up. However, in the chaos, two fat merchants slammed into her as they hurried to get away from the arrows. The impact sent her sprawling to the cobblestone street, momentarily stunned. Rolling over, she caught a glimpse of the mass of people who were standing around watching the spectacle play out in front of them. No one attempted to intervene. The hakra scrambled to her feet meeting up with Urith and Mivraa as they ran between two of the wagons, crouching down to avoid the rain of arrows. Fedelm helped the warrior remove his shield and spear hanging over his back, attached to his baudrik belt. He gritted his teeth, telling Mivraa to pull out the arrow. She looked around for the oncoming assassins before she quickly pulled on the shaft. Her haste caused the tip to cut open the wound wider and the warrior to yell out in pain. His tunic turned dark as the blood spread along his shoulder.

"I've counted at least four of them," Mivraa told them.

"Not for long," he told her as he slid his arm into the straps of his shield, gritting his teeth at the pain. He stood up with the Clovel Sword, momentarily leaning against the wagon. He saw a pair of the green-robed men trying to flank their position.

"Stay with Fedelm!" Without waiting for an objection, he took off from behind the carts, heading down the street away from them.

The fealharans immediately spotted the large figure in the green and red tunic running away from them. They sprinted after him like a pack of kuons chasing their prey. Urith cut through a scattering group of local citizens, turning up the alley between two buildings. Despite his wound, his frenzied anger kept him moving, and he liked his odds within narrow alleyway. He dodged past barrels and crates that dotted the path before turning up a blind alley. Instantly realizing he was trapped, Urith suddenly stopped, turning around with his sword and shield at the ready. The warrior decided to use the darkened area to his temporary advantage, hoping the fealharans did not know of the dead end. He could hear the running footsteps suddenly stop as the assassins regrouped. The

Esterblud's hopes suddenly faded as he heard the soft metallic sound of short swords being drawn from scabbards, along with slow footsteps as they closed on the alleyway. They were too experienced to run up the dark alley so he waited for an expected death, believing the death creepers would work their way into the dark alley in pairs. Trying to control his heavy breathing, he heard someone come near him at the edge of the dark gray plaster building. He took a gamble as the warrior suddenly charged into the group of assassins.

The closest enemy tried to dodge the longsword of the Esterblud warrior. His effort was in vain as the Clovel blade sliced across the fealharan's chest, sending the screaming man to the ground, hopelessly grasping at the gaping wound. Urith barely dodged another's swing of his wooden bow at his head, and the Esterblud threw up his Shield of Skool. He savagely slammed the edge of his heavy shield into his enemy's throat. The fealharan fell across a knee-high box, convulsing as he grabbed his throat to die a slow death. Unfortunately for Urith, as he pulled away, another assassin stabbed into his belly with a short sword. The explosion of pain sent the giant warrior back, lashing out with his long sword. He fell back into the wall; he was able to swing up his weapon, slicing into the exposed groin area of his enemy. The enemy cutthroat screamed as he slid to the ground in a fetal position, holding his bleeding lower abdomen.

Urith looked up in time to see the last assassin stood just a few paces away. The man gave a deadly grin, showing his discolored teeth, about to launch his arrow to finish off the Esterblud. Urith waited for the oncoming projectile, trying to raise his shield in time. However, the fatal arrow never struck. The giant warrior saw a flash of crimson and silver explode through the fealharan's chest. The man pitched forward face first on the stone pavement as Mivraa calmly pulled her spear out of the man's back. Fedelm stood behind the demigoddess as she watched in dismay at the blood spreading across Urith's belly. The hakra ran to his side, helping him lift himself from the ground.

"Come on, we need to leave this place now," said Mivraa as she helped Fedelm getting the giant warrior on his feet. The trio stumbled past the dying and dead assassins on the road, trying to escape other killers who might be in the crowd coming into the ally. Mivraa took the lead while Urith Fedelm's shoulder to help steady him as they followed the goddess down the alley. Mivraa turned the corner at the end of the lane, suddenly hearing a familiar low whistle, a sound missed by her companions. The tune caused her to pause momentarily, looking around to the source, but she could not see anyone.

Down at the other end of the alleyway, a crowd pushed into the narrow path, catching a glimpse of the survivors running away. The noise of the crowd grew louder as the initial shock of the battle, they just witness wore away. Behind them, temple and palace guards came running into the commotion, followed by various others. One of the interested observers in the mix was Lyncus, who had witnessed his men's wasted efforts to remove the Esterblud defiler and his companions. Coming up next to Cahmais noble was Pertac, the leader of the fealharans.

"Your miserable men have disappointed me," Lyncus told him. "It appears my father's money went to amateurs. The overlord will not be happy with your work."

"We will track them down and finish the job. I have access to more men," promised the man next to Aberffraw leader, keeping his voice as a whisper while the guards pushed past them. His youthful face belied his mastery of ambush and quick death. The fealharan knew he had underestimated the Esterblud along with the women who ran with him.

"No, I have a better idea. I will return to the tavern. You will gather whatever men you have left and meet me there." He paused, then turned to Pertac. "Before you return, make sure you cut the throats of those wounded idiots who still live. There is to be no record of this failure to get to back to my father through the spies in this city. We don't pay men for failure. Do you understand?"

The fealharan leader momentarily paused before he nodded his head, realizing his reputation and life were on the line. He walked back into the crowd milling around as Lyncus turned away, walking across open grounds.

Not long after their meeting in the plaza, the Cahmais leader arrived at the tavern, taking a spot at the table he used earlier. Only two men were left of his original group. Lyncus was drinking his second greenworm mead when Pertac arrived taking a seat next to Lyncus.

"It's been taken care of," the assassin quietly told Lyncus before he sat in the chair while the other men moved behind him in the shadows of the room. "No loose tongues to worry about."

"That's what I expected. Your following duties will be on an easier target. And I want the Esterblud named Urith and those who travel with him to carry the blame. You will wait here for me." Lyncus stared at the door of the tavern as if he expected someone to enter.

"Are we waiting for someone coming to the bar?" asked the assassin.

"Walking by the tavern," Lyncus corrected him, and Patrec wondered what this treacherous son of Asgurd intended for him.

~~~

Urith, Fedelm, and Mivraa arrived back at the Esterblud tavern as the sun reached its zenith. They took a long route through the city, following a winding path of alleyways and side streets, keeping away from the main roads. Fortunately, they met few people along the way, and none seemed to pay attention to the giant walking along with the two women. The Esterblud used his Shield of Skool to obscure the bleeding belly, but a close look at his face would reveal the agony with each stride. They quickly walked to the back of the room, were Helite stood behind the wooden bar. Urith asked him if a room would still be available. The warrior had assumed news already spread of their battle near the temple. He was correct as the man looked around the room and waved them to follow him.

"You must leave by morning," the tavern keeper told them, keeping his voice low as he led them up the stairs in the back of the building. "People are watching, and the news will spread. Those men in green are dead, and word is the giant Esterblud killed them."

"Wait, some of those assassins were alive, and they ambushed us," countered Mivraa at the information.

The tavern keeper stopped at the door to their room. "It doesn't matter. I heard that the wounded fealharan paid a price for missing their target. Those who survived had their throats slit. But more will come, along with the king's warriors, I'm sure." He opened the door standing aside as his gaze held the belly wound Urith covered with his arm. "Have no fear. I will have my boy bring you some water to help clean your wounds."

The women went inside, and Urith tried to thank Helite, who passed by him. The man nodded his head. "No need to thank me for I do what I must. The fealharans who are after you put me at significant risk. They have no honor, and my family will suffer if you stay. If they come early, I will send my boy to warn you. I'm sorry I cannot do more."

Urith reached out and pressed the man's shoulder as he walked by. "You have done more than anyone could ask," he said.

Once inside the room, Urith removed his tunic and chainmail shirt with Fedelm helping him. Mivraa used the last of her healing water from the god's Exyts Spring. Soon, the skin around the wound began to heal itself from the water, closing the line of raw flesh. Fedelm posted herself near a small window between the beds, keeping watch on the quiet street.

"You should be better in no time, now lay back and rest," the demigoddess told Urith after they had cleaned the wound. "Fedelm and I will keep watch from downstairs for a while. We'll bring food later."

Urith nodded before lying back on the bed, his long legs stretched over the edge. The two women silently left the room, stopping in the hallway.

"I wish Oslaf hadn't left," Mivraa said, sighing. "Since we still have sunlight left, I'm going to get us supplies for our trip. Keep your dagger at the ready in case those assassins track us to this place. It is apparent to those looking for us that we might come to this area of the city, but perhaps they won't have enough men left to hunt for us."

"You don't believe that, do you?" Fedelm asked the goddess, who lied when she nodded her head. "Wait, we don't have enough for any supplies. And my dagger won't do much against a fealharan."

"Don't worry, I have ways to get supplies, and I have my shawl to level things against any spies." Making her point, the goddess threw the black cloth of her shawl over her head, quickly turning into a middle aged woman. Mivraa hunched over, and gray hair fell into her face. "I won't be long, and I might be able to find out more."

Fedelm gave a thin smile. "Alright, I get it. I don't like it, but I'll find a spot to watch the front door. If anyone suspicious arrives, I'll get Urith out the back."

Mivraa nodded and went down the narrow staircase. She walked across the room with the surprised tavern keeper trying to figure out how the strange woman got into the building. Fedelm found a chair near the stairs, moving it in the shadows by the staircase where she sat. Only a few local merchants were sitting on a bench near the center of the room, watching the figure of the demigoddess leaving. The hakra put her hood over her golden hair to keep others immediately recognizing her. While she watched the room, she noticed the Esterblud tavern keeper give his young son a mug which he brought to her. She thanked him, giving the red haired child her last koinon. The little one smiled broadly at her and went back to help his father behind the bar. She took a drink and pushed the chair back against the paneled wall, trying to enjoy the nearly quiet room. But the thoughts of their near destruction kept coming back to her. It appeared that Satres had put enough money on Urith to entice the fealharans. It was difficult enough with the gods against them, but now assassins. While she was not the type of person who wished she could change things, she gave a little prayer to her father to any help he could find in the spirit world.

Down the street from the tavern, Mivraa walked along following a small, colorful cart being pulled by an ossane. The vehicle's driver smoked a thick cigar of rattail weed while flicking his wrist on occasion to keep the animal moving along. In the back of the wagon, the goddess could see cloth, stacked in bundles. The afternoon sun left shadows along the side of the road where a few peddlers had their carts out but mostly this path was quiet. She was heading to a spot in the city that she knew where a twisted lellowtere tree still grew. The goddess had not been totally honest with Fedelm. She decided she would return to the Sky Realm to retrieve more of the healing waters of the Exyts Spring. She knew it was a risk if any of the gods found her, but she felt she had to take the chance. The goddess had seen a vision in her dreams showing Urith in great danger during a battle. At first, she thought it was the fight with the fealharans. However, the more she thought about it, she came to the conclusion that something bigger awaited her lover. She was determined to provide him with any protection he needed, despite the risk. The Esterblud was worthy of such help.

The goddess found her way to the grand plaza, not far from where the battle with the assassins took place. She took an alleyway between two stone buildings to avoid getting too close to the line of merchant carts now doing a brisk business. She hobbled through the plaza to find the ancient twisted tree, looming up above the stone walkway. Mivraa glanced around at the open area, watching as a young couple, holding hands and looking perfectly continent, strolled along in the afternoon sun. The guards posted around the palace were too far away to see her as she went around the large tree while chanting a spell under her breath. With a flash of blue light, nearly invisible in the bright sunlight, the goddess disappeared from sight.

When Mivraa arrived in the Sky Realm, she was near the Exyts spring. The woman was immediately troubled by the lack of sound around her. Typically, the air was filled with the sounds of birds and songs of the water spirits soothing the gods during the afternoon. She walked from the twisted tree behind her, moving across the blue green landscape as a human, ignoring her god ability to fly in this realm. On one side of the field, she could see the few massive temples used by the gods, the white stones looking like snow monuments so vivid in the intense sunlight above the mountain tops. Ahead were the purple evertrees lining the stream which held the water she sought. However, as she got closer, she realized the babbling brook was silent as well. When she reached the edge of the stream bed, the demigoddess saw only dry rocks and sand where water would flow. The wind spirits, who normally would be so talkative, strangely remained quiet

"Do you like what you see?" came a familiar voice behind her.

Mivraa turned to see Wurms coming to a landing in front of her, his chiseled face bearing the same expression that their father often gave her. He softly stepped to the soft ground, his blue eyes sparkling and he ran his hands through his long golden hair, his head slightly tilted. He was dressed in his silver armor, which consisted of a silver breastplate over his long black tunic which hung to his knees.

"What has happened?" She asked, mindful that he was a spiteful little brother with her powers of transforming as well. He helped her lead the spirits of the deserving warriors into Haligulf when he actually felt the urge to complete his work. Usually, the demigod avoided his duties by running petty errands for their father.

"Nothing much, just following changes that our father has ordered. It seems you have forced his hand, so he ordered the water cut off along this stream. Apparently someone told him you visit this spot to help the humans."

She could tell from his smile that he was the one who informed Duwdamon about this. Soon she felt the presence of another behind her. Glancing back, she saw her half-brother, Uugor sitting on a small cloud like chair just above the ground. He bore the strong resemblance to the sky god, but his hair was cropped short. Yet, his vanity was legendary for he enjoyed the worship of humans, going into the temples to find women whom he would rape upon occasion. Not very bright, he could be easily manipulated by the other gods into using his powers over the waters and creatures within the Maflow Sea. His distaste of Mivraa was apparent in his scowl directed at her.

"The wind spirits told us you were here. Father had to convince the petty little creatures to tell us about your presence. Now we have the family nearly gathered up. Mother will be so happy to see you again," the voice of Ecarca sarcastically filled the air as his body formed from the earth next to her. The stones melted like water before turning into a human form. The earth god of Kamin's eyes glowed red with his hate evident. As earth god, he had the power manipulate the lands from the mountains to the farmlands toiled by the humans. It was his molten rivers of rock and occasional earthquakes which killed countless humans, sending many of their spirits to the underworld. Like his brothers, he had little use for his half-sister, finding her humanity a weakness. He believed a half-breed within the Sky Realm was something the gods should never allow.

"She is your mother; I'm happy to say. I come from better stock." Mivraa covertly tried to look for a way to escape as she was surrounded by her brother gods.

As if he could read her mind, Wurms laughed. "Don't think you can avoid us. Father asked us to escort you. It seems that your interference among the humans along with your disgusting display of loyalty to that person named Urith has upset the natural order. Your silly exhibition to save the human from the fealharan showed Duwdamon your weakness. And then, you failed to bring the Skool back to father. It was the last straw."

From behind her, Mivraa heard the sizzling sound of the godfire whip which painfully wrapped around her before she could react. The searing impact dropped her to her knees as her golden chain mail armor could not withstand the whip which sent shards of electric pain into her. Uugor, who held the other end of his father's whip, rushed forward encircling her body with more coils, his face excited at each jolt as she yelled out, but the brothers laughed in contempt.

"You will be taken before father for punishment," Wurms announced gleefully coming forward to punch the woman hard in the face, sending her to the dust. He looked at the others, pleased with himself for doing something he would never have attempted had Mivraa not been tied.

Uugor pulled hard on the whip, forcing her to scream out. "I've always wanted to do that. Your protection by father is over, dear sister." He spat the words at her as he kicked her in the head. As she fell into the black pool of unconsciousness, she remembered the low whistle she heard earlier. It was Wurms watching the assassins trying to kill Urith. It was evident her brother demigod went to their father with the news. It was the last thing she would recall. Her half-brothers continued to kick and stomp her, making sure to inflict the as much hurt as they could, knowing only a sword removing her head would kill her.

After she finally passed out from the punishment, Uugor roughly unwrapped the godfire whip from around her battered and bleeding body. He threw her over his shoulder, pausing to let the warmth of her body along with the drops of blood wash over his cold god form. It reminded him of what he missed about those times together in the gateways between the realms when he and Alrpan used the humans for their pleasure. The god's forms came from the elements outside of Kamin, but they were not human, despite the look they replicated so well. The gods could never replicate the devotion to another or the warmth and tenderness of a human body and spirit. Instead, they sought only the first echoes still housed inside their human form, the incessant need for violence and total dominance over their subjects. Uugor's thoughts quickly turned to his pleasure. He thought that it was unfortunate that their father waited for their return with the half-breed sister. Uugor enjoyed the warmth of the unconscious female and, briefly, considered raping her, even though the woman was his sister. He, like the other gods, considered this to be his privilege. An eternal deity right over any human.

"Come, brother," Wurms spoke up, knowing the thoughts in the earth god's mind. "Father waits for us, and Unis would not approve." Wurms rose in the air, turning to the temples as Ecarca followed along.

"Too bad," said Uugor slapping the unconscious demigoddess on her rear. As he rose in the air, he wondered what his father had in store for his human sister. It was the thought that made the cold creature smile.

~~~

Far from the peaks of the Neewar Mountains, Lyncus waited in the darkening tavern in Damicia, near the Cahmiama building where his brother stayed. The Cahmais warrior's blue eyes patiently focused on the street outside, waiting for a familiar gait to pass in front of the four panes of the window. When he saw his brother strolling along the street past his view, the Aberffraw leader reached out, tapping the arm of Pertac who looked up. Both men stood, their chairs scraping loudly in the nearly silent room. Lyncus whispered something to the man in green who nodded before scurrying to the rear of the building, his men following him. The fealharan pushed past the surprised lady behind the bar, heading out into the dark. Lyncus left through the front door, stepping in the wake of his brother's trail. As he kept pace behind Tuncel, remaining several steps behind, he was happy to see so few people left on the street, and his brother seemed lost in thought. Out of the corner of his eye, he saw the fealharan moving from the shadows near the corner of a building. The assassins began keeping pace with the long strides of the Cahmais diplomat, remaining slightly behind and closing in from the side. Lyncus slowed his pace as he saw another man stepping out of a tavern entrance in front of his brother. The man was dressed in the finest gray wools of a merchant, and he stopped on the edge of the road, giving a hearty hello to Tuncel. The diplomat looked up briefly and nodded his head before returning to his thoughts.

As he watched the scene unfold, a sudden inspiration struck Lyncus. He made straight for the et merchant who was filling his mouth with remnants of *kilishi*, greedily biting around the stick holding the dried smoked fish. The Aberffraw leader caught a glance at the fealharan closing in on his brother as he turned his attention to the man in front of him. Lyncus asked the man for directions to the Malhair House. As the man proceeded to explain where the sea traders' building was located, both men heard a desperate yell suddenly cut off by silence. Both men looked over at where the sound came and saw the back of the diplomat who was on his knees, holding his throat. The body fell to the ground as a single figure in a green tunic swiftly ran away, taking the first corner of the street and out of sight.

Lyncus and the merchant hurried over to Tuncel whose white-gray face turned to see his brother running to him. The man struggled to reach out to his brother, his lips asking for help as his blood drained away. By the time the men arrived, the darkness had descended upon Tuncel forever. In the fading light, Lyncus suddenly grabbed the merchant by the shoulder.

"Did you see that? It was an Esterblud who killed this man." He said to the stranger, who nodded his agreement, although he could only remember seeing a man in green. "Come on, gather help. No one is safe here." The merchant hurried back to the tavern, pushed along by the Cahmais warrior who forced himself to keep from smiling at the easy manipulation. He quickly steeled himself to repeat his lie to the oncoming flow of people coming into the street as they gathered around the body.

Urith awoke with a start with a small boy at the foot of his bed. His first reaction in the dark room was to react to the sound of the intruder by pulling his Sgian dagger from his belt. But the belt was gone, and he fumbled for it for a moment. He stared at the child who looked at him carefully. The warrior gruffly asked him what he wanted.

"My father says you must go. The cute girl is downstairs, getting food." He turned and quickly left the room as the man swung his legs over the side of the bed. The fog hung in his head as he tried to understand what the boy told him. Finally realizing something must be happening below, he swiftly threw on his chainmail and tunic, while trying to find his boots which had been removed while he was asleep. He noticed he no longer felt the pain of his wound; he reached to the spot on his skin where the sword had impaled him, still somewhat astonished by the healing that came from Mivraa's enchanted water. He looked around, struggling to find his boots, nearly falling over them near a chair where the rest of his equipment lay.

He found Fedelm downstairs speaking in whispers with the tavern keeper, Helite while the young boy who woke Urith was busy filling the mugs of mead for those locals entering the bar. The Esterblud decided it must be late in the evening. As he reached Fedelm, she quickly thanked the inn owner and turned, motioning for him to follow her as she gave him a bag to carry along with the other items he brought. She led him out the back of the building into the night.

"We must get to those ossanes you and Oslaf got earlier. Helite just told me that an Esterblud killed a Cahmais diplomat. He said the palace guards are moving into this part of the city looking for you." She continued down the alley to the quiet street. "Helite believes someone is stirring up the people loyal to Cahmais, who live in the city. Revenge attacks against Esterbluds living here could start. There is fear among the Esterblud people in this area."

"I don't understand, but I'll follow your lead. I don't know how I can be blamed unless the fealharans are spreading rumors," he said, trying to put his weapons into his belt as they hurried along. "Where's Mivraa? Is she going to meet us there?"

For a while, the hakra said nothing after they turned a corner surveying the dark street. She kept moving in the general direction where Urith and Oslaf went earlier. Finally, she pulled between two buildings.

"I haven't seen her since she left earlier. She told me she was getting supplies and wanted me to stay and watch over you."

"What?" his voice rose. "Why didn't you wake me sooner?"

"And do what?" she pushed his massive chest, but he barely moved. "I don't know where she went, and you couldn't go running around the city asking where she went."

He fumed for a moment before realizing she was correct. He placed his hand on her shoulder lightly, stopping her. "Sorry, you are right. Let me lead us over to the ossane trader and we can decide what to do there."

The pair took back streets and alleys while avoiding any city guards and street thugs, who hung in the night shadows. Their progress was slow, and it took up most of the rest of the evening. When they arrived near the traders' stables, Urith put out his hand to stop Fedelm.

"The guards have beaten us here," he whispered. She looked past him to see men in their silver helmets outside the stables. It appeared they were intent on hanging around as they stood about in small groups along the main road out of town. Urith took Fedelm by the arm and led her back the way they came. Safely away from the main road, he turned them up a small path which they could barely make out in the dim light. He stopped, turning to the woman.

"As much as I hate leaving our ossanes, it's too risky. Even if we got to the mounts, we couldn't just ride them out. We will be walking to get out of the city," he told her. "Hopefully, we can find a farmer or merchant along the way who might trade with us, but that will be difficult." Fedelm didn't get a chance to agree before he went on, "I hate to leave Mivraa but she is resourceful. She'll find us before we know it."

"Do you know how to get out of here?" Fedelm asked.

"I'm not sure," he admitted, "but I remember the wall wasn't too far away. We should be able to follow this path. I believe it will eventually get us close enough to climb over the wall." Urith began a careful trek into the dark as Fedelm followed, hoping the Fates would soon turn luck their   way.

Chapter 4: Victims

Oslaf arrived at the large palace temple in the city of Alurican not long after the cuggle docked during the late morning tide. He found Gerharn waiting for him at the temple. The Esterblud was surprised that the Vulthnals knew of his arrival when he stepped off the ship. Inside the main entrance, Gerharn introduced him to a large, round man named Sacamer, a local *satgert,* and advisor to the king. The man was medium height, stoutly built with a fat face showing seasons of soft living. Covered in an immaculate white and blue vestment which reached to his blue shoes, the man grunted his greetings. It was apparent to Oslaf that the man had expensive tastes. Sacamer took charge of Oslaf, telling Gerharn that he send the Esterblud to him later. Sacamer led him through the holy place and they followed the same route Oslaf took to meet the king. However, they went into the open courtyard where the statue of Ecarca sat. A few steps inside, they found an elaborately engraved bench where Sacamer invited the young warrior to sit.

"I understand you have made a difficult decision to join with us," Sacamer smiled, making Oslaf immediately uncomfortable. "It is none of my business, of course, but I thought I might talk with you. I expect you will provide us with information since you have already been within this area, you would know the inhabitants, I suspect."

"Not that well," Oslaf admitted. "Those under the thumb of the sea bandits were too afraid to talk with us. Plus, we left in a hurry. If you believe my uncle, they were part of the problem."

"I see. Which do you believe?" He asked, his brown eyes looked intently at the Esterblud.

"Well, I saw many who were more interested in working with the pirates than sympathetic our plight." Oslaf told him. He remained suspicious of the conversation. An unknown foreign warrior being treated as a near equal seemed incredulous to him.

"Not to worry, we will soon rid these provinces of the sea bandits." Sacamer declared. "Gerharn speaks highly of you. He believes you can help bring the Heptarc code among the other foreigners we are gathering. I was hoping I could count upon your assistance in this."

"You do me a great honor," Oslaf found himself blushing. "You have my word I will help, however, needed."

The *satgert* slapped Oslaf's thigh, sending an echo through the large room. "Excellent. I knew I could trust Gerharn. We have a need for steadfast warriors. You wouldn't know this, but I'll be traveling on this sacred mission. Come, let me take you on a tour of our temple. You will soon see we have the gods on our side."

The two men rose and walked into the back of the sanctuary, continuing to talk about the upcoming foray into the sea raider territories. During the discussion, Oslaf noticed how the leader of the temple would steer the direction of the conversation back to the points he apparently wanted to know. On the subject of his uncle, Oslaf kept his answers brief, making sure not to mention the Skool or the actual reasons for their travel to Eernicia. After a while, it appeared that Sacamer tired of his company. He turned Oslaf over to a young attendant, a boy with wide blue eyes and buck teeth wearing an oversized white robe. His escort kept tripping on the robe as he walked.

Eventually, Oslaf was led outside of the city to an encampment of tents. Hidden from the walled city, he soon recognized the contradiction in the army being created. The area was filled with a motley collection of young thugs wearing local garb along with a few foreign mercenaries. Many of the men he saw came from the lowest parts of Vulthnal society, probably recently released from the prisons. Those who looked at him merely nodded or they glared sullenly. As he passed the banners that hung above tents, he didn't recognize the symbols but he saw a group of peasants carrying nothing more than scythes and home-made pikes. To Oslaf, what he saw of King Barcal's army were men driven by visions of loot and plunder, not much different than the sea bandits.

Led to a large tent made of skins and canvas, Osalf was introduced to a few of Gerharn's warriors sitting around a fire. After the introduction, several of the warriors threatened the attendant unless the boy found them food. His attendant ran away when one warrior threatened he would slit the boy's throat and cook him over the fire. Coarse laughter followed the fear stricken boy as he raced away.

The leader of the group was a man called Moorscal who looked to be not much older than Oslaf. As he lit a pipe filled *ulcath*, Moorcal invited Oslaf to sit with him. The pleasant smell wafting in the air from the ulcath helped the Esterblud to forget the foul stench drifting over from other parts of the camp. The sweet herb was used by some of the hakras to communicate with the spirits.

"Yes, it is not much of an army, only a couple of hundred men is my guess," admitted Moorscal. His pale face sported a thin brown beard to go with his long greasy hair. "The king seems to think that the sea bandits will run away if he puts enough of these men in the field."

"Do you think so?" asked Oslaf, enjoying the fact they spoke his language well enough for him to understand. The alliance between the overlords of Vulthnal and Esterblud over the seasons brought tribes and traders together, giving many people the ability to understand both languages.

"It would be a better question for you," observed Moorscal. "Our captain, Gerharn, tells us you were captured and escaped from these bandits. He says there are only a handful of outlaws in the city."

There was some skepticism in his tone which Oslaf picked up on. No doubt his youth was being called into question by the warriors around him.

"My uncle killed their leader, a man named Thulmare," Oslaf told them. "I'm not sure who took over for the leader after we escaped. From what I saw, the pirates are a tough, hard lot who live well by robbing and pillaging the unarmed ships which come near the islands. I know that the pirates came from Regiussa and I would guess no more than thirty men were in the town. But I did see several ships in the harbor. If they had more men on those ships they could make problems for the king's army." He nodded out the front of the tent. "Many of those I saw outside this tent will run if they meet a group willing to fight to the death."

"So they have help from the villagers there as well?" asked Moorscal.

"I'm sure the townspeople were on their side. There were a few guards who appeared to be local. I would bet they will not be scared away easily. My suspicion is the sea bandits must stay in the area since they have few places to go where they can attack ships and steal the people and cargo."

Moorscal glanced over to his fellow warriors but said nothing. Several men seemed uncomfortable hearing this from an outsider, but they remained quiet as well. It was apparent to them that their overlord had no fleet of ships and only limited men to stop the bandits. Moorscal asked about Oslaf's capture and the young warrior gave them his account of their treatment. He told the story calmly, recounting their escape from the village.

Moorscal paused a moment as he refilled his pipe again. "What do you expect they will do?" He asked.

Oslaf considered the question, realizing they seem genuinely interested in his observations. It was the first time that a group of warriors thought to include him in such a discussion. He tried hard to make an impression on the men.

"If it were me leading the bandits, I would break up into small groups when I saw this army coming. Using my knowledge of the land, I would pick off stragglers and seek to destroy the small groups of those unproven men who carry little more than farm implements. Death would come to anybody who wandered away from the others while looking for food and water." He told them. Oslaf was deliberate in his thinking, using all of the experience he could remember from the seasons around Urith. "Then, I would attack at night and strike fear into the enemy's hearts. Such action would cause weak men to desert, leaving just a core group of mercenaries and the real warriors who might question their leaders."

Those warriors around the circle nodded as they murmured their agreement at Oslaf's assessment while an older man named Ywer spoke up, "That's just as Gerharn thought as well," he observed before lighting his pipe to smoke.

"I suggest we gather more weapons and armor for those joining this expedition. There should be enough time to shape up some of those men who could be warriors," Oslaf said. "Training from those with experience in battle will weed out those thugs who might bring trouble."

"Too bad we don't have that time," said Moorscal. "You were fortunate to get back to us before we left. Gerharn's told me we leave when the sun rises." Oslaf didn't have time to register his shock at the news when Moorscal broke up the gathering. He gave several orders to his comrades before he turned to Oslaf.

"You can take your bedroll into the tent," he said. "It's one advantage we have over the others in this army. Most of them will be sleeping in the open sky." Moorscal stood. "I'll see what I can find for food." He took the path back to the city while the others went about their duties.

Gerharn returned to the camp late in the evening after he finished with the king's council. Oslaf watched the man crossing into the light of the fire, signaling for the young Esterblud to join him. The pair went to a small tent where Gerharn slept. It was also his headquarters and a place where they could speak alone. Oslaf believed he could tell the man was not happy about their orders, but his new leader did not bother to explain his thoughts. Instead, Gerharn explained to Oslaf about his role within the group. He wanted him to be a scout, moving ahead of the main body of men led by the king. Oslaf was proud of the assignment, realizing he would ride armored ossanes with the other Vulthnal Guards. He smiled at the honor, thanking Gerharn for the privilege. The Vulthnal captain gave him a tired smile before sending Oslaf to join his men.

Morning came early for the rabble and fighters alike. Oslaf staggered out of the tent, joining Gerharn's men. He was bleary eyed after a rough night with little sleep. Vivid dreams, which he dismissed as nerves, kept waking him as he heard the slightest noises around the camp. He joined his new comrades and helped them break down the camp, packing the extra ossanes with the equipment and supplies for their journey. After a quick meal, they gathered up their armored mounts. The Esterblud received a large brown colored animal, scarred from previous battles. At first, he nearly took it as an insult before he realized the old war mount would be a natural fit for an inexperienced warrior in the eyes of the Vulthnal Guard. They had no experience with him in battle so it was evident he would need to prove himself.

Before long, the Vulthnal Guards left the camp, sitting proudly on their mounts. They tried not to notice the mass of the army that was still scrambling for their journey to Casab. Oslaf saw drunken leaders trying to organize reluctant, sullen men into rudimentary lines. He overheard Gerharns' bitter complaint at the rabble he saw, and it suddenly dawned upon him that Urith would have reacted the same way. The thought sent a smile to his face as they sped up their mounts to begin their mission. His uncle was right in his advice to stay close with Gerharn.

Not long after sunrise several mornings later, the leading scouts of the Vulthnal Guards arrived at the crossroads leading to Casab. They were forced to wait for the rest of the king's troops to catch up, leaving the complaining warriors with little to do. It was late in the afternoon when the main body of men arrived. Gerharn sent a few of his men along the sea coast to the village to scout ahead. He told them to report back if they noticed any sea bandits gathering. Oslaf could tell by the man's voice that he didn't expect any trouble for his men along the road which was in open country. Gerharn sent the rest of his men along the direct path to Casab. As they traveled, both Gerharn and Moorscal would ask about places along the road where danger from an ambush might lurk. At one point, Oslaf offered to take the point to which Gerharn nodded, watching him ride ahead. The Vulthnal Guard leader turned to his trusted aide.

"I have a feeling he can fight, Moorscal," he told him. What have you learned about Oslaf?"

Moorscal removed the pipe from his mouth "You know he can fight, it runs in the blood of their clans, these Esterbluds," he told Gerharn who nodded agreement.

"Also, he's smart and a little cocky, but that's to be expected considering he must try to live up to his uncle, the Clovel Destroyer," Moorscal said with a grin. "I've heard of this Urith before in stories from my family. He reminds me of you." He pushed his long brown hair aside to glance at his leader.

"You seem to know him well for the short amount of time you have been together." Gerharn sounded surprised.

"Not really, Oslaf appears to hide little and probably a bit too blunt for our leaders," said Moorscal. "But he's smart enough to recognize the men we have with us are too raw, coming along for the koinons and loot they can find. If the sea bandits figure this out, this may not end well." Moorscal had a knack for speaking the truth while remaining calm and steadfast, no matter the situation. It was a trait Gerharn valued.

"Perhaps," Gerharn replied, "however Sacamer seems to believe differently. Since the Esterbluds killed off the top two leaders of the bandits, they should not be difficult to overwhelm them with our strength. There cannot be too many of the pirates hanging around. They will know we are coming. They always do."

"Too bad Sacamer couldn't use his spies to find out who leads them now. But we both know that he must have lost a lot of koinons when the bandit Thulmare was killed." Moorscal's derision of Sacamer was apparent. He believed the rumors about the fat man's involvement with the bandits. "I'm curious why he decided to join the king in this campaign. He has never left Alurican with us on such campaigns before. I wonder what's in it for him. Too bad we now have two fools who lack the wisdom to lead us."

"Enough, my friend. It is not up to us to decide the king's council," Gerharn told him sharply. He knew Moorscal would not flinch from his belief, and he respected him for it. Like most people around the king, Gerharn suspected Sacamer used his position as the overlord's advisor to make sure the king never really attempted to attack the sea bandits. And now this hasty attempt to gather an army showed Gerharn that the king's *satgert* was not actually committed to defeating the sea raiders. It was a show of force for Barcal to demonstrate his power.

Still, Gerharn was the leader of the Vulthnal Guard. As such, his loyalty remained to his overlord, even if he might agree with Moorscal. He hoped the enemy would be too discouraged to put up a fight. Either way, it was up to him to lead and take care of the Vulthnal Guard. Gerharn spurred his ossane forward; soon it would be time to find a campsite for his men.

Just outside of Casab, the men of the Vulthnal Guard were waiting in their camp. Many were nervously wandering around. They knew a battle was coming after their scouts returned. While they waited, the men grumbled like warriors, complaining about whatever seemed to trouble them at the moment. Moorscal watched Oslaf, who was sharpening his sword, a routine that soothed the nerves of the young warrior. Both men looked up when they heard the distant echo of ossanes and men coming toward the camp. They could see a long line of men coming down the road with King Barcal and his large entourage leading them. Brilliantly dressed in a silver plate chest plate that gleamed in the sunlight; Barcal looked impressive. The king's head was covered with a silver plate helmet topped with white plumage while a purple robe hung across his chest and over his shoulder. Despite the distance, Oslaf could see the king enjoyed his triumphal parade as the man rode with his head held high, his face beaming. The fighters scrambled to their feet, hastily lining up in formation with Gerharn stepping forward to greet the king.

"How much further until we clean out the viper's nest?" Barcal asked with his eyes focused on the road ahead.

"Just up the road, my lord," Gerharn told him. "The village sits in a valley beyond the trees. I have the scouts out, and they are due to report back soon." He bowed to the king.

"Nonsense, it is a small village, so we need just to push forward now," Barcal declared. "I have an army behind me."

"Perhaps we should take a break, my lord?" asked Sacamer as his mount came alongside the king. "Then your army can become organized to trap those sea bandits in their nest. We wouldn't want any getting away from the justice you have planned." The fat man's voice was soothing to the temperamental king who seemed to deflate when he realized the wisdom of the words.

"Oh, very well," said the king sullenly. "Get these men gathered in their formations. I want the Vulthnal Guard to follow me as I lead the way into the village." Barcal turned his ossane to the shade of the large trees, trailed by his aides who quickly scrambled to find him refreshments.

Only Sacamer and two bearded strangers, wearing armor, stayed with Gerharn. They watch the king's men hurriedly push a cart near the king to lay out a place for him to rest while he waited. Oslaf focused on the men with Sacamer. Two different banners, one yellow and one red, were placed on either side of the grass field next to the trail so the men could gather around the leaders taking them into battle. The well-equipped warriors watched with some amusement as these men complained about their journey. Many were dressed in rags and they were lightly armed with just crudely made shields and short swords. None wore chain mail or wore helmets. Oslaf overheard his comrades saying the men were rounded up from jails and dungeons of Alurican and nearby villages. Gerharn noticed these men as well.

"You bring prisoners instead of warriors?" He asked, glaring at Sacamer.

"They are paying off their debt to the king," the fat man replied tersely. "They will be sent in after the warriors to search for survivors that can be brought for execution by the king. If they do their work, they will be set free."

Gerharn stared at Sacamer for a moment. When he turned his gaze at the leaders of the backcountry tribes, the two men grinned before turning their mounts away. Barcal made promises to release the prisoners in Casab where they would no longer prey on the merchants of his city. Gerharn turned away in disgust; he knew this would not help his troops during battle. He harshly ordered his men to break camp and get on their ossanes. Instantly, his men prepared their equipment for battle. Oslaf stayed with Moorscal, taking a final look at his weapons before gathering two extra spears to put on his baudrik belt which he slung back over his shoulder. Climbing on his ossane, Oslaf steered the mount close to Gerharn.

"Will we surround the village first?" He asked.

"No, we will lead the attack with the king at our lead," the Vulthnal Guard told him quietly. "That rabble Sacamer calls an army will follow us into the village looking for suitable prisoners for the overlord to sentence for crimes against his people."

"You appear to be concerned," Oslaf said.

Gerharn glanced around him. "Not for us," he replied. "You saw the village yesterday, the ships are gone. The sea bandits knew we were here. Those prisoners will be scavengers. This is not a battle, but vengeance for the king against these people."

"That is not a bad thing," Oslaf told him as he remembered his treatment. "I doubt that many of those people down there are innocents."

Gerharn gave him a surprised grimace before his voice hardened. "Then, prepare yourself to learn," he said. "These people are not as easily understood as you think. Hunger and isolation can breed resentment against a king. And now you have prisoners taking over this village when we leave. What do you think will happen then?" The Vulthnal Guard leader turned away his mount and rode off.

It took a while longer for Barcal's army to organize their two lines. Oslaf overheard from warriors near him that one column would follow behind the Vulthnal Guard, pushing along the main road as they pushed into the village. The other column would sweep around the forest, moving near the shoreline to cut off any escape. Gerharn's scouts returned, and he rode with them to inform the king and his advisors. They overhead the scouts confirming that the village was nearly deserted.

While he continued to make minor adjustments to the armor on his ossane, Oslaf glanced up to see Gerharn attempting to make a point to Sacamer and Barcal. The Esterblud guessed the leader of the guard was telling the king there was no need to attack the village. After a bit, the older warrior stiffly bowed to his king and stomped back past his men. Even though he barely knew the Vulthnal Guard leader, Oslaf could see the pent up fury of the man who reminded him of his uncle. His group of men pushed through the brightly colored aides and servants of the king with their mounts.

Oslaf was smiling at the coming battle when pulled his ossane near Moorscal, who was putting on his bright silver helmet over his long hair. There was a large difference in the Vulthnal helmet which had only a long nose guard and lacked the long side plate and chainmail of his helmet. After Oslaf put on his helmet with the *Estercetus* symbol, he realized how much he stood out among the guard with his green tunic and black helmet.

"Well, I'll be easy to pick out among the other warriors," he joked to his new friends of the guard.

Moorscal puffed on his pipe when he glanced over to Oslaf, deadly serious in his observation. "I don't think there won't be many warriors to worry about, the harbor was empty."

"Why have we wasted our time?" asked a red-haired man behind Oslaf. "They knew we were coming."

"The king will make a statement with this village" Moorscal said with a sigh as he knocked out the remains of his pipe on the pummel of his sword. "That's why Sacamer is here."

"What do you mean?" asked Oslaf, only to be interrupted by Gerharn, who swung his massive mount, covered in armor next to them.

"Follow me and learn," Gerharn told him bitterly. He pushed his ossane through the group of mounted warriors. The men followed in behind their leader as he led them to the trail running into the village. Ahead of them, they could see a band of archers, dressed in dark gray tunics, hustling to take up their positions along the tree line just outside of the village.

Oslaf could hear the sound of riders coming up fast, as the Vulthnal Guards filled in behind the king. It was Sacamer and his servant. The fat man was puffing from the short ride.

"I must ride with my king," he explained as he passed by Oslaf. He could see the quiet village below, an idyllic picture of timber frame houses and small buildings with the sea behind them. Despite the hate he held for those in the village after they fled, Oslaf began to feel an uneasy knot in his stomach. A quick look behind revealed the column of the king's recruited rabble following them. The other column was nearly out of sight as it marched through the thick forest of yan-yew and bluewood trees running along the ridge.

When King Barcal reached the top of the ridgeline, he pulled his sword and waved his men forward. Oslaf sped up his mount, and the group of Vulthnal Guards pushed their ossanes to keep up with their leader as they descended upon the quiet village. As the ossanes moved close, the sound of the cloven hoofs beginning to echo in the still air. Oslaf could see the archers had taken up a position in some trees not far from the outskirts of the wooden buildings and the ossane stable. A quick glance behind revealed the men on foot now running their line spreading out as they tried in vain to stay with the riders in front of them. Barcal waved his sword over his head, which signaled the archers. They sent a volley of flaming arrows into the thatched roofs of the buildings. Soon, the screams of the villagers mixed with the yells of the people trying to find buckets to extinguish the fires that were quickly spreading across the roofs. Before the people had a chance to run, a rolling wave of armed men charged into the melee. The inhabitants of the town suddenly realized the terrifying danger coming for them. Brown robed men, screaming women, and shocked children tried to scatter through the narrow streets. The king swung out his sword at the first panicked citizen in his path. The first enemy killed by King Barcal was an old woman who could barely see as she limped away from her smoke-filled home.

The Vulthnal Guard pushed in front of their king, plowing into the mass of people in the narrow main street. A few guards, distinguished from the villagers by their long shirts, colored blue, came out the buildings with short swords in hand. The guards quickly ran down the defenders, using the ossanes to trample them in the street. Oslaf noticed he was the only Vulthnal Guard, who tried to avoid those villagers unable to flee from the oncoming rush of warriors. He witnessed several of his new comrades slashing men wearing merchant tunics caught in the vise between the burning buildings and fighters. A wind change swiftly sending sparks and smoke over Oslaf and his mount which panicked the animal. His armored creature ran over a young woman trying to shield her daughter who lay in the street. He could not stop the battle hardened animal from trampling the woman with its hooves as it was trained. As he thought about jumping down to help the lady, Moorscal next to him. He ordered Oslaf to push on to the harbor. He reluctantly rode away from the badly injured females, the knot in his stomach turned into disgust. He braced himself, looking for men to fight.

The king's army, ex-prisoners along with mercenaries from the backcountry, entered the town. Some came after the Guards swept through while other came into the village from the forest. The rabble dashed inside those buildings not ablaze and soon the screams and cries of the villagers being butchered could be heard over the crackling roar of the burning buildings. As he rode through, Oslaf glimpsed gangs dragging men into the street where they beat them in front of their terrified wives and children. Some of the brutes pulled the women down in the muck, raping them in the street. Despite his initial urge to help the innocents, he passed the cages where he and his friends were once held as prisoners and decided the villagers deserved their fate. He spurred his mount forward.

Oslaf followed several Vulthnal Guards as they galloped toward the empty docks. Getting close to a trail, he spotted a man dressed in the blue of the bandits, trying to hide behind the wooden warehouses. He spurred his mount over to the trees, keeping his sword ready as he flushed out his prey from the hiding place. The man broke into a run, trying to get the water. Before the man could make it, Oslaf ran him down, striking him between the shoulder blades with his longsword. The savage blow sent the man to the ground, dying before the bandit fell face first at the water's edge. As Oslaf watched the blood flow from the massive wound, he felt the surge of satisfaction. Then, Oslaf realized the man was unarmed. He was running away; he had not even pulled his short sword out to defend himself. He wondered why the man panicked at the sight of the armored warrior.

He looked up from the bloody spectacle, seeing his comrades in the Vulthnal Guards riding out to the edge of the docks. They quickly struck down two guards at their posts who were clumsily trying to surrender, only defending themselves from the initial charge. Oslaf recognized the village guards were the same men who caged Oslaf and his friends for the pirates. There was a wave of satisfaction surging through him until he saw Moorscal jump down from his mount and nonchalantly remove the head of one of the guards. His new friend placed as a gruesome trophy on a nearby gate as the Vulthnal men laughed before turning their mounts and fanning out looking for more victims.

The action forced Oslaf to pause. While he had little sympathy for the fate of the men who caged him, he recognized there was no honor in their fight today. He tied his fate to the Vulthnal Guards who gleefully cut down surrendering enemies. As he watched the men begin milling around the docks and warehouse area, the sounds of the screams and fire slowly died away. The flashes of the brutality that he saw when he charged through the village came back to him. The purging slaughter people within Casab was a message from King Barcal. Oslaf carried no honor in such a message.

Oslaf heard movement nearby and noticed another figure moving among the brush and trees where the bandit had hidden earlier. He peered through the brush, seeing slight form and a flash of blue and yellow. He internally struggled with a rising question in his mind. Suddenly, he lacked the appetite to kill another unarmed person. Yet his duty must be to the guards. Oslaf spurred on his ossane at an angle to cut off the fleeing figure moving along. Despite dodging limbs and brush, he soon caught up with the fleet-footed person who broke away from the dense foliage, running toward the water. Oslaf steered his mount into the hooded figure, knocking them down to the sandy ground. He forced the ossane to a sliding stop, and he jumped down from his saddle. Holding his sword over the blue hooded figure with the yellow girdle around her waist, Oslaf wait until the hood fell away. Looking at him was a blonde woman whom he immediately recognized. Thulmares' *docke* or whore lay before him; the same woman who Mivraa let escape when they survived the ambush. She looked up at him with a mix of terror and defiance in her eyes. She refused to beg for mercy. Oslaf just stared down at her for a moment before he slid his long sword back into his scabbard.

"You have nothing to fear from me," he told her.

Catching movement nearby, he saw a small group of Barcal's army on foot coming toward them. Realizing the woman's predicament, he turned back, reaching down to grab her and she suddenly screamed at his actions. Oslaf clutched her hair, whipping out his dagger which he held near her face.

"Keep your mouth shut if you want to live," he told her fiercely. "I remember you were bedding the sea bandit leader. If this scum discovers your past with Thulmare, they will ride you until you beg for death. Then, they will mount your head on a pole to show the king."

He forced the hesitant woman on to his ossane when the first of the rabble arrived around him. By the bloodlust in their eyes, he could tell he was right about their intentions. They were looking to have her as a trophy for the group. Olsaf's warrior honor kicked in as he stood his ground, placing himself between them and the woman. The warrior code gave him a prisoner as potential ransom, and he was in the right to fight for it.

"Back off, she's my prisoner," he faced the growing group trying to mimic the growl of his uncle, hoping he was just a menacing. He shoved the dagger he held back into his belt. The trick seemed to work momentarily as the first men stopped in their tracks, their leering faces suddenly bewildered the Vulthnal Guard standing in their way.

"Boy, I don't give a koinon who you are, but I have seen the yellow girdle. She's a *docke* for the rest of us to use as we please." A loud voice came from behind the group. Oslaf could see the leader of the group as he came pushing through his men. It was a large man with a familiar face that Oslaf recognized at once. Ical gave the young warrior an evil look as he held up his sword and shouted out to the group.

"That's an Esterblud; he's a foreigner and a thief," he yelled to his comrades. "He stole my tavern from me and now he thinks he can take the spoils of our victory for himself. He deserves death for his crimes." The crowd rapidly grew menacing. The armed men started closing on Oslaf.

Oslaf lost his temper. All of the rage coming from the dishonor and foulness he saw around him welled up inside. As quick as a whip, his hand pulled his longsword from its scabbard, and in a single motion, severed Ical's windpipe before the man could react. The razor sharp blade sent warm blood across the group. They moved away as Ical fell to his knees, grasping his throat. As he died, the man fell forward with a thump in the sand. For a long, tense moment the ex-prisoners and tribesmen stared down at the dying man while deciding what to do. Oslaf faced them with his bloody sword at the ready.

"Every man back away now," Gerharn's voice thundered as he came riding up. When he arrived, he cursed them before telling the crowd that he would have each of them hung on the nearest tree. Backing his words, the rest of his Vulthnal Guards moved forward on their mounts to surround the group of men. Gerharn pressed his mount through, coming to a stop next to Oslaf.

"The next man who raises his sword against a Vulthnal Guard will die," he told them firmly. "He is here at the request of the king, and he will be judged by the king for his actions. Now, get back to the village and hope I don't come for you." Gerharn's actions caused the tribesmen to back away slowly.

You are to gather prisoners for the king's justice," he reminded them. "Now get to it unless you wish to stand before King Barcal." Muttering, the group broke up and the Vulthnal Guards pulled aside to let them pass. Dirty stares and mumbling came from the tribesmen as they stepped away.

"You will give your sword to Moorscal," said Gerharn after he turned to Oslaf. "You are now my prisoner."

Still wrapped in fury, Oslaf took a quick glance around. His chances to fight his way out were hopeless. Instead, he spoke up in his defense. "That cowardly *wearh* was the bandit leader who attempted to kill me at a tavern in Alurican. Then, he accuses me of thievery." He spat on the body.

"I'm sure what you say is true," Gerharn told him with a nod. "However, I have the rest of my men that I'm responsible for. We cannot have our Vulthnal kinsmen as their enemy. You will be placed before the king, and he will render justice." He turned his mount away and proceeded up the trail toward the smoldering village.

Moorscal got off his mount and walked up to Oslaf. "Give me your sword," he told Oslaf. "The girl will not be harmed. You have done your duty to protect the unarmed; you have remained faithful to Heptarc code

"Thanks for that," Oslaf said as he handed the man his sword. "We'll see if any others in this lot who remember such a code."

He began his walk to the village as most of the guards fell in next to him. He did not see Moorscal looking at his sword while Oslaf stomped away with the golden hair girl following him closely. Oslaf was resigned to meet his fate, but he also decided he would not go quietly. With a dagger in his belt, he would fight to the end. Perhaps that would wash away some of the stains that covered him.

~~~

Fedelm woke and sat up to look at the lights that outlined the skyline of Damicia, far off in the distance. Nearby voices woke her, and the graying dawn showed only thick brush from where the sounds came. Overnight, they were able to get over the short walls unseen. The travelers followed the road to Ffestini, walking a good part of the night until they reached the wooded area where the cover would allow them to sleep. Now, with the sun began its rising glow in the west, Fedelm decided to peek her head up. The voices she heard were out of sight so she quietly crawled to the top of the depression, pushing silently as she could through the brush. A group of wood-fellers with their ossanes had stopped to get water at a nearby creek. The men were laughing at a man who appeared to be the boss, told them to get moving. The leader was complaining about how much wood they needed to harvest and carry back into the city. From the conversation, the woman heard their route would be on the main road, a problem for her and Urith trying to escape notice. Fedelm slowly backed away, going back to their hiding spot.

"What is it," the warrior jerked awake when the girl slid next to him, causing Fedelm to press her cold hand over his mouth.

"Hush and listen," she told the man, her fingers touching the rough scar on his face. Despite the odd feeling it gave her, she quietly explained what she saw near the road before removing her hand.

"Are you thinking we must wait until they leave?" he whispered, and the woman nodded.

"They will be heading out in the same direction and will be coming back to the city later with their loads of wood. We will have to be careful not to run into them again. We are a pretty obvious pair." She smiled before turning serious. "I've not heard from Mivraa while we slept. I wonder where she might be."

The giant Esterblud's face grew somber as well. "That worries me. She's gone missing before, but I expected she would tell us something. It's too dangerous to return to the city." He was quiet for a moment. "I guess the best idea would be to continue on and complete what we set out to do. She knows where we are going. In fact, she might be heading there already. What do you think?"

Fedelm looked at him for a moment, the surprise evident on her face. "You've never asked for my advice before. What should I make of that?"

"Perhaps you are starting to wear on me," he said lightly with his permanent sneer softened to as close as he could give a smile.

"Well, since you ask my opinion, I say we continue on to the village. You could be right about Mivraa; she could have transformed into those wood-fellers for all I know. Maybe she' already waiting for us if she used those powers of hers to go through a gateway," said the hakra, trying to sound more confident than she felt. Fedelm felt uneasy after the demigoddess's disappearance.

The couple waited until the wood-fellers finished and continued on their journey, traveling along the road to the nearby woods. Urith and Fedelm chose to take a long circular route to avoid any chance encounter. Their route took them through the stumps of trees already clear cut by wood haulers over the past seasons. Devoid of most animals, their path meant they would be unlikely to come across hunters or other tradesmen. The pair kept in low-slung areas moving in parallel with the road before finally coming to the flat plains of Checeteria as the sun fell to the horizon. Stopping at the last of the stumps, they could see across the grasslands and the mysterious Neewar Mountains far away in the distance. The mountains, which separated Eernicia from Esterblud, were said to be the home of the Sky Realm.

"It's a long walk to Ffestini from here. I wish we could have gotten those ossanes," said Fedelm. "My father told me many stories of his time in this land, and he mentioned the long ride from his home to the capital."

"Well, perhaps we can do some trading. But I would be hard pressed to find something to trade since I'm down to just the weapons I'm wearing. I gave my last koinons to Oslaf for his trip." Urith looked carefully over the scenery as he spoke. He saw no settlements or farms in sight. The vast open grassland revealed little to him, but low, rolling land of blue and green grass. He did see what appeared to be a line of sparse trees.

"Maybe we can reach that stream before nightfall for water and perhaps some food," he said, trying to avoid the obvious in front of them. The warrior realized the open country presented them with additional challenges. On foot and exposed, a small formation of mounted warriors from the king would easily spot them and scoop them up quickly.

"We'll be alright," said Fedelm, recognizing the same danger. "I have the Clovel Destroyer with me," her eyes were sparkling as she ribbed the warrior. He just grunted, but she noticed his grin as he began walking toward the trees, barely visible on the horizon.

Both travelers were breathless from a long continuous walk they made to reach the stream just after the sun fell behind the horizon. During their journey, the hot sun baked on his armor and undergarments, causing Urith to stop and pull off his heavy tunic. Sweat covered the pair while their bag of water grew lighter. They kept their conversations to a minimum as each focused on moving forward, hoping to find water soon. No humans were seen as they crossed the grasslands, only the occasional *vensars*, scavengers flying high above them. Fortunately, the looming outline of trees was getting closer. Soon, they heard kuons yapping in the distance. Both knew they would need to build the fire soon for the vicious pack predators with two saber-like teeth were known to attack even small groups of humans. However, the animals were less likely to attack if there was a fire around. Squinting into the final rays of the sun, Urith noticed an area of brush which ran into the winding tributary of water. He led them to a relatively flat spot, located below the

112

surrounding countryside. It was a perfect place to start a fire using the brushwood nearby. Fedelm filled the water bag, returning to offer him dried *weamater*, given to them by their friend, Helite. As they lay back in the dense grass, the man and woman cooled themselves in the night air. The Esterblud warrior continued to worry about Mivraa.

"We should arrive in Ffestini during the end of Draenyna festivals for this land. According to my dad, the people still honor the sky gods with food and wine," Fedelm spoke as she lay on her blanket, looking at the stars in the clear sky. "This is fortunate for us that the village will be filled with strangers in their midst. I don't believe we should have problems there. We might be able to get us help when we get there. But I will need to go to the *satgert* of the temple there."

"I don't think that is wise," countered Urith. "Every time we get near one of those places, we run into trouble."

"Well, you seem to find trouble everywhere you go. But that's only because of your beliefs against the gods." She softly asked the question as she turned her head, waiting for his reaction. It was a slight surprise when she saw his face grow dark at her jest.

"Cursed gods are the problem. You would know this as well as I," said Urith. "I've made up my mind that anyone who sides with them is my enemy." His growl as deadly as his sword.

"Now, you don't believe that completely," she said, trying to soothe him. "Mivraa is on our side. And I'm sure she actually believes her father will side with us in the end. We need allies if we are to get the rest of the Skool. Too many are against us."

The Esterblud was quiet for a while, staring at her in such a way that Fedelm became uncomfortable. It was like he was sizing her up like the first time they met. Finally, his face softened a bit. "I'll agree with you about Mivraa, but that is because she is more human than god. She reminds me of the stories we listened to as kids about Mythrol. Heptarc's wife was probably smarter than he was. I remember how the skalds idolized her as the perfect woman in Esterblud."

"I wondered why you called her that name when we were captured," said Fedelm as she thought back to their encounter with the Vulthnal king. "I thought it odd at the time since many would hesitate to use the name for their children. It's just not done."

"Unfortunately, it was the first thing that came to mind," he said candidly. "I was surprised that the overlord didn't say something about it. I thought I made a terrible mistake when I said it."

Fedelm's face showed her surprise about the Esterblud admitting his mistake, but the warrior did not see it. The girl thought about the Esterbluds and their stories of Mythrol. Now she started to understand more about Urith's attraction to Mivraa. She brought herself back to the conversation as Urith continued.

"However, Mivraa has more faith in her god family than I can have. In all the stories, the gods act like a spoiled child and only act in their interests. We know they destroyed the village of Hyropda because they were trying to kill us. Mivraa doesn't consider that could have meant her life as well. Granted, she's as tough as they come, but she is not immortal and, despite the legends, I don't believe only a sword can kill her. Either way, you know better than the rest of us how the gods use us as their playthings."

Urith's words cut to the bone as the young woman remembered her rape and abuse by Alrpan, the underworld goddess, and her group of beorhs on their way to Du-Rinell. The thoughts hurt as she tried to push them away.

"So you don't believe the sky gods will be on our side?" She asked him, watching him as he sat up, crouching by the fire. He stared into the flickering light.

"No, you know the tales better than I do. Every song of the skalds and every story from the *satgert* tells of what the gods do for us and what the gods will do to us. If all the humans were slaughtered tomorrow, these infernal deities would be happy to build their temples to themselves upon our crushed bones," he declared empathically. Fedelm went silent as she thought about his words for a while. The words were harsh and uncompromising. The words cut at everything she ever knew. But there was some bitter truth in what he said.

"Would you like to sleep first since it appears we are down a few friends to keep watch at night?" She changed the subject as her eyelids grew heavy.

He now smiled at her. "I hadn't thought about it, but you give wise counsel. It looks like you are already comfortable there, why don't I take the first look around the area," he said standing up from the fire. Moving into the darkness, his voice echoed slightly as he told her he would wake her when he returned.

The young hakra continued to stare up at the night sky, trying to remember the stories her father told her about the ancient gods that traveled among the stars. The stars suddenly reminded her about the ancient myths of how the gods were cast out of the realms and replaced by those deities favorable to the humans. As her eyelids shut, the woman could feel the light breeze drift across her face, and she swore she could smell the scent of wildcress flowers which were her mother's favorite flower. Fedelm fell asleep with a satisfied smile on her lips.

It was the cold of the stone on her back, which Fedelm felt first, followed by the dull pain coming from her bound wrists and ankles as she hung against a tall pillar. The woman looked around the brightly lit temple, unsure of her location, but feeling she somehow knew it. Pacing back and forth in front of her was a handsome man with strangely bright blue eyes and long, thin golden mustache that hung down past his chin. The gods' eyes were cold as the stone on her back, and she could almost feel the sinister look he gave her. She knew the man, but could not repeat the name that rang out in her head. Around the man, sat others on finely cut benches, dressed in the same white robes and each looking at her with an undisguised vile hate in their cold eyes. Fedelm noticed how each of the beings shimmered in the sun rays streaming down, and they appeared not to touch the ground but seemed to be floating on air. In spite of her confused state of mind, she slowly began to recognize some of the gods around her, but she couldn't understand their hatred of her. What had she done to deserve such contempt? She could see Ecarca sitting on a bench, the same color as his brown skin. Uugaraa was on the other side of the woman; his seat adorned with symbols of the sea. He stared at her, licking his lips when she looked his way, the sea god's handsome face repulsive to her and she looked down.

Fedelm noticed her body was covered in golden armor and chainmail, but deep slices cut through the metal. She felt the pain of her ripped flesh below the armor. She took a deep breath as she knew she was experiencing Mivraa's plight. Somehow, the demigoddess was reaching out to the hakra in her dream state. The woman looked up at the family of Mivraa wondering how they could treat one of their own family this way. As if to emphasize the point, the sky god, Duwdamon suddenly lashed out at the body of Mivraa with a stream of electricity from his fingertips which sent the demigoddess into spasms of pain. Fedelm's vision went blank for a moment before she heard the words which echoed in her brain.

"You are no longer worthy to be called my daughter. The Triad knows your human weakness has clouded your judgment, making you dangerous to our realms," said the terrible voice of Duwdamon. "No doubt your human mother gave you these traits. If it was just your treachery to me, I could be merciful, and you would be utterly banished. However, it seems the underworld agrees with us you should pay for your transgressions against all of the gods. So they have come up with something special for you. It seems fitting given your betrayal."

"Curse you and your worthless family," Fedelm could hear Mivraa's voice in her head. "You are not worthy to be called a god. May the Guardians return to wreak their vengeance upon you!"

Fedelm could see the shock on the faces of those around her at her words. She felt the searing pain as Duwdamon lashed out with electricity again, which seem to continue forever. Finally, the torment stopped, and she felt the hands remove her from the column, letting her fall hard on the stone floor. A small cloud suddenly formed around her and she had the sensation of floating in the air. Above her stood her brother demigod as they crossed the sky. His thin lips compressed and his eyes fixed on their destination. The hakra felt a sharp pain in her bound wrists feeling the struggle of Mivraa, who tried to release herself from captivity. Wurms noticed the movement, smiling to himself as he kicked the goddess in the face, causing blood to splatter across his boots.

"No need to struggle, you'll have plenty of time for that," his voice menacing for its coldness as he wiped his boot on her arm. "I'm not sure if you heard, so I'm happy to tell you that our father wants you to appreciate fully the fact you are not a god. While you may have a few weak powers beyond the humans, you have proven unworthy of our realm."

He continued, "It was funny how badly Unis wanted your head mounted as a trophy in the great temple. I never understood why she didn't take care of you before. I was willing to help her but, instead, Uugaraa thought you should be given as a present to Caruun. You will be our token to help reconcile our realms. I must admit I was surprised when the underworld gods decided to help in your punishment." He looked down at the raw prostrate form of Mivraa; her eyes blazed with hate back at him. Her brother chuckled at her as he slammed his boot into her back and she jerked from the pain.

"I'll give you credit; you can take a beating that would kill any human. I suggest you get used to the pain." He reached down and pulled up her head by her hair. "By the way, with you gone, I now control Haligulf. You can be assured I will not be giving it back to you."

The demigod went silent as he let go of her hair and steered the cloud swiftly toward the highest peak Neehorsh within the forbidding Neewar Mountain range. These treacherous mountains of Kamin remained largely unknown and unexplored by the humans. The peaks which separated the lands of Eernicia and Esterblud ran like a serrated spine over the land. Fedelm could now see through the mistiness of the cloud as the two gods came to the high plateau, halfway up the rugged Neehorsh peak. The cloud settled into a twisted lellowtere tree which immediately opened the gateway into the human realm. Above them stood the high mountain of the Kamin dominion and it was now the dark of night. Wurms grabbed the demigoddess by the hair, dragging her forward as he held a blue light along a path leading up to the cloud quickly dispersed around them. They were in the human realm which meant the gods were limited to what their human bodies could do.

The red plateau jutted out from the side of the mountain for about a league with nearly vertical sides running down to the desolate sands below. Fedelm suddenly realized they were on top of the plateau, which could be barely made out in her mind and she saw Uugaraa and Ecarca waiting for them. She could feel steely fingers clamp around the neck of Mivraa while Wurms painfully lifted her by her bound hands. He dragged her across the dirt to the rock outcropping where large chains were embedded into the red wall that shot up toward the top of the peak. Mivraa struggled as much as she could, but her brother struck her savagely several times. His half-brothers, laughing as they came up to enjoy the beating of the helpless woman until she collapsed. Uugaraa got on his knees and rolled her over on her belly, lifting her by the waist. He laughed as Mivraa cried out and tried to fight, but the other gods held her face down in the dirt.

"Now that our father no longer protects you, we will let you be that human you want to be. Like all humans, you will be the slave to please us for a while," said the sea god as the others laughed.

Fedelm screamed as she experienced the terrible nightmare of Mivraa's ordeal. Again and again, the three gods took turns raping the woman warrior. They held no pity for a sister as they scornfully struck her repeatedly, anytime she struggled. Eventually, she collapsed from the torment. When they finally finished, the venerated Sky Realm gods looked down upon the battered woman, mocking her for her human failings while they put on their robes. Wurms used the silver dagger of their father to unbind her hands and pulled her arm up to the cliff face to clamp down one of her wrists in a shackle. He pressed down forcefully with screws until the demigoddess yelled out, vainly trying to kick at him. He laughed as he stripped her of the few remaining bits of armor and clothes she still wore. The demigod then shackled her other hand and ankles to the chains, pulling hard on the chains to satisfy himself the woman was securely attached to the mountain wall.

Wurms drew close to the woman, grabbing her auburn hair to lift her hanging head. The demigod enjoyed the fact the woman's eyes still held the fire of revenge. He forced her to turn her head to look at the edge of the plateau where Fedelm saw stair steps cut into the rock leading down the mountain.

"Near this place is the home to the *ranqels*, and I know you have heard of them. It seems our underworld friend; Alrpan gave this idea to Uugaraa. Father believes the underworld gods will consider your punishment to be a first step to bring the gods back together and to end the chaos of the lands. It seems a fitting tribute to the woman who joined with the humans."

His evil smile grew broader as his hair fell into his face, giving him the look of a madman. Fedelm felt the knot in her stomach, the realization of something even more dreadful was coming. Wurms stood up and placed the golden helmet of demigoddess on her head, taking special care to tighten the straps holding it on her head. The demigod then picked up her breastplate and chainmail, throwing it near the edge of the plateau. It would be in sight, but of no use to the vulnerable woman. He stepped back to enjoy his handy work as the naked, bloody woman hung by her wrists in front of him. As he walked away from his sister, his voice was ominous as the darkness that surrounded her.

"According to Alrpan, you will know much suffering and pain each night as the *ranqels* return from their travels to feast upon you. You see the humans leave a human sacrifice here each night for the beasts. Since you want to help the humans, Duwdamon decided you will replace their nightly sacrifice. Because you are part god, the creatures will not be able to kill you. So you will get the experience the agony of being eaten alive, only to be reborn again from the waters of the Exyts Spring." The evil voice faded away as the hoarse, desperate cries of the demigoddess filled the air. Her moans turned to screams when she heard wings saw creatures come forward from the edge of the plateau where they landed for their nightly feast.

In the darkness near the campfire, the sleeping form of Fedelm was struggling from the visions that enveloped her. She kicked out, struggling as she experienced the visions coming from her friend. So vivid was her experience that she screamed out which jerked the Esterblud awake. The warrior jumped up, his Clovel Sword at the ready in the dim light when he heard her yell. He had let her sleep when he finished his watch over the camp, feeling quite confident they were alone in this open land. Now in the dim reddish light still glowed from the dying fire he could see her thrashing body. He reached down to wake her, and the slight girl struck him hard in the nose which knocked him back. The warrior put his hand to his bleeding nose, surprised at the power of the small woman. Knowing her screams could bring unwanted company, he leaned over her, grabbing her to shake her awake. It took him a while before he shook the young woman out of her nightmare trance, her eyes blinking rapidly. She didn't recognize him at first, then suddenly grabbed him around the neck, hanging on tightly.

"Fedelm, what happened? Are you alright?" Urith struggled to breathe and tried to push her away, but her grip on him was like a vise as she trembled and tears streaming down her face. The giant wrapped his massive arms around her, whispering soothing words to her.

"It was terrible. I could feel them ripping me, eating me alive. I'm... I'm sorry but," she finally replied, her voice just a whisper. She paused for a moment before telling him more. "I saw something in my visions." She forced herself not to explain about Mivraa.

"What happened? I've never seen you react this way before." The warrior's expression showed his concern and it was something, in time, that she would fondly remember. "What did you see?"

"I'm not sure," she lied, suddenly debating with herself about telling the volatile giant what she knew. She realized that Mivraa must have known something would happen, which could change Urith's path and their future. The woman remembered the words of the warrior goddess and Fedelm decided she must protect Urith from himself.

"So much of it was unclear. I saw visions of the gods and images of the mountains. Terrible monsters that attacked me."

She shook her head, trying hard to believe what she told him. Then she realized she still held the big man tightly. Embarrassed, she let go of him, and he stared at her for a moment. She could tell by the puzzled look on his face that he didn't comprehend what she experienced. "You know I have to think about these visions. Give it some time," she stated gently, watching him in the dim light until he nodded. "Now why didn't you wake me for my watch."

"After the kuons had left the area, it was quiet, so I was pretty sure we didn't need it. Besides, I'm a light sleeper," he gave her his sneer smile. "Anyway, we have a long way to go so I decided we could use the rest before we leave."

"Next time let me know before you do that. I can hold my own on our trip." She feigned her displeasure with him, happy for the moment she was able to divert him from the truth. As she expected, he said he was going back to sleep, and she could pull her watch now. She quickly agreed, knowing well that she could not sleep after what she just experienced. The hakra made sure to tell him that he would be getting them breakfast then. As he grunted, he went back to his blankets where he went silent. Although she could not be sure he was actually sleeping, she watched his massive outline highlighted by the dying fire. While her body told her to rest, Fedelm was terribly afraid. She feared for what Urith would do when he found out about Mivraa. Although she could not admit it to herself, she was also scared of going to sleep and listening to the visions.

~~~

Oslaf walked past the dead bodies and the smoldering remains of buildings within a village called Casab. He took somber note of the number dead women and children that littered the streets. Few bandits lay among the innocents, leaving him with the heavy burden of his involvement in the deed. The Vulthnal Guards who walked with him paid no attention to the dead, causing the Esterblud publicly lash out about the slaughter.

"I sincerely hoped the Guards I rode with to this village believed in the Heptarc Code. It appears I was wrong," Oslaf enjoyed how some of some of the men, including Moorscal, looked away in embarrassment at his comments. However, it was a fleeting pleasure as he smelled the death in the air.

The group came to one of the few buildings which seemed undamaged during the orgy of destruction. Stepping out from the open door of the tavern, Sacamer looked down at the Esterblud, his face showing his disapproval of the warrior. Apparently, the word about the Esterblud's killing of the Vulthnal tribesman spread among the victors. Oslaf noticed how the man had his fat hands wrapped around a large silver mug filled with wine. He recalled the same cup used by the sea bandits. When he saw the gleam in Sacamer's eyes, the young warrior decided he knew who warned the pirates who knew the army was coming. It was too much of a coincidence that this fat man came along with the king against the sea raiders who left the village. Oslaf suddenly wanted vengeance as a way to atone for getting caught up in the politics of Vulthnal.

"I see you have made yourself comfortable," said Oslaf sarcastically. "I hope you didn't get your robe too dirty stepping over the bodies." There were a few muffled snickers as Sacamer stared back, his eyes narrowed at the insult.

"You have shamed the warriors of this exceptional group of men," stated the fat man. "Yes, it is already known that you have killed another fighter during an argument. There will be punishment for you."

"No, that was not a warrior, just a piece of street trash brought by you," the Esterblud interrupted when an idea came to him. He smiled to the *satgert*. "But my right to honor remains, no matter what you think. It was a *fealth*, and I'm fully justified in a fight of honor against a coward. I'm happy to accept the king's judgment on this matter."

The group around him began to murmur when they heard this. In the Kamin world, the young warrior had a point. Honor killing over insults could justify a fighter's actions. Gerharn rode up on his ossane, overhearing the young man's statement.

"Come then," the leader of the Vulthnal Guard told him. "Let us see what our overlord decides." There was something in the man's voice that told Oslaf he approved of the idea. As he passed through the group, he came between Sacamer and Oslaf. Looking down at the priest, the Vulthnal leader asked the fat man why he was not inside the temple.

"I'm sure the king would not be happy to know that one of his objectives remains unfinished." The Esterblud could see the fat man's face momentarily turn pale before he responded. Sacamer forced the silver mug into the hands of an attendant standing next to him before setting off to the wooden temple which remained unscathed during the attack. As the fat man nearly ran across the road from the tavern, Gerharn watched with a bemused look on his face, tipping back his helmet.

"I enjoyed that," he said Oslaf. "Now, let's go see the king."

The group moved forward again, with Gerharn in the lead and Oslaf walking between him and Moorscal. "For what it's worth, I agree with your defense of the girl. I tried to get the king to realize most of the enemy had left the village. Someone must have informed them of our presence. My scouts told me they saw many of the bandits were here when the sky went dark. Yet, this morning all of the ships are gone."

"And we still attacked," said Oslaf quietly.

The Vulthnal leader said nothing, and soon they turned the corner of the street. They could see the king relaxing in a chair, shaded by a small tent already set up near the two large posts marking the entrance to the village. Several of the former Vulthnal prisoners brought along were carrying off the bodies that littered the dirt street. Gerharn and his men stopped to dismount, and the Vulthnal leader led them to the king. The young overlord held a cup of wine in his hand and seemed content at his first victory. "I've already heard of your men's outstanding performance, Gerharn. You have my thanks."

The older warrior bowed his head. "You honor us with your words." Oslaf clinched his teeth, but he forced himself to remain calm, reminding himself not to lash out.

"We have brought the Esterblud to you for judgment. He fought well in the battle, but he killed one of the Vulthnal tribe warriors and claims he is justified because it was a *fealth*."

"So, you think you can decide an honor duel on your terms, my young friend?" The overlord's tone was light, but Oslaf felt the menace in his eyes.

"No, my lord," said the Esterblud. "However, that man was the same bandit which we removed from your city before. He falsely accused me and paid for it with his life."

The king sat up in his chair, leaning forward at the news. "So you are telling me, my advisors did not give me the fighters I asked for?"

"I cannot say what your advisors did, but I know this one man was not a warrior. He was a tavern keeper before becoming a mercenary, no doubt here for spoils of war." Oslaf made the decision not to express his real view.

"Don't think me stupid. I saw what those men did to this village. I've only seen a few bandit bodies and no prisoners for me to render judgment on. Either my advisors failed me or someone told the sea raiders that we were coming." Barcal looked back at the men standing behind him before turning back to Oslaf. Several of the advisors slowly began moving away like they were looking for an escape.

The king looked back at Oslaf, with a self-satisfied grin on his face. "But since I've won a great battle against this terrible scourge of my people, I'm willing to overlook your mistake. You have to remember that we must keep our tribal warriors happy since they will be settling here to help us maintain this village. No more will this area be a haven for pirates again."

"So that's the price of their so called help," Moorscal whispered sarcastically from behind Oslaf.

The king continued, "Now, since I've heard you fought well, I'm willing to give you back to Gerharn for judgment. However, our allied tribes might be unhappy at such a decision." He leaned back in his chair again, fully satisfied with himself, looking over to Gerharn. "What is your counsel?"

"I think a *frumkoin* might settle this, my lord. After all, it was an honor duel." The older warrior's face revealed nothing to Oslaf, but he understood the man was attempting to help him.

"Excellent suggestion, a simple blood penalty to placate our clannish friends," exclaimed Barcal. "Ten koinons should suffice." He looked satisfied with himself.

"My apologies, my lord, but I don't have such a sum," said Oslaf.

The overlord gave the warrior a cold stare. "Then it will be your possessions and banishment. My judgment is final in such things." He waved a dismissive hand, sending them away.

Moorscal grabbed the Esterblud's arm, leading him quickly away, telling him under his breath to remain quiet. Oslaf resisted, at first, wanting to attack the king, but he realized his temper could lead him into disaster. While he was able to use the long tradition of *fealth* to his advantage, but he felt no honor in the deed. The man was a thief and, no doubt, a murderer. Oslaf had killed the man before he could defend himself. Yet, something kept telling him that he must survive this trial and return to his uncle's side.

"Keep your temper," Moorscal whispered as he pulled him along for a few steps. "I would want to slit his throat as well."

Taking a deep breath, Oslaf nodded. "I'll follow your lead." He walked along with Moorscal. They watched the other Vulthnal Guards mount their ossanes and ride off, leaving the Esterblud wondering what he would do next as they walked around the village toward the woods.

"We are making camp outside the village," said Moorscal as if he read his mind. The guard leader took out his pipe again and stuffed it with *ulcath* from a small bag tied to his belt. With no fire to light the dry weed, he left it in his mouth as a reminder. "We'll grab some food and drink. I'm sure Gerharn will want to speak with you."

When they arrived at an open area, the Vulthnal Guards had already put up the tent for their leader and others were busy, working to set up their own tents for the coming night. Those buildings still standing in the village would be reserved for king's entourage. Moorscal gave Oslaf back his sword right before the two warriors stepped through the flaps of the light brown canvas to find their leader inside. Gerharn was sitting on a thick log, sitting on its end, which provided a small, almost throne-like chair. The gray-haired man looked up with they entered.

"Well, you have survived for the moment. However, we need to decide what to do with you now," the leader declared.

"I'm only sorry that I have not lived up to your agreement with Urith," Oslaf replied. "My uncle thinks highly of you."

"And you don't, I suspect." Gerharn's look sent Moorscal away. "Perhaps you would do things differently if you were in my place?"

The young Esterblud stared at the older man, wondering if his words were a trick. "I cannot know what is in your heart and mind," he said diplomatically.

The older warrior grunted. "Those are the words of a fat man who kisses the king's ass. I asked what you think." Gerharn could see the young man was struggling with his answer, avoiding the leader's eyes before finally speaking.

"Is it true the backcountry tribes will stay in this village?" he asked.

Gerharn nodded, "Yes, that is the decision of the overlord."

"I firmly believe you would not advise him of such a move. The king is ill served by Sacamer, either by design or stupidity.

"He is not stupid," replied the Vulthnal.

"Then, I would be going after those who advise your overlord poorly," declared Oslaf.

"And you think such a thing would be easy? Are you that naïve about the world?" The older warrior's face was turning red.

"Perhaps, but I was taught to stand for my beliefs, just as you. Gerharn, when my uncle told me about your steadfast stand against the enemy during your fight on the coast, it reinforced my natural desire to follow you. You were suspicious why this village was free of bandits. And neither of us believes that is a coincidence. Someone must have tipped them."

"With so many mercenaries coming with us, anyone could have told them," the Vulthnal leader countered.

"Perhaps, but do they benefit from this? I don't see how that means less loot for them to find. Something that keeps sticking in my mind was what Moorscal said to you. Remember, he asked why Sacamer came along with the king."

Gerharn's eyelids narrowed as he thought about the Esterblud's words. "You are accusing a powerful person." He paused momentarily. "But it's not your concern now. I would have liked to have you stay with us, but you heard the overlord."

"Yes, and I don't have the koinons needed. My possessions are what I wear," said Oslaf, carefully placing his hand on the pommel of his sword. "An Esterblud cannot willingly give up his sword. It provided by the family and engraved by the village elder. And my shield and helmet will remain on my belt."

"It is the same in our land," said the Vulthnal Guard. "Unfortunately, I don't believe our king thought about such a thing, so he left me in this quandary. I don't want to kill you for your weapons, but I must follow my king's command."

The two men stood looking at each other in awkward silence when they heard the scuffing of boots and Moorscal entered through the flaps. Hunched over, the smoke from his pipe covered his face momentarily as he spoke.

"My lord, I would like to take our prisoner here to his last meal with us. If a fight must occur, a man should die with a full belly, I've always said." Gerharn only nodded, happy the problem would be removed for a moment so he could think.

Oslaf sighed as he left the tent, following Moorscal. It seemed every path was filled with holes, causing him to fight just to leave this place.

"Thanks for your interruption," he told the one guard, he considered his friend.

"Come on, we need to get some fish for that feast I promised. I'm hungry."

Oslaf noticed they were walking toward the docks and away from the camp, following a trail through the thin yan-yew trees. He grew more suspicious as they approached two of the Vulthnal Guards standing at the shack off the side of the main road. It was the same building the Esterblud and his friends had found their armor and weapons during their imprisonment at Casab. Moorscal sent them back to camp, telling them to grab some food and return when they finished.

"There are weapons in this building which the bandits seem to have abandoned. I believe they are planning on returning," he explained to the Esterblud. "As for your problem with the overlord, I've been thinking on this. Our king puts you in a terrible predicament. You and Gerharn are too much alike, too honorable and too worried about following people who are not your betters," Moorscal said, smiling with the long clay pipe dangling from his mouth.

Oslaf felt himself nodding as they walked along the dock. He could see the Vulthnal's point. As they walked, he noticed a small sailboat near the end of the pier. The boat had a single sail with only room for a few people. He guessed that the sea raiders saw little value in such a craft since it was not suitable for the open sea with such an unstable design. But it did strike him that Moorscal led him to a potential way out as the young man continued to talk.

"Yes, some people believe the words of the gods, that some men are destined to lead. We see this in the role of our kings" The long-haired guard stopped just past the boat to knock out the remnants of his pipe on one of the knee high pilings. Placing his foot on the top of the gray piling, he refilled his pipe while making sure he left the smoldering remnants by his foot to relight his smoke.

126

"You talk like my uncle. He believes in the power of the warrior code over any words from gods." Oslaf told him.

"Your uncle sounds like a smart man. But too many times," Moorscal continued, "people follow someone who is born into their position. Not me, I support a great warrior, a person like Gerharn because of his loyalty to the Vulthnal Guard." He paid no attention to Oslaf as the Esterblud kept stealing glances at the boat.

"So, if Gerharn and I are so honorable, what's the answer?" the Esterblud asked. "I would rather chop off my hand than give up my sword, and I'm sure Gerharn knows this as well."

Moorscal continued to focus upon his pipe, not bothering to look up as Oslaf remained behind the Vulthnal Guard leader. "Well, that is because you both are following the rules set out by the ancients and now enforced by some ruler you don't respect. Now, if it were me, I would look for a way out," he put the pipe to his lips. "I can think of times when a prisoner suddenly gets the idea to escape. It's funny, some of the crazy ideas a prisoner can come up with when something so tempting is right in front of them. When you unleash yourself from conformity, you can do great things."

"I agree with you," said Oslaf, silently reaching for his belt, "and you have my apologies." The Esterblud struck his new friend in the back of the head with the handle of his dagger. The Vulthnal Guard fell forward on the planks, nearly tumbling into the water below before Oslaf caught him and laid him on the dock. The Esterblud sprinted a few steps, jumping into the boat and, with practiced expertise, pulled up on the halyard to lift the sail. The breeze was coming off the land, immediately filling the sail and pushing the boat forward. The warrior jumped over a tarp-covered mound to cut the line attaching the boat to the dock at the bow. The large man ran back to the stern, cutting the last line before taking the steering post connected to the rudder. The wind pushed the craft away from the danger. Looking over, he could see Moorscal struggling to his feet. The Vulthnal Guard was rubbing his head as he looked out at Oslaf, who gave him a wave. The Esterblud smiled when he saw Vulthnal wave back while watching the prisoner heading to freedom.

Movement from the gray canvas tarp caught Osalf's eye and the man silently pulled his sword. Keeping one hand on the rudder, he reached out and kicked the form under the canvas sharply. He heard a female voice let out a cry.

"Quit that, you fool. I'm coming along with you." Suddenly, a head emerged, looking up at him. It was the blonde *docke* he saved from the mob who struggled to emerge from underneath the canvas. He looked at his new passenger with amazement, turning his head to see Moorscal once again wave to him.

Chapter 5: Seeking Vengeance

Alrpan walked into the grand throne room of the underworld realm where Caruun sat upon his black throne, lost in thought, his sharp-clawed hand casually poking into the screaming souls encased inside the chair. Actita, the Vanth, followed Alrpan as he led a column of assorted foul creatures from the depths of the underworld. The Vanth carried his whip over one shoulder, the thick beorh-skin appearing similar to a long snake lying across his shoulders, nearly the same color as the brown hemp robe covering him. Usually, this demigod would be leading human spirits to the underworld to work in unceasing toil to their master. Now the beaked buzzard creature led monsters to appear before Caruun. The god of the underworld looked up, his vulture face showing the surprise at the creatures in front of him. Thin and tall beasts with white skin, the deity was surprised by such creatures which never existed before in his realm. He was not pleased.

"Why have you brought these things to me?" he demanded, then suddenly recognized the monsters. "Who is the one who brings forth such atrocities from the days of the Guardians?"

"I made them," said Alrpan defiantly. Her voice had a harsh edge, like a human clearing their throat. "They are here to begin the next part of the plan."

Caruun gave the woman his most unpleasant stare with beady yellow eyes. It caused the goddess to laugh at him. Her lack of deference was a dramatic, disconcerting change in his wife and not something the underworld leader could understand. She seemed to be mocking him now, and it was not something he would tolerate. He quickly stood up, towering over her smaller form.

"You cannot make such creatures." Caruun could not comprehend such power now in this goddess. Her primitive lust and carnal knowledge were her concerns. The element of fire was the thing Alrpan mastered. Now he found her capable of far more and he did not like this change.

"How dare you act this way? I control this realm, not you. Now remove these things from my sight."

Caruun turned around to sit back down when he realized massive chamber was suddenly silent. Even the mad spirits in the countless tunnels above him ceased their endless toil as if they could feel the tension filling the room. The surprised master of the underworld peered up, slowly turning around as he saw the shadows of souls floating around the honeycombed heights. His rage grew at this unforgivable blasphemy, a direct defiance of him. He spun around to face Alrpan whose continued laugh began to take on a deafening roar which caused the god to freeze. It was a sound he vaguely remembered.

"You are neither smart enough or powerful enough to rule this realm. While you and Duwdamon may have divided the world to your needs following your betrayal of the Guardians, your presence is really unnecessary now. Therefore, I've decided to relieve you of this burden." The beautiful woman with the red eyes pointed a finger at Caruun, and before he could react, the god was struck with a combination of fire and electricity. Taking the blast full on into his broad chest, Caruun was ejected away from his black throne, tossed across the room like a wounded bird. The god of the underworld landed at the feet of his son, Actita, who calmly moved out of the way. The new netherworld monsters moved forward to watch the coming fight, the musky scent of turmoil in the air.

Stunned by the attack, Caruun's form changed, taking on some of the elements from the Great Void. His dark flesh bubbled and one arm transformed into tentacles with deformed hands at the ends. A rancid smell filled the air as he struggled to recover. The underworld god glared up at Alrpan as she calmly strolled up to the throne. Caruun suddenly sent a massive blast of fire toward Alrpan, who coolly let the light blue flames envelop her attractive form momentarily. Then, the goddess sent the flames ricocheting back in the direction of the vulture-faced god. The flames broadened, becoming white with heat as they struck him. Caruun stood planted in the spot, enveloped with a consuming circle of white fire, his flesh writhing in shock and unimaginable pain. In an instant, the god of the underworld turned from a human-like creature into a blackened standing skeleton, frozen in agony. Alrpan sat upon the black throne, adjusting to get comfortable and with a quick flick of the wrist, Kriell returned the fury of white flame back into her finger as if the bolt was a fiery leash. An ancient Guardian revealed the power of *heliofire* to the beasts watching, their small brains hardly comprehending what they saw. For the first time since it was cast into the void, Kriell revealed to other this power to encase any creature in a living death, living upon the soul of the unfortunate.

In the quiet aftermath, Actita stepped over to the statue of his late father. There was no change in his buzzard face as he inspected the dark husk, his head tilting back and forth like a bird. Satisfied there was a new leader of his world, the Vanth stepped over to the foot of the throne.

"Master, what would Alrpan like me to do with the new trophy in this room?" The Vanth bowed before her.

"I've watched you Actita. You may have the strength and good judgment to serve me, despite your poor parentage." The beautiful form of Alrpan did not match the deep, gravelly voice coming from her. She stood, and stepped down toward the remnants of Caruun where she peered closely, observing the statue. The god could feel the evil soul still inside, unable to break free.

"Your first lesson will be to learn about your new master. Alrpan brought me from the Great Void, and I dined upon her weak power. Only Kriell has the power of a spirit stealer," Kriell told the Vanth. The beautiful human dissolved into the nebulous blob of its origin. The god's feet turned into tentacles, reaching to the blackened form of the encased god. Quickly wrapping around the legs, thick, slimy secretion oozed from the pores. Soon, the giant blob enveloped the statue to feed on the spirit inside. Reeking smells which emanated from the Great Void, Kriell ingested the remains of Caruun. Feeling the surge of another soul entering his hideous body, all of the thoughts and experiences of the former underworld master became one with the spirit stealer. Only the shocked image of Caruun's face remained, now outlined in the blob's body after the Guardian finished his feast. Now able to recreate an exact duplicate of the previous underworld leader, Kriell would begin the next part of its plan.

As Actita watched the offensive actions of his master, the Vanth felt nothing but coldness. The human emotions, such as love, tenderness, and family ties could not be understood by this half-god. Instead, he turned away to round up the monsters to stand before the ancient god who he whipped back in front of the black, oozing creature.

"Actita, we will continue to create these creatures from the spirits gathered," said Kriell, his voice barely recognizable as he lay in the gelatinous form with tentacles curled around him like many snakes. "You will begin sending them into the human realm of Kamin when the sun sets. We will let Sky Realm become even more desperate when they see the humans losing faith in their protectors. You will keep me informed of what you see and hear among the humans and spirits."

Kriell's hideous shape slowly transformed, sliding up to stand as an exact replica of Caruun. His head turned with blinking eyes as he tilted his beaked face, looking around the room. Then, the new underworld god strode confidently to its rightful throne. While this leader lacked the desire to extract exceptional tortures upon the hapless human spirits in the throne, Kriell held no empathy to those sub-creatures that existed inside his chair. Instead, the creature committed his attentions upon a need for vengeance. The remaining Kamin gods were his target. Those who control the realms may have gathered together with the humans to cast him and his fellow gods back into the void, but he would have his revenge. Alrpan and Caruun souls were slowly digested inside the creature, giving Kriell inside knowledge about their brethren. It was knowledge he would use to become the master of all the realms. The Guardians would return to their rightful place in the cosmos.

The Vanth bowed before his leader. "I need more of my species. I cannot bring more monsters back. I only one lone Vanth."

Kriell peered down at the hideous beasts that would be unleashed upon the humans, rubbing his chin as he considered the Vanth's request. The coming terror reminded the god of his past association with Aluric, the original creator of such monsters. Kriell briefly considered opening the portal to the Great Void to bring back other Guardians to help reclaim Kamin. But after removing two of the gods, he changed his mind.

"You make an excellent suggestion. However, we must forge more of your kind quickly as we have no time for breeding. Bring down some human females for us breed."

"I bring sturdy ones to whip better those monsters. Clovel not easy to bring to master." The Vanth bowed again and snapped his whip, sending the monsters scurrying back into the tunnel from which they came. Actita hurried after the creatures, sending wandering souls scattering as well. Kriell's buzzard form stood, eyeing the spirits around him. His displeasure was evident, and he held his clawed hand above him. The crackle of electricity surged outward filling the vast cavern, striking those human spirits who had mistakenly crept forward to watch the drama of Caruun demise unfold before them. With wails of torment and shocking screams, the souls floated away from the room where the master stood. Along with the wall of electricity that swept throughout the underworld striking all spirits. Following the initial shock, there was a message which came from the mind of Kriell and directed at the souls. It told them to stay in the dark recesses, away from their new master or suffer the punishment.

~~~

In the Sky Realm, the tension was evident among the gods who kept to themselves. The water spirits who served as their attendants remained hidden among the grand but empty temples of the sky. As cold as the white stones, he walked among, the spirit of Dughorm wandered as he did every morning since arriving. He carefully observed the engravings that lined columns and walls, and they told him much. The engravings were stories and myths of the gods, telling the prophet secrets never exposed to the realm of the humans. While a blind man in his final seasons as a human, his newfound sight showed him the arrogance and contempt of the gods. It helped with his prophecies as well.

Finished with his inspection of this side of the building, he heard the light sound of a spirit moving nearby. He recognized the sound of Caestia coming near him. The former record keeper still preferred to walk rather than soar in the spirit world.

"Need any more help on those engravings?" Caestia asked.

"No, I'm finished for now. I've learned more than I wanted to know our gods, but the engravings must be understood. You must continue your work."

The god's Oracle continued. "I will talk to the gods later. They will not be happy to know how the underworld continues to spread chaos and destruction throughout the human realm. But they will do nothing." Dughorm signed. "What of your time among the gods? Have you been able to record much."

Caestia came to a stop, again thanking Dughorm. As a simple record keeper in life, the spirit of Caestia would have been sent to the underworld. He was grateful for Dughorm's ability to persuade Duwdamon to bring him to work inside the temples. However, the record keeper was not pleased with what he learned.

"I've recorded those engravings on the parchments. But I don't know why you bother. We've just changed masters," his voice whispered. "It is one thing I remember most during my final time with Urith. The Clovel Destroyer always complained that the manipulation of the gods continued. Now I understand what he was talking about. Our new overlords act like children, wishing for this and trying to hide from the reality they find. It is too bad we are too weak to cast them out like they did to the Guardians."

"There is truth in your words, and it's growing far worse than you know. Recently, the gods have turned on one of their own." The spirit form Dughorm began to glow red from anger as he quickly debated with himself about telling Caestia what he knew. Unable to resist, the god's prophet continued. "Mivraa is being punished for siding with our brethren in the human world. I foresaw this, but I was powerless to stop it. Her father fails to realize the stupidity of his actions. The other sky gods welcome a chance to hurt one of their own, only because she is part human. They are savages. Not only cruel, vindictive but stupid since they don't see the genuine threat from below."

"Is there not something we can do?" the spirit form of Fedelm's father glowed with anger as well.

"Not directly, but these engravings give us knowledge that may prove useful. My trips among the temples have not been a waste. Fortunately, your daughter, Fedelm, aids us by showing me many things in her dreams and nightmares. The sky gods are doing great wrong, and I think it's time to let those Haligulf ghosts know. Great warrior souls will be useful to our cause, and we will need their strength in numbers. Let us make our way to Haligulf, to be among the warriors as they eat and drink."

Dughorm led his companion to soar above the temples as they flew to the Fields of Anord, which lay just outside of the ring of buildings. In the middle of the field sat the Great Hall of Haligulf where the noble warriors spent their eternity. The hall ran the length of the field, given refuge to the ghostly guests where they could find food, drink and shelter for which they had no real need. Slain during their life upon Kamin in glorious battles against their honored foes, the eternal life of a warrior consisted of daily clashes against their ghostly brethren until death or victory. Although pain, disease and age had long ago left these spirits, the shadows still held a great reverence for the timeless traditions of their past. Weapons of the gods they used and tore through their spirit flesh and bone just like they recalled when alive. At the end of the battle, those spirits which failed on the battlefield would be resurrected to drink in celebration with their friends and foes. Each warrior would spend their evening in the hall eating with their comrades while playing with the lovely water sprites who served them.   Many were female souls who were unable to get to Haligulf. However, they could be brought into the realm as servants to the gods, who turned them into large and small elementals with both form and substance. As such, they filled the realms with their tender care and gave beauty to the landscape. But, like the second side of a sword, some were used as playthings of the gods or to serve the pleasures of the dead warriors. It was the grand afterlife that all warriors of Kamin prayed they would reach.

When the two ghosts of the temples arrived at the outside of the hall, the fighting among the spirits was over. They could hear the riotous sounds coming from inside the Great Hall as they came to the twin wooden doors which soared above them. Each plank a massive tree trunk bandied together with iron bracing. The hall was topped with a high pitched roof of gray slate. Despite their ghostly form, they could not pass through the massive walls covered in blue clay plaster from the nearby mountains.

"Are you sure we should?" Caestia appeared envious. "I'm not a warrior."

"Nor am I anymore. Let us meet those who live in paradise and see their thoughts on our masters." Dughorm pushed open the large closed door with little effort.

Inside, they saw warrior souls sitting in long rows which lined massive tables that ran to the back of the hall. Dressed in the same armor in which they died, with their swords hanging on their belts, they drank heathmead from large mugs, yelling and singing. As they recovered from their daily battle, some of the ghosts were missing parts of their body or still carried their massive wounds. Around the tables, water spirits served them as they did for the rest of sky realm. The nimble female spirits placed large platters of roasted erba and fish on the tables while trying to avoid the men who grabbed for them. A night spent with a beautiful water spirit brought back the warming pleasures of the past. Also moving around the tables were ghostly skalds, warriors strumming familiar tunes on ancient stringed instruments and singing praises to the heroes exploits and, sometimes, offering the latest news of human battles which would add comrades to their midst.

Dughorm instantly recognized some of the great warriors of the past, including his dearest friend, Uolven. The Oracle of the temples could see the ghostly form of his old comrade sitting with another spirit away from the boisterous activities lining the middle of the room. He walked over to his old friend. Caestia, unfamiliar with the battle harden fighter's ways and uncomfortable in the loud chaos, swiftly joined Dughorm, gliding up behind him as he seemed mesmerized by the dead warriors enthusiastic drinking and eating.

"You look well, Uolven. Haligulf seems to agree with you," yelled Dughorm over the ruckus around them.

Uolven looked up, his eyes squinting from the double vision created by his drink. "Dughorm, you old traitor. What brings you to the lower classes? How is my son?"

Dughorm's spirit clothes glowed blue as he smiled at his friend. "You never will let me forget that I became a hakra, eh. Urith is alright but seriously troubled. May we join you?"

The old warrior's tunic glowed slightly green as he bid them join him. "Come and sit down. Have some of this heathmead we can toast my son.

Dughorm took the mug, already filled with heathmead. "I salute you, old friend. It is well that Alrpan released you from the underworld. I heard terrible things."

The dead Esterblud scuffed. "That wench should have had her head removed long ago. It was good news when I found out she lost her power by taking on my son with the Skoll. It wasn't very difficult once Mivraa came for me. Snuck me out right under their noses."

The hakra told Uolven what happened to Mivraa and the man in green became livid. After a series of oaths and curses, he calmed down long enough to tell Dughorm to point the Skool directly at the Sky Realm. "That should take care of the mess," the drunk warrior pounded the table with this empty mug.

Caestia tried to change the subject. He held up his cup to Uolven The gods are merciful to give us such a drink."

Dughorm heard a grunt of disapproval beside him. He looked over to find himself next to the soul of Heptarc, the greatest hero of Kamin. It took a bit for the shocked old warrior to realize he was looking at the great destroyer of the Guardians. The hakra, who helped establish the three realms, slumped over his drink. As Heptarc looked down at the thick mug, his nearly transparent face showed a weariness in his reflections.

The soul spat out a bitter laugh. "Merciful gods are they? Here we languish for eternity, and you give thanks like they are worthy of such praises." The former man took a long drink, placing the mug down on the table, but the object made no noise. "It's like this heathmead, made of the Exyts Spring water. It numbs us to the point of oblivion and heals us for the next morning where we try to slaughter each other. And the endless cycle continues."

"And what better way to live," said Uolven, spilling the dark brown liquid in his mug as he raised it with an exclamation. "We suffer from nothing. Food and drink spring eternal for us and the maidens are beautiful. Now we live to a victorious exhilaration over our slain enemies or bitter ache at defeat from their hands."

"That's just the point," the great hakra declared slamming his mug down again, irritated it gave no sound. "We are nothing but muses. We wander around a circle of trees like nature spirits with no sense of purpose, only remaining to please ourselves. We just exist." His bleary eyes looked over at Uolven, "Do you remember the touch of flesh? Do you remember the warmth of love or the simple kiss from your child? Uolven's ghost shook his head, suddenly remembering his wife who could not come to the Sky Realm. Heptarc tried to stagger to his feet before landing back on the bench. "No, I don't recall them anymore? How is this eternal bliss?" He waved his hand at the chaotic scene around them.

"Was this not what you asked for?" Dughorm spoke up. "Stories told to us since our youth says you brought peace to the realms through your agreement with the gods."

The spirit of the great hakra suddenly became entirely focused, glowing red. "No!" his voice raised, trembling with anger. "That is the great lie. The truth is, my dearest wife taught me the way to enter the Great Void. My spirit came to find for those gods fearsome enough to send the Guardians back into the void."

He stared intently at those around him. "Here's the real story. When my wife discovered that a human could enter the Great Void using a talisman, I came upon the spirits of Duwdamon and Caruun, who agreed to remove the Guardians. They would get the other entities to come into the world. But once they took our form, they found sensations and desires they never knew. Their powers made them arrogant when they came into our world. The new gods suddenly decided to betray me, conveniently standing aside when I struck the Guardians with a blast from the Skool."

The founder of the warrior code gave a rueful smile as he remembered his last time among the living. The other spirits watched in disbelief. This tale went against everything they knew. Many of those in Haligulf felt no need to understand the past.

"It is now clear; I should have used the Skool upon all of those we call gods. However, before I realized it, the Skool shattered, killing me and sending pieces across the lands. The next thing I remember is rising from my mangled body, watching the gods standing around me with their unused weapons. I tried to force them to honor their word, but they laughed since they knew I had no ability to cast them out. They just divided the realms amongst themselves. I remember how Duwdamon and Caruun drew lots to determine how they would send the human spirits to the realms."

Heptarc shadow momentarily turned to the pale white, shivering as if he could feel the cold. "What I was able to bargain for was this great hall. Since the sky god was so pleased with my work, he decided the greatest warriors would come to join me in this eternal bliss to be served by elementals like the water spirits." It was a bitter, mocking laugh from the hero, which could be heard over the din.

The phantoms of great men around Heptarc went quiet as they reflected upon his words. Fooled by generations of lies, the news came as a great surprise to Caestia and Dughorm. It steeled the Sybil's resolve against the gods.

"So, all of this world and the three realms is a lie of the gods?" echoed Caestia aloud. "How is this possible?"

Heptarc peered up at the thin figure on the other side of Dughorm. "I don't know you, but you seem like one of the humans that helped keep the lies alive. When you were human, did you wear the scarlet robes of those who bowed to the gods?"

Caestia quickly admitted he worked for the Sacred Overlord as a keeper of the records. That news elicited a contemptuous scowl from Heptarc while Uolven growled at him. The sound reminded Caestia of Urith's mannerism.

"You are in the wrong place, record keeper. You are among warriors now. I should give you a sword, and we shall see how soon I can cut you down," said Uolven.

"Don't embarrass yourself, my old friend." Dughorm calmly informed the drunken spirit. "Caestia is a name you know. He is the man who helped discover the Shield of Skool with Urith. He died bravely in the battle against an army of Aberffraw warriors. Some of those warriors are here."

"Then, you have my thanks, my new friend," exclaimed Uolven. "I've only heard some of my son's latest adventures. Please take a drink and tell me more about your life." Before the record keeper could speak, he was interpreted by Heptarc.

"So that's the one I heard about," exclaimed the apparition of Heptarc, his red eyes brightened at the news. "Those warriors who died by the Skool made it to Haligulf, and they spoke of a man who fought alongside his daughter." The hakra stared at the wraith of Caestia for a long moment as he shook his head as if awakening from sleep. No longer was the hero content to wallow in self-pity.

Heptarc looked at Dughorm. "I've heard of you, a warrior and a seer. You died terribly at the hands of Satres. Yet, you somehow became the Oracle of the Sky Gods. Now, why would you mingle with old warrior spirits? I cannot believe you missed your time among fighters."

"Heptarc, you are the first hakra, so visions must still come to you as they do to me. Is that correct?" Dughorm took a full mug given to him by a cute water spirit who passed them.

Heptarc nodded slowly, "I can still see things which bother me."

Dughorm lowered his voice, leaning closer to the hero. "Then, if you have a reason to avenge your betrayal, I have some ideas I would like to discuss with you. I think those spirits in Haligulf would have an interest in helping those in the mortal realm."

"I sense you are a cunning man. I sense you are here for a purpose. You have seen something, haven't you?"

Dughorm smiled before taking a drink of his heathmead.

~~~

As the small boat holding two strangers sailed along the coast of Vulthnal, Oslaf kept a constant watch for storms which were known for their quick and deadly appearance in the area. The skiff they sailed in was barely large enough to hold a few fishermen, and it was designed to remain close to the coast. It had such a shallow draft, which meant it could quickly become swamped if they hit rough seas. Despite the slight size, the single-mast vessel made progress moving across the Maflow

Sea. They had no maps and only rudimentary knowledge of the coastline, but Oslaf was an old hand in the ways of the ocean, learning from his tribal elders who took great pride in their seafaring ways. Esterblud awareness of the sea and ships was an extension of their warrior prowess. Oslaf sat in the stern, lightly holding the rudder as he kept looking at the sky and the sail which appeared dark gray from the light of a sun hidden behind the clouds.

"We will need to find food soon," said Henther. Oslaf just grunted, not noticing it was the same trait he picked up from as his uncle.

The young fighter remembered the morning he and the girl escaped on the vessel. No doubt the girl's life would be in peril had she stayed in Casab when the Vulthnal Guards left. Oslaf guessed Moorscal put the woman aboard the boat to guarantee her safety and, thereby, keeping his promise to the Esterblud warrior. He smiled at the way the wily Vulthnal planned their escape, hoping he would be able to repay a debt of gratitude to Moorscal in the future.

During their time together, Oslaf learned the woman knew the Esterblud language well enough, and he learned her name along with many other things about the village and her time with the bandits during their journey. Letting her speak as much as she wanted, Oslaf noticed she never talked about herself, only those things he might have wanted to know about the land of the bandits. She admitted to becoming friends with the sea bandits, especially Thulmare who, she said, rewarded her with exquisite jewels and clothes from his plunder. When she spoke of that Oslaf remembered how she had tried to alarm more bandits before Urith killed her lover. The recollection caused him to remain suspicious of her.

It was her way of living, by keeping men or women satisfied for a few koinons, which bothered him. His life might consist of bloody survival using his skills with weapons, but, at least, his existence could bring honor and glory. However, the woman used her body to survive in their violent world which he considered contemptible. While he realized the weak might have only a few options, the Esterblud felt they should rise above such circumstance. The dockes were chattel, barely above a slave, to be used and discarded as the man desired. Frowned upon by the *satgerts* of the temples, no man would marry such a woman if they had any ambition to be a warrior and leader.

Oslaf decided she was a liar as well since she was dressed in the same long blue robe they saw her in before. If the bandit leader was so good to her, he wondered why she could not have left Casab using the valuables she supposedly had. In his eyes, she lacked any honor or virtue, two of the traits most highly prized by the warrior code. In Oslaf's beliefs, a person's word was a contract and bond with another. Not something to be discarded upon a whim. Yet, as he watched her, he had to admit the woman was beautiful. He especially liked her eyes, so expressive and green. The young warrior decided he must remember the bad things he believed about her past.

"You should have brought more food with you. I'm heading to Eernicia," said Oslaf, trying hard to keep his attention on the sea. He knew they had few provisions when they started. "It's only a few nights away from Eernicia if the wind holds."

"And what do you propose we drink?" replied the blonde woman sarcastically. "With no rain, we will be drinking the sea water soon. I don't intend on dying out here just because an Esterblud decides it."

Oslaf had to admit the woman was correct, although he would rather cut off his hand than agree with her. "The land is that way," he pointed to the rocky shore far off in the distance. "You can swim there if you want. We have enough heathmead until tomorrow. If these winds stay with us, we should be near the border between Vulthnal and Eernicia soon. We'll look to find a place to land."

"But won't that will put us near the swamplands of Larcal?" The tone of her voice caught his attention. Oslaf looked at her, trying to read her expression.

"I'm not sure," he admitted. "But it appears you know these waters better than I do. Why does that matter?"

The woman paused, biting her lip slightly. "It does not matter, but I know this area well. Leave it at that."

"No, I will not," said Oslaf hotly. "During our time on this boat, you told me little about yourself. I don't care about the sea raiders, the village or this cursed land called Vulthnal. The people of this nation are either cowards, bandits, or fools. If the gods came out to wipe this area from the world, I would thank them." The Esterblud noticed her eyes narrow at his rant.

"I suppose you think that of the man who saved us. If so, the tales of the Esterbluds must be right, you are a savage, ungrateful thugs who smell of erba dung."

Oslaf forced himself to suppress the sudden urge to throw her overboard. The woman was correct about Moorscal. In his fit of rage, he quickly forgot about the people like Gerharn, Wiga and other Vulthnal people who helped him and his friends during their journey. He went quiet, and his face turned red as he stared up at the sail. Suddenly her words about the smell of the Esterbluds made him laugh. It started out as a chuckle, which he tried to subdue, only to laugh out loud. Henther looked at him like he was going crazy, her face growing pale. The look she made caused him laugh even harder. Finally, after his side hurt from the fit, he became quiet, his eyes watering.

"You don't have to worry," he told the woman, giving her a sheepish grin. "I'm fine, really. Your description of me is quite insulting but equally colorful. It struck me as quite funny." He grew quiet for a while as he thought about how to handle the woman. He realized they would need to at least get along for a while.

"Listen, I will accept your advice since we need to survive. But don't assume I will forget my capture and my friend's treatment at the hands of those sea bandits you pleasured. Your loyalty to those vermin means I don't trust you."

Henther's green eyes gave him a hard look, but he could tell his words did have an effect. However, the slap of the waves and the creak of the sails were the only sounds along the water as they refused to continue the conversation. Each person stared at the water surrounding them.

After the sun reached its zenith, Oslaf quietly spoke to her. "Now, let's start again. Why do you have a problem with Larcal? I cannot land this on those rocks, and the port of Alurican is off limits since we escaped from the overlord of the land. If you have a better place we can land, tell me."

Finally, she took a deep breath. "No, you are correct; there is no other option for us. We land in Larcal, or we die on this boat before we can reach Eernicia," her voice could barely be heard. "I know the area because I come from there,"

"So, is this a problem for you?" he asked. She shook her head but remained quiet. "Well, perhaps we will get rain before then, and we can bypass the area." Realizing the woman would not go further, he decided to change the subject.

"Anyway, I say we use a bit of our remaining food for bait, and we might be able to catch us a meal. If you get the food, I'll rig up a line for us to fish with."

Henther nodded and carefully moved forward the rocking skiff to get the bag with their remaining supplies. As she did so, Oslaf stared at her lithe body, pleasantly distracted by what he saw and thoughts of Fedelm came back to him. He absently began to compare the two women, noting that the *docke* in front of him was quite a bit taller with long slender legs and arms. As the women rummaged through the bag, he noted her exotic olive tone skin and her aristocratic manner. As he watched her, the woman briefly looked back as if she was troubled by his staring. The warrior liked her wide, expressive eyes and thin lips. He also noticed she had a slight crook of the small nose as if broken at one point. Oslaf guessed her past held a darkness that Fedelm would not have known. He suddenly realized that it was the first time he had thought of the hakra woman since he left Urith in Eernicia. The thought surprised him as the woman came back to the stern holding a piece of the remaining food they had. He hoped they would be lucky enough to catch a fish as he heard his stomach rumble at the sight of the food.

Two mornings later, Oslaf wanted the calm seas back as he and Henther tried landing the skiff among rolling waves. They were coming on to the black sand beach, not far from the marshes of Larcal. The dense clouds whipped rain into their faces while the increasing winds and white caps left them no option but to come ashore. To stay in the open ocean with such a shallow draft boat during a storm would be suicide. After gliding onto the beach, they struggled, trying to pull the skiff out of the surf. Oslaf was able to get the craft tied off to a large rock pile to anchor the boat while Henther gathered the water and food bags along, wrapped in the canvas tarp she had hidden during their escape. Able to retrieve his weapons and shield before they moved inland, Oslaf led them to the only mound he saw on the flat land. They climbed to the top, looking for any potential spots where they could find shelter. As the driven rain pelted them, the pair could make out only a barren green landscape of marsh weeds and tall grass, with much of the distant view obscured by the low clouds. Henther pointed a grove of trees, and they pushed through the tall vegetation which slowed them while pelting droplets of rain stung their exposed skin. Soon they were running for the trees trying to get shelter before the full weight of the storm struck them. Bursting through the first line of bluewood trees, they found the ruins of a farmhouse with only a chimney still standing. They quickly pushed the remaining wood leaning against the old fireplace and anchored one end of the tarp they carried to the stone. Oslaf attached the other end of the tarp to a tree that grew near where the center of the house once was. The makeshift roof provided them with some protection from the heavy rain as they sit close to each other on a flat rock near the tree. Neither said anything as they listened to the pounding rain, trying to avoid the swirling mist of cold air the whipped around them. It was unusual to have such a cold wind come in with the storm, and they lacked any blankets to keep warm, so both shivered when the breeze lashed at them.

Oslaf looked at the open hearth of the chimney, then began crawling on his hands and knees around the damp grass under the tarp for kindling.

"Do you have any idea how close we are to the border?" he asked as he crouched down, picking up small broken limbs that remained mostly dry.

The girl shivered, crouching down to help him in his search. "I'm sure we are close. It's been awhile since I was in this land, but I think this farm should be near a road which leads to the village of Greman. That is the village which sits nearly on the border between Vulthnal and Eernicia."

The Esterblud crawled back to the hearth, throwing in the wet twigs and branches he found as the girl added her load to the pile. Oslaf pulled out his strike rocks from the small pouch attached to the baudrik belt, which ran diagonally across his chest and over his shoulder. He felt inside the bag for any tender, but it was empty.

"Well, we will need to find something to light, or we will remain cold and wet," he looked around. Before he could think about a solution, he heard the sound of ripping clothes as the girl was shredding the yellow cloth girdle into smaller pieces. Her eyes were hard as she glanced at him, tugging and tearing at the fabric. The Esterblud took each strip and rubbed them hard across the edge of the rock they sit on until the fibers were thin and separating. Piling strips together near the damp sticks and wood the young warrior struck the rocks together until a spark caught the cloth on fire. It took a while, but they were able to coax a small fire in spite of the whipping wind and rain. Oslaf found a large branch which he broke into small pieces to use. Finally, they watched the flames as the fire grew to warm them.

"You know how to build a good fire," he joked. However, he could see no laughter in her eyes as she stared at the remnants of yellow cloth nearly consumed by the flames. Feeling awkward at her lack of response, the Esterblud found a log which he dragged over so they could sit on to face the chimney while they waited for the rain to pass their shelter. As he sat, listening to the rain, he opened one of the water bags and began filling it from the stream of water pouring off the canvas above them. His stomach growled reminding him; they had not eaten for a while. Using their last piece of food, they caught two small flat face fish which they hungrily ate raw. Oslaf was about to say they needed to find food when the girl spoke up.

"You should know that my people come from Greman." She had quietly moved next to Oslaf. The Esterblud could not think of anything to say so he remained quiet. She gave him a glance before continuing. "Since we left Casab, I've thought a lot about what I should do, where I should go."

"Do you want to return to Casab?" asked Oslaf carefully.

"No! I don't want that. The sea bandits will return when the king's men leave, and I will soon be the property of whoever leads the bandits now. You know that."

"I thought they treated you well, buying your jewels and clothes? I would believe that you would want to return." He said, remembering her story from earlier.

She quickly turned to him, apparently ready to lash out, but when she saw the honest confusion on his face, she paused, then looked away.

"That is only partially correct. I wanted you to think I had some worth. I could not tell what your intentions were, but you looked like you might kill me just for being there." She stared at the fire. "Most of the men in Casab are dung eaters. But occasionally a man would treat me well, like the man you killed."

"He was helping you?" Oslaf gave her a pained look as he realized the bandit was only trying to help her escape. The image of the bloody body came back to him. "I'm sorry, I should have realized this."

Her lovely face grew hard as she thought back to the village. "It doesn't matter. Jimal thought he loved me, and I saw a way to leave that town through him. The bandits were in chaos when they heard the king

145

and his army were coming. Some wanted to stay and fight but most wanted to leave for a while and return when the overlord left. They heard a story of a fat man who would be waiting for them after the king left, to help them as he had done before. Jimal thought if he remained after the sea bandits left, then we could escape by hiding in the woods and taking an ossane to follow the army back to Alurican. We decided no one would be looking for us, and we could lose ourselves in the city. Jimal hid as the bandit ships left the harbor, but he was delayed getting back to me when the attack came. We saw you coming, and he tried to catch your attention so I could escape. He was a fool."

Oslaf could tell the woman held no bitterness in the words; it was an observation. "So he meant nothing to you? Just a means to an end?" He could see in her aristocratic profile; the women tensed at his words, hardening herself as she nodded. He did not believe her.

"But why did run from me?" he asked. "You were trying to leave; you could have hidden out and given up after things calmed down in the village."

"What type of joke is that?" she grew red with anger. "I've been in such villages before when they are attacked. There is no mercy for people like me. The powerful take what they want…. As many times as they want." Her voice trailed off as she seemed to recall painful memories.

"You knew better than that when I held off those men to keep you from being a trophy for them," said Oslaf.

The young woman paused, regaining her composure. "Maybe… but I could not be sure if I was to be your trophy. I didn't know what you had planned for me; I still don't. You forget, I've seen what you and your uncle can do in a fight. After what the bandits did to you and your friends, I thought you might slit my throat for revenge."

Gusts of heavy winds hit their makeshift shelter, nearly ripping their canvas roof away. Oslaf grabbed at the flapping tarp and got it reattached to the limbs while Henther helped hold the other end. Now thoroughly soaked, they gathered next to each other, sitting on the log after Oslaf added more wood to keep the fire going.

"I guess I would think the same," the Esterblud conceded as he came back to sit with her. "So, you don't trust me, and I'm not sure of you. No doubt, my uncle would have some wise saying for me if he were here." The Esterblud warrior racked his brain for something witty to say, but nothing came.

"Look, I have no intention of making you do anything. You can leave any time for you owe me nothing," he said.

"Well, that's something, I suppose," she responded bitterly.

He turned to her. "What do you want from me?" he asked, exasperated. "You came with me to save your skin. Now you're mad because I said you can go. Why don't you go to this village that you say you come from?"

"None of my family or those in the village know I'm alive." She looked down and quietly said, "Or what I am."

At last, Oslaf fully understood. Henther was a person without a land or home, probably not even a real friend. It was something he never considered. Not an idea that he could actually understand. He grew up with people he trusted, learning to follow the warrior code. But, he recognized the pain and anger that she held inside. He had seen similar reactions from Urith after the loss of his wife and child.

"I think I understand," he muttered. "Listen, it's your choice, but I'm traveling to Eernicia. Join me on my trip and perhaps you can find your place there. Just like you burnt the yellow piece of cloth, a new beginning in a new land for you. No need to be a *docke* while you are with me."

She looked at him, her wide eyes immediately narrowed with suspicion. "And what do you get out of this?"

"Just a partner to help in our travel," he smiled at her. "I need to find my uncle, and I don't know this area of the world. If you know this place as you say, then we can be a team until we reach Damicia. Perhaps we can learn from each other?" He waited until she carefully nodded before he turned to look at the rain and wind which continued to whip around. Henther turned back to stare at the fire, thinking about his words, but continuing to believe none of them.

~~~

Lyncus landed upon his homeland of Cahmais, in the capital city of Uugaraa on the morning tide. Dressed in his elegant blue tunic and outfitted in silver armor, the man combed back his long curly blonde hair with his hands, whistling to himself. As the sole heir to the throne now, he considered it his good fortune to arrive on such a beautiful morning. It was as if the gods approved of him giving the sad news of his brother's death to his father. He expected his father would break-down at this news, immediately taking solace with wine and food. It would leave him, even more, opportunities to extend his power throughout the kingdom. The thought made him whistle even louder as he walked down the plank to the dock. He saw Pertac, the fealharan leader, quietly following him. His whistling suddenly stopped as he remembered the fealharan assassins were the weak link in his plan. Unable to pay him off in Eernicia, Pertac left the rest of his men in Damicia, coming aboard the ship and he had remained in the background on their voyage to Cahmais, saying little to the Aberffraw leader. Nevertheless, the assassin leader was a reminder to Lyncus that he must come up with the koinons promised. It was something Lyncus thought long and hard about during the journey. While he knew finding the money would be impossible without the king finding out, he had come up with a plan to keep from paying anything. He waited for the fealharan to pass near him.

"Meet me at the tavern near the end of the docks tonight when the watch changes," he said under his breath. He saw the man nod as he walked past, quickly losing himself in the crowd of sailors and merchants. Lyncus continued his walk, whistling again as he sought out the guards who were dressed in dark blue robes, sitting on a bench at the end of the dock. They paid little attention at first until one of them recognized him. Nudging the other guard, they immediately stood for him as he arrived.

"Welcome back, my lord," said the man who recognized him.

"Good to be back. Can you find me an ossane?"

"Use one of ours," offered the man, pointing over to the line of the mounts standing across the street from them. "We can get an escort for you."

Shaking his head, Lyncus hurried across the road, getting upon the animal and spurred it toward the fortress at the edge of the city. He pushed the animal along as fast as possible through the crowded streets, often delayed by the trader carts, stopped in the narrow streets. However, Lyncus knew the city well and took advantage of the alleyways, roughly pushing aside the people who might be in the way. Some of lower classes in the city might have been tempted to say something until they saw the royal colors on his tunic and cape, leaving them to mutter under their breath. Finally, he reached the main road which led to the stone fortress, home of his family. Coming to the massive wooden gate entrance, which stood between twin white stone towers, he jumped down from the ossane. He gave the reins to a surprised guard as Cetral, head of the castle guard, ran up to meet him.

"My lord, your return comes as a surprise. I hope your journey went well."

"Where's my father?" Lyncus demanded.

"He is in the Great Hall with the merchant and guild elders of Uugaraa." Cetral quickly moved to the side as the man walked by him.

"That is good," said Lyncus, stopping to look back at the confused man. "I need you and your men gather up the rest of the king's advisors at once. Have them gather in the throne room. There will be no excuse for these people not to be there."

He continued on his path while Cetral ran off with his assignment. Lyncus knew the man was competent and intensely loyal to the royal family. After going through the gates, he entered a large courtyard of neatly cut bushes, the crunching sound of his boats leaving footprints from the meticulously maintained pebble drive. The main house rose in front of him, and he took the stone steps two at a time where a guard opened the twin doors for him. Passing through the entrance to the hall, he followed the tall archway with its stone lintels and columns lining his way. Lyncus entered the great groom at the end of the corridor where he interrupted his father, King Asgurd talking with elders of the city. It was a formal meeting around the long table as the guild leaders were dressed in a colorful assortment of robes and tunics, each based on their specialties in trade and commerce. The king gave him a glare before starting to speak again; Lyncus came around the large table to catch an attendant holding a large jug of wine. He talked to the man briefly, and the man discreetly went to the side of the king, whispering in his ear as one of the guild leaders was striking up with a long speech in tribute to the leadership of the king. Lyncus went to a corner of the large room, waiting for his father. Soon the fat man joined him, holding his goblet unsteadily in one hand.

"This is most inappropriate, my son. Could your news not wait?"

"No my father, for I have terrible news from Eernicia. I'm afraid that Tuncel is dead. He was assassinated by an Esterblud," Lyncus told him.

The fat man looked at him blankly for a moment as if he could not understand the words. Then the king of Cahmais did something unexpected. He dropped his cup and fell to his knees with a wail of despair that echoed throughout the great hall. Lyncus was caught off-guard by the reaction of his father. Instinctively, he reached down to help bring the man to his feet again, embarrassed by the response.

"Father, you must get a hold of yourself," he kept his voice at a whisper as he helped the king lean against one of the massive stone columns. Their position mostly hid them from the view of the curious people staring at the corner of the room. "You are a king, and you must not let those elders see you like this."

Asgurd was silently crying, his mouth opened as if he wanted to scream, but nothing came out at first. He turned his head and body to the column which became a crutch for him to hold himself erect. Finally, a moan came from the man, and then the words, "My son, my son," he kept repeating over and over as his son watched with growing disgust. Lyncus knew such a reaction would never come from this man had it been his death. Tuncel was his first and his favorite. A sense of bitter satisfaction ran through the killer standing behind his father. He signaled for one of the servants to come over, telling the young boy to escort the king to his chambers. He helped the attendant and the king along the marble floor to back stairs which led to the second-floor rooms. After the king was out of sight, Lyncus returned to the grand hall where he apologized for the king's absence to the crowd. He decided to take advantage of this unexpected occurrence.

"Forgive my father's departure, but we have received terrible news from Eernicia. My brother was assassinated by an Esterblud warrior named Urith, one of their king's favorites," the Aberffraw leader told them calmly.

The expected outbreak of indignation and cries of revenge was sweet music to Lyncus as he played the patient grieving brother. He told them he expected swift justice for this outrage and that his father had already called his advisors together.

"Please let your people know the king hopes for their cooperation and help during the coming events," he told them, making it clear that something big would be coming.

He left the room to bravos from elders now ready to support whatever action their leader decided. It also meant he could begin moving on his plans while his version of his brother's death was spread far and wide among the land. Such beliefs would cement his presence at his father's side. He had to suppress a smile as he walked into the throne room, for things were coming together as if the gods themselves were helping him.

During his meeting with the king's advisors, the war fever was at a pitch, unaided by Lyncus, who continued his role as the concerned son of the king. He guided the conversations around the best strategy for the coming war. Halfway through the meeting, the king had entered, looking disheveled with red-rimmed eyes. He was carrying a large cup of wine and staggered while he struggled to sit in his chair at the end of the table. The meeting continued as the advisors brought up their ideas and concerns about forming an army large enough to invade Esterblud. At one point, the treasurer brought up the costs of this invasion and the king threw his cup at the thin man, nearly hitting him in the head.

"I've lost a son to these cowards, and you tell me about koinons," the king staggered to his feet, yelling at the cowering men. "I don't want to hear anything from you, but how my army destroys this offspring of beorhs. I want their heads on post lining the roads as we march into their capital. We will lay waste to any tribe allied with Penhda. I want those miserable killers, Penhda and Urith suffer a slow death by torture. Then, I want their skin flayed from their bodies, mounted for display, and presented as a trophy to me to spit on. Is that understood?"

As the king sat in his chair, the shocked advisors looked at each other. They expected a battle, but their king had just ordered the full destruction of Esterblud. This was something far beyond the raids and minor battles over the years. It would take more men and weapons than they had. Once they accepted their task, they realized they could be masters over one of the strongest kingdoms in Kamin. Soon there was a steady clapping of hands on the table. The king gave a brief smile before lapsing back to find another drink, offered to him by his son.

As the group broke up, Lyncus directed Cetral to another room where he could speak privately. He told the head of the castle guard about the fealharan following him on the ship. Lyncus told the guard; he wanted the man picked up at the tavern that night.

"You will take enough men to get him," Lyncus said to him. "He is an assassin so if you need to kill him, do it quietly. He had something to do with the Esterblud, so I want him taken out of the city to a spot where we can question him." Cetral nodded and began to walk to the door, but he stopped at Lyncus' next words. "Make sure you don't speak to anyone but me about this. I don't want my father to know about this person before we are ready." Lyncus could not see the suspicious look that Cetral had on his face, but the man left to complete his duty.

~~~

Urith and Fedelm arrived in Ffestini at the height of the Draenyna festival, finding the small village overrun with swarms of farmers, herders, merchants and others who wanted to celebrate the height of planting and growing season. It was a scene of general chaos on the streets where revelers offered their thanks to the sky gods. However, the debauchery and open carnal acts which occurred during this ancient festival were only half-heartedly supported by the leaders of the temples. Urith believed such support was due to the increased offerings to the gods along with increased spending within the temples. His giant frame moving through the sea of people allowed Fedelm to slide in behind him as he pushed through. Most of the people paid no attention to the Esterblud, other than to offer drinks or act like they were best of friends with the strangers.

Fedelm, on the other hand, had to watch out for groping hands or worse. As they passed near a small shrine, three drunken farmers tried to corner her for their pleasure. Before Urith noticed she was missing, the young woman had kicked one of the men in the crotch while gouging another man in the eye. When the giant warrior arrived back to help, the woman was going after the third man, who ran off into the crowd. Urith smiled as he placed his hand on her shoulder, leading her away. Impressed, he realized he was growing quite attached to the woman.

The pair of travelers finally reached a small temple dedicated to the sky gods. The engravings on the large boulder near the temple told a story of how Heptarc killed a Clovel monster at this spot during his journey from the lands of Gwendak. The temple, composed of an unusual blue crystal rock, was a circular stone structure of columns which supported a flat roof. A few locals in the crowd explained to those who asked that the gods created the stone structure in memory of Heptarc. The structure stood on a small rise in the center of the village. The pair followed the throngs of people who pushed to get inside the open structure. The columns, used to support the roof, had long flutings showing on the outside, painted with gold paint. As they walked up the blue-gray steps, they could see the large reliefs of the sky gods carved into the back of the stone columns. Each god of the Sky Realm was looking down in harsh judgment upon the worshippers inside. Even Urith felt uneasy as if the gods would suddenly reach out to grab them.

Now Fedelm led the way, pushing through the crowd that milled around while Urith tried to stay with the determined women. They soon reached the center of the shrine where a wooden platform was overflowing with various items left as their sacrifice to the gods. There was the glint of silver, bronze and gold scattered on the platform. The warrior cynically thought about the large number of koinons such items would bring to the priests when the *satgerts* collected the items at sunset. He saw Fedelm lay a small piece of cloth on the table while she began saying a prayer that he did not recognize. However, he did remember the fabric. It was a piece of cloth she removed from her father's tunic when they buried Caestia at Du-Rinell.

Urith felt awkward as he had no prayers to give so he pulled off his heavy shield and leaving it next to the table. He sat cross-legged beside the kneeling Fedelm as he quietly thanked the spirit of Caestia for his wisdom and sacrifice. He remembered the former record keeper to be as brave as any warrior he knew. Lifting his head, he patiently waited for Fedelm to finish. He watched her quietly crying, the tears falling down her cheeks. It was a sight of tenderness and loss that he could feel deep inside from his own pain in the past that suddenly welled up in him. He tightened the grip on his Clovel Sword, willing the pain of his own losses to go away.

When Fedelm finished, she looked over at Urith, who sympathetically smiled at her. The woman smiled back, appreciating his presence. They got to their feet with Urith pulling his shield back over his shoulder as they started to move through the crowd. He was about to say something when they heard a scream ring out, and then other terrified screams broke out among the crowd as well. Amid the rising panic, Urith saw the reason for the screams. Red eyes came alive with the engraved god figures staring down at the crowd. The columns began moving as the whole structure shook back and forth as if something was erupting from below. People scattered, trying to run from the temple as Urith felt the eyes of the stone god upon him, and suddenly he could hear a roar coming from the statues around them.

"Bring me the Skool or you will be destroyed." The words rang out in his ears as he grabbed Fedelm, joining the mob escaping from the shrine. The two travelers were about to reach the edge of the structure when they could hear the rumble of the roof collapsing. Large fragments of stone came tumbling down, striking the worshippers who fell to the temple floor with a sickening thud. One column, engravened in the figure of Duwdamon toppled toward Urith, who pushed Fedelm hard through the crowd, allowing them to get out before being crushed by the stone. However, worshipers behind him were not as lucky when the thick stone roof landed on them, their shrieks of terror suddenly cut off.

Safely away from the structure, the stunned crowd scrambled about, and the rumbling almost immediately ceased. Dust filled the air along with the cries and moans of the injured. A few people in the crowd ran back to help those pinned under the wreckage, including the two travelers. Urith, maddened by what he witnessed, pulled away the fragments of stone, cursing at the gods for this destruction. Fedelm used her command of the native language to gather others to help and she guided the angry warrior and other stout men to areas where they could free people trapped under the rubble. As he approached one of the men dressed in the white robe of a priest, he saw a man's leg crushed under part of the massive column. Despite the obvious pain, Urith noticed the man kept looking at him. When they were able to roll the column enough to free him, the man passed out at Fedelms' feet. The hakra suddenly recognized Imenal lying at her feet. It was hard to tell at first with his face and body covered with the blue-gray dust that still clouded the area. She bent down, using the cloth from her robe to wipe his face.

"We need to get him to a *mhoda*," she said, turning to look up at the Esterblud. The warrior was about to say there were others needing help, but the look in her eyes told him to follow her lead.

"I'll get him; you find someone who knows where a healer can be found." He reached down, picking the tall man up, keeping the mangled leg dangling. The warrior knew a physician was unlikely to save it.

Fedelm was able to find one of the *yolma*'s attendants; a young boy named Jewn, who survived the destruction. The boy immediately led them to the home of the local *satgert*, several houses down the street. Inside, Urith placed Imenal carefully on a bed in the back room of the small dwelling. Fedelm sent Jewn to find the mhoda, or healer while she told Urith more about the man lying unconscious on the bed. While she had briefly mentioned her and Mivraa's encounter with the temple leader at Damicia during their walk through the open lands, she now told the warrior more about Imenal and her family. She also told Urith that the man in the bed was no friend of the Sacred Overlord. She could tell by the expression on the warrior's scarred face that he was suspicious, but he continued to focus on cleaning the injured leg. There was little blood coming from the foot, but the bones were badly broken, and the ankle was deformed.

"Why is he here?" Urith wondered aloud. "This is nothing but a small village and temple. He must have another purpose."

The girl looked down at her friend, suddenly concerned about how much she really knew about him. "Perhaps," she conceded. "But we won't know until he wakes."

"You can ask me now Fedelm," came a voice. "I'm awake now." The two travelers turned to the man who was in obvious pain.

"How are you feeling?" asked the hakra before realizing her words were insufficient.

"I've been better," said Imenal diplomatically, giving a weak smile. "What happened after I passed out?"

"You are in the home of the *satgert*. Urith brought you here, and we have Jewn getting a healer." Fedelm was looking out of the small window for the village doctor to arrive with the attendant.

"Now, why are you here?" Urith spoke up for the first time. "Someone of your importance doesn't come to this village unless you have a reason. It is too much of a coincidence that you are here when we arrive." The Esterblud's cold stare reinforced his words.

"You are correct, but it's not what you think. I came to help you." Imenal explained.

"How?" asked Fedelm turning back from the window.

"Rumors in Damicia are rampant about a scarred Esterblud had assassinated a diplomat in Damicia. But I saw you and your friends attacked by the fealharans that very afternoon. I witnessed this big warrior take an arrow or two in the courtyard, barely escaping with his life." The *yolma* tried to adjust himself in the bed, but a wave of pain caused him to groan.

"You have good friends who protect you, Urith. I was just able to see Fedelm and Mivraa help you escape those assassins." Imenal gazed at Fedelm before looking back at the warrior. "I'm no warrior, but I doubt that any man could be wounded like you were and then calmly come back to assassinate a Cahmais diplomat later that night. It got me thinking that someone else must have a reason to try to kill you and then,

155

kill a Cahmais diplomat. Too much of a coincidence, wouldn't you say." Urith slowly nodded agreement as he thought back to the day.

"Fedelm and the goddess of Haligulf didn't just stumble into my world." His voice was nearly a whisper as he took a deep breath, trying to stay still. "Either the gods are up to something or the Fates were warning me of something. I began searching for you and your friends to offer protection in the temple, but I missed you at the tavern in the Esterblud area. I spoke with the man named Helite who told me what happened. He confirmed you were in the tavern during the killing."

He stopped when the physician, a small woman, came into the room. She immediately bowed at her patient, immediately giving him a green herb to chew on to relieve the pain. Imenal braced himself for the healer's touch, and Fedelm told him they would leave for a while since they had many things they needed to discuss. The man's look to Fedelm indicated something unspoken that the Esterblud wanted to know more about. For a brief moment, he wondered if he was jealous and dismissed the thought. Urith motioned Fedelm to come with him. The woman gave Imenal a quick squeeze on his shoulder, telling him they would return soon. When the two travelers entered the main living area, Fedelm sent the young attendant back in to help the mhoda with his treatment of the leg.

"So, what do you think?" she asked the Esterblud.

"He seems to be telling the truth. Are you sure about him?" His tone indicated the warrior was concerned about Fedelm's closeness to the stranger. "Anyway, we still have to figure out what he knows. He seems to have much to say, and something in his look towards you made me wonder if he has something to say to you as well."

He turned his back to her and walked over to the open window that let in the sounds of the festivities that continued in the streets despite the destruction so close by. Fedelm was about to say something about Imenal, but the shield still strapped on his back suddenly caught her attention. She did a double take, realizing something was different about the round wooden and iron object. The silver Skool seemed to have expanded in size, filling nearly half of the wooden circle, covering over some of the flaking red paint. She practically yelled at Urith, trying to point while he quickly swung it off his back to see what she was looking at.

"By the gods," he said as she came up next to him. "Look, there's a new engraving with a fine line. It appears like another piece became attached. But how it never left me since...." He racked his brain wondering where he might have picked up the piece. Then, it struck him. "The temple," he said as she nodded her agreement.

"Can you make it out?" she asked. Urith shook his head and showing her the shield.

"No, I see better at long distance, but your eyes should be able to make it out. It appears the same type of symbols and letters as before." The Esterblud went to sit in a chair near the window. "I remember leaning the shield against the table in the temple. It means the piece of the Skool must have been on the table when we arrived. But who could have left such a thing?"

"There must be gods on our side," the hakra declared, her attention focused on the shield.

"Curse the gods, they just shook apart a temple," he growled as remembered the screams of the dying. He told her about the warning voice in his head at the temple and asked if she heard it. Fedelm looked at him, telling him she only heard the screams of the people. The Esterbluds' face grew dark. "I've had enough of these coincidences. As soon as we find another piece, the shrine is destroyed and killing and crippling more people. I'm running out of patience with this. Curse the gods," he said again as he sat the shield on the table.

Fedelm squinted at the fine lines of the engraving, trying to make out the word. She struggled with the symbols for a while before the word came to her. It was *doltais*, meaning justice. But the question was whose justice. She told Urith what she found, but he said nothing as he continued staring at the window into the sky. Fedelm went back to studying the Skool. Her focus was on all of the tales she had learned about the object since they left Du-Rinell. Most of the stories she heard were conflicting, but one stood out. The Shield of Skool had, even more, power. If Urith came to control this force, he would be nearly as potent as the gods. And, potentially, more dangerous.

"You will need to take care in remembering your dreams," she told the warrior. "I have a feeling that there will be more visions about the shield. Since you are the one that controls it, I believe other enchanted words will be revealed to you soon."

The mhoda entered the room with the young attendant and told the group that Imenal was resting after giving him *geju* root which deadened the pain while letting him sleep. She told them there was nothing she more she could do for his leg; it was permanently damaged. She went on to say that she put a splint on the ankle, and it would take some time before the man could travel. Fedelm asked when they could talk with him, and she told them when the sun rose. The healer left, leaving the room in momentary silence.

Fedelm wondered aloud why the priest failed to come back to his home. Jewn spoke up, telling them that the *satgert* died in the temple with several others, crushed when the roof collapsed. He told them that the villagers had already removed the bodies to be burned in grave pits near the temple. The boy looked worried as he revealed the villagers believed someone in the village brought down the wrath of the gods. Although nobody knew who the anger was directed toward, Jewn stated the gods were upset, and prayers should be led by someone in the village. Fedelm changed the subject back to the boy's master, telling him that he should remain with Imenal to make sure he stayed comfortable the rest of the night. The woman promised they would stay there if he needed anything. This seemed to reassure the boy, and he left the room to keep watch over Imenal. After he had left, Urith moved over next to Fedelm, who still held the shield.

"We need to find Mivraa," he said. "The local *satgert* is killed, and one potential ally is nearly killed with him. We barely escaped with our own lives. This is more than a coincidence. The gods are hunting us now. They must be getting nervous about this god weapon."

Fedelm pointed to the shield, "We also have a riddle on our hands. We know the other piece says *gcothrem*. So what does justice and vengeance engraved upon your shield mean?" she asked. "Does anything make sense to you?"

He shook his head as he looked down at the silver pieces which held so much power along with the burden it carried. He walked over to the window again, as he looked out feeling the weight of the human world on him.

"Urith, about Mivraa, I need to tell you something." Fedelm came next to him and put her comforting hand on his broad shoulder. "I've had some visions about her, and I haven't told you everything. They have been hard to piece together."

158

"Does this have something to do with your dream the other night?" he asked.

"Yes," she replied. "I know Mivraa is in trouble, but I haven't been able to determine where she is. I know I should have told you sooner."

"Urith turned on her, his temper rising. "What has happened? What do you know?" His voice grew menacing.

Fedelm told him what she saw, avoiding the rape and beating the brother gods did to their half-sister. The girl worried he could become fixated upon revenge. After she had finished, she knew she was right by the look of his hard, gray eyes. The Esterblud wanted blood. His massive frame seemed to wind up, looking like a black *bater* about to attack. His hand was holding tight to the grip of his sword as if he wanted to pull it from the scabbard to destroy something.

"So, Duwdamon decided to punish an excellent warrior and person for helping humans?" his growl became as death. "And the rest of the dung eaters called gods, helped him? I swear I'll remove their heads personally for this." The giant man's scarred face filled with hate and contempt against the deities. He had lost a loved one before to the gods; he vowed that it would not happen again.

"Listen to me carefully," said Fedelm, feeling an almost desperate need to calm him down. "In Damicia, Mivraa asked me to watch over you if something happened to her. She told me she feared for you and what might occur with the power you carry. I only kept some of the vision from you for this reason. I'm not sure where we can find her yet. We need to have patience until we find out." Urith remained quiet for a moment, his face unchanged, but she could tell her words were slowly getting to him.

"I'm trying my best to track her location, and we will go to her. You need to trust me. I promise that I'll gratefully hand you the Skool to destroy the gods." She reached out to touch him, but he pulled away, taking the shield as he walked from the room. Heading out the entrance to the street, he realized she was correct. He knew there was little he could really do at the moment. But he was enraged and needed time to think, vowing to find a way to settle his score against the gods.

Wandering through the streets, the Esterblud paid little attention to the festival, which continued despite the temple tragedy. Eventually, his travel took him to the burning funeral pyres, near the grave pits. Soon the bodies would be consumed, leaving nothing but ash and bits of bone to be placed in clay jars. Since the people died an unworthy death, each pot would be put in the pit, unknown but to the gods. Disgusted, he knew their spirits would enter the underworld to be tormented. He turned away and went to the local stables nearby, checking on any mounts that might be available to purchase. Plenty of ossanes were available. However, his lack of funds meant they would be walking when they left the village.

Suddenly, an idea came to him. The warrior decided to act as an arms trader who came to the village in search of potential buyers. The ruse worked well enough as he spoke with people, learning much about the local community. Jewn was right, the people talked about their anger at the gods. Some blamed the destruction on the debauchery that came to the village while others claimed the foreigners failed to provide proper sacrifices in the temple. Either way, those who suffered under the sky realm saw little reason to bless their gods, feeling that the deities wanted the humans to hate them. While Urith did not consider himself a *satgert*, he knew the energy of the souls and the offerings to the gods kept the realms in balance. And this balance was falling apart. As he thought of the conversations, the dark streets finally led him back to the wattle and daub home of the dead *satgert*. Inside, he found his companion asleep. The man felt as exhausted as the woman after all of their travel and the day's events.

Early the next morning, the sound of pacing woke Fedelm. Sitting upright next to the empty blankets on the hard stone floor, she could see he had not slept well. As she stretched, he noticed her movement, and he stopped pacing.

"You dreamed last night. What did you see?" His question momentarily surprised her; then she realized he must have watched her all night.

"It was the same dream as before," she yawned, thinking back as she scratched her head. "The mountains are unlike anything I've ever seen, high in the sky and showing red rock. She is chained to the highest mountain, and I know it is very remote and rugged for I saw only a small trail coming up from the highlands which I can observe in the distance. I could see the flicker of lights so there must be a village nearby."

His large frame sagged momentarily, and then an idea caught hold of him, and he knelt next to her, staring into her eyes. "You said the highest mountain made of red rock. The range between Esterblud and Eernicia might be a safe bet. I've heard of some of the areas are unexplored; it might be a spot for gods to hide. And they say the rock is red like the sun at times."

"But where do we start?" Fedelm asked. "North to South, you told me that range would take a full season just to ride between the villages. We cannot leave her to the Fates guiding us."

"Look, it's a start, and we have to try something. We should be able to learn something as we go. Sitting around here isn't going to find her," the Esterblud said pointedly.

She looked at him cautiously, unsure how much to push back on his idea. She knew his stubbornness well. "How do we get there? Walking will take that us much longer. Plus, we will need supplies. I can't imagine that the mountains will welcome us with abundant food."

"That's what kept me up some," he admitted after a brief pause. "And I have no answer but to keep moving from village to village as we go to the area."

Fedelm reached out, holding his arm. "Listen, I'll follow you wherever you want. But we have to believe that something will come, it always does. You know just rushing out of this village goes against all the things you have been trying to teach Oslaf." She smiled at his surprised expression. "Yes, I've been listening on those long rides."

The giant warrior looked into her blue eyes. She was a loyal friend like few others. He felt ashamed that he once strongly considered killing her. Her misguided alliance with Alrpan and Satres even after he and Oslaf rescued her from the *Gallaeci* in Ynyover was a distant memory. While they were thrown together for only a short time, he now felt like they knew each other for ages.

"Let's go check on Imenal," Fedelm interrupted his thoughts, using his shoulder to lean on as she stood next to him. Urith nodded before standing as well, thinking of their next moves. She continued, as she walked to the bedroom. "Maybe he's better, and he can tell us more about what he knows."

They found Imenal propped up on the bed, his leg bound in cloth with wood splints on either side of the leg, from the toes to his mid-thigh. His face was pale, but he seemed in good spirits. His attendant, Jewn, had just finished feeding him broth made of *weamater*. The smell of the sun-dried slices of salted *duelill* meat filled the room. The boy looked exhausted as he went back to sit in the chair where he slept earlier.

"So you want to know about your friend and what I know?" Imenal gave a weak smile after they entered the room. He saw their surprised expressions and pointed to the wall. "The walls are thin and sound carries very well. I heard your conversation. Well, at least, I listened to some of your discussions. The confounded root the healer gave me is powerful, and I'm not sure what might be a dream and what is real," said Imenal.

He directed his gaze at Urith. "Now I understand the burden you bear, my friend. I didn't thank you for saving my life. And now I realize that you have rediscovered the Skool. I always thought it was a legend, but it explains why Satres was after you and Fedelm. He must have branded you *wafaoils* to make his job easier."

The leader of the Damicia Temple went on to explain how the Sacred Overlord was sending out instructions for the *satgerts* to track the Esterbluds. Imenal told them of rumors that the fealharan, who attacked Urith in Damicia, were led by a central Aberffraw leader. Imenal said he heard the man immediately left the city after his brother, a diplomat, was killed, not even bothering to stop by the temple for the death rituals."

"Wait a moment," Urith moved toward the disabled man. "Do you know what this person looked like?" The wounded man paused a moment, trying to remember.

"Lyncus," said Urith emphatically after Imenal described the man. "I know I should have killed that dung eater the first time we met. I let the Hepatic code stand in the way. You say he left Damicia?"

"Yes, right after the assassination. I heard tales that a fealharan were with him. Look, I can tell you want to find him, but it wouldn't do any good to go back to Cahmais. You and your friends are branded as temple defilers who would be hunted and killed by anyone at any time. I suggest you continued to travel the backcountry to stay alive," Imenal advised.

"That is what bothers me. Why are you helping us?" Urith asked, his suspicion still evident, although he had to agree with the man's logic. The leader of the Damicia Temple impressed Urith, and he seemed to be telling them the truth so far.

Imenal glanced over to Fedelm whose face was asking the same question. "I can see why you are suspicious. It appears everyone is against you. But that is not true. Some of us have seen things in our dreams that shake our reality."

"What do you mean," Fedelm interrupted.

"You're not the only hakra around," the temple leader told her. "I believe I've seen some of the things you have as well. I saw a chained Mivraa on the cliff you were speaking about."

Chapter 6: The Struggles

On the side of the Neehorsh peak, Mivraa began her morning ritual, bathed in Exyts Spring water by members of the Death Bearers. The cycle of torment would start again just as it had for so many dawns. The spring water of the gods would immediately begin to heal the woman's missing flesh and raw muscle. Each night, flying monsters, called *ranqels,* would land to feast upon the chained demigoddess, tearing and ripping at her naked flesh, like *vensars* upon carrion. The flying winged creatures with their ugly beaked heads were created from the souls of those condemned to die for their hideous crimes. Released from the underworld, the long, lean skeletal monsters, covered with black leather-like skin, enjoyed their feast upon the living goddess. Mivraa could not die from such dreadful wounds. Instead, she felt the pain and agony of near death from the loss of blood and tissue, her arms and legs nearly devoid of flesh. After the monsters had finished, the demigoddess endured the rest of the night half alive, wishing for death.

In her foggy, nearly unconscious state each morning, the demigoddess could hear two of the Death Bearers climbing the treacherous trail to sprinkle her with the same healing waters she used on her personal friend's injuries. The men and women, dressed in black robes and wearing starched white turbans, remained to watch the enchanted magic work to rebuild her body. The cult members proudly wore the black flag of death around their necks and remained oblivious to her suffering or her mutilated body. No matter how she begged them to let her loose or, later on, to kill her, they would only smile before they forced her to drink the spring water, which immediately began to revive her, reforming her body and flesh to whole again. The water would satiate her hunger and thirst a short time, but the cramping and pain of starvation would creep back by nightfall. As the sunrises and sunsets stretched together, the demigoddess tried everything to get help from the Death Bearers when they arrived, chanting prayers to their god, Kriell. It was a name she did not know, but soon she began to curse this cruel god who provided such people to help in her torture. Her curses against Kriell fell upon deaf ears as these foul humans obeyed their powerful master.

As if the nightly suffering was not enough, the heat of the afternoon brought the burning of the sun on her pale skin along with a growing thirst for water. The constant bites of *tantus*, small six legged insects that swarmed from the nearby rocks, became just another torment of many. Despite the torture, at first, her spirit remained strong as the goddess focused her efforts on escape. It was soon clear that the chains and bindings were impervious to her strength. As the day and the nights became nothing but a repetition of unfathomable pain, she changed her strategy. One of her strengths was the ability to see visions of others. Now she attempted to focus on communicating her terrible nights into visions for her friends to find her. Mivraa was alone in a vast, forbidding mountain range and unable to guide them. Her terrible plight forced her into despair. Some of the time she was able to concentrate on her memories, like Urith's scarred face and gray eyes, which somehow reassured her that the Clovel Destroyer would come eventually. She also saw Fedelm and Oslaf in her dreams on occasion. Strangely, she would have dreams showing other faces, people she knew such as Dughorm or Caestia as well as others she did not know. When she was able to think clearly, she wondered if she was going mad from the torment. Eventually, as a cycle of torture continued, the demigoddess turned her attention to thoughts of revenge against the sky gods. Much of her day became consumed with how she would strike down those responsible for her suffering. Nothing else mattered.

After the Death Bearers went away, the goddess could again feel the rough and cold stone against her back, now completely healed. The healing rebuilt her physically, but her mind remembered the agony of near death. At times, she used the time to concentrate upon her revenge. Other times she tried to remember details from the night before, to send out to her friends. Mivraa recalled the twin moons of Kamin rising above the mountain peaks and the face of a stranger appearing before her. His short blonde hair and oval face she did not recognize, but he was reaching out to her. He was handsome, and her sixth sense told her he was not a threat, maybe even a friend. His green eyes locked on hers for a moment, and she knew he must be a hakra. In his eyes, she could sense his extreme pain which momentarily allowed her to feel for the plight of someone else. She saw stones falling around the man and the image of a familiar giant lifting her. Somehow it gave her a comfort that she was not alone, Urith was near. Soon, Mivraa could sense they were sharing the same vision, much like the demigoddess had done with Fedelm on occasion before.

As the sky grew dark, the goddess hoped she could share her plight with the man, sensing his questions, though neither spoke in her dream. She looked around her, giving him all that she could see while trying to remember all of the images from her trip there. Her eyes focused upon the weighty chains that bound her and the steps where the Death Bearers came from each morning. They continued to exchange such views and thoughts when she realized the man was getting weak as if something was dulling his senses. After a while, they separated, and Mivraa felt alone with her thoughts. The light gave way to the coming of the night, and she felt the panic fill her as she watched the last rays of purple hue leave the sky. She heard the flapping of leathery wings and the faint high pitched shriek of the *ranqels* and the goddess took a deep breath as she braced herself for the torment to come while praying for her friends to find her soon.

~~~

As Imenal told Urith and Fedelm his visions about Mivraa, the Esterblud began pacing the floor, his eyes staring down at nothing. Fedelm carefully sat upon the edge of the bed, listening to the descriptions. She was brought to tears as she remembered her own visions from her friend, feeling inadequate at her inability to help the goddess. Fedelm asked a few questions when Imenal spoke about the views of the mountain and trails. The two hakras went into as much detail together as they could to make sense of their dreams. It was when he spoke of the Death Bearers that Urith stopped them and looked down at the *yolma*, his face showing the anger.

"If what you say is true, we know where she is," he growled. "My king spoke of these urine drinkers hiding in the Neewar mountains. And both you and Fedelm spoke of the highest peak. If so, there is none greater than the height of Neehorsh according to the skalds."

"Yes, I've heard of this as well," exclaimed Imenal, before groaning at his effort. "A *satgert*, um… I forget his name. Anyway, he claimed to have been chased out of the area by these people. I wrote to the Sacred Overlord about this just last season. Of course, he seemed preoccupied and never responded."

"Good luck with that," said Urith sarcastically. "Listen, if they are in that area, they should be easy to find. I've seen a few of those fanatics brought before Penhda for judgment. They are happy to give their lives to help some wretched god. I don't remember the name, but it was not even a proper god that I've heard of. These cult members are a venomous lot and happy to inflict death on those who don't follow them. They tell the villagers to submit or die to their cause."

"What did your overlord do with them?" Fedelm asked although she suspected she knew the answer.

"We found out they had killed a *satgert* along with some village elders. The vermin remained steadfast to the end, claiming they would die as martyrs, and they would return with their god. So, Penhda had them dig their graves very deep before they were buried alive as punishment," the warrior told them. "They were put face down, so it made them that much easier to meet Caruun in the underworld," Urith smiled at his grim joke as he focused on the next journey. "Now we need to find supplies and ossanes to find Mivraa." Urith started for the door as Fedelm rose to join him.

"How? You have nothing to get them with," asked Imenal, which caused the pair to stop. When they looked at him, surprised until he knocked on the thin walls again to remind them as he smiled weakly.

"I wish I could go on this trip with you. Instead, I can help you as I lay in this bed. Take Jewn with you to get what you need," he told them before turning to the boy who listened quietly in the corner of the room. The boy's eyes were wide with the information. "You will have the merchants come to me for payment since I'm now the *satgert* for this village." The boy nodded and ran in front of the two travelers. Fedelm looked back at the man, holding the door open after Urith walked out. Imenal motioned for her to come to him and she walked to the bed. He handed her a small medallion on a gold chain. When she held it up, she could see the *helois* or bloodstone in the middle, outlined with the symbols of Imenal's family along with an odd phrase.

"I cannot accept this," she said, trying to give it back.

"You don't understand," he replied as he forced it back in her hand. "This is a talisman used by my grandfather in defense against powerful beasts. It's called a *dyriya*. I didn't want to speak in front of your friend, but the power in this object could be used to stop him."

"Who, you mean Urith?" her voice hushed as she looked back to the door. They could hear the warrior's booming voice as he talked with Jewn in the other room.

"Yes, we both know he now carries the power of the gods and will only grow stronger as the Skool is pieced together." The man hurried his words. "Say the phrase *teinidh cadhla* with this talisman in both hands and you can weaken any human, perhaps even stop spells or enchantment over them. I cannot guarantee it will work against everything, but it is some defense for you. Now take it."

He stopped as he listened to the front door open. "You can show the medallion for help at any temple. I'll send word around you are protected by this. There are plenty of others that don't follow the Sacred Overlord. Just ask the satgert about the health of Imenal. If they say, I'm traveling to Regiussa, and then you know you have an ally."

"I don't know what to say," said the woman. "But wait, what if you go to Regiussa?"

The man smiled at her. "Don't you know? There are no temples in that barbarian land. Now go with my blessing. You will know when you need to use the amulet. I have foreseen trouble ahead, and you will have your work cut out for you.

Imenal's face turned somber. "I heard what you told Urith earlier, and I sense a deadly purpose arising in that Esterblud. Keep a watch on whether he no longer follows the chosen path for him. He is destined to find the entire Skool. This is not in doubt. But, I suspect that makes him dangerous to all humans. My visions about him were not clear but consider my words. He is mortal with many human frailties. He could take over Esterblud and make himself overlord with that shield he carries on his back. I'll pray for the Fates to help him make the right choice. However, if he is half the warrior I've heard about, nothing on that mountain will remain alive when he finishes. Take care of yourself," he told her gently.

"I will," she said, "and take heart. I've learned to trust that giant killer of men and beasts. There's more to him than just his quick temper and his Clovel Sword. I've seen good deeds in him as well. He shows great honor to those deserving, and he carries a desire for helping the weak." She closed the door telling herself what she just said must be true. However, as she joined Urith going out the front of the home, she somehow felt like she had just betrayed the Esterblud.

The unlikely pair of travelers left the small village, sped by Jewn's ability to find the right merchants for them. Imenal's attendant was bright and an excellent negotiator, able to haggle with the best of the merchants for his master. Fedelm enjoyed watching the boy, dressed in his white robes, using his master's authority to get them three ossanes and all the supplies they needed. As they were leaving, she bent down and gave the boy a quick kiss on his forehead which greatly embarrassed him. The horrified look he gave her even put a smile on Urith's lips.

Seizing advantage with their rested, long-necked mounts and plenty of sunlight left, they galloped along at a quick pace toward the border of Eernicia and Esterblud. Earlier, when they talked with the ossane trader, the woman in charge told them it would be several sunrises before they reached the border of Esterblud. Fedelm asked Urith if he knew exactly where the Neehorsh peak would be, and he admitted he did not know the precise location. But he told her that he remembered a village called Kanhan which was overrun by the Death Bearers a few seasons before. Since the village lay near their path, he told her they would be able to find out more information there. While Urith's plan seemed reasonable, the woman felt doubt nudging her about the warrior. She worried if his rage over Mivraa's treatment would overcome his usually sound judgment. As they rode through the open land, she noticed the Esterblud remained even more brooding than usual, like he carried the burdens of the world. She wondered if Dughorm's confidence in this warrior was misplaced. At times, the giant warrior scared her with his inclination to lash out. He had possession of the Skool, the Djeed talisman, and the Clovel Sword. How could one man not succumb to the vast power he held?

~~~

Near the border on the other side of Eernicia, Oslaf and his new partner, Henther, entered the place called Greman. While the girl had called it a village, the Esterblud looked at the few buildings on either side of the old road and decided her term was generous. Forced into the community after finding their skiff lost to the sea during the storm, at first, they wanted to blame each other for the loss of the boat. But when Oslaf had found the rope sliced by the knife-like edge of one of the rocks, both of them realized the Fates had again worked against them. After some tense discussion, the new allies decided they must walk into the village on their way to Eernicia to find some means of passage. Fortunately, the storm allowed them to refill their water bags which tempered some of the hunger pains. When Oslaf pushed the girl to show him the way to the village, he could tell she was not happy about the upcoming reunion with her past. Shaking his head, he reached down to grab the few items they had, rolling his green tunic within the makeshift bag. Better to be a simple mercenary traveling between towns, he decided as he remained concerned that the Vulthnal King might have put out a bounty upon him.

The first thing Oslaf noticed about the hamlet was how quiet it was. An empty road held no ossanes, and the only sound was the sound of whistling, which came from the middle of a small building. Henther led them to an entrance where the top of the frame held a broken sign showing a mead cup. The wooden doors were open, and the musty smell of sweat and mead struck them when they entered the room. It was a tavern with no patrons, only a middle-aged man sitting alone. The whistling man played a game of *chemmy*, a strategic game using pieces of carved bone on a small, round board. The pieces represented warriors, and their placement indicated he was playing against two other players. The gray-haired man looked up in surprise at his new visitors.

"Please come," he said eagerly, "yes, come to the table and rest yourselves from your weary travel. I must confess I heard no ossanes. Although, I must admit I was distracted by the complicated game."

The man quickly went behind a slab of thick wood where he pulled up two mugs for his guests. He nodded for them to join him as he poured the heathmead from the small cask sitting on top of the bar. Oslaf pressed forward now as Henther wanted to vanish, only reluctantly following him.

"Pretty quiet," the warrior observed the long, narrow room which revealed a few tables with uncomfortable benches on either side of them. In the back, Oslaf could see a few thin wooden boxes scattered about the cobblestone floor. He rightly guessed the supplies were not coming to this hamlet frequently.

The tavern keeper placed the copper mugs in front of them. They were tarnished but clean. "It's always quiet here since the guilds stopped the merchants from using the road between Damicia and Alurican," said the tavern keeper, his thin face turned grave for a moment. "But we do well enough when the travelers come through for the festivals. So, where are you heading?"

Oslaf took a long drink, then complimented the man on his drink. The tavern keeper immediately brightened and lied to them, saying he received his supplies from a local merchant who took regular trips to Damicia.

"How far to Damicia?" the warrior asked.

"Only a few sun cycles," the man replied, "if you need a place for your ossanes I can find a good place out back of the building."

"We are traveling on foot," the warrior told him as he gave the other mug to Henther after she failed to pick it up.

The tavern keeper looked at them as if they each had two heads. "It is far too dangerous for you and your girl to go through the Larcal marshes, especially at night. You must find an ossane to get through the area before the sun drops."

"Well, we have only a few koinons," Oslaf took the last drink of his mead. "I don't see how that will happen. Anyway, we are hungry, so I would rather use my last koinons on some food. Is that possible?"

The tavern keeper immediately apologized and told them he would have his mistress get food ready for them as he scurried off to the back of the building. Oslaf turned and moved over to the nearest table as Henther followed him, sitting next to him on the bench, which was just a split log, roughly sanded and uncomfortable as he expected.

"Well, you were quiet," the Esterblud told Henther. "Any ideas?"

"If we need ossanes, find out who might have them," she told him. "I'm sure I can get them for us."

"I'll ask, but do you have any koinons?" Oslaf looked at her suspiciously.

She batted her pretty eyes, giving him a sweet smile. "I have found I don't need such things if I need something. I can get them."

"You burnt your yellow belt," he reminded her. "And I don't need a partner that forgets that." Although he acted nonchalant, she could tell he was upset at the thought. Using her beautiful face and fine figure to achieve what she wanted had become second nature to her, and his reaction was strange to her. However, she decided she wasn't going to start starving due to his beliefs.

"Well, if you have a better idea, let me know," She replied haughtily. "I don't need a partner that gets me killed because of his stupidity."

"Better to die with honor…" Oslaf shut up as a small lady with gray hair come from the back holding two platters. The woman sat the dishes in front of them, and they smelled the pickled fish covered with herbs. She looked at them sympathetically.

"I heard you are traveling by foot. You should really find another way," she told them as she watched them eat ravenously. I know," she exclaimed at a thought, "I can check with one of the local boys. They might have an ossane they can sell."

Oslaf smiled at her, thanking her. "I'm sorry, but we don't have anything to trade. Perhaps I could work for it?"

The older lady shook her head as she looked at the large man. "I doubt that. You don't look like a farmhand to me. Besides, most folks around here need the work for themselves since we can't get the spices out of the swamp now. Too dangerous. And we don't have many folks coming through since the troubles began."

"Troubles?" Henther spoke up for the first time.

"Yes," the gray-haired woman's voice lowered to a whisper as she leaned forward, stretching out her rough hands to brace herself on the edge of the table. "Just started up recently. People used to hunt in the bogs for spices. You know, *pap* and *quith* are famous here." Oslaf wrinkled his nose as he thought of the bitter root called *pap*. He hated it. But he smiled and urged the woman to continue.

"Well, I probably shouldn't tell you this, but once people go in, they never come back. Mind you, that's happened before with strangers, but not local folk who know the marsh area like the back of their hands. My man don't like me talking about it cause it scares folks." She looked behind her to ensure the tavern keeper remained the back of the tavern before continuing.

"But we need someone to know about it. Nobody coming from Alurican with our overlord off acting important chasing bandits on the other side of the land. Both of you seem like nice folk, so heed my warning, you need a mount to speed you along. Maybe you can find us some help."

"Ok, if you can find us a deal on an ossane, we will get you some help. I'll take your advice and not wander in the bogs at night. Do you think you can find us something?" Oslaf asked.

"You don't worry about that," the woman said earnestly. "We'll work out something. You finish up while I find out what I can." In a flash, the talkative lady was out the door, yelling back to the tavern keeper she was leaving.

Gordon Brewer

"Looks like you made a friend," said Henther sarcastically.

He shot her a glance. "You can always walk through the marshes by yourself." She bit her lip, unsure how much she could push the young man. Henther guessed Oslaf had his uncle's temper. Despite her reservations about him, she liked his apparent honesty and openness. But she knew from bitter experience she could not trust such men, especially warriors.

As the sun fell behind the trees, the travelers were walking back to the tavern after meeting some of the other hamlet's inhabitants looking for any traders or merchants going to Damicia when they ran into the inn keeper's wife. She told them of a farmer who had a spare animal he would sell to them. But, as expected, his price was far beyond what they could pay. Still, the woman told them to stay the night since the farmer would be leaving with his wagon to Eernicia. She told them she could not promise anything, but they could find the cart across the road when the sun rose.

Oslaf thanked the older woman who blushed slightly, "Is there a cheap place to stay around here, other than the ground outside?"

She told them not to worry, they could use the room above the tavern. Then, the plump woman went into a long, detailed explanation of her work to secure their passage out of the village as she guided them back to the building. Oslaf decided their presence gave the woman something to fuss over as he watched Henther suspiciously eyeing their passage upstairs.

The room the two travelers shared that night was cramped and cluttered. However, it was better than the damp ground outside in the Esterblud's mind. He was happy that the owner had decided to let them stay for nothing. While the warrior was sure the man's wife had something to do with it, he promised himself he would find something to pay them for their kindness. Henther, on the other hand, looked at the small room with the low ceiling with visible distaste. While better than some of the places she endured to satisfy men to get koinon, it still reminded her too much of her past. She knew she could not sleep outside. Still suspicious of the young warrior, she refused to undress. Instead, she used the wet smelling wool blanket she took from the skiff, to cover the dirty blanket where she lay. Facing the brown plaster wall, she covered herself with the blanket. During the whole process, she continued to complain about the accommodations.

173

Oslaf wanted to give her a sharp retort, but his mind was blank, and he was tired. So much had happened to them, and he really did not understand her sudden fussiness about the room after spending so much time on a narrow boat. He decided to let it go and get some sleep, hopefully thinking that one of those visions that Fedelm told him about would come to him and help guide him.

Screams from outside the building awoke Oslaf and Henther late that night as the two moons of Kamin peaked to the north. The strong moonlight cast a pale light over the town and the marshland. The Esterblud was the first to the tiny window, still sweating and breathing hard from his own nightmarish dream. He glanced out over the area with his sword in hand. He could just make out two-legged shapes entering the buildings across the road where the screams were coming from. Other tall, thin shapes moved out of the tall grasses of the swamp, moving across the road. Quickly Oslaf barreled out of the room, grabbing his shield on the way. Running full speed down the narrow stairway, his bare feet felt the worn floorboards which creaked as he stepped into the tavern near the entrance. A quick glance over his shoulder revealed the wide eyes of the innkeeper and his wife hiding behind a table in the dim light. The warrior only wore the thick, padded canvas undergarment having removed his tunic and chainmail earlier. As he went to the door, the Esterblud heard the sound from the stairs and he turned his head to see the golden haired form of Henther enter the room, holding his battle ax in her hand.

Standing near the entrance when the first beast crashed through the thick wooden door, Oslaf found himself dodging the heavy door which shattered from the blow. In the moonlight, a tall, gaunt creature which looked similar to a *cruba* entered the room, sniffing the air. Its humanoid head held extra wide jaws of razor-sharp bony ridges, much like a turtle. With long arms ending in three extended claws, the warrior saw the vicious yellow eyes and white skin of the beast just before it attacked. Despite his initial surprise, the Esterblud was able to defend himself with his shield when the creature sliced at him with its clawed hands. Using his sword, Oslaf struck down on the creature's arm, the beast grunted savagely as the arm sailed across the floor, splattering him with blood. Unfazed, the animal tried to clamp down on the warrior's shoulder. Instead, its massive jaws took a hunk out of his shield, cutting through the iron and wood like butter.

Oslaf spun away from the gnashing jaws that came at him again and was able to slice down on the head of the monster with a wide swing of his longsword. The creature fell to the floor with a massive wound on the hard skull. However, as he was about to strike the beast again, he saw the head suddenly healed itself, and the creature swung out its arm, partially catching the warrior in the thigh with its claws. The Esterblud backed up, becoming cautious after seeing this monster healing itself. Confirming the fighter's suspicions about the creature, the tall form slowly rose, now with its severed arm fully replaced. Oslaf had to look at the other arm on the floor to see if somehow he was dreaming. Unfortunately, the nightmare continued as the monster attacked him again. The warrior parried away a couple of claw strikes at him as he realized the creature was intelligently searching for Oslaf's weaknesses.

"I'll chop you to pieces, cursed beast," he breathed hard, steeling himself for the next attack.

The monster came at him again and this time, the warrior jammed the tip of his sword into its neck, driving the blade deep. The creature howled, backing away. Oslaf seized the initiative and moved forward, slashing at its middle, slicing through the thin flesh. Bending over slightly from its wound, Oslaf looked at the yellow eyes and suddenly had an idea spring to mind. Remembering what Urith had done to the cruba that attacked his uncle at Du-Rinell, the warrior waited. When the creature moved toward him, Oslaf stepped into the beast, pushing the longsword deep into the eye socket. Howling in desperation, the monster tried to swipe at the warrior, but Oslaf finished it off by driving the blade deep into the creature's brain.

Pulling out the sword, the Esterblud heard the yells and screams outside. He ran out the shattered door and saw one of the beasts taking a massive bit out of the shoulder of a dead man it held in its claws. The Esterblud attacked the monster immediately, driving his sword into the back of its neck, trying to kill it. However, he missed the sight of another monster who moved in behind him. The creature was nearly on him when he heard Henther scream a warning. He tried to step away, but caught a hard strike across his back, momentarily knocking the wind out of him as he landed flat on his belly. He lost his grip on his sword still stuck in the neck of the beast. Oslaf looked up and saw Henther land his battle ax in the back of the creature. The white face monster howled at the deep wound and swung around to attack her.

Henther was trying to raise her ax for another swing as the monster moved in to rip her apart. Oslaf scrambled to his feet, sprinting to cut off the beast. He arrived just in time to run his battered shield up under its razor jaws forcing the creature to miss the woman. She hacked at it again, giving it a glancing blow as man and monster went by in the bright moonlight. She saw her first strike had already healed. Oslaf used the momentum of the creature's rush to push it directly into the heavy timber building. The beast slammed headfirst into the frame, and the Esterblud used the edge of his shield to drive into the back of his neck. The neck snapped as the armor nearly decapitated the monster. The snapping sound could be heard over the screams and growls in the night air. Bouncing off the side of the building, Oslaf turned to find the other monster.

Outlined in the glow of flames from a burning building, Henther frantically backed away from the razor-jawed creature attacking her. Oslaf saw his sword embedded in the back of the creature's neck. Despite being winded, he felt a burst of energy run through him as he ran toward the beast, coming up from behind. He grabbed his sword and before the creature could react, he pushed the blade up into the monster's brain. The razor jaw fell face forward into the ground without a sound. "There are more over there," cried Henther, pointing to two lanky forms ripping on the walls of the building away from the flames. Inside, the trapped villagers yelled and screamed, penned between the flames creeping along the building and the ferocious creatures trying to get at them. With sword and shield, now in hand, the Esterblud ran to the terrifying scene. Henther joined him, ignoring his protests. He thanked the gods as the creatures remained fixed upon their prey, oblivious to the two humans closing on them.

Oslaf's sword stroke came down on top of the skull of the nearest monster, splitting it wide open, sending parts of the black brain matter across the area. Before the beast could heal, he hacked down through the creature's neck, beheading it. The other white-faced beast charged at him. Fortunately for Oslaf, the fearsome claws barely cut his padded shirt. Henther struck the back of the fiend, causing it to face her as she planned. Seeing his opening, the Esterblud warrior jabbed his sword into the base of the skull, thrusting upward. The last monster fell face first at the feet of the woman who was holding her battleax to strike at it again.

The adrenaline still rushing through him, Oslaf noticed movement from behind the building and moved to investigate. As he got closer, he could make out a familiar figure entering the high grass at the edge of the marshland. He heard the splashing coming from the figure running through the water and muck. The Esterblud stopped at the grass line, thinking he might be running into a trap. He heard the sound of the footsteps continue on until the sound was lost in the noise of the night.

"What did you see?" Henther was breathing heavily as she came up behind him.

Oslaf turned to her. "A Vanth that I've met before," he told her. "I think that might explain these creatures. They must come from the underworld. Are there any more around?"

"No, I think they have been destroyed. The tavern keeper and his wife got some of the people away from the fires. Now, we need to help them get those flames from spreading to the rest of their homes."

Nodding, the Esterblud joined the woman as they went to burning buildings. They joined the small group of strangers, using buckets of water to put out the burning building. The sun rose over the horizon in the west before the flames were finally extinguished. Then, the group began the grim task of removing the charred bodies of the wife and her child caught inside the burning structure. While the young Esterblud was used to seeing death, this attack struck him to the core as he helped carry the charred body of the boy. The burnt flesh smell stuck in his mind. He walked by Henther, and he noticed the woman was silently crying with tears coming down her face. The bodies of wife and son were laid next to the man Oslaf saw being eaten by the monster. The townsfolk quickly buried the bodies in a shallow grave since cremation remained the way to the gods reserved for warriors alone.

When they finished, the men and women wandered slowly over to the tavern. Oslaf stopped by the open well in front of the building, cleaning his face and arms from the full bucket of water sitting there. He felt the bracing cool liquid dripping from his face and hair, enjoying the sensation as he tried to fight off a sudden weariness that enveloped him. Henther was standing behind him, observing his movements.

"You look like you've fought such monsters before," she noted, coming up close to him and lowering her voice. "I've overheard some of the villagers. You have impressed the people with your bravery. Many men would have run from those beasts." He could tell from her tone that she had difficulty reconciling his actions to save the villagers and his part in the brutal attack on Casab with the Vulthnal Guards.

"I need a drink," Oslaf ignored her words as he walked into the tavern. Inside, he met some of the remaining members of the village, old men who patted him on the back and had a heathmead brought to him. They spoke with him, praising the Esterblud for his courage, before telling others who slowly drifted into the village. They said they would tell the skalds who came through the village about Oslaf. Satisfied with their actions, the village men returned to their families who came into the somber room.

As he drank from his mug, the warrior noticed Henther was talking with the people, leaning over to comfort them. He could tell she had a natural, soothing touch despite the cold mask she wore. Her words helped calm the lingering fear as the sunlight came through the dirty glass. She was still dressed in her robe which was covered with dirt and soot. And her face was covered with soot as well. He could see her talking with one of the village women who said something about the warrior which he couldn't hear. He just saw her give a quick smile, patting the woman on the shoulder. She walked over to join him at the table.

"Now that you are a hero, it appears the village will find us an ossane." She told him, but Oslaf said nothing as he stared at the mug he held. He seemed as if in a daze.

She went on, "If the tavern keeper's wife is correct, we can be in Eernicia by nightfall. So are you leaving?" she asked quietly.

"Why would I stay?" he asked, mostly to himself. "I have to find my uncle."

"Who will defend these people when you leave? Or don't you care?" She challenged him with her words.

"Don't put that on me," Oslaf told her, tired of the constant fight with her. "You cannot understand this, but I have to leave." With his words, he rose from the bench and moved off to the room to pack. On his way up to the chamber, he stopped at the bar and confirmed with the tavern keeper that he would be able to get a mount. The man smiled, shaking his head energetically as he assured the warrior they would have an ossane for him and his girl. Too tired to argue with the man about the woman with him, he thanked him. As he climbed the stairs, he thought about Henther's words and realized his decision was not as easy as he

178

thought. He was genuinely torn by the warrior code which told him to remain.

Inside the room, he put on his green tunic, fully aware the Esterblud symbol would become the talk of the village when he left. Despite his reservations about leaving, he was proud to know his fight would be remembered by those of the hamlet. Rolling up his few remaining items into his bedroll, Oslaf put his helmet on his belt. Henther silently joined him, rolling up a blanket from her bed. He could tell by her silence that she remained upset with him. But he refused to worry about her feelings.

"So you are coming along as well?" He asked her.

"Yes, there is nothing here for me. I told you that." She tied off her blanket and left the room as he grabbed his black helmet and followed her out.

Soon, they were on the road toward Damicia with Henther sitting behind the warrior on their new ossane. The rest of the village had given them great send-off, ignoring his Esterblud tunic. They had food and drink enough for the journey. Oslaf thanked them for their generosity, promising he would send help to their hamlet when they reached Damicia. As they moved quickly through the moors, the misfit pair remained quiet, each lost in their own thoughts. When the sun rose to its zenith, Henther suddenly asked him a question.

"Why do you need to find your uncle? Was it something to do with your dreams?"

Oslaf stopped the mount, "What do you mean?"

"I heard you in your sleep. You seemed to be talking with someone." Her tone indicated suspicion.

He paused, wondering how much to tell her. "Yes, it was a vision I had. While I know a hakra who sometimes explained about visions, I've never felt a dream like this before." The Esterblud spurred the mount forward, remembering they needed to get out of the moors before dark. Even with their victory over the razor-jawed monsters, he did not want to meet more of the creatures.

After a long while, he decided to explain his vision. "I saw my friend in terrible pain, chained to the side of a mountain," he blurted out. "Listen, I'm not a hakra or a madman, despite what you may think. That's why I'm telling you. If I'm having these dreams, something must be very wrong. All I know is my uncle will be in the middle of it. I can guarantee you that much." His voice trailed off as he thought about what the vision told him and where is uncle could be located.

"I heard you yell out which woke me before the screams. You said something about Mivraa."

"Yes, I saw a vision of Mivraa, who was chained to the mountain. I have to help since I know my uncle will be on his way to find her."

"So now you know a demigoddess?" The girl's skepticism was evident.

Oslaf smiled, telling her she knew Mivraa as well. "You should remember her. She transformed into your rival *docke* and then kept you from helping Thulmare during our escape."

Oslaf rightfully took her silence as surprise. Not many people in the world of Kamin could claim a demigod as an ally. Henther suddenly felt confused about her companion, wondering if she made a mistake by coming with him. In her experience, putting trust in the Fates led people into dangerous situations.

"So, you have a dream, and now you are searching for your uncle. While he might be a great warrior, what you are attempting doesn't make sense. Where I come from, you don't run your life on dreams," said Henther.

Oslaf grunted. "Perhaps you need to change your thoughts about such things. You might not believe this, but since my uncle and I met Fedelm and Mivraa, I've learned you need to trust in the Fates sometimes."

"Ok, so you believe in this dream you had so you will leave the village to their own devices. Now how will you find your uncle in Damicia?" The woman asked.

"Listen, it was not an easy decision to leave, but I meant what I told the villagers. There is a small Esterblud community in the city; I will find someone to return to this village. Young warriors who want to make a name for themselves, and they can get their chance. Plus, I can tell them about the Vulthnal Guard needing help against the bandits. Some will come here; I'm sure of that. Plus, someone in Damicia will know when my uncle left for Ffestini. We should not be that far behind him." At least, that was Oslaf's hope as he spurred the mount along the road.

~~~

The gates of the Citadel of Br-Ynys were open, and a small crowd lined the sides of the cobblestone road leading into the massive fortress.

Those in the crowd pressed forward to look at the two lines of blue and silver clad Aberffraw warriors parading past them, led by King Asgurd of Cahmais with his son next to him. Both men were mounted on immaculately decorated white ossanes which were symbols of the peaceful alliance between Ynyover and Cahmais. Only a few old men and women in the crowd recalled the same uniforms arriving at the Citadel some twenty-five winters before. An event which led their warriors into the disastrous Necropolis War. On this morning, King Asgurd and Lyncus were enjoying the pomp and pageantry for entirely different reasons. Lyncus had sent a messenger to Satres before their army's arrival, giving him a general idea of their plans. The king's son remained cautious in his planning, stopping any rumors from coming back to his father through the various spies planted in the Holy Overlord's troops. While he controlled this guard, he knew his father placed individual families in strategic positions over those who patrolled the lands of Ynyover. Given what was at stake for Lyncus, extra caution was prudent.

King Asgurd, on the other hand, enjoyed the spectacle in grand fashion. He remained sober throughout the long journey from Cahmais, refusing the luxuries of wine and women on the trip which surprised his servants and his son. A deadly focus came after the death of his firstborn, and he meant to make Esterblud pay for it in bloody revenge. To the surprise of Lyncus, each night the king took his son into his confidence. Explaining his military and political strategies to remove the loathsome Esterblud from the control of their lands, Lyncus knew his father's goal was the complete annihilation of King Penhda's kingdom and the extermination and enslavement of the people. At first, Lyncus thought he might have gone too far in his quest for the crown by keeping his father alive. However, as he listened to the old warrior, he became convinced that Cahmais could dominate the Kamin lands. His father remained a valuable tool for the young warrior who saw himself becoming master over most of Kamin and he gladly welcomed the idea.

While the rest of the kingdoms reacted with shock at the assassination of the king's son by an Esterblud warrior, Asgurd immediately sent messengers to each of the territories asking for their support against King Penhda. A surprise attack upon Esterblud by land, covertly backed by sympathetic rulers in Vulthnal and Eernicia, had the possibility of removing the Esterblud kingdom once and for all. It was an opportunity welcomed by overlords who saw a chance to expand their own influence.

Satres stood on a platform in the courtyard to receive his guests. Surrounded by his Majireef, a council of hakra, who were loyal to him alone, the assembly provided spiritual guidance to the *satgerts* throughout Kamin. The red and gold robes worn by the elders within the group provided a grand spectacle to welcome the oncoming line of warriors. While Satres personally despised this display of power that the King of Cahmais held over him, he realized he was in no position to stop it for the moment. However, unknown to these allies, Satres remained in close contact with the underworld gods and the Vanth continued to give him hope in their brief meetings. In fact, Actita was becoming a regular visitor to the Citadel, giving the Holy Overlord instructions which the creature said came directly from Caruun. By knowing the ongoing work of the underworld to create chaos in the lands, Satres saw opportunities for his future. He was content to play underling for both sides. He knew from the coming chaos a leader of the new order would emerge. The thought sent a smile to his lips as Satres welcomed his visitors when they dismounted from their mounts. He bowed to them formally showing what the priests in the Citadel suspected.

"I hope your journey went well, my friends. We welcome you and your men to our home."

The king proudly stepped forward to shake the arm of the overlord. "We thank you for your generous hospitality, my friend. My son informs me that we will have many of our men arriving, and he has asked you for a place to shelter these men."

"Yes, your messenger came, and we have already begun clearing the woods outside of Grimma harbor. We believe this will keep spies from being able to give away your buildup of men in the area. It is out of sight of the Citadel and the port." He motioned for them to follow him. As they walked through the Ynyover guards holding their halberds in attention, he continued. "I've put my personal guards around on the trail to this new camp, and I've also decided to put our more inquisitive visitors in less accommodating locations."

"What do you mean?" asked Lyncus.

Satres smiled at the young man. "I've sent them to our fortress in Mugga. Our council instructed these diplomats and their families that I will be going to this remote village for my health. So, I've sent some of

my attendants and guards there with instructions to keep a watchful eye
on these diplomats." The warrior returned the smile at the thought of
envoys attempting to find comfort in the rugged fort on the remote border
between Ynyover and Cahmais. It was the perfect location to get certain
people from reporting the events back to the other overlords and the
shipping guild.

After reaching the entrance, the small group, consisting of the king's
war council and attendants, came forward, and they were introduced to
Satres and his council. The Sacred Overlord turned to Pepalin, his trusted
advisor, and told him to accommodate the visitors. The party went into
the fortress while the servants, attendants, and the guards followed. As
they walked, the king spoke to Satres about various items they would
need for their invasion of Esterblud. He assured the thin man such
assistance would mean bounty to Ynyover, allowing them to expand the
country's borders into some of the lands of Esterblud. Satres happily
agreed, knowing such a permanent solution benefited him and his role.
All that remained was the gathering of an overwhelming number of
Cahmais warriors to invade the lands of Esterblud. Asgurd told him they
would soon enter the lands of their common enemy and place the head of
King Penhda upon a spear to be paraded throughout the lands.

Late that night, long after his guests were asleep, Satres met with the
Vanth, Actita, deep in the bowels of the fortress. They held their meeting
in the *sidhera*, a plane between the realms, established by the magic of
the gods. Arriving early, Satres sit in one of the ornate chairs which
encircled the large table, glancing at the colored stones on the table top.
The stones showed the symbolic god forms of Caruun and Alrpan along
with other creatures of the underworld. At first glance, it seemed the
stones no longer held the fiery colors that he remembered in the past.
Taking a closer look, he became convinced the colors had changed,
becoming the color of ash. Hearing the Vanth enter the room, he quickly
dismissed the thought, assuming it was a trick of the oil lamp lights
filling the room.

The creature stood across the table from the overlord, its arms
crossed, listening as the man told the underworld messenger about the
coming invasion. Satres informed the demigod that the Sacred Overlord
would ride with the warriors as they entered the Esterblud lands. The
Vanths ugly rat face remained fixed on the human appearing to look him
over for lunch. The beady eyes of the Vanth along with their long snake

hair sent chills down the back of the Sacred Overlord. After finishing his report, Satres asked the demigod when Alrpan might join them. The question brought a kind of smile, exposing wicked teeth.

"Alrpan not able to come anymore. I the only one you are talking to."

Satres asked why, but the Vanth just ignored him as the creature walked back through the red curtain into its realm. The overlord stopped a sudden urge to follow the demigod. He knew his power was too limited. While a human might enter the gateway to the other realm, it was a one-way trip. Only certain spells combined with talismans would allow a person to come back from the sky realm or the underworld. Even if Satres entered another realm, his human frailty would never allow him to stand up to a god. In his rise to power, the Sacred Overlord never bothered to discover spells or talismans used by others to achieve their aims. Instead, he used allies and friendships to achieve his goals. As he stared at the curtain, he decided he would have his trusted Majireef Council change their focus away from finding the Esterbluds who had the Skool. Instead, they would begin to use their visions to spy upon the Underworld and Sky Realm gods. He was convinced there was more going on there than he knew, no doubt, information which could be useful to his needs. If the demigoddess of the Sky Realm was helping the human trash who stole the Skool, perhaps his council could find a weakness to exploit. One thing he remembered well from his study about the gods, each was vulnerable, and a smart human could exploit such weakness.

As he sat at the table, he wondered why he never thought of such a thing before. It was clear he would need to keep an eye on the other realms. Alrpan and Caruun were apparently ignoring him now, merely sending an underling demigod to receive his reports of events in the human world. He decided if the gods thought they could just use him to advance their own cause, the gods had underestimated this human.

Satres rose to return to his suite of rooms where he expected Lyncus to be waiting. Since the young man was without his wife, the Sacred Overlord guessed that they would be enjoying their special relationship through the night. The thought excited him if only for the unthinkable shock which would occur if others knew. Sex among the same gender was taboo in the many cultures making up Kamin. Especially among the *satgerts,* such exposure would mean imprisonment and torture before banishment of a priest. In some lands, if two people engaged in such activities, it would mean instant death. But to Satres, the acts had nothing to do with love. He simply saw sex as a method of pleasurable control, and he was happy to use it to his advantage with women or men. With Lyncus, he found a kindred spirit.

As he walked the stairs up through the bowels of the Citadel, his padded slippers created soft shuffling echoes to mix with the dead quiet. As he thought of his young lover, he knew the young man was focused on his own needs and the overlord felt the raw quest for power in the person. Satres was sure that Lyncus had something to do with his brother's assassination. The Sacred Overlord's *yolma* in Damicia reported that Lyncus was suspected in the death of the fealharans, and only one of the assassins returned with him to Cahmais. Satres reached the carved door of his rooms as he came to the conclusion that the young warrior was setting up his future. He opened the door, and as expected, he saw Lyncus there, lying in the massive bed. As he closed the door, the question that ran through his mind was what the young warrior's plotting would mean to Satres and his plans for the future. Control in the bedroom only extended so far when it came to controlling the many tribes of the lands.

~~~

It took Urith and Fedelm nearly four sun cycles of torturous riding across the flat plains of Caeteria to reach the winding path leading into the high mountains of Neewar. Another three mornings passed as the pair pushed up into the range of high valleys which led them to the outskirts of Kanhan.

Before they had left the village, Urith had pulled out a short sword and scabbard from the back of his mount. Handing the weapon to Fedelm, he explained it was something he should have done sooner. "I used Imenal's name to get you this as Jamal, and I went looking for weapons. It should be light enough for your size and still slice through some armor. You will need to learn to use it."

Fedelm was momentarily silenced by the giant warrior's gesture. To an Esterblud, the giving of a weapon to another was one of their greatest symbols of respect. She took it and attached the scabbard to her waist belt. Sliding out the short sword which was about the length of her forearm, she waved it around, getting a feel for the weapon as she had seen the warriors do so many times before. It was a fearsome weapon compared to her dagger.

"Why did you give this to me now?" she asked at the time.

"I should have trained you before now. You have been unable to protect yourself at times during our journey." Urith looked down, and she thought he was embarrassed by admitting to his mistake. It was the first time she had seen him do that, and it was a memory she kept.

During their trip, each night before they slept, Urith worked with the girl on her techniques and trained her in basic fighting skills. However, he was not a patient teacher, often growling at her when she failed to grasp a move. She tried to understand his frustration since an Esterblud warrior continually developed and honed their warrior skills from an early age. Despite her lack of ability, by the time they reached Kanhan, Urith told her she might be able to defend herself. It was not a ringing endorsement, but Fedelm took it well. She remembered how often Oslaf failed to please his uncle despite having trained with the scarred faced man from his childhood.

When they reached the outskirts of the town, they pulled off the main trail. Urith took the reins of his ossane and followed a small footpath to the top of a large outcropping of gray and white boulders. From the vantage point, they overlooked the valley, overlooking the village which lay at the base of the highest peak of the range Neehorsh. In the fading light of the afternoon, the Esterblud warrior was laying on his belly on the warm rock watching for moments from the village below. Fedelm lay next to him, wondering what he was looking at.

During their journey, Urith had said little to the woman, aside from his continued harassment about her inadequate warrior skills. While she tried every approach she could think of, it was evident the stubborn giant was not letting her into his thoughts. She found this to be troubling. He had a frustrating way of not saying things that he was thinking. When she thought about it, she sometimes wondered why she cared about trying to understand the man. His massive scar left him less than handsome, and his vicious brutality scared her on more than one occasion. Yet he had qualities of honor and fierce loyalty to his friends along with tenderness and warmth he continued to hide from others as if he wasn't worthy of such things. As she watched him scan the area below, the woman realized that she was as closer to this man than any others she knew.

"Do my eyes deceive me or do you see a black flag down there?" He could feel her staring at him, so he turned to her. She quickly looked back at the village.

"Hard to tell with the calm air, but it seems like I see something black on a pole near the center of town. Is that what you mean?" Fedelm glanced over, and he nodded. "So what's the plan?" she asked.

"Right after dark, we go into that town and introduce ourselves." His grim tone underscored his determination.

"The dead cannot tell you where Mivraa is," she warned him. "Besides, this looks familiar in some ways. As I think of it, my visions felt like I was looking down from a spot that looked halfway up the mountain. If so, that means she might be near there," she said, pointing darkened areas that could be ledges or caves on the mountain side.

He stared at the area she was indicating. "That makes sense. We can see several possible spots," he agreed as he looked up at the eastern sky. "We don't have enough time to get there before dark. Curse the worthless gods. I'm afraid she will be up there another night."

He was silent for a bit as he thought about it. "We need to circle around that side of the village," he indicated a place which was near a trail, "and see if we can pick up any spots they move from. We can't see much at night, so I think we find someone to help us find the correct path to Mivraa."

"But how?" she asked.

"You said they go up every morning, so I go into the village and find someone to take us up at night," He told her.

"What if they won't go?" Fedelm asked.

Urith gave her a sneering grin, and she knew death was stalking the people below.

They mounted their ossanes and slowly followed the road toward the village. Urith found a trail leading to the village, and they got off the animals, walking the ossanes to the village. They kept climbing along the trail, the red soil of the landscape nearly barren between the mountain and the village. They stumbled across a small patch of blue-green grass hiding between some large boulders that provide a natural pen for the mounts. He tied the animals off in the green area, watering the animals before they left.

"I don't suppose I can keep you with the ossanes until I get back?" he asked Fedelm.

She shook her head. "You might need my visions to ensure we are going to the right place. Besides, I can take care of myself."

He knew there would be no further argument, and he had to admit he liked the idea of her coming along. "Very well, but remember you are not a master of the sword. If you need to use that thing, use both hands and keep your wits about you," he grunted as he turned back on the path. She glanced at the weapon again and slid it into the scabbard, then swiftly caught up next to him.

The pair followed a footpath until they reached an outcropping of flat rocks that were piled up next to another walkway leading up to the summit of the Neehorsh peak. The sun fell behind the mountain range, darkness settling fast across the valley. In the distance they could hear the grunting of *rangifers* nearby, the slight wind carried the smell of the boars to Fedelm's nose causing her to scowl.

"At least, I don't smell that bad anymore," he joked, keeping his voice low. She grinned back, telling him that she thanked the gods for it. It had become a running joke between the two since they first met. Growing serious she asked what they would do next.

"That footpath appears to lead up to the mountain top. I'm going to the village and find someone. You stay here until I return," he told her. She could tell by his tone it would be fruitless to ask to join him. "I'll give a couple of whistles when I come back so don't skewer me with your sword," he said, then quickly moved down the path to the village. She watched his large frame outlined by the few lights coming from the town. Soon, he disappeared.

The moons had not risen, leaving the blackness of the night to envelop Fedelm. There was no concept of time, just the occasional sounds of the nighttime creatures. The woman sat crouched, leaning against stacked stones that provided a marker pointing out the two footpaths. The air grew cold with the altitude and night, and Fedelm put her arms inside her robe, trying to remain warm. She couldn't smell the rangifers anymore, so they must have moved off looking for food. Her stomach growled, and she wished they had brought along a bag of the smoked meat they left with the mounts. After waiting for what seemed to be half the night, she heard the sound of shuffling footsteps coming from the path. Fedelm pulled her sword and moved behind a nearby boulder when she heard the sound of a muffled whack with a slight, muffled squeal. She could barely make out two figures outlined by the little yellow lights from the village. Then she heard a quick succession of low whistles. Seeing the familiar shape of the giant warrior, she came forward to meet him. A smaller man fell at her feet, pushed down to the ground. Urith opened his hand to reveal a green glowing *tribolrock* and pointed the dim light on the man at their feet.

Dressed in a black robe, she could see the bearded man's face was bruised and bleeding, his white turban hung in tatters on his head. He was trussed up with his hands tied behind his back, near his shoulder blades and they were connected to a rope that ran tightly around his neck. If the man tried to drop his hands, he would strangle himself. A piece of cloth was stuffed into his mouth to keep him quiet. Only the blazing hate within the man's eyes kept Fedelm from reaching down to help him.

"Here's one of these Death Bearers. He made the mistake of not coming silently," Urith whispered to her. "Looks like there are more of these vermin controlling the village. Now he takes us to Mivraa." He grabbed the man by the rope, lifting the choking person to his feet.

"I will kill you slowly if I don't like your answers. Do you have Mivraa on this mountain?" The man refused to say anything. Urith slammed his fist into his face. "I can do this all night," he growled. He pulled back his fist to strike him again, but the man recoiled, nodding his head.

"I thought so. Now you will lead me up the mountain to her," the Esterblud said coldly. The bearded man tried to mumble something and Urith pulled the cloth from his mouth.

"No yelling or I'll skin you alive, very slowly!" Urith pushed his Clovel Sword to the man's throat.

"I don't mind dying for my gods. But you will die along with the woman you call Mivraa," spit out the man. "It is *gcothrem*. The Sky Realm's vengeance upon one of its own and you cannot stop it."

Urith stuck the rag back in his mouth. "We'll see about that. I would like to take out a couple of gods right now. Now get moving." Urith pushed him forward, telling Fedelm to light the way with the tribolrocks. He and the prisoner followed along, slowly moving up the steep path; the group could feel the land fall away on one side of the trail. The green glow did not emit enough light to see much further than a few paces around them. The Esterblud kept his hand on the rope around the man's neck, pushing the bearded man going forward. When they came to a fork in the path, the man, at first, refused to go any further. However, a couple of turns by Urith's fist around the rope sent the choking man to his knees, as Urith knelt next to him.

"Don't test my patience," Urith growled to him as he pulled out the rag from the man's mouth. "Either you take us to meet your *ranqels*, or I let them feast on your carcass. What will it be?"

The bearded man's face was turning blue as he stared at the Esterblud. However, the man was not ready to die yet. He finally nodded his head, believing the beasts would finish off this upstart. Urith pulled him up to his feet, and the Death Bearer led them up the trail to the left. Above them, in the night air, the group suddenly heard the sound of flapping wings. As they looked at the sky, Urith could see the vague outline of shapes as the stars were momentarily blacked out when the monsters flew toward their prey. The bearded man gave them an evil chuckle, telling Urith he would soon meet his death. The Esterblud pushed him faster up the trail, telling Fedelm to hurry. The woman tried to move quickly while trying to keep from watching the narrow path. It was a dizzying path which seemed to drop into oblivion. She tried not to think about what they might find at the end of the trail.

Feeling the effects of their higher altitude, Fedelm slowed to catch her breath, and she noticed Urith was breathing heavily as well. She could no longer see any lights in the distance, only pitch black all around them. Only the glow of the rocks in her hand and the dim starlight above them allowed them to follow the steep path. The woman could not tell if she was close to the plateau that she remembered from her dreams.

Suddenly, they heard the harsh echoes of screeching above them. At first, the sound seemed far away, but the noise soon escalated as more creatures appeared to be fighting over something. They could hear a pitiful human scream that was cut off and the pit in Fedelm's stomach grew at the animal sounds for she knew what they were fighting over. Urith realized it as well as he pushed his prisoner past Fedelm, grabbing the tribolrocks from her. Prodding the Death Bearer in front of him with his sword, they continued up the sloping footpath.

Reaching the top, the group stumbled out on flat ground where they could hear the creatures scrambling around with scratching noises and the sound of pitiful moans combined with the clanking noise of chains. Urith pushed his prisoner toward noise as he could barely make out shadows of movement. Instinctively unhooking his helmet which was attached to his waist belt, the warrior quickly put it on. Soon, he could see three humanoid shapes with wings crouched over with their backs to him. As the glow of the tribolrocks revealed the horrifying scene to Urith and Fedelm, the long-armed creatures turned, their red eyes glowing menacingly at the intruders. One stood and leaped toward them, it's long, lean skeletal body moving quickly to cover the distance as the other creatures turned back to their nightly feast. Urith threw down the bearded man at monster's feet. The man began screaming ritualistic words of his cult. The *ranqels* stopped, turning its blood covered hooked beak as it looked down at the cowering prisoner as if it was considering its options. The Esterblud noticed the black leather-like skin of the creature had blood dripping across the front.

"Help me, please."

The familiar voice drifted to the group, and Urith attacked the *ranqel* in front of him immediately. He swung the Clovel Sword in a wide arc, sending it down on the creature's shoulder, nearly cutting through its arm, one wing and into the chest. The monster barely squawked as it fell across the screaming prisoner. As Urith quickly ran the several steps to reach the other creatures which turned to face him. His furious swing at the first beast was wildly out of control, and he only clipped the monster. The creature managed to swipe its claw at the Esterblud's hip, striking him just below the waist on the side. The fearsome claws cut through the padded canvas and causing the warrior to drop to one leg. He could feel his blood streaming down the leg.

The other *ranqel* jumped on the warrior's back, but the beast was unable to cut through the wood shield with its beak. The Esterblud warrior flipped the creature over his shoulder, immediately impaling the monster after it landed on its back. The creature screamed, desperately trying to reach out to strike at the human as it slowly died. Forced back by the attack of the last monster, Urith whipped out his long Sgian dagger from his belt while trying to hold off the strikes of the other monster. The creature came at him, using its wings as a weapon, striking at the warrior with long swipes while it came in closer to inflict more damage with its claws.

Urith so focused on the creature, failed to notice the bearded prisoner pushing away the dead *ranqel* which lay on him. Freeing himself, the Death Bearer crawled over to the impaled body of the other winged beast. His beady eyes fixed on the engraved weapon; he reached for the Clovel Sword. His attention momentarily drawn to the deadly battle going on between the giant warrior and the beast, the Death Bearer wrapped his fingers around the grip of the sword. A massive shock went into the man, sending blue charges from his body into the ground. Wrapped in agony, his scream never got out of his mouth as his hand burned from a searing heat. The bearded man fell away from the sword, dead before his body hit the ground.

While the battle consumed Urith's attention, Fedelm avoided the fighting, going directly to help Mivraa. When the woman came up to the demigoddess, she did not recognize the curled up bloody mass of mutilated flesh. Mivraa was severely mauled with her blood spurting from the many massive wounds created by the *ranqels*. Stifling a shocked gasp, Fedelm quickly pulled off her robe and used it to try to cover the woman who fought to stand. Grabbing her dagger, Fedelm struggled to remove the bracelets that chain the goddess to the wall of stone. Unable to do anything with the dagger, she resorted to the pommel end of her short sword. It took several tries of slamming the weapon on the metal, but she finally broke the chain holding the bracelet. Mivraa fell into Fedelm's arms. In the dim glow of the tribolrocks scattered on the ground, the hakra tried to stem the flow of blood while softly whispering comfort to the injured woman. Fedelm looked up occasionally to watch the battle, hoping Urith would soon finish off the monster.

Urith sidestepped the beast coming at him, avoiding slashing claws heading toward his skull. The giant warrior jumped into the side of the passing creature and embedding his dagger into its neck. Falling over with the dying monster, Urith suddenly felt a fire-like pain in his mid-chest. Quickly getting to his feet, he could not see his talisman lit up white, but his quick look down suddenly reminded him of his Clovel Sword. A glance around the area revealed the prisoner's corpse positioned next to the body of the ranqels, the man's hand still holding the sword. The Esterblud could see the man's dead eyes staring at him in the faint light, traces of smoke floating up from the body. Urith step over to retrieve his sword, wondering what had happened. Never before had the Clovel Sword done such a thing. He carefully pulled it from the body of the monster, half expecting it to shock him as well. He cleaned the blade with the shirt of the dead man and slid it back into his scabbard.

Urith was dumbfounded for a moment, sliding his hand on the sword handle when the sound of crying broke through his trance. Turning back, he could barely see Fedelm holding a robed wrapped body. His stomach sank as he realized it must be Mivraa. He sprinted over to them, dropping to his knees, trying to understand how to help the half-eaten creature being held by Fedelm.

"What can we do?" Urith's face was white looking at the nearly stripped shell of a woman who lay in Fedelm's arms. His initial shock turned to a smoldering anger. Fedelm lowered her head close to the whispering Mivraa. After she had finished, her shredded head fell back with a low groan. Fedelm looked up at the Esterblud.

"She says the Death Bearers bring Exyts Spring water every morning so they must have access to it nearby. Mivraa says it must be coming from a *sidhera* which leads to the Sky Realm," Fedelm kept staring at Mivraa with tears rolling down her cheeks. "She tells me to find a twisted lellowtere tree down the trail."

"So that's how the gods travel," said Urith surprised he had never bothered to ask Mivraa about it. He looked at them. "Then one of the Sky Gods is helping this trash," he nodded over to the dead body of their prisoner.

Mivraa tried to nod, but Fedelm stopped her, telling the goddess to rest.

"Can she hold on?" Urith looked at Fedelm.

Fedelm whispered yes, and Mivraa slowly lifted her hand for the warrior. He softly took it, and he could barely hear her whisper.

"You forget I cannot die. I'll stay awake just to watch you kill the *cawalds*."

Urith smiled at the insult the goddess gave the death cult. It was a word richly deserved for them since it could mean either a coward or little dick. Either way, it was a word truly offensive to a warrior. He tenderly put her hand at her side and told her to rest.

"The sun will be rising soon, we will get the healing water, and I'll make sure to bring the *cawalds* to you." With his words, he put got back to his feet.

The warrior retrieved the tribolrocks, taking the rest of them to Fedelm. The demigod's eyes were closed as she drifting out of consciousness.

The trio remained that way until the first glimpse of the rays came from the highland plains below them. Mivraa was sleeping with Fedelm still cradling her in her arms, her back against the rock wall that went straight up. Urith rose quietly and went over to look down from the plateau, stopping by the bodies at the edge. He sent them tumbling over, down the long drop to the valley floor. The Esterblud went back over to the other side where the footpath came up and waited. Soon, far down the valley near the village, he observed two figures coming up the winding walkway. He gave a little whistle and motioned to Fedelm that he was going down the path. The woman nodded, mouthing approval.

Assuming the twisted lellowtere tree would be close to the trail, Urith moved rapidly down the footpath, pulling on his helmet and running his hand through the straps on the back of his shield. He reminded himself to stay focused and armed. His need for revenge upon the monsters nearly caused his own death. Still ashamed at his lapse, he now centered his mind upon his next objective which was staying as quiet as possible and out of sight of the black robed people coming. His sole focus was to ambush them and get the healing water for Mivraa. He rounded the next turn and saw the twisted tree at the fork of the two paths he and Fedelm came to earlier in the night. Its roots were coming out of the hard packed gray soil like a brown spider web. Urith quickly found an ambush spot for himself. Despite the narrow footpath, he was able to drag his large frame up above the small tree using a narrow ledge of an oversized boulder. On one side, the Esterblud could watch the tree while his angle kept anyone from seeing him from below as they walked up the trail. There he waited, feeling the sun rays warming the back of his neck and listening to the distant squawking sound of birds echo from the valley below.

Hearing the shuffle of footsteps coming from the trail, Urith quietly pulled his sword. Suddenly he felt the warmth coming from a small area of his chest again. He glanced down quickly to confirm that the Djeed talisman, given to him by Dughorm, was glowing. He looked back to lellowtere tree just in time to see a human shape suddenly emerge from behind the tree. The Esterblud's muscles tensed as he watched the god whom he did not recognize step in front of the tree as the Death Bearers came up the footpath. Dressed in bright silver armored breastplate over a long black tunic, the man looked young with his long golden hair hanging over his shoulders.

Remaining out of sight, the warrior silently crept forward, ready to spring before he quickly ducked back as the deity glanced back. Urith slowly sneaked back over the boulder edge to see the god hand over a water bag to a woman dressed in a black robe. Immediately, the Esterblud sprang from his hiding place, jumping down the short distance to the footpath behind the two Death Bearers.

The warrior immediately jabbed his Clovel Sword into the upper back of the taller Death Bearer, who went down with barely a sound. He scarcely had enough time to withdraw his sword from the body before a flashing sword came at him from behind the blinding armor of Wurms. Suddenly on the defensive, the Esterblud countered the rapid strikes with his sword. The man with the silver breastplate took another long swing of his sword at Urith, who ducked and slammed his shield into the gods' armor. The explosive force that came from the shield sent the demigod flying backward, sending his body into the trunk of the lellowtere tree and causing the shallow rooted tree to topple over.

Urith caught the movement of the Death Bearer out of the corner of his eye, and he was on her like one of the black baters that hunted in the mountains. Using the pommel of his sword as a club, he cracked the small woman's head, and she fell unconscious. When the warrior scrambled to face the deity again, he saw only the trunk of the tree as the man had disappeared. The fighter ran over to the tree bitterly disappointed about the escape. The warrior had to satisfy himself with the healing water. After picking up the water bag lying near the unconscious Death Bearer, he paused, holding his bloody sword over her neck. Finally, Urith decided to keep her alive. Hoping she might have some information, he picked up the small woman, whom he threw over his shoulder, and began limping along the long path up the mountain.

As the trail neared the plateau, Urith was forced to stop, his wounded leg burning like fire from the cuts of the *ranqels*. Hearing a pitiful moan coming echo from above, the warrior pushed himself up the rest of the way, forcing himself to the top of the flat area. He dumped the woman on the rock ground and quickly brought the Exyts Spring water over to Fedelm. The woman gently pulled herself from under the demigoddess, carefully opening the robe which revealed the devastating wounds. Large swaths of skin and muscle were gone, showing gray bone and darkened dry blood. Taking the bag from the warrior, Fedelm poured the water upon the wounds causing Mivraa to grimace and groan in pain. It was a rough start, but Urith watched as the flesh immediately began to heal. Thousands of string like muscles quickly spread over the exposed bone and muscle before miraculously weaving themselves into fresh skin.

Underneath the skin, which rippled while the new muscle twitched as they rebuilt from the damage. Fedelm gave Mivraa a drink from the bottle which helped the woman regain her strength.

Urith heard the Death Bearer girl stirring, and he went over to her as she awoke, holding her head in pain. He forced the girl over on her belly and quickly searched her for any weapons before tying her hands behind her back. To emphasize her predicament, he dragged her over to the side of the mountain, letting her view the *vensars* below feeding on the remains of the prisoner. The bodies of the underworld *ranqels* they avoided.

He told her to think of her fate. "Mivraa is unchained and swiftly heals now. You and your people have done a great wrong to warrior goddess. I will let her decide what to do with you," he warned her. The girl looked up at with a combination of confusion and defiance in her brown eyes. She was a small thing, probably only a few seasons older than his nephew. However, Urith had no compassion to those wearing the black robes of the cult. He simply turned away and returned to his friends.

Chapter 7: Darkness Falls

A gloomy green of the underworld light struck Actitas' sensitive eyes when the Vanth entered the large cathedral-like structure. The creature immediately noticed Kriell sitting upon his new throne, still filled with the tormented spirits of humans. Immediately, the black nebulous form of the Guardian changed, and the image Caruun appeared, his buzzard face cocked like a bird as it watched the Vanth approach.

"Are my plans proceeding as expected?" The underworld god asked, its rasping voice echoed in the silent dome. The Vanth was not comfortable with the silence since the anguished souls were forced into the dark caverns for other uses.

"Yes, my lord. The chaos is coming as you say. Satres say he joined with the Cahmais king. Says he looks for Alrpan." Actita wasn't sure how his master would react to his words.

"So the human wants the female god does he? When we arrive in the Kamin world, I will be happy to join them," said the spirit stealer with a mocking laugh. "Pitiful humans are not good for much, but we will continue to make them our pets."

The Vanth gave a sickly smile from his rat face as he continued. "But something more happened. *Ranqels* say human hero found the Sky Realm goddess. He killed many to set Mivraa free."

Kriell lifted his head at this news. It was unfortunate the demigoddess lived, but she was of little importance to his plans. In fact, this development might ensure the chaos continued in the Sky Realm. He knew keeping the gods focused upon Mivraa worked to his advantage.

"Very well, keep me informed about her whereabouts. She may be a key for us to sow more discord with Duwdamon. Now, are you expanding our collection of creatures below? I've placed enough of my power into your cave for all of the human spirits that worked the tunnels above. I expect progress," Kriell's statement had warnings for the Vanth as well.

"I build many from Bloodstone power, but underworld spirits weak. It takes many to make a creature. Only foul souls make good monsters like Clovel," Actita reminded him. "Many beorhs and *crubas* we have."

"I know what you have," the god snapped at him. "Did you put the Clovel to guard the entrance to the underworld?" The Vanth nodded vigorously while the underworld leader paused, thinking about Satres and his work.

"Good, there will be no mistakes in our plans. I'll add more to your mix of spirits soon," the deity assured the Vanth. "Soon the humans will descend upon each other. Blame will fill their world and many will die in revenge and vengeance. We will have enough fresh souls to begin filling the underworld with our creatures. Now, keep your beasts moving out at night. The humans are incapable of stopping our plans so keep your attention on the Sky Realm."

Actita cocked his rat face like his master, slowly nodding as though he understood the idea. Bowing to his master, he turned away, heading into the bowels of the underworld as his small brain tried to grasp what the god was planning. But the Vanth remained unable to understand what the deity meant. It did not matter to the demigod as Kriell was the boss and the Vanth understood his role. Moving into the darkness where the Vanth felt comfortable, he instinctively felt for his whip to keep back the tormented souls that frequently came moaning and wailing as they sought relief from the living. But these spirits were gone. Each transformed into hideous beasts and monsters by the power of the Bloodstone cavern and Kriell's knowledge of the ancients. It was a power that Caruun and Alrpan were unable to match. Entering the vast antechamber that led to the human realm, he could hear his monsters agitating for their nightly prowl to rape, maim and kill their former species. Any humanity that was left in the spirits scattered when the monsters were created. When they let these beasts roam in the night, the Vanth knew he had aligned with the powerful one able to overtake the realms.

While Actitas continued with his work in the lower chambers, Kriell kept his thoughts focused on the future. Already in control of one realm, his larger ambitions lay in front of him. While he built, he also kept the Sky Realm divided. The combined unity of the Sky Realm and the Triad of gods could stop his designs. And as long as Duwdamon, Uugor, and Ecarca continued to press their fury upon Mivraa, the better for him. The underworld god foresaw little threat from the Sky Realm's prophet. A human could hardly be able to see the future the Kriell had in store for them so the underworld lord dismissed the idea he could be exposed before he was ready. Seeing how the Sky Realm used them, the god decided it might keep a few of the hakras around as his pets to maintain his control. Otherwise, he saw little use for the human realm. Better to let the land run free with his beasts than have it overrun with those unworthy beings he used to build his monsters. Either way, it was not something an ancient god would worry about as he leaned back, closing his eyes and licking his lips at the thought of his moves.

~~~

Wurms, the new leader of Haligulf suddenly appeared upon the Fields of Anord as the daily battles among the human warrior spirits finished. As normal, much blood and gore covered the vast expanse of soft grass. The demigod paid no attention as he walked over the bodies and limbs in his way. Wurms failed to notice the spirits of Caestia and Dughorm were talking among the warriors who won their battle over their brethren. When he reached the edge of the field, he took the marble walkway to the temples of the sky gods, leaving bloody leather sole footprints upon the white stone. Although he could fly within the realm, he was distracted by the experience of his encounter with the Esterblud upon the Neehorsh peak. A human should not be able to hold more power than a god.

He quickly scurried past the high white columns of the main temple, heading to a spot where his father would likely be. Entering the building through the large open doorway, he spotted Duwdamon pacing the floor, his chin in his chest. He appeared lost in thought. Wurms approached him, looking for any of his sibling gods or the elementals, like the sprites, who might be listening in. He knew from experience many ears were listening to overhear his father's conversations.

"I need to talk with you," he whispered, glancing around expecting other gods to come out of the shadows. The room was filled with small blue columns acting as walls to the interior of the temple. The Sky god's yellow hair seemed pale in the intense beam of light coming in through the open windows.

"What is it? I'm busy." The sky god didn't bother to look up.

"Mivraa has been found by the usurpers, those Esterblud humans," the demigod interjected. "I think they may have released her from your punishment."

"And why are you here? I would expect you to take care of this. I assume you have sent the defiler's spirits to Caruun and returned Mivraa to her rightful place." The chilling tone of Duwdamon's voice struck the half human side of Wurms.

"I cannot give you such news." Wurms realized he should have come with more than an excuse, but he could not stop now. "I'm afraid the human is even more powerful. They struck me with the shield that carries the Skool and knocked me back through the gateway. It closed from the damage created by the god weapon he carries." Wurms felt proud of himself for the quick, if not totally, convincing lie.

His father stopped his pacing at the news. "More powerful you say," he looked over to Wurms, who eagerly nodded. "That must mean they have found another piece of the Skool, despite your brother's destruction of the temple. This is not good. The humans may now be our greatest threat."

"But father, they are just humans. Not a threat to your realm." The god of Haligulf seemed shocked by the statement, but he slowly realized that the bolt he was struck with was far beyond a human's capability.

Duwdamon gave his son one of his knowing glances. At times, he considered Wurms to be an imbecile. "You forget what the Skool will do when they find the remaining pieces. A human will have more power than the Sky Realm and the underworld combined." The sky god turned away as he continued. "No, we must stop them now. We have to find them." An idea struck him, and he turned back to Wurms. "You will go find Uugor and Ecarca immediately and send them to me."

The demigod turned away only to be halted by a shout from the sky god.

"I'm not finished; you fool. After you find your brothers, you will then go back to the Kamin world to find the humans carrying the Skool. Don't do anything to arouse their suspicions, just find them and report back to me. Is that understood?" When Wurms nodded, Duwdamon sent him away.

As he stood watching Wurms leave, he was briefly reminded of his human mother, whom he raped so many seasons ago. Now that Mivraa was cast out, he would go into the human realm for a woman to bear a child for him. He would find a more suitable person, this time; he told himself. His god wife, barren after their two sons, refused to bed with him since he had found the company of spirit women to be superior to his needs. Again, he would be forced to improvise. He could not afford another worthless son or daughter with the power of a demigod.

Reflections about his wife forced the sky god to return his thoughts to his brother god, Caruun. The underworld legions were causing problems for him. From the whispering winds, he heard the prayers of the humans asking for help for missing loved ones. Now, the sky god understood Caruun was sending out the monsters. While, Caruun or Alrpan enjoyed striking fear and dread for their own calloused reasons, the stories coming to him were becoming far too numerous. Also, rumors of monsters not seen since the Guardians floated in the winds of the Sky Realm. These creatures were designed to inflict fear and panic, along with many deaths. Such a pattern did not make sense to him. He thought the underworld gods would be satisfied just to spread fear and replace those spirits whose energy eventually vanished into the Great Void. Duwdamon guessed his underworld brother was after revenge. While he could understand the need to attack the Esterblud, who had hurt Alrpan, the Sky God could not fathom what made the underworld gods seek out other parts of Kamin for destruction. He hoped their anger could be pacified when he accepted their idea for punishment of Mivraa. The sky god knew the distaste they had for his daughter, and he hoped her punishment would calm the realms. Still, no change had come, and something gnawed at the back of his mind. An old memory combined with something the Sybil told him about the ancients.

The deity glided through the open entrance to the courtyard where the Exyts Spring now flowed again. He sat on a small stone bench near the stream, dropping his hand in the flowing water. Feeling the surge of energy from the mystic fluid Duwdamon's thoughts turned to the prophet named Dughorm. The spirits' visions, which he dismissed at the time, began to push into the god's thoughts. It still seemed ridiculous to him. However, he had to admit the oracle was accurate with his visions since arriving. Dughorm's talk of the Guardian continued to bother him. Kriell was an ancient one. Had this god returned, Kriell's anger would be pointed at all of the gods for his betrayal. When Duwdamon, along with his brothers and sisters, deceived the ancients to rule over the realms, there was always the chance the Guardians would seek their return to Kamin. But no portal to the Great Void was known, and none had been found since the sky god knew the gateway destroyed by the human named Heptarc during the Great Passing. As he continued to stare into the water, he could see a vengeful deity like Kriell waiting for the right moments to return, and it would explain some of the news he continued to hear. He could not believe his brother god, Caruun, could be able to ally with such an entity, so he kept coming back to his belief the gods' prophet had to be wrong. Suddenly, the sky god sensed the presence of his wife.

"You look troubled," She told him, her regal face showing no sympathy. He looked up at her and wondered what she knew. Unis, as the supreme goddess of the cosmos, had insight into the other gods using her powers of mind control and dreamscape. While she lacked the seer capability of the humans, the woman could enter the minds of nearly any creature, becoming master over their actions. The creature could be exceptionally ruthless to those who opposed her, and she only thought of the enjoyment of the daily baths in the Exyts Spring. It kept the blue hue of her skin while retaining the vanity of youth and beauty. She was the symbol of love worship in his realm and the humans. Each morning female water spirits would gather around her acting as her servants when she emerged from the temple to the large spring lake that fed the stream. He knew those thin, long sprites were her lovers as well. However, the god creature was not interested in the pleasures his wife enjoyed, by either man or woman. Their marriage remained an agreement to maintain the realm, a fact that she was happy to remind him about.

"The humans are becoming a threat to us. It appears they have found another part of the Skool," he returned to gaze into the water flowing beside him.

"That is bad," she agreed, her blue eyes growing hard at the thought of humans spoiling her routine. "Are they not destroyed yet?"

He looked up quickly, his eyes flashing. "Your sons failed to kill them at Hyropda when they destroyed the village along with half the coastline. Now, I hear the so-called overlords hunting the group seem as incompetent as your sons."

She glared back at him, "Don't blame my children for the interference of your half-breed offspring. Mivraa helped them escape from the village. At least, she's been taken care of. Now I suppose you want me to find a way to fix this mess like I took care of the other." She floated around him, mocking him. "Duwdamon never gets his hands dirty."

The sky god rose to his full height, towering over the woman who did not back down. While her husband could inflict much damage to her, she knew him too well. He could not afford to anger her or her sons.

"Remember, the Triad is what you need most right now," said Unis, daring him to strike her. She could see the intense rage in his blue eyes. Then he suddenly smiled, an action which caught her off guard.

"You are correct my dear, and you have given me an excellent idea. Since we failed to destroy the humans before, it is time for the full weight of the Triad to be used. You will become personally involved with this. With your powers to find and destroy them, the insolent heroes will no longer trouble us." His voice was as smooth as the north winds that blew over the Sky Realm each night.

Unis stared at him, "And what makes you think I would help you on this little adventure of yours? I'm much too busy for such unworthy duties. I'm a god, not one of your human offspring."

"Since your place in the realm is at stake as the rest of us," he smiled with no humor, "I would think you will find some time. Besides, it would be a good way to be with your sons."

She turned away, thinking about her husband's words. If he was asking her to help, it must mean he had other plans as well. Suspicion filled her, but the goddess knew she needed the other gods, including her husband, to keep her world as she liked it.

"Very well, I'll think of something. Send my sons to me and we will take care of your mess." She walked away, her long dark hair flowing in the slight breeze. Duwdamon watched her leave with narrow eyes, regretting her necessary involvement in his plans. While Unis was instrumental in their removal of the Guardians with her skill in reading their minds, he could not trust her. He knew the goddess was more dangerous to him if she and her sons suddenly got ambitious. It was better to let her alone but, for now, he needed her. But he decided she would be closely watched.

The two sons arrived at the main temple not long after their mother left. Duwdamon was inside and sitting upon the throne as a reminder of his authority. The sky god could tell from their hesitant glances that Wurms had told them the news and neither son wanted the wrath of their father.

"Since you know the story, what are your plans?" he asked them, menacing and impassive like the statues carved in the human temples below. Each deity looked at the other knowing the question could explode upon them. Neither said a word, at first, each waiting on the other. Finally, Uugor spoke up.

"Wurms told us what has happened," the god of the sea agreed, trying to play the diplomat. "We must remove the human threat."

The cold stare from the sky god made him uncomfortable. "You should have done this already. Instead, you have been diverted by Alrpan's promises, whatever they are." He stopped the man from saying anything in protest. "I know of your trips to the gates of the underworld, so don't bother lying to me. Chaos is spreading across the human realm and, with the power of the Skool in human hands, it can spread into our realm. It could destroy everything we have. As I've told you before, the underworld wishes this instability, it benefits them. Caruun has made this clear to me before." Duwdamon saw them look down, unable to face him as he continued. "You will now join your mother, goddess of the Kamin realm, to find those with the Skool."

The two gods nodded at the news. "We cannot fail," said Uugor, clearly pleased.

"Her power to control the minds of humans will bring them to us," injected his brother god. "I've seen her send the humans into madness before. It is truly a delightful sight."

"For your sake, I hope this is true," replied Duwdamon, his face remaining grave. "Be warned, I will not accept your failure lightly this time. Now, go to your mother. I don't care what you do with them. Just remove them as a threat."

"And what of Mivraa?" asked Uugor. "She has escaped and will inevitably side with them. While not a real god, she can be dangerous as well. She knows us well."

"If she sides with them, you may do as you please," replied her father.

"What about the Skool?" The god of the sea was enjoying the idea of being unleashed upon the humans and his sister. Even better if he was able to retrieve the weapon for himself.

"It cannot fall into the hands of the underworld," said Duwdamon. "While the legend says no deity can hold it, I don't believe it. So, if you find it, it will be brought to me. Is that understood?"

The two gods agreed happily to his demand, although neither had any intention of giving the weapon away once they found it. Both gods gave a quick bow to the sky god before taking off in search of Unis. Their departure reminded Duwdamon of a time when Wurms and Mivraa were young, eager to escape into the next adventure. Now, two of the most powerful gods along with their ruthless mother would be searching for a small group of near powerless humans traveling in the backcountry of Kamin. Had he any pity, the sky god might have felt sorry for them.

~~~

"My master can…," the brown-haired woman struggled to speak as Mivraa continued to press slowly on her windpipe with both hands wrapped around the woman's throat. The demigoddess, now fully recovered and dressed in her shiny black robe, held the woman off the ground by her neck. Her feet kicked out in the air, the Death Bearer's face had grown ashen, and Fedelm put her hand on the warrior goddess, yelling for Mivraa to stop the assault.

"You can't find out what she knows if you kill her," she reminded the woman warrior.

Mivraa let the woman drop to the ground, watching her holding her throat and gasping for air. Fedelm kneeled down to the woman, telling her that she would be treated with mercy if she told them the truth. The woman looked up, and her defiance showed again on her face.

"I wish to join my master in death, so your threats are no good to me," the woman gasped out at last. "We know the future since we have seen the signs. The *ranqels* come to us as foretold by the prophet, and they will return to claim you."

Mivraa was about to pick the woman up again, but Fedelm grabbed her arm. The hakra asked about their prophet. "How can Death Bearers know about the future? You are not prophets."

"Our spirit knows all. We don't need false visions of humans who live as slaves to the sky gods," the woman seemed keen on letting them know all about their cult. Urith walked over to the group, after finishing healing himself using the last of the god's spring water on his wounds, whispering in the ear of Mivraa. There was a flash in her eyes. However, she reluctantly nodded in agreement.

"Who is this prophet that no one but you and your village seem to know? When my king buried the first group of you, none of your people talked of a prophet, only subjugation to all non-believers on the orders of your master. It seems like your beliefs change with the wind," Urith mocked her.

She sat up her face red. "How dare you? I saw the prophet arise from the lellowtere tree. A human who came to tell our people about the next world."

"And what did this thing look like?" Mivraa spoke up, convinced that Wurms must be involved. "Let me guess, a young man with flowing yellow hair."

The woman looked at the warrior god confused. "No, the goddess appeared as a beautiful woman, at first, looking like the engraving of the underworld goddess I've seen in the temples. Then we saw her transform into a beast with a bird face and yellow eyes. The bird creature told us of the coming of a goddess who would be feasted upon by the *ranqels*. When mighty winged beasts arrived as foretold, the prophet came again, showing us of the correct path. No Sky God has such power."

As the others stared at her, she continued her tale. "I know you won't believe me, but the prophet told us the coming future. The gods will be consumed during the turmoil. The prophet said only those who follow Kriell would obtain peace through death in the new world."

Fedelm wanted to laugh at this tale despite the sincerity of the woman. She was obviously crazy. Urith just grunted his disbelief. Only Mivraa was quiet for a moment as if something the woman said caught her attention. But the goddess was not in a forgiving mood. She reached down, grabbing the woman by the collar of her robe and dragged her over to the chains embedded in the side of the mountain. Finding one manacle lock broken Mivraa forced the woman to her knees and clamped the woman's ankle in the only working iron bracelet. The demigoddess gave the chain a tug to make sure it remained embedded in the rock.

"Well, you can meet your fate with the *ranqels* when they return," said the demigoddess, her tone dark and icy. "Maybe your god can save you before they come tonight." Mivraa walked back to the others, leaving the woman to scream her prayers to Kriell, telling them she gladly waited for a martyr's death.

"I don't understand how these *ranqels* came to this mountain," Urith spoke to Fedelm as they watched the scene. Neither interceded since they both saw the punishment as just. "Dead outlaws that come back as these malicious beasts is something from the ancients. We know it's the work of the underworld, but this Kriell is not a god of the underworld, is he? And what of Caruun and Alrpan? Is the chaos of the underworld working against us now?"

Fedelm said she didn't know. "It makes no sense to me either," she agreed. "I've no idea who this Kriell could be, but Alrpan is tricky, perhaps she is fooling them along with Caruun. Seems to be something they would do."

"All I know is this; it's time to change some things. The Fates have led us to the Skool," Urith told her. "I just wonder what's in the hearts of the gods anymore." He didn't see Fedelm's confused expression at his words, turning to Mivraa, who joined them.

"I don't give a damn about their hearts, except when I rip it out of their chests. I'm going to wipe out those that did this to me, said the warrior goddess in a cold, unforgiving tone. There was something in her voice neither of her companions recognized. Mivraa started down the footpath leading from the mountain. Fedelm tried to ask if the goddess was fully recovered for the coming trip. Mivraa disregarded the question, focused only on the village below. Urith and Fedelm quickly followed her down the trail.

Fedelm took one quick glance at the chained women who defiantly spit in her direction when their eyes made contact. The hakra felt an urge to release the Death Bearer from her certain death. But she also remembered the bloody, pitiful body that was Mivraa and she knew the others would never agree. She suddenly hated the brutal nature of her world as she listened to Urith telling the demigoddess about their long search to find her. Mivraa paid little attention. She stomped along the path, focused on finding the rest of the Death Bearers.

When they reached the fork at the trailhead, Urith had difficulty convincing Mivraa to go with them to the ossanes. He was only able to persuade her when he mentioned their food and water was with the mounts. The trio traced the trail back the long-necked beasts grazing on the grass. Urith pulled his bag of water and gave it to the goddess. Mivraa refused, saying the healing water was enough. As the warrior gave the bag to Fedelm, he felt they were being watched. He climbed a nearby boulder to get a better view. However, a careful scan over the trail he could see revealed nothing. But the feeling remained. He told the women of his thoughts. Mivraa only nodded while she rearranged the saddles and bags so the demigoddess the use of the third ossane. The demigoddess pulled her long silver spear of crystal from her black robe and swung herself up on her mount. Urith grabbed her reins and told her he was sure someone was spying on them since they had walked down from the peak.

"I believe we should press on to the den of the *ranqels* in the old mines of the East," he told Mivraa.

Mivraa immediately interrupted him. "No, I want the head of each wretched member of that cult. Anyone who came up that peak to watch me humiliate myself begging for death, I will cut their throat."

"Your vengeance is justified," Urith conceded, patiently trying to keep the warrior goddess from making a mistake. "But we are only three people, and we don't know how many are in this village. Let us take it slow and scout out the place. Besides, something is happening between the gods of the realms."

He could see he was not getting through. "Look, you know I'm not the type to stop you from your revenge. I'm only asking you to calm down and think. I've never heard of this Kriell, but that woman we left was describing Caruun and Alrpan. They are the ones who must control these monsters that hurt you. We find those beasts and we know who is behind your suffering."

"I know who did this," the demigoddess gave the warrior a furious glare he had never seen. She was a goddess filled with a ruthless, cold vehemence. "The ones who put these vermin to punish me will come next, this I can promise."

She pulled the reins from his hand, then grabbed a spare shield from its hook on the saddle and pushed her arm through the leather straps. "Now you can come with me or stay here. I'm going to the village." Mivraa sped off on her mount, leaving her comrades looking at each other.

"I think you said I'm the one with the uncontrolled temper," said Urith, trying to make light of the events but his face was somber. He avoided the pleading look in Fedelm's eyes. He knew, like her, that Mivraa was dangerous, to them and to herself at the moment. Their eyes eventually met, and he took a deep breath. "I have to join her. I owe her my life several times," he said as he put on his black helmet. He jumped on his mount and hurried after the demigoddess. Fedelm paused before she took a deep breath and climbed on her mount, turning the animal to follow them. She knew she had really no other options as she dug her heels into the ossane's flank.

The warrior goddess had already reached the outskirts of the village when Urith finally caught up. As their animals kicked up dust entering the center of the village, the slight wind sent rolling clouds of dust through a long line of single-story buildings made of faded red mud bricks on either side of them. Each building had small dark windows, many of them open to the elements. The Esterblud noticed the streets were eerily empty of any people or animals. Urith came up alongside the woman's mount to slow her, but Mivraa saw a figure in a black robe and white turban, ducking behind a corner between the buildings. The goddess spurred on her mount, paying no attention to Urith's warning.

When the group rounded the corner, they saw the person running down to the back wall of the dead-end street, appearing to be cut off. Mivraa saw her chance and rode headlong toward the figure. Seeing the rider coming at him, the figure swiftly shot over to a doorway, ducking inside just as the black ossane neared. The warrior goddess jumped down from her mount, heading to the door, finding it barred. Urith and Fedelm arrived as the demigoddess slammed her fist into the wood before turning back to them. She was about to say something when she noticed movement at the entrance to the alleyway. A large wagon was being pushed into the entrance from the street, blocking their exit. Mivraa pointed to what she saw when flames begin to envelop the cart.

Cries filled the air with the name of Kriell as lines of Death Bearers showed themselves on the rooftops around their trapped victims. The villagers, dressed in black robes, were well armed with spears along with a few archers. Glancing at the buildings, the trio could see no way to retreat or escape. But they could hear the sounds of footsteps above them as their enemy closed in. Taking up positions closer, the cult members began throwing their spears down at the trio. Fortunately, nearly all of the first wave of spears missed the mark as the villagers were hampered by the overhang of the roof. However, one spear struck the ossane carrying Urith. The mount fell down on its side, landing on the Esterblud's leg. The warrior cursed loudly from the pain of his twisted leg under the animal while Fedelm jumped down behind her panicked mount, avoiding the spears while looking at some way to escape as archers moved to get better positions on the roof nearby.

"What have you done?" she shouted at Mivraa who struggled with her mount as well. However, the goddess's eyes remained on the villagers, intent on finding her first kill.

Fedelm pulled her short sword from the saddle, running to help Urith. Mivraa jumped from her the black mount, going to help the trapped Esterblud as well. With their combined strength, they helped pull him out from under the dying ossane under the increasing number of arrows and spears flying at them. Urith grabbed his shield and a spear from the saddle, and somehow the trio avoided the arrows coming at them. They pulled behind the black mount held by Fedelm. However, a spear landed into the side of the animal, and it reared back in pain, briefly pinning the warrior and the goddess into the stone wall behind them. Leaping away, the mount ran blindly away from them, leaving them exposed. The man and woman pushed in with the hakra behind the last ossane, all desperately seeking a way to escape the onslaught of projectiles coming at them, moving along the wall to get cover from stacked firewood.

Fedelm saw the window next to her, then grabbed the large man by the arm to show him they could escape through it. He glanced, then shook his head. He knew he could never get through the small hole, but the discovery gave him an idea. The warrior told Fedelm to stay with the mount as cover, even if it was killed. Pulling himself from under the eve of the building, he found an overconfident archer leaning past the edge of the roof. A quick flick of his wrist sent his spear into the man's chest, and the man fell next to them. Urith ran out to retrieve his spear as the archers repositioned themselves along the rooftop.

"I'm going to clear the roof," said Urith, "Stay close to the wall until I get back."

Limping the few paces over to the nearby window, he pulled himself up using the top of the window ledge as his foothold. He took a glancing blow from an arrow that struck him in the side from an archer across the alleyway. Scrambling to avoid other arrows coming, he pulled himself over the edge of the roof where black-robed figures ran toward him. Unsheathing his Clovel Sword, he limped toward them while a volley of arrows came toward him from the other rooftop. His large shield protected him as the projectiles bounced off the metal covering. Several of the bearded men pulled their sickle swords, and he gave a death sneer which they could see under the visor on his helmet. He knew their leaf-shaped short swords were no match of his longsword. Their only hope was their numbers which might give them the victory.

"I trust you are ready to die like vermin," his low growl could barely be heard as the black-robed men suddenly charged him with their screams of death.

The Esterbluds' long sword whipped through the air and two men were cut down with two wide swipes. Although hobbled by his leg, Urith swung his shield, striking another enemy in the face. The man fell off the roof to the ground where he landed in a heap near the two women. The Death Bearers on the rooftops gave their full attention to the Esterblud now, and they came running to his position. Several of the enemies were coming up behind him, leaving the warrior in the precarious position of fighting from two sides.

Below the Esterblud, Mivraa, and Fedelm were no longer dodging arrows, but a horde of screaming cult members began running down the alley. Both women knew they would be soon overwhelmed. Unable to see Urith fighting above them, Mivraa told Fedelm to get the shield from the mount. Then the demigoddess almost lifted the young woman on to the high back saddle.

"Charge into them and I'll try to keep them off with my spear," Mivraa said calmly. The warrior goddess climbed up behind the hakra who thought it was a suicidal strategy. "Urith can join us if we can break their line," Mivraa spoke in her ear.

"Yes, this worked so well before," said Fedelm sarcastically. She was thinking back to the charge she and Dughorm made against the Aberffraw warriors to save Urith and Oslaf. The old blind man and the hakra were immediately captured which led to Dughorm's death.

"This isn't the same," said the goddess with a slap on the animal's flank and the two women charged at the mass of black robes coming at them.

As Urith fought another wave of enemy striking at him with short swords, he failed to see the arrow shot from a nearby archer. The tip hit him from behind, embedding deeply into his injured leg. Stumbling, he fell forward, his sword slicing through the leg of a female cult member trying to stab him with a spear. She screeched in agony as two more Death Bearers rushed at the fallen warrior. Urith struggled to a knee, letting one of the men impale himself on the Clovel Sword while using his shield to deflect the others' sword stroke. Sparks flew from the shield as the running enemy passed him and, in a strange pirouette, he got to his feet behind the man and suddenly began pushing him forward. The unlikely pair ran headlong into the next line of archers that were coming from behind.

Urith fought through the pain of the arrow still in his leg, moving the Death Bearer in front of him who took arrows in the belly and chest when they crashed into the line. The action gave the Esterblud time to cut down two more of the lightly armed men as they attempted to scatter. At the same time, he caught a glimpse of the dramatic charge by Fedelm and Mivraa, which gave Urith a crazy idea. As the enemy gathered around him, Urith began screeching like a mad man. Recklessly flinging his sword and shield around to strike them, the onslaught from the giant caught many of the remaining cult members off-guard. Showing that not all of the cult members wanted to die, several of the black robed villagers suddenly peeled away from the fight, either jumping down from the roof or running away for the safety of the other side of the rooftop. Two men still in the fight were quickly cut them down by the charging warrior. When the edge of the Shield of Skool slammed into one of the men, it nearly severed his head. While Urith fought the first man, the other jammed his short sword into the back of the exposed Esterblud. Fortunately, the chainmail stopped the tip from going deep. Urith swung his sword, striking the man in the head with the pommel. As the man staggered back, the Esterblud warrior sliced him across the belly, sending the screaming man to a slow death among his entrails.

Urith forced himself the next couple steps to the edge of the roof, glancing at the ossane carrying Fedelm and Mivraa ran into a mob of black robes. The giant warrior struggled to get down from the rooftop, his injured leg revolting at his movement. He tried grabbing at the arrow with his shield hand. Slick with blood, he only succeeded painfully sliding his hand over the shaft, yelling at his futile effort. When he saw more cult followers moving back toward him on the rooftop, he made an awkward attempt to jump to the ground. When he hit the gravel, he felt his leg turn to fire as his landing broke off the shaft of the arrow. Fortunately, part of his fall was cushioned by the dead ossane. Pushing off the animal, he somehow maintained his balance. Painfully, he struggled forward in a limping jog toward the two women, oblivious to the few arrows shot at him from the roof.

Mivraa had sliced down several of the enemies with her wicked double tipped spear as Fedelm plowed the ossane through the mob. As the crowd of white-turbaned men gathered around them, the ossane began to panic, its long neck rearing high above them. Fedelm struggled to turn the animal, and one of the Death Bearers grabbed onto the reins, sending the mount onto its back legs and lashing out with its front cloven hoofs in defense. The animal crashed into the mob, kicking down a few unfortunates who were crushed by the weight of the ossane. However, the crowd began to stab their sickle swords into the beast, slicing deep into the animal. The ossane tried to bolt away, leaving Fedelm unable to control it as the panicked creature struggled to turn into the alley where Urith came toward them. A black robed figure started to drag down the women by grabbing their clothes only to be stabbed by Mivraa.

Suddenly the ossane received a spear into its heart and immediately went down, sending the women hard onto the ground. Struggling to hold on, Fedelm fell face first, unable to reach out quickly enough to keep from striking her head. Mivraa was able to use her spear to help balance her landing, popping up swiftly to impale a large man trying to swing at her with a short sword. The demigoddess stood next to the semi-unconscious Fedelm, yelling to the cult members surrounding her that she wanted Kriell's head. The response from the crowd turned into pandemonium as they pressed forward to kill her. The goddess swung her spear in a methodical fashion at the heads of her attackers, and the blood flowed on the ground around her as she inflicted maximum carnage on the unshielded cult members.

Still, they came on and their mass of bodies soon overwhelmed her, their swords striking at her in the back and arm. Mivraa yelled out in pain as she felt herself being taken down to the ground. Struggling, she heard the roar of Urith as the warrior flung his large body into the mass of cult members around Mivraa. His attack sent men and women flying, and she could feel the weight being removed from her back. She pushed herself back to her feet to join the Esterblud warrior who was now the center of the mob attacking them. His initial charge and his massive sword strokes sent enemy blood flying, soaking his black helmet and green tunic. However, more of the Death Bearers joined in the fight to destroy him and Mivraa. Several of the wounded clung to his legs and trying to take the giant warrior to the ground, screaming their final death cries as he sliced and stabbed into them. Losing his balance, Urith fell back into Mivraa, and they both landed on the ground as a wave of attackers struck them. The Esterblud warrior was able to roll over, slowly and painfully rising to his knees and using his shield to fend off the continued swords strokes coming at him. Exhausted by the wounds and feeling his strength quickly ebbing, he heard the voice in his head tell him the words.

"Da Umca Mivwar," he spat out from his dry mouth, feeling the sudden heat of the amulet on his chest inside the chainmail he wore.

The explosion that shot from the Shield of Skool was far stronger than he remembered. A blinding white flash shot from his shield. Just as before when he used the weapon to destroy the Aberffraw warriors at Du-Rinell, the deadly stream of energy slammed the shield back into Uriths' chest. However, now, the blast slid him along the ground. The light focused like a huge tunnel through the mass of Death Bearers around him. Those caught in the explosion were immediately vaporized, leaving only their gray ash floating in the air. Those who looked at the intense light of the Skool were temporarily blinded, their screams filling the air while others were choked by the dust of their incinerated comrades.

Mass panic ensued as the cult members struggled to flee. Urith got himself to his knees, looking in stunned disbelief at a huge blast hole that had cleared the alleyway of any living thing along with a portion of the buildings. At first, he could hear nothing, his ears still ringing from the explosion. Then he heard the screams and cries as he watched those blinded by the light who stumbled over each other in panic. The villagers running away ignored the few cries of help which could be heard in the wreckage of the buildings.

Mivraa pushed off a couple of the dead as she struggled to her feet, ready to kill more of the cult. Only a few wounded remained alive, and the woman quickly ran to them, savagely cutting their throats. No one remained within reach as she watched the remaining people scattering, heading into hiding. At first, she felt like running after them, to hunt them down. Then she observed Urith, covered in blood and dust, on his knees trying to pull a body off the struggling Fedelm. Hesitating at first, the demigoddess moved over to help Fedelm get to her feet. Groggily, Fedelm joined Mivraa helping the giant warrior to his feet and she saw how severely wounded the man was. Mivraa held out her arm to help the Esterblud walk.

"Help Fedelm and gather what you can. I'll find some ossanes for us," Urith told her as he wearily pushed past her offered arm. His anger returned as he knew how close they came to death from an ambush, a mistake unworthy of an experienced warrior. While it was not an intentional snub to the demigoddess, Fedelm saw how Mivraa reacted, and the hakra felt a strange sense of satisfaction. Urith hobbled through the wreckage to the street as Mivraa put Fedelm's arm over her shoulder and they trailed behind. The hakra asked her what happened.

"Urith unleashed the Skool, of course. It was fortunate he did," said Mivraa.

"We wouldn't be in this state if you hadn't wanted revenge." Fedelm felt a growing fury as well as she shook off the fog of her headache. "You ran us into a trap, and now he has to save us, yet again."

Mivraa flushed at the indictment against her. "Don't tell me what I should do," she snapped. "No one said you had to join me."

"Maybe not, but what else would Urith do. He warned you about the village. Perhaps you might not die, but you nearly killed the one person who could destroy the gods. Remember that next time." Fedelm yelled back as she shook her head. The hakra pushed Mivraa's arm away. "I can walk on my own," the small woman told the goddess defiantly.

Ahead of them, Urith had turned down the street toward the edge of the village to the stables he saw coming into the town. He found a few of the animals there, each one milling about, fearful beasts who smelled the scent of blood in the air. He opened the gate, went inside the pen, taking three halters while talking in a low, calming voice. He was able to coax them into the leather straps, leading the three of the animals from the pen as the women came up.

"We're doing this bareback and no supplies now," he told them gruffly. "I'm not going back to see if we have anything left since they may regroup. Fill the water bags and keep watch for any more of those dung eaters who may be around."

Fedelm took a white and tan mount while Mivraa took another from Urith. They led their mounts to a water trough out front of the small building that held the trader's office. As expected, nobody came to greet them, so Urith took several water bags hanging nearby. While he filled the water from the trough, the women kept watch for any Death Bearers, but the village was eerily quiet. The Esterblud splashed some of the water on his face and hands before struggling to climb on his mount after attaching the bags to the saddle. As Urith kept watch, the women quickly cleaned up the blood from their hands and faces as well from the trough. Just as they got ready to leave, Fedelm ran into the shack. She came out with a sack, telling them she found some items they could use.

Turning the ossanes to the east, they left the village, each rider expecting another attack but not a sound was heard. In one fateful blast, it appeared the core of the death cult had been destroyed by the Skool. And Urith hoped the need for vengeance within Mivraa was satisfied. He knew the next time the demigoddess focused solely on revenge; they probably would not be as lucky.

~~~

Satres and Lyncus were discussing the upcoming invasion of Esterblud during their late breakfast. Dining on erba meat served with exotic purple cycress leaves, both men commented favorably on the Aberffraw wine they held in their hands. Despite the outward appearance of camaraderie, there was an underlining tension between the two men. Neither wanted to face the fact they now had mutually exclusive goals. Each man fixated upon paths that only met on occasion and deep down they knew this. But the game they continued to play if only because they needed to maintain the act.

"The king will be wondering where you keep yourself all the time," Satres told the young warrior. "It is risky to continue to meet each night. And our servants can find reasons to wag their tongues at the wrong times. Neither will do us good."

"I'm not worried about my father," said Lyncus. "His dedication is upon revenge against the Esterblud's for my brother's death. As long as I keep the forces coming in from Cahmais and make sure they continue to be equipped and trained, he will be happy. Those who might talk, I make sure to find plenty of work for them away from the Citadel."

"That is quite wise," agreed the Sacred Overlord, taking another sip of wine. "However, this secret remains dangerous for us both."

"Relax my friend, a little danger is good. It will keep us on our toes." The young warrior's face beamed at the idea, confirming Satres' suspicion about the man. He seemed to be interested in their secret affair only to satisfy a rebellious streak against his father and his kingdom. The Sacred Overlord disliked knowing this, but he realized he was in no position to say anything. Both had the sword of the executioner dangling above their necks if the truth were to come out. The real power of the Citadel rested with the Aberffraw warriors who now controlled the kingdom. The warrior world of Kamin held a vicious hatred for homosexual affairs. Torture and death were the standard sentences for such discovery, even for the son of a king.

"I've scheduled a grand send off for your troops when we leave for the Esterblud lands tomorrow." Satres changed the subject. "I must see that my council has prepared the *satgerts* for moving into the lands your troops will conquer. I have sent out emissaries to make sure the other overlords see this invasion as entirely justified. I think your brother's death has opened the eyes of the other rulers throughout Kamin. They now understand you cannot trust the Esterbluds."

Satres could tell by the satisfied expression on the young warriors face the news pleased him. The Sacred Overlord knew far more about the death of Tuncel than he let on. He never told Lyncus about how much the Aberffraw leader talked in his sleep nor the information that came to him from other sources. It was valuable information Satres believed would be useful in the future. For now, he would play his role as subservient to the Cahmais King and his son.

"This bodes well for us," agreed Lyncus, smiling. "I'll make sure to inform my father of your work. I'm sure he will be quite pleased."

"I'm appreciative of such words. The Ynyover people grumble about all of the warriors roaming in the land. There are some complaints about the shortages. I'm afraid some will soon begin to ask questions about our partnership." Satres had heard rumblings already, however, nothing that would shake the faith of his council so far.

"No need to worry," Lyncus told him, quite arrogant in his attitude. "Late yesterday I received word that many of our ships carrying food and supplies have left Uugaraa. They will stop here before long, and my men have been instructed to unload part of the supplies so we may use the ships for ferrying troops to help with our invasion. My father expects that you will be able to use these supplies to reward your friends."

"It seems you and your father have planned for everything. I must go now as I have some of my advisors waiting on me. I'll meet you at dinner after giving sacrifices to our allied gods." Satres excused himself, then put on his long red robe before leaving his chambers to walk the short distance to the stairway leading to the main hall. He slowly strolled along, his head down as he thought about his plans for the Majireef Council. Their influence over the many *satgerts* throughout Kamin would be vital in the instructions he received from Caruun.

After entering the main hall where his advisors and ministers waited around the long table, he was so pre-occupied that he stopped in the middle of the room. Suddenly aware of the eyes upon him, he reddened slightly. "My apologies for being late," said Satres as he turned to take his place at the head of the table. Settling himself in the large ornate chair, he continued. "My sole focus has been to convince our Aberffraw guests to leave as soon as possible."

There was a low murmur among the people around the table. They were well aware of the complaints coming from their villages and leaders of the temples. Satres went on to tell them about the supplies that were coming as well. This information gave a boost to the men sitting around the table, and they began to clap their hands on the table. Satres took advantage of their approval to lay out his upcoming plans.

"When the Aberffraw warriors leave, they will be changing the course of history on Kamin. We must take advantage of this to expand our influence into the lands of Esterblud. We all know how their king has opposed the control of our temples for many seasons. Now, I'm convinced that with control of Esterblud by the Aberffraw army, we will soon have the temples under our guiding hand. I ask that this council begin planning for this development." The Sacred Overlord felt the energy in the room surge at his dramatic words. He also knew his position grew more secure with this news. An expansion of his small kingdom at the assumed defeat of the Esterbluds would send his name across Kamin. It was a small step to his greater ambition.

While Satres spoke to the council, Lyncus was heading to the other end of the citadel, still feeling quite happy with how his plans were moving along. While he knew much work remain for him to overcome his father's power, the man was aware that his ability to use Satres and his guards provided the young warrior the influence and information he needed. He smiled to himself when he thought how easily the Sacred Overlord could be manipulated to meet the Aberffraws' needs. Lyncus knew the older man was playing him a fool. But where Satres valued the closeness of their relationship, the young warrior considered the older man foolish. The son of Asgurd believed the thin man was no different than his wife. Only useful to achieve his goals. Ultimately, Satres would not be needed when Lyncus became king. Through his wife, Althran, the Aberffraw leader already had significant influence in the Majireef Council. Coming from a prominent family, the ambitious woman he married at the direction of his father knew everything within the council and the Sacred Overlord failed to realize about wife held control over several members. Lyncus already knew much of the Sacred Overlord's plans for Esterblud. And even better for the Aberffraw was the detailed knowledge he had about Satre's within the council.

Since Satres made deals with Alrpan and Caruun, many of the members resisted the thought of underworld gods dictating the future for them. And some of the visions coming to hakras within the council cause grumblings against their current leader. Since it was the hakra body who decided the fate of the Sacred Overlord, Lyncus's wife strove for her husband to become the next Sacred Overlord. Lyncus decided it was a natural destiny for him. Once the Esterblud's were dealt with, his father would suffer the fate of his brother and Lyncus would be King of Cahmais. With Ynyover controlled by the Aberffraw tribe, there would be a need to bind the kingdoms together using the power of the *satgerts*. He could either control Satres or become the Sacred Overlord. Lyncus knew it was ultimately a choice between him and Satres. His lover would have to be taken care of in due time. But for now, the son of Asgurd enjoyed the game he was playing.

Lyncus entered a small room at the end of a long hallway, passing by two columns where the leaders of his men were gathered. His men were sitting around a table, chatting about their upcoming trek. Their golden hair leader sat at the right-hand side, purposely avoiding the chair at the end of the table, reserved for the king. Lyncus raised his hand for silence, and the men listened with eager anticipation. While they knew some of the plans, the Aberffraw leader proceeded to tell them of the news from his conversation with Satres. He also continued with King Asgurd's plans. The king and his advisors decided to use the main force of fighters who would invade Esterblud from the south. While they advanced quickly, they would use ships to bring another mass of warriors to overrun the fort from the north. It was an unusual plan for the Cahmais army to be using ships to land combatants far from the main force invading the land. By capturing the main fortress in Eran, the Aberffraw would ensure the division of the Esterblud tribe, causing a fracture to their alliance with the other tribes of the south. This would guarantee the conquest of all the Esterblud territory. It was a bold plan, unusual in its scale and coordination. The young warriors in the room gave excited shouts, pounding the table with their fists in approval. Their leader smiled at the electrified fighters.

"Pray you, give such spirit back to your men," Lyncus told his leaders. "For now, this information does not leave this room. We will tell those on the ships after they leave port. You will not inform our warriors who are with us on our trip. There is no need for them to know anything at this point."

After the room had quieted from the initial excitement, the men asked a few questions, but it was evident they were ready for their mission. When they finished their planning, Lyncus left the room with his men, leading them to the stairs below to drink heathmead from the cellar stores. They made quick work of opening a cask and the group's leader happily handed out the mugs from wooden shelves lining the wall. It was part of his ritual to maintain their loyalty as a generous benefactor, another step on his ultimate goal. Holding up his mug, he drank in salute to his men, who offered up their cups in tribute to their leader. Shouts of thanks were offered to the gods for their eventual victory over the hated Esterbluds.

Chapter 8: The Lands of Neerwah

Fedelm cleaned the numerous wounds on Urith that evening as the sun set behind the Neewar Mountains in the east. Stripped of his bloody tunic and chainmail, the Esterblud wondered why the woman was taking out her frustrations on him as he stood leaning on a small tree trunk. As she was squatting down next to him, the woman used a strip of coarse cloth and water the back of Urith's leg. The warrior had to grind his teeth at times from her rough handling. Still upset at what occurred earlier in the village, she continued to bump into the arrow shaft as she cleaned the tender area. In her eyes, there was no reason to put themselves at such risk to get revenge against the cult. Finally tired of the pain, Urith told Fedelm to pull out the arrow, and he put his arms around the trunk. He barely had time to ready himself when Fedelm grabbed the shaft and quickly yanked it out. The pain caused the giant man to roar, cursing in Esterblud. As he tried to walk off the pain, Fedelm was trying to follow along on her knees while attempting to wrap the wound. It was an awkward scene that caused Mivraa to smile briefly before returning to her shell.

The demigoddess was thinking about how close the giant warrior came to death. However, her need for revenge nearly got him killed. The demigoddess was willing to risk it, but Urith needed to survive. It was not the thought that gave her comfort. She had her own business to take care of now, and the only human she cared about was suddenly in her way. The thought surprised her. However, the warrior goddess could never forget the abuse, rape, and degradation at the hands of her family. Her redemption would only come with their deaths.

Drawing a deep breath, Urith suggested that the Fedelm help with tending to Mivraa's wounds while he worked on binding his leg. Earlier, he had given the hakra woman a fishing hook from his belt, and he did not like the idea that she would soon be stitching up some of his other wounds. He knew Fedelm was upset, so he also knew it was not the time to bring it up. Urith decided he would bring up their fiasco after they healed, which was going to take a while. His deep wound from the arrow hurt like fire and Mivraa had quite a few long gashes as well. While she would recover with her half god breed, there was no Exyts Spring water to heal them quickly now. They would need time and rest to recover.

When Fedelm moved over to the demigoddess, Mivraa simply let her shawl fall away. Urith caught sight of the naked goddess and his eyes held on to the view momentarily. While he held her naked body before, he saw a different woman now. The warrior goddess had no compassion or tenderness in her eyes; instead, they reflected only pain and anger. He limped over to sit on a flat rock near them. Mivraa saw the warrior look away, thinking it was out of deference to her. Fedelm noticed this exchange as well, and she tried not to show her annoyance at Urith. The blonde woman wanted to shout at the giant man for being a fool. Why would he follow this goddess into oblivion while the rest of the world needed him? Fedelm tried to remain focused on the task at hand. Neither woman said anything, although each had plenty to say.

After binding his leg, the Esterblud warrior slowly pulled his padded undergarment top over his head to reveal his massive chest, covered in red stained sweat from the superficial cuts. The dry desert air cooled him, and it felt good.

"I wish we had thought to find some heathmead in the village," he joked as he took a long drink of water from the leather bag he held. "Once we cleanup we will have to get a fire before nightfall. It will be cold by morning. Luckily, it doesn't appear that anyone is following us."

He watched the trail from their high vantage point down along the valley floor. The terrible Neehorsh peak remained visible high in the sky behind them. While the Esterblud was satisfied that nobody attempted to follow them, he was concerned about finding water and food for they had little of either. Now in Esterblud, he knew there were only a few places where water and supplies would be available in this desolate land. He explained his concerns while he cleaned off the sweat and blood from his upper body.

"Are we sure where we are going?" Fedelm asked as she used the fishing hook and a bit of fine twine that she carried to mend a nasty gash near Mivraa's shoulder. She took some satisfaction in hearing the demigoddess suddenly suck in a deep breath and clutch at the rock she was sitting on. It was good to see the warrior goddess feel some of the pain she caused others, thought Fedelm.

"I'm not sure of anything at this point," conceded Urith. "All I know is we got Mivraa away from the mountain. And the Shield of Skool is even stronger than before. The force of the blast was able to push me along the ground."

"You know the gods will stop looking for you once they discover your escape," Fedelm said to Mivraa as she finished cleaning Mivraa's back wounds.

"Yes, and I won't stop looking for my opportunity to get them," said the demigoddess bitterly. "My father is no more, and I have no allegiance to those who live in another realm."

"So what are you wanting?" Urith asked as he limped over to several dead wstinga bushes, avoiding the blue-green thorns as he carefully crushed the bush limbs under his boot. He picked broken branches to use a tender for a fire.

"We cannot keep charging into ambushes for vengeance against humans who believe in this god or that," he intentionally kept his voice thoughtful although both women knew he was serious. "My shield is halfway filled with the Skool. That must mean we are getting closer to our goal. We have to quit thinking about deities and trust in the Fates and the visions. What's are our next path?"

Mivraa gave him a glare at first before she took a deep breath. Slowly, the demigoddess told them of a vision she had during those terrible nights on the mountainside as she lay near death. She described the scenes of Kamin where the old gods, known as the Guardians, waded into the temples to cut down cowering humans for sport. Then she told them of another vision where such entities could no longer bend the humans to the god's desires. As she spoke, her voice grew soft and, Urith could see her eyes glisten.

"I saw the future world, and it was so different than our world now. This is what I seek, and the only way this will happen is to destroy these cursed gods. That is my path now," said Mivraa coldly.

The surprise from the goddess's admission caused Urith and Fedelm to look at each other. A new world would come. It was something they never considered. The humans wondered if Mivraa's vision could be correct. Fedelm walked over to the Esterblud to finish cleaning the wounds on his back.

"Are you sure what you saw? Do our paths follow together?" Urith asked Mivraa, who paused before she shrugged her shoulders. This was the first time since they began searching for the Skool; they considered the implications of their quest. Before, the weapon was a tool to stop the gods. Now the purpose of the Skool was clearly seen by one of them, and it was a fearful thought, even to the hardened warrior who held the power. The group went quiet for a while, thinking of Mivraa's words. Fedelm quickly finished scrubbing the dried blood and sweat from the giant's back. He gritted his teeth as she stitched up a deep gash near his neck. When she finished, Urith turned to her.

"Your turn now," he said. He noticed that Fedelm tried ignoring the long bloody gash that ran on the back of her robe near the pelvis. Protesting, at first, Urith forced the woman to turn, and he lifted the wrap revealing the deep wound. It would need to be cleaned and would require some stitches. He led her over to Mivraa, telling her to take off the robe as he used water to clean the area. Mivraa slipped on her black shawl, standing in front of the topless woman and gave Fedelm a grin as she took the fishhook and string from her. Neither woman noticed Urith staring at Fedelm. The hakra fixed a cold glare on the demigoddess who reached around her, handing the instruments to Urith and he began washing the wound. Fedelm gritted her teeth when the warrior began to poke the steel into her flesh; still she refused to call out. She looked into the eyes of the demigoddess, and she could tell Mivraa was enjoying her suffering. It was payback for the harsh words said by the human to a warrior goddess.

When he finished, Urith broke the quiet spell as he hobbled over between the flat stones throwing the brush to the ground. He went over to the trail which passed by and found several limbs from a large dead stump of a tree.

"Well, Mivraa you have laid out a path which is straight and narrow toward revenge," said Urith as he limped back to them, returning to the future. "But I need to know we are on the same side."

"You know I'm with you. It's the only way we have to stop from being hunted." Fedelm, putting on her robe, believed Urith was sneaking glances at her. She quickly dismissed the idea when she saw the expression on his face while he talked to Mivraa. The giant warrior seemed genuinely perplexed about his companions.

"Perhaps the Skool might solve our problems with the gods. I'm asking that you remember that?" Urith continued to stare at the goddess who sat on a rock, wrapping herself in a blanket. Mivraa said nothing for the moment. Urith painfully knelt down with the wood and used a spark stone to light the brush. Soon, there was a fire glowing as the sky turned dark.

"I don't have an answer for you," said Mivraa finally, "I will kill my family, I swear my oath upon that. But if you are going to face the gods and their monsters in your quest, I'll be there. I can guarantee I'll be with you."

"But these words don't help us right now," Fedelm reminded them. "We need to think this out and quit falling into disaster after disaster. I believe we need a plan to get ahead of the Fates." She looked over for support, but Mivraa looked away. The warrior goddess might agree with her, she said nothing, still upset at young hakra.

"Well, I'm open to ideas. But I also know we need armor for Fedelm," interjected Urith, "She won't last long against beasts like the *ranqels*. Somehow I'm sure more creatures will be coming from the underworld." Then a thought came to him. "I seem to remember something in myths. When the gods changed into human form, they would come into our realm wearing the armor forged before the Guardians. Could we find such things?" Urith leaned back against one of the bags which Fedelm had already pulled off the ossanes. While he thought he knew the answer, the Esterblud looked over at Mivraa.

"You must be talking about pieces scattered within the Temples of the Sky Realm," Mivraa said sleepily as she slowly and painfully laid out a blanket near the saddle by the slab of stone. She carefully laid down on her back, attempting to avoid pressure on her wounded areas. Looking at the stars above, she continued. "I've only seen on occasion. Wurms showed me a room which held several shields and armor pieces when we were young. I remember he said the weapons haven't been used since the time of the Guardians. Anyway, who knows what enchantments were left in the weapons." She looked back at Urith showing her disapproval. "I know what you're thinking. You're wondering if it's possible to get to them for us. I tell you it's not. No living human gets into the Sky Realm, let alone past the spirits that wander through the temples."

"What spirits?" asked Urith. "I thought only the gods reside there."

Mivraa smiled to herself. "There are many secrets you don't know. Spirit sentinels keep watch over the Sky Realm, spying on those who come and go. They are attached to the living plants in the realm and controlled by Unis. I learned how to bypass those spirits who watched over the Exyts Spring. That was how I was able to get in and out of the realm with the healing water. But, somehow, Wurms must have found out. That's how they captured me."

The trio grew quiet again, each trying to overcome the weariness falling over them from the fight earlier. In many ways, they were still lost and only knew they must follow a path that seemed predetermined for them. Finally, Urith stood, putting his undershirt back on. The padded fabric finally dried and he soon had pulled on his battered chainmail and blood stained tunic as well. He cinched up his belt which held his Clovel Sword. The women looked at him, wondering where he was going, as he began to hobble to the ridge. It gave a better view of the area around them.

"We need rest as I'm sure we will feel the aches tomorrow," he said. "I'll take a look around just in case our enemies are nearby." He did not say who the enemies might be, but he felt the strong urge to so something before he fell asleep as he sat upon the ground. Something pushed him to keep watch over the group.

The twin moons had risen in the north casting a pale light over the ridge where Urith sat with his back against a large, flat boulder, desperately trying to stay awake. At first, he was going to take a quick walk around the camp. The sounds of the restless night gave him cause to stand watch for a while. He felt eyes watching their camp, yet he could not place exactly who might be spying on them.

His body yearned for a rest. His injured leg throbbed, keeping him awake every time he shifted his position. After a while, his weariness overcame him again. His head lulled to the sounds of the night, and he did not hear the soft steps coming from behind him. When Fedelm placed her hand on his shoulder, he instinctively whipped out his dagger, nearly cutting into her. Recognizing her white face in the moonlight, he quickly apologized as he sheathed his blade.

"No need to say anything," she whispered, kneeling next to him, the concern evident in her face. "You should be resting. Your wounds were the worst, and they need healing. Anyway, you look terrible."

"It's the moonlight," he joked grimly. "Besides, someone has to keep watch over the camp."

"No, you sleep," the hakra said. "I've slept some already. Rest yourself, I'll keep watch."

Too tired to argue, the warrior just nodded his head, turning his body slightly to rest his head on his arm, as he leaned back against the rock.

Fedelm was going to say something about it being warmer near the fire, and then stopped. He would not have heard her words. He was asleep.

As Fedelm sit next to him, she looked over the valley which appeared ghostly in the pale light. Nothing moved in the shadows falling across the open prairie as the night was unusually quiet. Far off in the distance, the hakra did see a small fire. However, she dismissed it as any threat since it appeared so far away. She listened to Urith's shallow breathing while she mulled over all the recent events. She could not tell her friend why she woke in the middle of the night. The grim visions still filled her head, and nothing she could think of gave her any comfort. She knew that something terrible was coming. The death and destruction of the village kept gnawing at her as well. She inadvertently ran her hand through Urith's long hair as she tried to reconcile his need to support Mivraa even at the risk of everyone around him. And now Dughorm is sending her visions which were terrifying and confusing.

"So what am I supposed to tell you?" she whispered as she looked down at the sleeping giant. "You love a goddess who will get you killed because she is now consumed with the idea destroying her father and brothers. She risks everything that you are destined to achieve according to Dughorm. Yet, I know we need you to live. Maybe even I need you."

She looked back at the stars at the sudden thought. She shook her head at the idea of needing the sneering warrior. He was calloused and brutal.

"But you are more complex than that, aren't you?" she asked aloud. "And I'm not the same little girl who left the Citadel. Now, I'm just another misfit trying to do right in a terrible world."

Turning back to look at the dark sky, the woman wondered aloud. "Still, will you listen to me? That's the question."

When the sun finally rose in a brilliant red haze, Fedelm was bleary eyed. She stood, stretching from the uncomfortable position leaning on the gray slate rock, oblivious to the purple hue in the morning over the camp. While she watched over Urith and the valley during the night, she had come to several conclusions about their path. The hakra knew they must find the *ranqels* now. The vision from Dughorm confirmed that. He showed her the den of the monsters and a disturbing view of an underworld realm with Alrpan and Caruun somehow twisted together. Fedelm knew something was amiss, and she could not understand the significance yet. As she thought through the events, she knew that the

Fates were either being merciful or somehow playing a deadly game with them.

With the red dawn flooding over their camp, Fedelm went over to the campfire to add a few pieces of wood to help rekindle the fire. Despite her weariness, she knew the others needed rest much more than she did. Her wounds were minor and, other than the few stitches, she only carried a headache out of the battle. The woman scrounged through the bag which she took from the ossane shack. She found a few salted Erba strips for them to chew on until they found more food. Sitting near the growing fire, she watched her sleeping companions and did not see the dust rising from the trail leading to their camp. Partially dozing, Fedelm did not hear the two ossane riders until they were pulling off the trail toward the camp.

"Hello. Do you have room for some fresh meat for breakfast?"

Oslaf had a large grin covering his face as he slid off his mount. A red robed woman climbed down from another mount behind him as the young Esterblud nonchalantly threw over a saddlebag filled with food to a shocked Fedelm, who caught it on the fly.

"Where's my uncle?" he asked the hakra.

From the ridge above came the voice of Urith. "It's about time you showed up. It seems like you are always arriving after we need you," he growled in pain, slowly standing up. Stiff and sore, his injured leg nearly gave out on him. He forced himself to limp down to meet them, waving Fedelm away as she stepped forward to help. However, his limping leg looked worse, and he sucked in the air at each painful step down the dusty brown ridge to the camp.

"Urith, by the gods, you look terrible," came the voice of Mivraa from behind Oslaf. The young warrior looked around to see the auburn haired goddess trying to stand as well. He noticed she did not look much better than his uncle, both sported bruises, on the visible parts of their bodies.

"It only hurts when I walk," Urith joked through a grimace as he carefully sat on a rock by the campfire, straightening his injured leg. "Now, where have you been and who do you have with you?"

Oslaf could see that his uncle did not remember Henther, so he decided to let her story wait. "Well, it's a bit of a long story. We ran into Imenal at his temple in Damicia. That's how we knew which trail to find you." He walked over to the fire, standing above his uncle. "Let's get some breakfast and I can tell you everything."

Using the supplies the new travelers brought, the group sat in a circle on the flat rocks, sharing their meal and stories. Oslaf reintroduced Henther to the Esterblud warrior and the other two women. He noticed the quick looks Fedelm and Mivraa gave each other, and he hoped Henther did not take offense. Oslaf was firmly attached to the golden-haired girl who was little older than himself. During their time together, she slowly learned to trust him, telling him some of her painful past and the young Esterblud quickly learned to rely on her. He carefully watched the others, wanting to make sure none of his friends might insult her.

"I must admit I hardly remember you," said Urith as his gray eyes gave the young girl a once over, "but I do remember your loyalty wasn't with us at the time." He turned back to Oslaf before Henther had a chance to respond. "Now tell us how you got here. I suspect you have something more than just your *sakreta* to enlighten us with."

The warrior brightened and enthusiastically told them about his travels with the ragged army of King Barcal and how Henther became his companion. His description of their escape and travel by the small skiff caused Urith to smile with pride. When Oslaf told them of their fight with the monsters near the swamps of Larcal, Mivraa suddenly interrupted.

"Those are Kronogs," she said, her eyes wide. "Those beasts haven't been heard of since the age of the Guardians. It's unbelievable. I've never heard of Caruun having such power to fashion such creatures."

"Well, I can tell you they are deadly and damned hard to kill. Fortunately, they are not terribly smart," said Oslaf.

"But that doesn't explain why these things are now coming from the underworld realm," Urith stated as he inadvertently groaned when he moved his swollen leg. He smiled at his nephew. "You did well for it appears you didn't have much help."

"Oh, I had great assistance," Oslaf looked over to the woman in the red robe. "I couldn't have done it without Henther. She has been as good a warrior and companion a person could ask for during our journey. It was Henther that figured out how to find you."

The others looked at the former *docke* with some surprise. The woman averted her eyes at the stares coming from the rest of the group. "That's not true," she protested. "Oslaf took us to the Esterblud tavern owned by Helite, and he told us what had happened in Damicia when you left. It was good you have a friend there. The people of Cahmais have been stirring up resentment against the Esterbluds since the assassin struck."

Oslaf interjected again. "That is true. I had to stay hidden among our people. Henther decided to check out the area near the temple. She learned more about the assassination of the Aberffraw diplomat," he explained. "While she was talking the local merchants, she noticed the wagon bringing Imenal back to the capital. Word quickly spread about his rescue which came with the help of some giant Esterblud in Ffestini."

Oslaf turned his smile to Urith, who was preoccupied with removing the bloodstained bandage from his leg. "Anyway, Henther was able to get me into the temple to meet with Imenal. He gave us his story and told us you were heading this way, so Imenal sent us along with supplies and another mount."

"What happened to you?" The young warrior finally asked. "When we entered the highlands yesterday we heard what seemed to be a distant earthquake. At first, we thought the gods had destroyed the village when we saw the main street. However, I guessed it was you when I saw the way the buildings were leveled. It appears the villagers have left."

Urith looked up at his nephew. "Yes, we found another piece of the Skool in Ffestini before the gods tried to bring down the temple on our head. When we got to the village, the Death Bearers nearly got us, so I was forced to use the shield against them."

Oslaf could tell his uncle was leaving something out, but he skipped it. He was more concerned about the swollen leg of his mentor and asked about it. Urith dismissed the question, focusing instead on their upcoming ride. He asked if they had enough supplies to continue on.

"We brought enough to feed an army," said Oslaf proudly. "And we have some heathmead and weapons as well, courtesy of Henther's ability at bargaining. She would make an excellent weapons trader."

"I'll bet," the reply from Fedelm suddenly caused Mivraa to cough, trying to suppress a laugh. Henther gave both women a cold, deadly stare, but she remained quiet. Oslaf was about to say something when Urith interrupted.

"Well, we must get moving as we have a long way to go," he slowly stood and began to limp over to the ossanes. He knew where the conversation was going, and he was determined not to allow the women to start splitting up his group into camps. He was too old of a warrior not to recognize the underlying hostility. It was also evident that Oslaf had great faith in the blonde he brought along so he would defer to his nephews' judgment for the moment. The lad seemed older and wiser despite only being away for a short while.

"Tell me where we are going?" Oslaf swiftly caught up to his uncle. "I've heard only bad rumors since before Damicia. There is so much turmoil going on that I'm not sure if the gods even matter now. The merchants are saying that traders are missing when they travel, and whole farms are wiped out."

"We are on the way to the mines," Fedelm interjected. Urith glanced at her, and the hakra told the group about part of the vision she received from Dughorm.

"Then, as we travel I'll explain what the gods are doing," the giant gave a brief glance at Mivraa, "and you can tell me if they matter or not. However, I can say the *ranqels* are real, and they are controlled by the gods," Urith's voice grew bitter. "Fates are leading us to each place for a reason."

Oslaf was not sure if his uncle spoke from a feverish mind. However, he had to admit some of what he said made sense. The young warrior was learning that fortune came to the lucky at times. And, so far, they were lucky. However, he wondered how long this would last.

"You know I'm with you, but what about our overlord? We are in Esterblud now, and he will soon know of our arrival. Shouldn't we go to him first?"

"And tell him what?" Urith asked as he limped over to his ossane, spreading his blanket on the animal's back. The Esterblud told Oslaf to hand him his saddle. Urith began cinching up the thick leather straps as he explained. "Do we give our overlord half of the Skool? How do we explain we only met Satres, the Sacred Overlord when he attacked us in Cahmais? How do we travel to meet with a king who might not be happy with the idea of the power I carry on my back? The Skool would be very tempting for him."

"King Penhda would certainly understand that Satres is unworthy of meeting him. Certainly unworthy to lead Ynyover."

"That may be true, but do we give this Skool to be used in a war between to lands? On top of that, you just came from Damicia. I have the cloud above me over the death of that Cahmais diplomat," the older warrior wiped the sweat from his forehead with the back of his hand.

"We are accused by many, and we are unable to defend ourselves. I've thought on this. The king cannot welcome us back with open arms without risking trouble with the Cahmais King. If you think about it, we were the perfect scapegoats to be blamed for this." Urith hooked his black helmet to a belt on his saddle before slowly pulling himself upon on the mount. Fedelm and Mivraa quickly gathered their bedrolls as they recognized the Clovel Destroyer was leaving.

"Enough chatter for the moment, we need to get to the mines of Neerwah." The giant warrior nudged his beast forward, starting toward the trail which crossed the highlands.

~~~

The demigod, Wurms, waited for the group of humans to leave before he turned back to the twisted lellowtere tree for his return to the Sky Realm. He wondered what his brother gods would say when they realized the humans traveled to Neerwah. Unable to get close enough to overhear their plans, he could only guess they would be after the *ranqels* that made the abandoned mines their home. But the demigod remained suspicious since it was one of the few places in Kamin in which they could reach the underworld realm directly. With Mivraa alive and fully committed to the humans, he knew many of the sky god's secrets could fall into Caruun and Alrpan's hands. Now, the humans had parts of the Skool and appeared to be going to the underworld. He wondered if perhaps Mivraa would betray the sky gods to Caruun. Nothing was beyond her revenge, the demigod thought.

When he arrived back in the sky realm, he made sure to inform his father before finding his brothers and Unis in the smaller temple where they made their home. Walking across the colored stone mosaic floor, he entered the rooms of Unis through elegant blue silk curtains. He saw the goddess lounging half naked on her bed while her sons lay around her in a similar state of undress. Each creature was drinking the god's wine and looking quite sated, pleased with themselves.

"I've found the location of the Esterblud and the Skool for you," he told the surprised group. "They are heading to Neerwah where the *ranqels* come from so it appears they follow Mivraa."

"You dare mention her in our presence," Unis gave him a glare. "It's bad enough; she escaped her punishment. It appears you have forgotten your place in this realm."

Wurms stared back. "I know my place well enough. I also know that you haven't attempted to track down those humans who are dangerous to this realm. You have been telling Duwdamon you are waiting for me. So I let him know where the usurpers are. You can talk with the sky god about your plans. He waits for you and your sons."

The goddess of the cosmos quickly thought about using her power to send the demigod into a mental breakdown; then she dismissed the thought for the moment. She would have time later for a little revenge upon the insolent Wurms. The goddess had no love for any half human, especially bastard children of her husband.

"Then, you may show us the way," she said, the venom dripping from her voice. "We don't want to let them escape and blame you for such a failure."

Wurms frowned. He had little option. To refuse her would allow the goddess to make trouble between him and his father. "Very well, when you and your sons are ready to travel, I'll be at the gateway near the Fields of Anord."

He turned and quickly left, happy to remove himself from their sight. He could not trust them so he decided to find someone who might be able to help him. Instead of taking the path to Haligulf, he took the footpath to along the Exyts Spring where the ancient elemental spirits resided. Since a young child, he learned how to bribe the spirits who filled the reeds and flowers along the shore. With the proper motivation, the spirits could become as flesh and blood as a human which the gods would take advantage of at times. The elemental spirits had a significant weakness which was also a great strength. It was the insatiable need for dreams. Imaginings and vision were their food, able to refresh and energize the spirits. And Wurms held the power to draw the dreams and aspirations out of the warriors who lay wounded on the battlefields. He fed on their spirits, and this allowed him to supply the elemental spirits in return for their inside knowledge of the gods. Intertwined with the elementals of the other realms, the spirits of the reeds and bushes knew every vision and every dream held by souls. With such knowledge, Wurms decided he would protect himself from the wrath of his family. And as he learned about the future world, he realized that the instability of the realms and the chaos of the human world moved faster than the sky gods recognized. And the number of monsters coming from the underworld grew each morning. That was news even his father did not know. And Wurms intended to use such knowledge to stay on top, no matter who came to power. For now, he would play the trusting fool for the others.

Unis took her time dressing, coming between her lustful children in a flowing white robe. While she watched her lovers, she took the time to comb her long brown hair, which she fashioned into a chignon using gold hairpins. While she prepared herself, her sons put on their elaborately adorned chest plates and belted leggings which came to their knees. Over their shoulders, they wore a long cloak fastened with a fibula over one shoulder. While they could easily destroy the humans with their powers over the elements on Kamin, each god decided to carry their own particular weapon as a symbol of their divine power. Ecarca, as ruler of the land, favored the war scythe which was the long blade of a scythe mounted on a long green rod. The tip of the knife held an exotic looking silver metal wash over the darker metal underneath. The sea god, Uugor, decided upon a long harpoon which held a razor sharp, crystal barb on the end of the dark blue pole.

The sons joined Unis at the temple entrance, and they floated across the steps, moving across to the finely cut stone path leading to Haligulf. As they appeared in their regal display skimming along the ground past the Fields of Anord, the daily battle fought by the spirits of the warriors came to a complete stop at the spectacle passing next to the spirits. Even those wounded upon the ground took time out from their attempts to staunch the bleeding wounds to watch the gods floating by. They seldom saw such grandeur despite their close proximity. Of course, the sky gods held their heads high in dismissal to those human souls staring in curiosity.

They were joined by Wurms when they arrived at the gateway. He held his place away from the group, acting even more deferential than normal. The other gods failed to notice this. They also did not see the new object around the demigod's neck. It was something given by one of the elementals along with several tidbits of useful information.

"We will travel near the mines of the underworld gateway and wait for them to arrive," said Unis, who took charge repeating the words of Wurms. She then laid out the plan for them. "When we trap them, I will take over the mind of the human giant who holds the Skool. Remember, when we control the god's weapon, we control the realms."

"But he doesn't have all the pieces to the Skool yet," said Uugor as they entered the gateway. "What good does this do us? We should just have Ecarca use the mountain to grind them into pieces and take it as our weapon."

His mother turned in front of him, placing her hand on his cheek. "But we cannot find the other pieces, you fool," she said lightly. Yet, there was hardness in her tone. "Don't bother trying to understand, my pet. I will get us what we need, and you will just follow along. I need your power over the sea and water, not your brain."

Wurms suppressed a laugh at the words as he passed through the back of the lellowtere tree to enter the world of the humans. Within an instant, he came from behind the twisted trunk of the tree near the trail into the mines. As the others followed him through, the demigod looked around for any sign of the humans.

"They have not arrived yet," he told the others. "I have an ossane close by that I took from a person so I can find them."

"Go find them while we make ourselves comfortable," hissed Unis as she looked for a place suitable for her comfort among the rough rocks scattered about the area. It was evident she had little concept of living in the human world where the laws of the natural world interfered with her desire to float in the air.

Wurms gave her a withering glare, which he knew meant nothing to the goddess but felt good nevertheless. "I'll find out where they are and let you know." Stepping down to a footpath that followed the edge of the slope, he proceeded to the spot he left his stolen mount. He found the animal near the body of the human that Wurms killed the sunrise before. The beast was grazing on the sparse blue-green grass, its reins still held by the stiff hand of the dead man. Ignoring the confused spirit of the dead man, the demigod retrieved the ossane and soon he was heading down the western road to find the Esterblud.

~~~

On the second morning of their journey to the mines of Neerwah, it was apparent that Urith was in no shape to travel further. His leg grew worse overnight, and Urith was apparently trying not to move it when he gingerly sat up from his resting place. At first, he sought to remove the cloth dressing from around his leg, which bit into the flesh because of the swelling. After painfully fumbling with it, he quit. Fedelm saw his leg and immediately moved over to help the injured warrior despite his protest.

"It's severely infected," she observed as she kneeled by him, staring at the swollen area near the knee. "Let's hope it's not blood poisoning. Now lay back and roll over so we can look at the back of your leg."

Instead of the resistance, Urith nodded and used her help to roll over on his belly. Fedelm could not lift the breeches cuff high enough to see the wound, so she pulled her dagger and cut through the back of the pant leg. When she cut through the bandage, she found an ugly red and purple puncture wound which oozed a bloody puss. At first, the hakra wondered if the Death Bearers had put something on the tips of the arrows but she decided against the thought otherwise Mivraa would be showing a similar reaction.

"I think the tip broke off inside. Urith did you see a whole arrow when you pulled it out?" The hakra asked. Urith shook his head, trying to look back at her. "I was a little busy at the time, so anything's possible when I landed and the shaft broke."

"Well, we have no healing water, so if this gets worse, your blood will become poisoned." Fedelm looked at the others who gathered around in a circle. "Are we close to a village with a healer?" Oslaf said they were, at least, five sun cycles before reaching such a village.

"So it's too far to get a village mhoda. I'll take my chances with you, Fedelm. I trust you. No matter what, if the Fates allow me to die then I will be happy to go after Caruun in the underworld," said the warrior with his death sneer. They knew the warrior believed he could take on the god of the underworld. Urith awkwardly looked back at them. "Fedelm, you know as well as I do that an infection wouldn't get this bad so quickly unless something remains in the wound. Put a dagger blade on the fire and let's cut it open to see."

She stepped around so he could see her better and he could tell by her face that she was unsure about this. She was good with herbs and roots. The woman was not used to cutting into people like a healer. "It's ok, do what you need to. Just let me get some leather to bite down on."

Oslaf helped his uncle pull the leather baudrik belt from over his chest. "I trust you not to remove my leg accidently," Urith joked to Fedelm. The hakra gave him a half smile; she knew he was just trying to steady her. Directing Oslaf to have one of the bags of water ready, she asked Mivraa to find clean strips of cloth. Fedelm went to the fire, pushing her dagger into the hot coals. She saw Mivraa staring at her and wondered what was going through the demigoddess' mind. Oslaf handed Urith the bag holding the heathmead which the older warrior thanked him for. He took a long drink from the bag, giving it back to him.

"Let's get this over with. We don't have much time," he growled, steeling himself as the rest of group watched on. Their eyes followed Fedelm as she retrieved her dagger from the fire, its blade smoking and dull red.

"Now get ready," warned the woman. Urith put the leather strap in his mouth, nodding as he grabbed the rock edge. Fedelm took a deep breath, poured some water on the back of his leg and told Oslaf to hold the limb tight. She cut into the puss filled wound, trying to keep the sickening stench of burning flesh from gagging her. Urith groaned, and his other leg began moving as Henther grabbed it, pressing down with all of her weight. Mivraa moved over to the Esterblud's torso and pressed her hands on his back, whispering into his ear. The hakra cut and dug into the muscle as the others had growing difficulty holding the large man down. Finally, she found a small piece of metal shard buried near the bone. It had taken several tries before she was able to pull the bit of arrow out. She could feel the man beneath her shudder and relax when she removed her knife. She washed water over the area before placing several golden flower plant tops over the wound to help cure the infection. The hakra bound them under the broad strip of cloth she used as a bandage. She hoped the golden plants would speed his healing although she only heard tales of the plant's power.

When she finished, Fedelm looked up to see Mivraa running her hand on the back of the warrior's head. While she still resented how the demigoddess nearly got them killed, it was apparent some of her feelings for the Esterblud remained. It made her wonder about her own feelings about the same man. But for now, personal feelings must continue to be suppressed until they found the Skool.

"How is he doing?" she asked Mivraa who nodded.

"It'll take more than a little arrow to hurt me," she heard his growling voice.

A smile crossed her face at his words. "You need to rest," said Fedelm. She cleaned off the dagger as she walked back to the campfire. Henther joined her, remaining quiet and observing her as she held the water bag over her hands for her. Fedelm glanced up at the girl who appeared little older than herself. However, the hakra could see the hardness behind her blue eyes.

"You haven't said why you joined this crazy journey," the hakra took the bag from the woman.

"No, I've not." It was a short answer, and it told Fedelm that Henther had not forgotten the slight when they were introduced.

"Look, I'm sorry about what was said," Fedelm paused slightly. "You are new to our group, and you weren't exactly friendly to us the first time we met."

"Meaning, you don't know whether you can trust me or not. You wonder if I've just attached myself to Oslaf," said Henther. "Well, that's for you to figure out. I'm here, and I'm not going anywhere." The woman turned, walking back to the young Esterblud, who was kneeling by his uncle's side. Fedelm wanted to lash out at the woman even though she realized she was right. She watched as Mivraa walked passed the former *docke*, eyeing her suspiciously as she came over to speak with Fedelm.

"Urith is resting," the demigoddess said as she approached. "Actually, he went right to sleep. I think he was up all night with the pain."

"That's good. I'm pretty sure I got everything out of the wound, and the flowers are supposed to speed the healing. How are you doing?" asked Fedelm. "You were in pretty bad shape yourself."

"I'm a goddess, remember. I'll live, just sore," said Mivraa. "What do you think about Henther?"

"I'm not sure," admitted the hakra. "She seems to have a lot of resentment against us, but that's understandable. She appears loyal to Oslaf and he's convinced."

"He's also young." The goddess turned to look at the couple. "With all of the intrigue and turmoil going on, I'm not sure it really matters at this point. It's hard to trust anyone."

"Yes, I can see that," admitted Fedelm as she thought of Mivraa's change.

Mivraa turned back to the hakra. "I see you mean me as well. Let me ask you something. You haven't told Urith about all of the visions, have you?"

Fedelm lowered her eyes and turned back to the fire, busying herself by putting away her dagger and kneeling to put the remaining clean cloth into a saddlebag. She could feel Mivraa staring at her.

"I've told him all I understand," she said.

"So, am I the only one that seems untrustworthy now?" Mivraa sat next to her, her gray eyes carefully watching the face of the hakra. They had been together long enough to realize when the other was lying. Fedelm's light freckles would turn slightly brighter.

"He suspects more than the *ranqels* are there," countered Fedelm. "I saw no reason to explain more."

"So what happens when he finds out a gateway to the underworld is there? Do you think he will continue on back to Esterblud and his king?" Mivraa paused as if thinking about this herself. "I suspect he will continue on into the underworld and go after the gods and beasts there. He will see that as an opportunity to stop the monsters and come back a hero to his lands."

The demigoddess took Fedelm's silence as agreement. "So what do your visions tell you? My dreams see something coming to destroy us. Without the full Skool, we cannot survive."

"Then, you know we must focus his attention on the next part of the Skool," the hakra told her. "And I believe you are the person to help us do this. But you cannot let your need for vengeance overpower what we seek. Other gateways exist to the Sky Realm and Urith will follow you if able."

Mivraa's face showed that the goddess had not considered such thing. Fedelm spotted conflict in her eyes. "Very well, you have my oath. We will see this through and protect Urith. I can wait a while to get my revenge." The demigoddess stood up and walked away, her mind on what she had just promised.

After Urith had rested for a bit, Oslaf and Mivraa helped him to a blanket down near the fire. The giant warrior was shivering with hot and cold spells. Oslaf piled on his blanket as well, watching his uncle wrap the wool covers tightly around himself. While Urith slept, the group decided they must wait until his fever broke before traveling again. Oslaf said he would scout around for any signs of water or food nearby, and Henther immediately stated she would be with him. Mivraa volunteered to find more wood for the fire while Fedelm stayed to watch over the warrior.

As the group went their separate ways, Urith could hear them talking as he drifted in and out of sleep. He could feel the cooling touch of Fedelm as she placed her hand on his sweating forehead. The touch calmed him, and he seemed to drift like a god above the fire. All around him was the blue of the sky and the sudden feeling of freedom, like the soaring of a vensars above the world. In his dream, he could see the mountains so far away, and he somehow knew they were unknown to his people. He felt like he wanted to go there, to forget all the trials and to seek out a new world to start again. Yet, while he thought of this, an image of Fedelm crossed his mind and then he saw Dughorm. The old warrior stood next to Caestia, and he smiled at them.

"Both of you look well," he told them. Then, a thought suddenly struck him, and he was concerned. "Have I passed into the spirit realm?"

Dughorm smiled back, "No, my friend, you are still quite alive. We come to you in your sickness. We have a plan."

They suddenly faded from his view and next he saw a small, strange blue rock shaped like a star with familiar letter engravings cut into it. The words looked similar to the engravings on the amulet around his neck. He heard the voice of Caestia telling him to remember his words.

"*Calduworm Actus Umbara.*" The words were repeated three times.

"The words are for defense against the powers of some gods. You will see old friends soon, my friend. The powers of Ecarca will help us form an army to stop the chaos from below," said Dughorm.

"But the gods oppose us," replied Urith silently. "Only Mivraa helps us."

"They will not help you willingly. We will ensure they don't know this when they do give assistance. Fedelm will learn more as you continue to the mines. But be warned, that the greatest threat comes from below." Dughorm's voice began to echo, and Urith could sense fading away. He saw a dark entrance of rough-hewn rock and on the dirt floor where he saw a running silver stream of metal.

"Wait, don't go," he shouted. "Tell me more." But the voices of Caestia and Dughorm faded quickly, and a final image appeared before him. It was the Citadel.

~~~

The next morning, the warriors lined the narrow road outside the Citadel of By-Ynys that ran toward the lands of Esterblud. Splendidly dressed in their finest blue tunics, King Asgurd and his son, Lyncus, led their contingent of men. Just behind the two Aberffraw leaders rode the Sacred Overlord, looking impressive in his red and gold tunic and cape of gold. A few aides followed him as they passed by the line of warriors that soon fell in behind to follow them out down the hill. Other Aberffraw warriors had already boarded their ships and sailed to Esterblud with the high tide. They would be landing near Eran to overrun the fortress. By this time, the Aberffraws expected the rest of the Cahmais forces, led by the King, will have taken over the southern city of Gramcan and cutting off any hope for the southern Esterblud lands. The leaders and their warrior were confident that their secrecy and planning would lead them to ultimate victory over the unprepared enemy.

King Asgurd waved Satres forward to join with them. When the thin man pulled next to him, on the opposite side of Lyncus, the king told him he had news as he handed the curled parchment back to Lyncus.

"I just received a dispatch from the King of Eernicia," he said. "That damn Merkhan says there is doubt about whether the Esterblud killed my son. Can you believe this? He says the *yolma* of his temple has told him that the fealharan were involved. What is going on with your priests? How can they not understand the truth?"

Satres thought immediately about Imenal, who was the leader of the temple in Damicia. The *yolma* had not shown any disloyalty before. He glanced over to Lyncus. He saw the man's jaw was clenched tight, the muscle on the side of his face twitching slightly. It explained more to him than their nights together. Lyncus lied to him, yet he could not afford to let the Asgurd's wrath point to his only surviving son. He thought quickly to come up with a passable lie.

"I'm not sure. Imenal is quite trustworthy. But, if I recall correctly, the fealharans are known for their green tunics. It would seem those in the city were mistaken by the clothes they saw. It would be a fundamental error given the fear many have about those assassins."

Asgurd grew quiet as he thought about Satres' words. Finally, he seemed to accept the reasoning from the Sacred Overlord when he changed the subject.

"It doesn't matter, either way, the Esterbluds caused my son's death. Merkhan goes on to say that it appears the group of usurpers has returned to Esterblud. That proves what the one called Urith is involved. Apparently King Merkhan is a bigger fool than Penhda. He couldn't even capture the Esterblud when he had him in his city," said the king.

Satres thought it convenient how Asgurd forgot that the usurpers with the Skool had escaped from Cahmais not long ago.

"How does he know this?" Lyncus spoke up for the first time.

"It seems they have destroyed the village of Kanhan with the Skool. I thought you would be pleased to hear this news Satres. The village was filled with Death Bearers."

The Sacred Overlord nodded. "Of course, I'm pleased that such infidels are gone. They cannot spread their malicious lies when they are no longer alive. My council knows the damage just a few of them have done. This is part of the reason why they support this invasion. It will lead to greater control over the temples in this backcountry area."

Satres paused as he thought on this. "However, the fact that the Skool was used is a problem. No doubt Urith will be seeking out his king. But the destruction of this cult could make him into a hero. There is much turmoil in the lands and those who have the Skool could quickly become the stuff of legends."

"Impossible!" the king barked as he adjusted himself in his saddle, causing his ossane to slow due to the weight of its rider. "The people would never follow these people. They go against the gods. I will not rest until they are destroyed for what they did to my son."

"I understand, but I thought you should know about my concerns," Satres tried to soothe the rising temper of the king. "I merely speculate about the minds of those who pray in the temples. My reports from the *satgerts* tell me the people are looking for help from the gods. If the gods do not calm the many terrible things spreading across the lands, the people will begin to follow someone who appears to have great power."

"What he says makes sense, father. I've heard rumors from my men about unsettling things coming in the night," Lyncus defended his friend. "But it could be used to our advantage as well."

The king was slow at times. However, he understood when his son had an idea that might be useful. "All right, you have something on your mind. What have you come up with?"

"I believe if my king takes over Esterblud then the people will have their new hero. We can take care of the usurpers at our pleasure. We can use the power of the *satgerts* to ensure the people accept this new king," said Lyncus, stroking the neck of his mount. He looked over to Satres and gave him a wink which the king failed to notice. Asgurd was thinking about the advice.

"Your suggestion is a wise one, my son. I think I don't give you enough credit for your quick wit," the king told the warrior. Lyncus only nodded, smiling for his father while he fumed inside. Still, he was grateful that Satres brought up an interesting idea. A king as a hero to the people suited his plans quite well. Even better if a new king became such a hero he thought.

Chapter 9: The Mine

When the sun rose on the third morning of their journey, Oslaf was quite awake. He knelt over the sleeping form of Urith, who finally broke his fever during the night. The nephew was so focused on the great warrior that he did not hear Henther come up behind him.

"You've been awake all night, haven't you?"

Oslaf peered up at her, trying to shield his eyes from the morning glare. He put his finger to his lips as he stood. He took her by the arm and led her a few paces away.

"He's been fighting the fever all night," he whispered. "He seems to be finally resting. I wanted to let him get as much sleep as possible. He's been delirious for too long. I wasn't sure he would recover."

"You do him well. Are you Esterblud's always so caring?" She asked him sarcastically. He could tell by her expression she was needling him.

"No, sometimes we eat our children to appease the gods," His eyes lit up his tired smile. She smiled at him.

"Speaking of eating, I'll get food from the bags for our breakfast. It'll be dried meat and berries again," Henther looked around at the other women sleeping. "It appears the others did not sleep well, either."

"No, I heard Fedelm speak out at one point," Oslaf saw the woman's eyes grow hard at the hakra's name. He placed his hand on her shoulder, and he noticed the woman didn't pull away. "I forgot to thank you for coming along."

She smiled at him, "I had nothing better to do. Besides, I couldn't let you keep traveling alone with those women." She indicated the sleeping forms with her head.

"You have nothing to worry about," he told her. "There was nothing there, and I'm over her."

She patted his hand, turning serious. "I know that your silly man. I'm worried about their visions. You said yourself that the gods are devious. I know you trust the women, but who knows whether they are being led into a trap?" The woman walked away, letting him think on her words.

Urith awoke after the others, feeling weak as a newborn bater. His padded clothes were damp from the fever. He was terribly thirsty as well.

244

The man slowly turned over and sat up, noticing the others gathered near the fire. Mivraa spotted him first. When he asked for water, she grabbed a bag by her foot and quickly covered the few steps to him.

"Are you feeling better?" she asked as he took a deep drink.

"I'm better but weak," he admitted as he tried to fight the slight dizziness he felt. "Give me a bit and we'll see how it goes."

"There's no hurry," Mivraa told him. "We can take our time."

"No, we can't. The Skool is at the mine. I've seen it."

"It can wait," said the goddess.

"No, he's right." Fedelm walked up. "I saw it myself. My father and Dughorm came to me last night, and they are up to something. I can feel it."

"I know I'm not a hakra," said Urith, "but I hope they can come up with more than they showed me. How about some of that heathmead?" He pointed to the bag Fedelm held and the woman handed it to him, warning him that he needed water. The giant warrior grunted before took a large swig. The firm kick from the liquid helped revive him enough to slide on his baudrik belt over his shoulder and put on his sword belt which lay next to him.

"We will leave today, I....," he declared, stopping when he saw the expressions on their faces. "Listen, I only look like a helpless whelp. I've got a bit more left in me. It's only a short ride."

"You need to rest," protested Oslaf, who joined the discussion. "You're as white as the clouds."

"Let's get some food and we can talk," said Urith, holding out his hand to Oslaf, who reluctantly helped him to his feet. The giant slid his shield over his back. Oslaf knew the discussion would be one sided as he knew his uncle too well. He helped the big man over to the fire where Henther handed Urith a large piece of dried meat. Nibbling, at first, the giant warrior quickly grew hungrier as he ate. The conversation consisted of small talk as the others found food for themselves. Holding the piece of meat in his mouth, Urith rose and made his nephew help him toward his ossane. It took him a couple of times finally to lift himself onto the animal. He asked his incredulous nephew for his black helmet which he hooked to his belt.

Satisfied, he made his point to them, he took a large bite out of the meat in his hand for effect, giving them his sneer smile as he slowly set off. "Now, as you pack, I'll scout out our path."

The others looked at each other before it suddenly dawned on them the Esterblud had left them in a scramble to break camp and catch up with him. Mivraa grinned as she watched the formidable human steer his mount onto the trail. He was truly worthy to be a leader of Haligulf, standing next to Heptarc.

For all of his bravado, Urith remained weak, and his mount responded as if it knew, keeping the pace down to a slow trot. The warrior peered across the hilly land, seeing nothing but brown, mostly barren ground intersected with patches of low brush on occasion. Movement far up the hill caught his eye, and he observed the human figure between boulders. It was enough of a glance for Urith to realize someone watched them. However, he decided against doing anything about the spy for the moment as the ossanes of his friends came up the trail from behind.

It had not taken long for the rest of the group to break camp since most of their supplies were already packed. As the collection of animals settled in for the journey, Urith waited a while before the Esterblud told everyone about their spy. Oslaf immediately wanted to confront the person among the boulders, yet Urith urged restraint. It was something that surprised his nephew.

"Whoever is watching us could be a Death Bearer or a spy for our king. Either way, I think we should wait for nightfall after we reach the mines." His face was showing the strain of the travel. "If the *ranqels* are at the mines, the creatures may do our job for us by killing the person I saw during the night. Otherwise, this spy may tip their hand before we get there. Either way, we can capture him when the time is right."

"I don't agree. There's only one of them," said Mivraa. "If we catch them now, we can find out what they are following us for."

Suddenly Fedelm spoke up against Mivraa. "The last time you ran us into a trap. I say we follow cautiously. There's no telling who else might be around." The demigoddess gave the hakra a glare, but the young woman stared back defiantly. Urith just grunted at them.

"Well, we might be able to trap them before the mines," suggested Henther. "The road and terrain might allow an opportunity to grab this person. One person cannot scout ahead for themselves, and it may be possible to circle around them. And we would soon know if others are with the spy."

"We have a natural warrior here," Urith looked impressed as he turned to view the woman riding near Oslaf. "I like that idea. If we can find a place, I suggest Oslaf and Mivraa hold back to trap our prey while I act as the bait. After all, I'm the weak one in our group." He laughed at the amused looks from the group. They never considered the giant warrior might become bait for a trap. Mivraa looked over at Oslaf, who nodded his agreement.

"Make sense to me," said the demigoddess. She turned her attention to Henther as the ossanes continued along the rocky road. "Where did you learn such tactics? This is not something a *docke* learns."

"No, but a daughter of Kirowan would," Henther told them boldly. The shock of her words momentarily stunned the traveling companions enough to bring their ossanes to a stop.

"How is this possible?" asked Urith, his typical growl softened at what he heard.

The woman said nothing, spurring the ossane forward through the ossanes as she took the lead. Her companions looked at each other before slowly following her. It was stunning news that the daughter of a renowned Vulthnal general rode with them. They remained silent for a while as Oslaf spurred his mount to catch her.

"Well, you've shocked us. I assume that was the idea. Now, what?"

"I'm not sure," she conceded. "Do you believe what I tell you?"

"Of course. You've never lied to me before, and I see no reason why you would now," said Oslaf. "But you will need to explain to the others before long. They don't know you as I do."

"I know. Just trust me to do what's right. It is a painful past."

He moved his ossane close to the woman's and placed his hand on her forearm, giving it a squeeze and she smiled at him. She was still unsure what she would tell them since she held so much inside. For some reason, she felt a need for them to learn to trust her. Somehow, it had become important for her to join them, even if she was unsure why.

He released her arm and let his mount drop back with the rest of the group where he tried to calm their concerns. The young Esterblud looked around; taking notice of the area of the open country they rode as the trail continued into the highlands in the distance. He saw his uncle's head nodding from the regular cadence of his mount's steps. Fedelm and Mivraa grew quiet as well when the young Esterblud slowed his mount for them to come alongside.

"She will tell us more when she is ready," he explained to the women. "You will learn she is as trustworthy as you."

Fedelm sighed, "Henther seems to be as remote as your uncle at times." Mivraa nodded slowly in agreement when Oslaf looked at her. The demigoddess put her black hood over her head as shade from the warm sun.

"Maybe, but she fought monsters with me, so she is fearless. What she said is good enough for me," said the young warrior. He looked at Mivraa. "You are probably more alike than you think. I only know parts of her story. What I do understand is she's had more than her share of sorrow."

A sleepy voice from behind them agreed. "If she is the daughter of Kirowan than there is much to know," said Urith. "Her father was one of the greatest of the Vulthnal warriors. I met him before. He was a skilled and fierce warrior." The warrior unconsciously rubbed his scar as he fought off the sleep. "I heard rumors he died after returning to Vulthnal. His family was cruelly treated following his death. It would explain why she ended up where she was."

"So, we're handed yet another riddle," said Fedelm, reflecting upon their journey. "I wonder what else the Fates have in store for us."

"Well, whatever it is, we need to have someone who is a warrior on point," Mivraa said. "Henther may have some experience, however, we cannot assume she has the knowledge of a fighter."

"I'll take the point," said Oslaf, eager to stop the conversation. "Besides, it'll give me more time to be with her." He smiled at the women and spurred his ossane back to Henther. The young warrior was obviously happy to be going back to his companion.

Mivraa looked for a shadow to cross Fedelm's face as the Esterblud rode away. She saw nothing. The demigoddess wanted to believe that the hakra still held some feelings for the young warrior since the attractive woman was growing too close with Urith for her liking. The warrior goddess would not let herself believe she could feel jealousy. And the demigoddess remembered the recent condemnation Fedelm spoke against her. This was something Mivraa could not forget. The goddess did not suffer insults from warriors, let alone a small human woman. With the natural rights of a god, she considered the giant Esterblud the only real match for her when they finished their quest for the Skool. It was an accepted state for the strong to remain with the strong. Until then, Fedelm would remain an ally. But it was becoming apparent the hakra did not understand that Mivraa would determine who remained with Urith.

The fading rays of the late afternoon created deep pockets of shadows between the crevices of boulders which lined the road. The group knew they were getting close to the mines when they came across the first waste tailings that littered either side of the twisting trail. The barren slag piles of gray stood out on the red-brown soil, and soon the gray filled the landscape. Oslaf had come back to the group with Henther, speaking briefly with Urith, who stopped the group.

"We have someone following us, and it appears Oslaf caught sight of a man moving ahead of us at the last turn," he told them. "He thinks we are running into an ambush."

"By whom?" asked Fedelm, "You destroyed the cult."

"We can't be sure of that," said the giant warrior. "Besides, we have many against us. I can't believe I'm saying this." He paused. "I've seen this trail before on my dream. If I'm to believe Dughorm, we must be very close. So, I'm taking the lead."

"Are you up for it?" asked Fedelm.

"We'll soon find out. I'm the bait remember so we'll go in two groups. I'll go in with Mivraa in case it is one of the gods. The rest of you will follow us. Stay out of sight until you can get the advantage on them. I think Mivraa and I can keep them busy." He gave them his death grin, reaching down to Oslaf's saddle to get a spear. He looped it over his shoulder.

"I'm not sure how much it will do to a god, but I'll try to give someone heartburn. I think my shield might do that." He winked at Mivraa. She gave him a wink back as she noticed how sick he still looked. She decided she would have to stand up for both of them.

"I only wish I had some more weapons. Let's go," said the demigoddess, pulling her spear from out of her black shawl. She turned her mount up the trail and looked back at Urith.

"Keep back enough to let us get their interest," reminded Urith to his nephew. Oslaf nodded, watching the Esterblud and demigoddess go forward into the trap. They waited until the two were out of sight.

It was not long after they traveled along the up sloping trail before the two lead riders came upon twin large blue-gray boulders which appeared as a natural gateway. They pushed their mounts past the rocks as Urith mentioned that it looked to be a perfect spot for an ambush. Mivraa agreed, intently watching for movement in the rocks and shadows that wrapped around them. The trail opened to a fork in the path, one on the right leading up a steep angle upward and the other heading around off around the mound. Urith guessed this constricted trail must have been used by the stranger that Oslaf spotted earlier. He took the steep uphill trail and Mivraa pulled in behind him. She felt someone was watching from behind. Her quick glance revealed nothing. As if he read her mind, Urith turned and whispered to her.

"I get the sense the net is closing on us." With his words, he put on his helmet and slid his shield over his forearm. Mivraa put on her golden helmet as well while making sure her spear was available for quick retrieval. The mounts continued up the narrow path which opened into a wide piece of flat land as they crested the ridge. Suddenly, they could hear a low rumble which sounded like thunder. The animals reared back in fear as both rider and beast felt the ground began to move under them. Jumping down from their mounts, the two warriors grabbed their weapons while they tried to control their ossanes. The ground began to shake violently, and the beasts went into a full panic. Trying to move was nearly impossible with the ground shuddering in rolling waves under their feet. The soil beneath them vibrated so quickly before they knew it, the dirt turned into brown liquid, swallowing the humans and ossanes. Struggling to remain upright, the human warriors were soon up to their waists in the hardening earth while their mounts had their long legs pinned below their elongated bodies. The screams of the ossanes pierced the riders' ears, so loud they could hardly hear their own cries to each other.

Suddenly the quake stopped, and the pinned humans remained stuck up to their waist, unable to pull themselves from the ground. As they struggled, they did not see the three gods of the Sky Realm walk forth with an air of triumph in their arrogant manner.

"As I predicted my mother. These humans are quite harmless when the elements are used against them," said Ecarca as he kissed Unis on the cheek while they walked arm in arm to their prisoners. Uugor laughed at the struggling humans when he emerged from the shadows nearby.

"Since the others must have taken the other trail, we'll let Wurms lead their allies to this spot and we can finish them off my sons," Unis turned her eyes to the Esterblud. "Your helmet may protect you from human weapons, but it is of no use against my thoughts. Don't worry, I have something special in mind for you."

Urith focused on pulling up the Shield of Skool, which was partially stuck in the ground at his side. Suddenly his mind went blank as the goddess took control, sending him into convulsions as she sought out his darkest fears and secrets. The goddess laughed at what she found inside her prey, her mind sending the man all terrible things she planned for him. Inside his mind, she whispered how she would make him kill all of his friends slowly before she took the Skool from him. To emphasize her control, she made him turn his head to watch as Ecarca knelt next to Mivraa, who desperately tried to stab at him with her spear.

"My son, you can do what you want with the half-god, just make it quite painful for the others to watch when they are captured," said Unis. The earth god gave an evil smile and placed his war scythe tip at her chest, giving it a quick jab. The metal blade easily cut through the armor she wore, entering her flesh slightly and Mivraa cried out in pain.

"Damn *cawald*," thought Urith to Unis. "Come try that on me, you worthless *docke*." The goddess looked at the Esterblud warrior and began to send searing waves of torment and pain into the human's brain. The giant Esterblud's body shook with violent spasms, kicking up the shield attached to his arm as he flailed about. The goddess promised him that her son would flay the human warrior alive for such disrespect to her.

Suddenly, there was the yell of the Esterblud war cry as Oslaf charged into the area followed by Fedelm and Henther. The young Esterblud rushed his mount at the surprised earth god who sprung up at the onrushing animal. Ecarca was spreading his arms as he brought forth his power over the land. Again the land below the ossanes rumbled and quaked, but Oslaf was able to let his spear fly at the deity. The point of the weapon struck the god's knee between the bright armor he wore. The sudden yell from her son caused Unis to break away from her fixed attention on Urith and the earthquake immediately stopped. The Esterblud warrior wasted little time as he directed the front of the Shield of Skool toward the earth god and Unis.

"*Da Umca Mivwar*," yelled Urith. In the next instant, a blinding light shot forth from the shield and struck the Ecarca with its full force as the earth god tried to pull the spear from his leg. His chiseled body was enveloped in flames, and his screeching could be heard over the roar of the Skool. The blast hurled the deity high into the air, tumbling over the huge boulders and falling out of sight. Both Unis and Uugor took part of the explosion, which knocked them back several paces. Unis landed against one of the large rocks, sliding to the ground. However, Uugor, the sea god bounced off the rock and quickly attempted to impale Oslaf with his harpoon spear. The young Esterblud was barely able to avoid his death by swinging up his shield which shattered from the force of the god's weapon. Oslaf was thrown off his mount by the force, landing near the struggling Mivraa. Springing up with his sword in hand, the young Esterblud began a fierce battle with the god.

Fedelm and Henther slid off their ossanes at the start of the quake, each pulled a short sword and started racing to help their comrades buried in the ground. Out of the corner of her eye, Henther caught sight of a blonde man in armor running from the shadows to attack Oslaf. She veered her body into his path just in time to slam into the man. The impact sent both of them sprawling across the ground. Falling painfully down on her shoulder, the woman yelled a warning to Oslaf, who immediately backed toward her to shield her. Her right shoulder felt like it was on fire, forcing Henther to use her other hand, awkwardly holding the short sword. Wurms quickly got back to his feet and charged her, but the young Esterblud saw this from the corner of his eye, and he sprinted away from a surprised Uugor. Oslaf ran the few steps to take the fight to Wurms. The god and human crashed into each other in front of the woman in a desperate struggle.

While Henther was helping Oslaf, Fedelm got to Mivraa first. She struggled with the demigoddess trying to pull her from the solidified quicksand around her. After several attempts, she dug and pulled until the demigoddess forced herself from the hole. Oblivious to her wound, Mivraa grabbed her silver spear, and immediately launched herself toward Wurms, who saw her coming. He broke from his fight with Oslaf, letting Uugor rejoin the battle against the young Esterblud.

"You have fun killing the humans," yelled the demigod to his half-brother god. "Mivraa is mine." Wurms ran at his mortal enemy with his twin bladed spear in hand.

Fedelm rushed over to help Urith out of his hole, who was aided by the blast of the Skool, which loosened the dirt around him. The woman pulled on the warrior's tunic, helping him make the final push on to the top of the ground. Once he got out of the trap, the giant Esterblud pulled up his Clovel Sword and began moving toward Wurms.

Then, he stopped. The warrior suddenly turned, lifted his arm and attacked Fedelm. The hakra screamed, just dodging a vicious swipe of the Clovel Sword at her head. Even behind the helmet mask, the woman could see the man's eyes were wide, his mind lost in a sort of trance. Fedelm circled widely around the warrior as the big man attacked her and the woman tried to defend herself with her short sword. The Esterblud sought to draw in closer, and she could see he would slightly hesitate with each step, struggling inside to regain control. Behind them, Fedelm saw Unis staring directly at the warrior trying to kill her. Realizing the goddess had not been affected by the blast, she suddenly raced at the goddess to strike her down. But the goddess saw her coming, and she sent the giant warrior into Fedelm's path. He tackled her near the feet of the goddess, quickly getting on top of her. Fedelm struggled to escape. However, his bulk and strength made it impossible for her to move as he put his massive arm around her neck. She could feel his hot breath on her ear, and she began to panic, forgetting her amulet, as he slowly began to squeeze. Rising to his feet, he held her like a rag doll with one arm locked around the throat and the other pinning her arms at her torso. His face smiling with enjoyment at her struggles as Unis stepped up to meet them. The goddess instructed the giant Esterblud slowly crush the young woman in his arms.

Several paces away, Mivraa and Wurms were in their own death match. Seasoned fighters from their involvement in Kamin battles, they were circling around, each looking for an advantage. Wurms carried a similar spear as his sister, and they locked on each other with hate filling their faces.

"You may have gotten away from the *ranqels*," the demigod said to his sister, "but I'm going to do much worse to you."

"You talk like a man, but you kiss an unworthy god's ass each night," she replied, mocking him. "Besides, I've seen your little *calward* in action. Now I'm going to cut it off and stuff it down your throat."

As expected, he rushed her at the insult, and she quickly tried to push her spear point into his armored chest. Unfortunately for her, the blade glanced off the breast plate, and he was able to counter her momentary advantage. They broke from the fight and circled again. Taking a stutter step, Wurms attacked and struck the demigoddess full in the shoulder, pushing the spear tip through the mail. Mivraa whipped around the back of her spear and caught him in the helmet, the metal striking metal sound barely heard above the din of the other fighting. Wurms backed off to clear the fog from his head. Then, he noticed Ecarca limping forward as he crept to rejoin the battle. The wounded god, scorched from the Skool blast, let his desire for revenge overrule his injuries. Able to retrieve his war scythe from the ground, he slowly crept into position behind Mivraa. Getting closer while Wurms kept the warrior goddess busy, Ecarca searched for the right moment when he would strike. The god was skillfully using the gathering shadows to his advantage as the sun quickly fell behind the mountain.

Mivraa spotted a quick glance from Wurms at something behind her. Feeling the tug of her sixth sense, the woman faked a lunge toward the demigod in front of her, suddenly dodging to the side as she turned to meet the charge of Ecarca's long pole weapon. The surprised man was unable to react in time as the warrior goddess used her razor-edged spear to slice into the demigod's shoulder. Letting the man's momentum push him by, she jumped behind him, pushing Ecarca into Wurms. The gods collided, knocking each to the ground.

Mivraa caught a glimpse of the talisman Wurms was wearing around his neck, exposed by his fall. Memories of vision suddenly washed over her as she recognized the amulet and its power. Almost in slow motion, she looked over to see Urith slowly squeezing the life out of Fedelm, with his death's grin on his face while Unis gleefully watched on. Her dream became her reality, and Mivraa suddenly became enraged. She immediately attacked Wurms, who was trying to lift himself from the ground. He attempted to fend off her ferocious assault with his spear, but the woman kept the advantage, raining down blows on him with both sides of her spear. Each blow she inflicted was in retribution for each flashback of pain and humiliation she endured. The demigoddess found an opening when Wurms tried to stand. Mivraa faked a move one way, and when the demigod struck out at her, the warrior goddess brought down the long, razor edge of her spear across his chest. Before Wurms was able to counter, the goddess of Haligulf slid the point of the spear into his groin. She smiled as he screamed, carefully twisting the spear to inflict more pain, reliving some of the abuse she endured from him on the mountain. She pulled out the spear as the man dropped to his knees trying to stop the bleeding. When he looked up, he saw Mivraa coldly smile and with a sickening flick of her weapon, Wurms lost his head.

The bloody head of the demigod shot across the ground, landing at the feet of the wounded Ecarca, who was trying to attack again. The god was unable to slow down, tripping over the head and falling face first on the ground. Fortunately for the god of earth, Mivraa paid no attention at her advantage as she swiftly scooped up the amulet, along with dirt and blood as she raced toward Urith. Hoping she wasn't too late, Mivraa could see the bulging eyes and blue face of the dying hakra. The warrior goddess raised her silver spear and sent it hurtling toward Unis. The sky goddess was so intent on controlling the giant Esterblud she failed to see the spear coming until it was too late. The weapon struck her in the shoulder, knocking the goddess on her back. Urith immediately released Fedelm, who fell to the ground in a heap. The Esterblud instantly dropped to his knees and tried to revive the woman. Fedelm turned to her side coughing and wrenching, trying to catch her breath. Urith looked up as Mivraa joined them, his face showing a mixture of horror and disgust at what he nearly did. She handed him the amulet covered in the blood of Wurms.

"I saw this in my vision. Now put it on and remember the words of Dughorm," she told him. "I'm going after that pitshog for what he did to me." She turned back to find Ecarca, who ran into the shadows. The woman ran near the boulders looking for him. Momentarily stunned, Urith quickly put the talisman over his head and around his neck with the other. He picked up the Shield of Skool and the Clovel Sword to begin looking for Unis in the deepening shadows.

As the others were fighting their battles, Oslaf and Henther had their hands full with the Kamin god of the sea. Uugor was shaking off their human weapons like raindrops striking a rock. Unused to the techniques of the humans, nevertheless, the god felt no fear as his armor could not be penetrated by massive attacks from the young Esterblud's weapon. Worse, the harpoon the sea god used sliced through the Esterblud's armor in several places, the crimson spots of the man's blood showing on the padding. Henther was acting as more of a diversion since she was not able to get close enough to do any real damage. As the battle went on, Uugor could tell the humans were tiring. He smiled savagely as he struck another blow at the warrior and took a glancing shot from the fighter's sword.

"Once I finish you off, I'll make sure your spirit is used as my personal slave. Then, I think I'll use your little woman to mate with before I feed her to the *ranqels*," the god cackled at his words.

The words enraged the tiring Oslaf, and it gave him an inspiration, recalling a trick from his uncle. Dodging to the inside of the fearsome harpoon when the deity lurched forward, the Esterblud aimed the tip of his sword up under the helmet mask of the god. His aim was true, and the tip plunged into the eye of the god. Unfortunately, at the same time, the god was able to jab his short sword into the belly of Oslaf. Uugor screamed from the pain, the echoes filling the area as he pulled away, his hand over the wounded eye that streamed his blood. The young Esterblud staggered back, his eyes wide with the realization of his own injury. Falling to his knees, he observed the sea god quickly back away into the shadows while Henther ran over to help the Esterblud.

With the dark blanket of the night covering him, Ecarca ran out of sight. Mivraa, unable to get to help Oslaf in time, ran after the sea god, but her quick search found no trail. She went be wounded Oslaf, disgusted she was unable to finish off her god brother. The demigoddess joined Henther, who was trying to see the full injury struggling to get Oslaf to remove his hands from his bleeding belly.

"We need to get a fire started to see how badly he's wounded," Henther told the demigoddess. Mivraa immediately pulled her tribolrocks which gave off a green glow. It helped them see the extent of Oslaf's wound as Henther ripped off a part of her robe to help staunch the flow as Mivraa kept watch for any more attacks from the wounded gods.

Barely seen in the failing light, Unis pulled herself up to a sitting position on a rock staring in amazement at the wound in her shoulder. Her astonishment at the damage the weapon had done to her and the other sky gods left her in shock. While the wound would not kill her, it was painful. However, she had no time to regret the lack of the Exyts Spring water. As she sat there, her eyes turned a glowing red as Urith was nearly upon her. The Esterblud warrior could feel her trying to enter his mind again.

"*Calduworm Actus Umbara,*" he said aloud and felt a surge of energy rush through him. Suddenly the woman's thoughts disappeared from his mind. Then, the sky goddess realized she now saw death in front of her with a sneering grin. The goddess of the heavens was unable to control the massive human who would surely kill her.

"Prepare for your death," Urith growled at her.

"You wouldn't dare harm a sky god," Unis stood up to the human, still perplexed that she could not control him. Urith stopped suddenly, and she saw an evil grin cross his face. Before she could react, he slammed is fist into her face, sending her to the ground. Senseless, the goddess felt the man rolled her over, face in the dirt while he penned one of her arms behind her.

"Being a god, no doubt you will recover from your wound. But now you will be my hostage, and if you try to enter the minds of any of my friends, I'll take your head off." He growled close to her ear. She was about to say something, and he twisted hard on the arm, causing her to cry out.

"Shut your mouth or I'll mount your head upon a pike for me to show my king." He pulled off his baudrik belt and tied her hands tightly behind her back. He used his sword to cut off part of her elegant robe which he used to tie her legs together. Finally, he cut off another long strand of her robe to trussed her hands and ankles together behind her. While a deity would be much stronger than a human, he was sure this goddess was not going anywhere. For one last measure, he stuffed a last bit of the robe-cloth into her mouth. She was livid at her treatment but unable to stop it. It was a humiliation she vowed not to forget.

"You will remain quiet. It will give you time to feel what it's like to be powerless," he told her as he picked her well-endowed body up and threw her over his shoulder. He walked toward the green glow which he recognized as tribolrocks of Mivraa. "Make no mistake, you *scunce*," the Esterblud continued talking to her. "I still want your head to display in front of Duwdamon. I've grown tired of the gods and your ways. Be warned, if you make me angry again, I might give you to a bunch of warriors to be used as their slave. Better yet, I might have you used in target practice for their spears." He could not see the bitter, frightened rage on the goddess' face. For the first time, a human took a goddess as his prisoner.

Ecarca had seen the giant Esterblud capture his mother and despite his initial urge to try to help, he reconsidered. Still wounded from the Skool and unable to use his powers over the earth, he racked his brain for a solution as he watched the human humiliate his mother. Suddenly he thought of a way he could use this to his advantage. He would return to Duwdamon and have his father extract vengeance upon the humans.

Such a violation of a sky god meant that his father could not allow the humans to exist as a partner anymore. He knew his father would inflict a terrible revenge on the humans, and he would be by his father's side to help. Skool or not, the earth god had little doubt that his father would know of a way to defeat this god weapon in the hands of the human. He consoled himself that the humans had the Fates on their side, yet he knew the tide would soon turn. Then, he would use humans and extract a gruesome revenge. And the earth god had something special in store for the Kamin world when he healed himself at the Exyts Spring. He watched his mother on the shoulder of the human and overheard the man's words about using her as a slave. That alone would bring the heavens down upon the world when Duwdamon heard this. The earth god smiled to himself as he left his mother to her fate and hobbled back to the lellowtere tree to return to the Sky Realm.

At the same time, Uugor was struggling through the shadows of the boulders, unable to see well in the dark and holding his hand over the devastated eye that still sent waves of crushing pain into his mind. The sea god was confused where the rest of his god family was located. He whispered to his brother and mother as he worked his way up the mountain. He assumed they would move to higher ground to regroup. Suddenly, in the distance, he saw something move, and he had to wipe his uninjured eye to confirm what he saw. It was Alrpan. He saw her wave to him and turn away, her nude body moving quickly up a trail toward the mine where the *ranqels* slept. Of course, he decided as he followed her barely able to see her shadow in the darkness. She must have watched the battle and came down to help him. Suddenly he lost sight of her. Then, he heard her whistle, and he continued to follow. The slope increased, and he could see a large dark hole where the entrance to the main Neerwah mine lay exposed. He saw movement at the opening as a small form went inside. It was good she was taking him to safety, he told himself. Perhaps the underworld goddess could help restore his eye. After all, she had been able to restore herself from the damage inflicted by the Skool.

Soon, the god of the sea topped the crest of the slope and slowly entered the mine. It was pitch black, and he whispered her name. The god heard a rustling echo repeat her name, and he continued on. He suddenly saw a green glow as a tribolrock lit up several paces away. Confidence growing, he walked toward the light where he saw the shadow of a familiar figure, her face hidden in the darkness with red eyes glowing. When he got close, he saw her face, cold as the polished stone of the underworld floor.

"I need your help, Alrpan. The human with the Skool scattered us," he told her. "I know you were able to rebuild yourself. Teach me how to restore myself." The deity pleaded with the other.

"The Skool didn't do that," said the disguised Kriell, mimicking Alrpan's voice. "I saw you struck by the young Esterblud. You are not worthy to be god if you cannot defeat a single human."

Uugor came closer to the underworld goddess. "It was a lucky strike," the sea deity told Kriell. "While we were surprised by their skill, I took care of the young Esterblud. He will be joining you soon. But you saw the power of the Skool and the damage upon my brother. All I ask is that you help me. Remember that I have helped you so many times. I took your words of punishment for Mivraa to my father."

The goddess placed her cold hand on the cheek of the sky god and nodded slowly. "Yes, I will give you what you need. Just relax and close your eye." She removed his helmet, dumping it on the hard packed cave floor as she licked her lips in anticipation.

Uugor did as he was told and Kriell, in the form of Alrpan, spoke soothing words of comfort. Her feet suddenly changed into tentacles which slowly worked their way around the sea god and quickly raced up the ankles of the sea god. It took several seconds for Uugor to realize that something was amiss as he felt the soothing appendages of the new underworld god slid around his thighs. When the god opened his uninjured eye, he no longer saw the beautiful vision of Alrpan. Instead, he was face to face with a black globule that was quickly wrapping around him like a snake around its prey. Unable to move, the sky god tried to call out. However, he could not breathe from the viselike hold the gelatinous blob attached around his chest. Soon the slimy black covering enveloped his head. In the dim green glow providing a backlight, the body of Uugor slowly dissolved in the nebulous form of Kriell, another god spirit stolen for use by the powerful Guardian.

~~~

Below the mine, Urith used the last of his strength to carry the goddess over to his friends who were gathered around the wounded Oslaf. Still not fully recovered from his wounds and fever, the giant Esterblud felt his leg burning like fire when he roughly sat the tied up bundle from his shoulder on the ground. He had fought on adrenaline alone, and the energy left him. An overwhelming need to sleep struck him.

"How is Oslaf?" he asked in the yellow campfire light as he sat next to the goddess.

"He's doing well, but it's a deep wound. Luckily, I could smell nothing from the area, so I don't think the harpoon went into the intestines," whispered Fedelm, who came over to look at what Urith brought with him. "Henther is quite skilled, and he is resting now."

She saw Urith look over to Mivraa, using a rag to wipe the gore from her armor. "Don't worry, she wasn't severely injured, the blood comes from Wurms," Fedelm continued her assessment. "We were able to get the ossanes out the traps. None of them appear to have injured themselves in the panic, so we still have a way out of the mountains." She raised her voice slightly, pointing at the bound god. "Why did you keep that thing alive? What are you doing?"

"We have a hostage and some bargaining power, I hope." He slapped the goddess on her rear for effect. The bound woman jerked at the humiliation of her predicament. Her godly rage grew as she kept thinking of her revenge upon the Esterblud. For now, she was forced to bide her time.

"Don't be too sure about that," said Mivraa entered the discussion with a grim smile on her face, flecks of dried blood covered her. "Duwdamon will not be easily persuaded to do anything he doesn't believe is in his best interest. Why do you think he sent her out here? He thought her power over the mind would allow her to control the Skool. If not, he would be happy let Unis perish. There is no love known in the Sky Realm."

"This is may be true. However, it is better to bargain from strength. We've been following these worthless creatures around for too long."

Above them, Mivraa suddenly heard a familiar sound of wings, gathering in the distance. "I know that sound. The *ranqels* are coming," she told them.

"I nearly forgot about them. Gather around Oslaf," said Urith as he struggled to his feet with the aid of Fedelm. As he put on his helmet again, Mivraa asked about Unis. She wanted to leave her as prey for the beasts coming, but the Esterblud would not hear of it. "We need to keep our hostage somewhat undamaged since we have no healing water."

Mivraa reluctantly agreed, dragging the helpless goddess over to the fire, taking some satisfaction watching the woman struggle as her blue hued skin scraped across the loose rocks. Urith took a quick look down at his nephew who was struggling to rise. He wanted to fight, forcing Henther to keep him down. Urith placed a comforting hand on Oslaf's shoulder. "We have a defense against these monsters by using the amulet," he told them. "Oslaf, I'll call you if I need you. Rest yourself for now." Henther looked up, and Urith could see the thank you in her eyes.

As if they heard the humans talking around the fire, the flapping sound of wings grew stronger. Urith quickly told them of his vision and plan. They would remain in a circle while he would use the power of the new amulet that Mivraa took from the body of Wurms. "We have this large boulder behind us and others on either side. I want to force the monsters to come together as a group in front of us," said the giant warrior. He told them he didn't know how long the spell would last so if the beasts broke through, they must be ready to use the spears to drive them away.

As the leathery monsters descended upon them from the mine, only the vague outlines could be seen in the night sky above them. The movement could be heard, and then several of the humanoid beasts swooped down trying to use their power clawed feet to grab at the people around the fire. When Urith finally saw them, he yelled out the words of the spirits.

"*Calduworm Actus Umbara*," said the Esterblud and immediately an invisible force surrounded him and those near him. Three of the *ranqels* tried to land upon the humans, striking a transparent wall and bouncing away like rocks skipping off the water. They screeched and flapped off a short distance away and tried again with the same result. Two more of the beasts landed nearby, beady eyes watching them. The other came down in the dark, out of sight, and soon the group could hear a screech and the creatures watching them run into the night where the body of Wurms lay. Soon there were more screeches and Mivraa understood.

"They are gathering around the body of Wurms and signaling for others to join them," she told them. "I thought they only went after the living." She turned to Urith. "Here's your chance. Give them some time and more of those filthy things will come to the body. Then you can destroy them at one time." The fierceness in her expression showed her desire for revenge upon the underworld beasts.

"Do you want to join me for this?" he asked her, although he doubted she would have stayed with the others. She looked at him like he was a fool and he just gave her a dumb grin. Urith pulled off his defensive talisman from Wurms and gave it to Fedelm.

"You should be able to keep the others safe with this until we get back," said the warrior. "Keep an eye on Oslaf, he needs to rest." Fedelm agreed, telling Urith to take care of himself. She nodded at Mivraa, who was looking into the night when she said it. It was evident the hakra still did not fully trust the demigoddess yet. Urith turned back to Mivraa. "Come on, let's finish them off," he said as the two warriors pushed into the night toward the sound of ripping flesh.

Several steps into the darkness, Mivraa reached out to stop the Esterblud. "I hear more coming," she whispered. Before long, they heard more of the beasts coming and from the sound, they would soon be overwhelmed with the *ranqels*. Pausing until as the noise quieted, the two moved forward several paces. They stopped when they could make out the dim outline of the monsters fighting among themselves over the remains of the demigod. Despite her hatred for Wurms, Mivraa shivered in remembrance while watching the monsters rip apart the body. She whispered over to the giant next to her. "Destroy them now."

Urith pushed forward the Shield of Skool, pointing at the group. He said the words and the blast that shot forth from the shield temporarily blinded the two warriors as he tried to focus the beam back and forth on anything that had wings. The white light blasted into the group of *ranqels* sending the monsters into a dusty oblivion. Their bodies evaporated into the night, the ashes scattering to the wind after the explosion stopped. He covered the area with the death ray, and suddenly it finished, leaving an uncanny quiet over the area. Only the breathing of Urith and Mivraa could be heard in the stillness.

After a while, the Esterblud pushed himself up from the kneeling position, his leg now stiffening on him. He could feel the pain returning, and he knew he needed to rest, his body still feeling the fever. He felt Mivraa move past him, and he asked where she was going. "I'm going to check on the body," she said. The demigoddess pulled her tribolrock to light the way, walking over to the area where she killed her rival and found nothing. The body was destroyed along with the monsters. But she felt no pity for the loss of a brother, only a smoldering revenge that still burned inside.

On her way back to Urith, the goddess tripped over something. At first, she wondered if it was Wurm's head before she saw the outline of a long pole in the green light. Bending over, she grabbed the war scythe left by Ecarca and decided she would keep the weapon as a trophy, thrusting the shaft into the ground a couple of times to get a feel of the armament. Surprisingly balanced, she flipped it around a bit and wondering why she never saw Ecarca use such a weapon before. She put the scythe over her shoulder and joined Urith, who looked pale, even in the green glow of her light. She showed him the bright silver blade, telling him of her discovery. He paid little attention, his mind on something else. She sat the weapon next to his shield as she said they should return to the camp.

"No," said the warrior. "We must go to the mine and make sure we have destroyed the *ranqels*. Otherwise, this fight will be for nothing. We don't know how many are left, and we need to make sure those beasts are stopped from attacking more people."

"Quit acting like a hero. We should wait until the morning," said Mivraa. "Ambush them like we expected to do this morning. Remember, the visions seem to show the mine is the place of the next part of the Skool."

Urith nodded. "I agree, but I'm going up to that mine," said the Esterblud firmly. "I've had enough of this, and I'll finish it tonight. You can stay or go, but this will be done now. All I ask is your tribolrocks."

Mivraa sighed as she pulled out a few more of the glowing rocks for Urith. He took them and placed his hand on her shoulder. "Listen, any other time I would agree that your plan is smarter than what I'm saying. But I'm telling you I'm finished with these gods. It's time to destroy a gateway. I don't give an ossanes ear for whether that damn Skool piece is inside the mine. I'll use what I have to close every gateway on Kamin."

She watched him hobbling away, surprised he knew about the shaft being a gateway. The goddess was also shocked about his words concerning the Skool, but she was reluctantly proud of his words. She started up the dark path, following the green glow of his light.

It took longer than the pair thought when they finally reached the entrance to the mine. The opening was nothing more than a large hole burrowed out of a solid wall of stone. While they decided that all of the *ranqels* were probably destroyed by the Skool blast earlier, each putting on their helmet just in case they found more than they bargained for. Mivraa was now leading the way with Urith trying to keep up with his limping gait. She stopped momentarily before entering the blackness, her green lights disappearing out of his sight for a while. As Urith went in, he thought he heard the echoing shuffling sound, and suddenly Mivraa was running past him.

"That place is filled them. Get out of here," she cried as she pushed him away from the entrance. From the dim green glow, he could see the black winged creatures moving forward on their hands and legs, their monster beaks opening to reveal a white mouth as they made the hissing sound which seemed strangely similar to a snake. Urith tried to run away, but one of the creatures was too fast, landing upon the warriors back as it tried to use its massive dark gray beak to strike at the man's neck. The Esterblud flipped the beast off of him, swiftly pulling his sword and turned to defend himself from the others swarming out of the cavern. Urith brought up his shield in time to ward off another *ranqel* trying to slice at him with its claws using powerful legs and arms. The wood of the shield held and the beast was suddenly sent backward by an electrical bolt from the Skool that flashed momentarily in the night.

Mivraa joined Urith with her spear slicing into the first monster that attacked. She continued to pull him back between jabs with her spear, yelling for him to get out of the mouth of the mine. The Esterblud backed away, realizing they would be quickly overwhelmed unless he used the power of the Skool. Above the screeches and hissing coming from the mouth of the tunnel, he yelled for Mivraa to back away when he said the spell. He did not wait for her reply as he moved back several paces and thrust the front of his shield directly toward the mine entrance.

His words, *"Calduworm Actus Umbara,"* could be heard above the creatures' din and Mivraa shielded her eyes, still backing away and trying to remain upright on the narrow trail. The blinding white light turned blue, and the blast unexpectedly pushed back against the giant warrior holding the shield. He nearly lost control of the weapon as a concentrated furnace of light and fire struck the monsters. Anything in the path of the light immediately disintegrated and the ranqels pouring out of the tunnel were lost in the light. The huge trail of white fire coming from the Skool blasted into the tunnel and across the rocks at the top of the entrance, sending down massive boulders to crush those monsters still trying to get out of the cave.

However, the massive landslide started by the Skool came tumbling closer to the two humans who were rapidly backing away from the area. Urith was having a difficult time controlling the shield from the recoil of streaming fire and electricity. Even his massive arms and body could barely keep the shield in control. Something had increased the power of the Skool into a genuinely terrifying weapon capable of slicing through rock.

Finally, the light went out, and they could hear the mountain, continuing to come down on the mine combined with the screams of those monsters who were dying under the avalanche of rocks. Urith could not make out the path of the dust the swirled around him, but he could see the green tribolrocks of Mivraa, and he moved closer to her. Together they continued to back away until they felt they were a safe distance away.

"Well, that's one way to do it," Mivraa was trying to catch her breath as she frantically searched around in the night for any of the monsters that might have survived. "What happened?" she asked. "I swear that was even stronger than the time earlier."

Urith said nothing as he was looking over the Skool on the front of his shield. Even in the dim green light of the tribolrock he held, he could see the silver metal disc had filled in with another piece. It was too dark to see the details, so he turned the shield to her and told Mivraa what had happened. She came up to see the sight with her green light.

"Somehow it appears we have another piece of the Skool. We'll check it out when we get back to the camp," he told her. "And we will have to check this area out when sunlight comes. I don't hear those monsters anymore, so they are either dead or trapped."

"Like I said, that was one way to do it," she repeated, appearing slightly stunned by what she had witnessed. The power Urith held was both breathtaking and tempting. The goddess came next to the warrior, and he put his arm over her shoulder as she guided them back to the camp.

Chapter 10: Going Home

East of the mines in the city of Eran, the overlord of Esterblud was spending that late-night listening to the arguments of his advisors in the vast hall of his castle. Frantic word had reached him about the Cahmais invasion coming from the south, and he grew tired of the back and forth from his ministers and advisors. King Penhda sat upon his dark brown throne, his feelings growing as dark and twisted as the spiral engravings that ran along the arms of the chair. He ran his hands through his long gray hair in exasperation.

"Enough of this bickering," roared the leader suddenly over the din of competing voices. The room went silent as the outraged king pointed to Brihar, the head of the Gramcle tribe, the rippled muscle of his massive forearm tensed in anger. "Gather as many warriors as you can find and have them on the road to Gramcan before the next nightfall. You must cut off the Aberffraw scum before they surround the city."

"But we must gather as one force, my lord. The spies are telling us that the Aberffraw army is as many as the leaves," said Brihar. "I haven't enough warriors to stop such a force."

The gray leader of the Esterblud kingdom scowled at the mild rebuke. However, he trusted the man standing before him as loyal, so he kept his temper. Brihar was a renowned leader of the Esterblud tribes. Unlike many of the warriors who led their clans, the small, slight man was deadly quick and smart. Known for his fierce temper and battle skills, he became a leader through sheer will and determination.

"You will not be alone. You will be joined by myself and the rest of the *Geniht*. We will gather the fighters from my tribe along with way. The Eranis tribe will fight with you, and we will be enough to handle the Aberffraw. Now go and meet us at the Tibra River crossing."

The man bowed and quickly exited the grand hall, his boot steps echoing in the hushed room. The rest of the king's entourage turned back to the king. A short, round man dress in an elegant red robe rose to address Penhda.

"What of Eran and your fortress here?" asked Feeral, the king's royal hakra. "My visions show a threat from where the north winds blow will come into the lands."

"No need to worry, my old friend. I've received no news from the towns along the border with Eernicia," the king assured him. "Besides, the Eernician warriors remain close to their king as you saw in the messages from our diplomats in Damicia. We have the Esterblud tribe between the border and this fortress. No army could cross the Neewar Mountains without me knowing about it."

"Perhaps it's not an army?" suggested the hakra. "The rumors about the Skool and the man who carries it are spreading throughout the temples. It is said that the Sacred Overlord and King Asgurd are searching for it. If either person gets it, then all of Kamin would be threatened.

"Have you not been listening? Both men are said to be among the warriors invading our land from the south. I have a real fight coming from Cahmais," said the king, his patience growing thin. "It is not an illusion about a mythical talisman, but real iron blades and sharpened spear tips my warriors must face."

The king could see his hakra was unconvinced. The man remained quiet, sitting down on the bench where the *satgerts* and skalds quietly whispered among themselves. It was clear they shared the religious leaders' suspicion. Penhda had little patience for such weakness, and his brow wrinkled. He leaned over to whisper to his son, Alcarlic, who nodded before leaving his side. Another advisor spoke up, telling the king that the wagons for their journey were being loaded overnight and would be ready in the morning. As the king nodded his approval, his son, dressed in the green tunic of the Geniht, went to the far end of the room where he spoke with others dressed in the same colors. The group of warriors spoke among themselves before fanning out among other advisors. When they sat next to the advisors and hakras, their presence made it clear to the others around the long tables that any questions which undercut the king's wisdom were not allowed. The room quickly grew silent from the intimidation. The overlord smiled at the silence, and he told them that he expected the fighters to be mounted at dawn for their journey south.

"Know this," said the king in a rousing voice, looking across the room, "I don't care if the so-called Sacred Overlord joins this rabble, we will drive the Aberffraw scum from our lands." There were loud claps of agreement from hands striking the tables along with yells of encouragement when he rose to leave the hall. Several of the older warriors gathered next to him, escorting their leader while displaying their undying loyalty to all in the corridor. The rest of the combined leadership of Esterblud, Eranis, and Gramcle tribes that made up the Esterblud kingdom gathered in smaller groups to discuss their plans. The king would have his warriors, and they would begin sending their men against the Cahmais invasion. King Penhda expected nothing less and those in the hall would cooperate.

Feeral stopped Alcarlic momentarily, ensuring that the warrior was reminded of the hakra's loyalty to his father. He told the eldest son of Penhda that his visions were showing him a growing threat to the king, and he wanted to make clear this threat was not coming from King Asgurd. Alcarlic gave him a careful look before speaking.

"We seem to have threats from all around us according to your information. But the king cannot follow visions when we have a real enemy pushing into our lands," said the warrior.

"You have threats within as well," Feeral took the large man by the arm, leading him away for more privacy. When he was sure they were out of earshot, he continued. "I've received word from one of our loyal *satgerts* who was driven out of the village of Kanhan by the Death Bearers. He sent me a message from villagers who are spreading tales of a giant Esterblud in the Neewar Mountains. The warrior appears to have the Skool."

Alcarlic turned with interest at his words. "Are you telling me Urith is returning home?" he asked.

"I'm not sure," the round man admitted. "But who else could it be? We have all heard the many tales coming to us concerning his travels across Kamin. We know the Sacred Overlord says he killed the Cahmais diplomat in Eernicia. Now there are rumors about his role in saving people in Ffestini, and now he could be at the border. It would appear he's returning. No doubt, he will not be happy on the reason he was sent to Ynyover in the first place." There was a hint of suspicion in the man's voice.

"I cannot believe he would return for he knows my father will have him stripped of his tunic and his head put on a pike," said the warrior. "He trusted Urith like a brother, having him the mission to Ynyover only to attack the Sacred Overlord in the Citadel." He paused to look around. "Do you believe the Clovel Destroyer turned into an assassin and is planning on sneaking back into Esterblud? For what purpose?"

The round man's eyes lit up with the interest shown by the kingdom's second in command. "Urith has a wicked temper, but I doubt he is an assassin. And he remains popular among many warriors," Feeral reminded him. "As a leader within the Esterblud clan, he could cause the king problems. Perhaps lead an overthrow?"

"That's nonsense," declared Alcarlic, "Urith was never interested in politics and running a kingdom. He only wanted to fight."

"Maybe this is true, but what would you do if you have the power of this Skool? Does it not seem a strange coincidence that he comes in the back door while our greatest enemy stands at the front door?" asked the king's hakra. "I would guess King Asgurd would be happy to strike a deal with someone who could stand as a replacement to our overlord." He could tell in the momentary pause that Alcarlic was seriously considering his words.

The warrior finally spoke. "It is something we must keep an eye on. But you will keep this to yourself, and I will talk to the king about it."

"Perhaps we should tell him together?" suggested Feeral. "Your father is suspicious of the hakra's abilities. This could eliminate such doubts about me."

Alcarlic smiled smugly, knowing that the man wanted more access to the king. "I'll be happy to let him know of your talk with me." The warrior turned, walking away from the disappointed hakra and feeling a sense of satisfaction. While he did not like Feeral, Alcarlic considered him a smart man who could be useful with his visions. But he was also ambitious enough to give his father pause. As the warrior walked through the stone corridors toward the suite of rooms where the king made his home, he thought of his shared distrust of *satgerts*, hakras and others who dealt with prophecy and the gods. Still, the words of the fat man would make sense if they were about anyone other than Urith. Alcarlic had grown up watching the Clovel Sword warrior in battle and in council. He knew Urith had little interest in the intrigues that went on around the throne of the king, presenting honest and direct answers to the king. However, the warrior was not a natural fit to go on a diplomatic voyage. He was as shocked as many others in Esterblud at the stories coming about the warrior. Now, it made no sense for Urith to attempt to return as an ally of the Sacred Overlord unless the stories about his attack on the Citadel were untrue. By the time Alcarlic reached the large, dark doors of the king's quarters, he had formulated a plan.

King Penhda was readying for bed when his son entered after an announcement from the guard outside. The king's young personal attendants were moving in well-executed coordination as one boy pulled the woolen sleeping robe over the large man's torso which another boy was pulling back the sheets on the large mattress. Another attendant finished his daily duties of cleaning of the king's weapons which he hung on the wall next to the bed. Alcarlic noted that it would be another lonely night for the king as his beloved wife, his mother, had died a few seasons before. Like his father, he missed the frail, happy woman who could brighten a room with her presence.

"What is it?" the king asked, his green eyes narrowing. He knew that something must be wrong for his son to enter at the late hour.

"I was speaking with Feeral, my lord. It appears he believes that Urith is the threat coming from the north."

The king gave out a hearty laugh. "Urith a threat," he spat out the words between his laughter. "That old fool just wants my attention. You should know better than to come to me with such idiotic things."

"I must admit I was suspicious of him as well. However, his words have some logic," said Alcarlic. The warrior went on to tell his father of the discussion. When he was finished, he could see his father's puzzled expression.

"No, Urith is not the type to oppose me, even with such a great weapon. If he returns, it is to clear his name. And he would never ally with the king of Cahmais over the tribes of our lands. He has too much hate for the Aberffraw," said the king after he thought about it. "If it is Urith in the north, he must be coming back to explain his actions to me."

"But he sent no word to you about his actions," replied Alcarlic. "Beyond what Feeral just told me, one of our spies in Vulthnal sent us word he was there with a small group talking with King Barcal. And why not just return by sea straight to Eran? Instead, he appears to be going overland and coming in through the lands of his tribe. That would seem to fit what Feeral is saying."

Penhda scowled at the news. "Yes, this is something to consider." The king dismissed the attendants and moved to sit on his soft bed filled with the finest Vulthnal wool. He pondered what his son told him. He looked up to see the excitement in the man's eyes. "Ok, I know that look. What do you plan?" he asked.

"I will send out men to find him and return him under guard to this fortress," said Alcarlic. "He will be unable to start any problems if Feeral is correct and you can have him executed when you return from your victory over the Aberffraw army. You have already made it known among the diplomats in Eernicia that he is an outlaw. His execution as traitor can be shown as a reminder to his friends who lead the Gramcle tribe."

"The plan is sound, but we will wait until he explains himself to me personally," the king decided. "If he carries this weapon, he does me well by returning. I can spare him if he shows such loyalty to me. Make sure no harm comes to him until I return from the south."

The king sent his son away and laid back in his bed, thinking about his old friend. Penhda still did not believe Feeral's vision since he had seen the hakra misread his dreams too many times. Still, a king must protect himself, Penhda decided. He always considered Urith to be the most trusted warrior he had. However, the death of the Cahmais noble in Eernicia quickly led to the invasion of his lands from the south. It left the king with limited options. Any possible betrayal must be dealt with quickly. The king laid his head on the pillow thinking of the countless battles they had fought together over the seasons. Yes, he decided, Urith was an old, loyal friend, but a king could never be too careful.

～～～

The next morning, Urith to the voice of Henther, who was talking softly to his nephew. He looked over to watch the woman carefully tending to the young warrior, and it struck him that she was more of a mystery than he first thought. Oslaf could do far worse, he decided. Henther felt the warrior staring at her and she looked over with a smile.

"He's complaining that he's hungry," she whispered.

"Then, he's doing fine," Urith smiled at Oslaf, who gave him a wink. The young man looked weak, his face ashen. However, he seemed better than when Urith nursed him back to health in the lands of Ynyover. The older Esterblud suddenly realized that the young warrior had picked up some of his habits. "Well, don't get too comfortable," he told his nephew, "we will have some riding today." With his words, Urith got up stiffly from his blanket, taking several attempts to stretch out his injured leg. Despite only healing overnight, the bleeding had stopped. The warrior only felt a slight fever. He noticed the bound Sky goddess was staring at him with hate in her eyes and the rag still in her mouth. The

Esterblud responded to her look by giving her his death grin. He always considered the look to be his scars' biggest asset. Mivraa was asleep next to the goddess, with one leg over her to act as an alarm if Unis tried to escape. Fedelm was dozing in a sitting position near the warm ashes of the extinguished fire with a blanket over her shoulders. The giant warrior guessed the hakra must have spent the night watching over the camp. He stepped softly to the blonde woman and placed a hand on her shoulder. Fedelm laid her head on his rough hand, and he felt a sudden emotion run through him. The feeling confused him.

"Go sleep for a while," he whispered. "I'll keep an eye on things." The girl murmured agreement as he helped her lay down on the ground, bringing the blanket over her. He suddenly wanted to stroke her hair. When he looked over at Mivraa, he decided against the idea. The warrior did not see Henther watching him with a slight grin on her face. She seemed to understand the man's dilemma.

Urith went to wake Mivraa carefully, ensuring she would not lash out at him with the spear in her hands. When her eyes opened, he asked if she was ready to check out the abandoned mine. The Esterblud told her about Fedelm, so they asked Henther to watch over Unis. The warrior goddess gave her the talisman to protect her from the power of the goddess. Urith considered it quite an accomplishment for Mivraa to trust Henther already. When they began their trek back up the trail, Urith noticed how Mivraa was carrying the war scythe trophy with her and her spear was now carried over her back. Something on the war scythe blade caught his eye. The silver that covered the tip was gone leaving only the base metal underneath. He mentioned it to the demigoddess, but she simply shrugged, saying the polish must have been removed during the battle.

As they went up to the ruins of the mine, Urith was still hobbled by his leg. However, he insisted it was getting better after the warrior goddess asked him about it. She was about to say more when they suddenly stopped in mid-sentence. The pair stared in awe at the amount of damage that was now visible in the sunlight. A massive piece of the mountain had a large gash on the rock face like a giant sword had sliced through. As they wandered the area, they were able to find a few of the ranqels smashed under the boulders that came down onto the trail. They realized how fortune had smiled upon them in the dark.

"A couple of steps either way and we would be flattened as well," said Mivraa. "It appears the Fates like you. First, you somehow find the other part of the Skool and then we are missed by this landslide."

Urith nodded, "We were lucky. I'll take that over skill sometimes. And we closed a gateway to the underworld which is a start. Let's go back and tell the others over breakfast." He turned back down the path. Mivraa asked him what he meant by a start, but Urith did not answer her.

"We need to get to Cilgarran. I know of a healer there for Oslaf plus I believe we can get what we need for our next part of the journey."

"What do you mean next part of the journey?" asked Mivraa. "Fedelm hasn't seen a vision has she?"

"Not that I'm aware of," he confided. "But whenever we've stumbled upon another piece of this puzzle something is shown to us."

"Damn the gods," she replied, not thinking of what she said as she racked her brain for ideas. Urith absently grinned at her comment as he was thinking of his shield's sudden increase in power.

"Wait, I think I understand now how the other piece of the Skool came to us," exclaimed Urith as he stopped. Mivraa nearly ran over him. While Mivraa waited for him to explain, the Esterblud warrior suddenly began to laugh, his loud snorts sending echoes up the valley. He saw her giving him a confused look, and he forced himself to stop with some difficulty.

"Look at your trophy of the sky god. The blade was silver, right? And now it's gone. Remember the night you set the scythe on my shield. It reminded that I had to move it so I could get the shield to put on my arm." He looked at her waiting for a reaction with a smile on his face.

The realization slowly came across Mivraa's face. "You mean Ecarca carried the Skool to us? I had it in my hands the whole time?"

Urith nodded his head as he pointed to the war scythe tip she held up to look at. "Look at the tip. It's the same base metal as a sword. It struck me at the time I first saw it, that the weapon's edge was too brilliant, but I just thought that must be something in the way it was made."

Mivraa suddenly pulled out her chest plate, looking down at her chest area. The wound she received from Ecarca was above her left breast from the scythe cut appeared to be gone. "You have to be right, the cut from the weapon is gone. I should not have healed this quickly."

Urith pulled her close to him, wrapping his massive arms around her. "It appears the Fates looked down upon you as well. Let's go back and get ready for the journey. We have a long way to go yet." Suddenly he gave her a kiss, saying he wished they could stay away from the camp for a while. Mivraa just smiled slightly, pushing away and told him there would be time later. The discomfort coming from the demigoddess was brief but not lost on the warrior. Her wounds at the hands of her brothers were fresh and painful. As he followed her back to the camp, his mind raced through all the lost opportunities. He hoped they were not lost forever.

~~~

Inside the massive white temple of the Sky Realm, Duwdamon pacing around the room that morning and the god was in a foul mood as he floated across the chamber to his throne. With his wife captured and another son injured by the usurpers with the Skool, he was yelling in the empty hall. The great god of the sky could not understand how his plan had failed. Worse, his realm was in critical danger if the gods of the underworld decided to challenge him. He had taken the injured Ecarca there during the night, yet the healing waters were unable to restore the lost powers of the sea god. Even the elemental spirits which came forth to look at the wounded god offered few answers. He heard nothing of Uugor either beyond of his wounding. All the incessant talk coming from water spirits who resided in the reeds near the Exyts Spring revealed nothing to him of his sons' location. The ruler of the sky decided the humans must have captured Uugor as well.

If Caruun found out about this weakness, it could spell trouble for him and the realm. And if that was not enough for the god, Dughorm, the prophet, revealed to the sky god of the new struggles of humans throughout the Kamin world as beasts and monsters were coming from the night to defile the sky god temples, raping and killing the humans inside. Duwdamon paid considerable attention to this news since humans were leaving the temples and their offerings were no longer enhancing the sky god's power. Quickly, the symbiotic relationship between the gods and the humans was being torn apart.

As he sat upon his throne, he heard the soft noise of Dughorm joining him. The oracle was far too interested in the sufferings of the humans than the Duwdamon liked. And the prophet continued to remind the sky god of the danger of Kriell although the god had yet to see any substantial proof of this. As far as Duwdamon was concerned, Caruun and Alrpan were the culprits for the troubles among the humans.

"I'm sorry to bother you, my lord, but I've learned that the third part of the Skool was discovered by the warrior called Urith," said Dughorm.

"How did you learn of this?" The sky god became suspicious since the prophet could not have left the realm.

"Uugor came to tell me this morning," said the oracle.

"You mean my son came to you? Why didn't he come to me?"

"I have no idea," confessed Dughorm. "He simply let me know this and left. He looked to be heading back to the human realm. He told me that the Vanth called Actita wants to arrange a meeting between you and Caruun."

"A meeting, eh." The sky god tugged at his long mustache as he thought. "Perhaps a meeting would be good for us to restart things. If I can get Caruun to join with me against the usurpers than we can stop our biggest threat to the world we know." The sky god heard the prophet lightly coughing in disagreement, but the spirit of Dughorm remained quiet.

"You still believe Kriell is here, don't you?"

"Yes, my lord. As I've told you, the visions are clear, and he is stronger now," said the prophet.

"If I accept your words, then why would Caruun wish to meet me?" The god looked down at Dughorm.

"Because if the spirit stealer gets close enough to you and destroys you, the realms will no longer matter. Kriell would control everything," said Dughorm, his face grave.

"But Caruun would not allow this since Kriell would be a threat to him," the sky god said mostly to himself. "Unless they are working together like you told me."

"I don't believe I said this, my lord. I only stated he was back from the Void. Do you believe he would be in the underworld working with Caruun and Alrpan?" Dughorm tried to keep the skepticism from his voice.

The sky god did not notice since he was convinced of his superior wisdom. "Of course, it makes sense now. Well, since Caruun wants to meet, then I say we make this happen. Since Uugor has already left, then bring Ecarca to me. We will set up a meeting for our godbrothers. I think we can guide them to the correct solution then." The sky god smiled smugly at his plan while Dughorm just bowed and left the temple with a bit of a grin on his face.

When the Dughorm found Ecarca kneeling by the Exyts Spring, the deity looked healthy, unlike the burnt mass of flesh that entered the temple during the night. Dughorm told the earth god of his fathers' instructions. He made sure to point out the information about Kriell before mentioning his brothers return during the morning.

"I'm glad that Uugor returned since he was injured by those worthless humans," the god declared. "He must have stopped by this spring for his eye."

"I saw no one enter the area around the spring," said Dughorm, keeping the surprise of the comment from his voice. His mind immediately became suspicious of the god he met during the morning. "But perhaps he was here before I arrived."

However, the earth god was not listening. "My powers have not returned," he complained. "I swear that I will be cutting my bitch sister apart slowly and feed her to the humans."

Dughorm stiffened at the words before smiling to the god. "I'm sure your powers will return soon. Remember, Alrpan seems to have recovered from her encounter with the Skool." He watched the earth god brighten at the news. "I'm sure your father will want you to find Uugor after you arrange a meeting with Caruun. You should go to him now."

As he watched the earth god glide away, Dughorm's face turned sour as he thought about his continued distaste for these gods of the Sky Realm. He walked through the gardens that surrounded the spring and when down the path toward the Fields of Anord where the great warrior spirits would be doing their daily battle. The prophet had seen the future many times in his visions. They were so clear since he came to the Sky Realm. And since his treatment by the sky god since they met, the former warrior made sure he was using the visions to help those who needed it most. His friends were in danger, and he was happy to send these arrogant gods to their own destruction.

~~~

Kriell returned to the underworld in the form of Uugor after his side trip into the Sky Realm. He used the journey as a test of his new powers. Also, he carried a flask of water from the Exyts Spring with him. The Guardian considered the water only good thing in the realm of the sky gods. He had use of the healing water in the next steps of his plans. The trip to the Sky Realm above also proved the deity was now capable of achieving all of his plans. There remained few obstacles in his control of all the realms.

Yet, the god was troubled when he witnessed the human use the Skool to blow down half of a mountain and destroy the *sidhera*, a gateway to the realms. Kriell knew well the power of the Skool, and he realized that these humans could be a problem if not destroyed. He wondered where they would be going since the information he had was old. The spirit of Alrpan, which he ingested as he came out of the Great Void, offered him little in her knowledge about the humans. Only her powers were useful to Kriell's plans for the Sky Realm. The deity needed a trusted ally to find those humans. Actita would be the supporter he needed. The Guardian called the Vanth to his side.

"Is something needed?" the rat-faced demigod asked of Kriell.

"Yes, you will find that man called Urith who has the Skool. Only follow him and let me know where he and his group go. Your stealth in the night should allow you to get close enough to their camp to listen to their plans. Report to me before the morning rises. Do you understand?" The god dismissed the Vanth when the rat face nodded.

The god pointed to a beorh nearest him, one of the many that surrounded the round cavern near the walls. "You will find your leader and have him come to me," Kriell told him. The beorh ran away as the god leaned back looking around. His new underworld looked much different than when Caruun was in charge. The unfortunate spirits of the underworld were nearly all transformed into assorted hideous monsters to be used as his hordes against the humans and the Sky Realm. By sacrificing some of his powers of transformation, the god of the Great Void used the malformed and degraded human souls in the underworld to recreate a world lost by the Guardians so long ago.

Kriell remembered his betrayal by the traitor gods in a pact with the one called Heptarc. Once the three realms were his, then Kriell would bring out his brother and sister Guardians. The god began to let his form turn back into the natural dark blob, still enjoying the feel the souls of those traitor gods now inside of him. They would suffer in their permanent prison inside him. Kriell was content to let their spirits slowly, painfully wither away until the spark of life was entirely consumed by him. It would be perfect vengeance for his humiliation long embedded in the dark spirit of the god.

The leader of the beorhs came to the black fleshy mass of tentacles lying across the throne, bowing deeply before his master. When the monster's spirit lived in human form, he was known as Reppir. It is a name still known in the lands of Kamin for his infamous deeds. As a ruthless leader of the Regiussa tribes, the warrior king took great delight in the infliction of pain and suffering upon his people. Torture and maiming of his enemies became a specialty under his rule. The songs from the Skalds rang with hideous accounts of roads into his kingdom filled with unfortunate victims, dying a slow death impaled upon sharpened poles. The sick soul of such a madman was quickly transformed into the leader of the beorhs. Reppir now joined his new master with a single-minded focus to remake the realms of Kamin into a single realm of death.

The black globule that covered the throne turned its two eyes down on his obedient servant. He was satisfied with this new leader of his hordes, the worst soul culled from the others in the underworld. Now he would unleash this fiend upon the world of the living.

"I've lost many of the *ranqels,* so I expect you to find me more spirits. You will begin staging your beorhs near the gateways of the lands they call Esterblud and Ynyover. Also, you will send off the crubas into the areas around the Citadel. Soon, you will send your beasts into the human realm. Leave nothing alive. I want the number of spirits to overwhelm the underworld."

The creature called Reppir croaked enthusiastically, unable to speak since the beorhs primitive form did not allow such vocals. Kriell dismissed the monster who hurried away to its duties. Then, the god began to transform into the form of Caruun for his next trip into the human realm. The chaos must continue to keep the humans from seeing the end of their world was near.

~~~

Aberffraw warriors had returned from scouting the Esterblud countryside, trying to find the main group of fighters coming to stop their invasion. Their reports to the King around the morning campfire that morning told him that his plans were going even better than expected. The king, Lyncus, and Satres were seated comfortably in the small chairs at an elaborately filled table. All items were being carried in one of many supply carts for the kings' comfort. The leader of the scouts told his leaders of finding only small numbers of warriors within the villages that lined their way to Gramcan. Lyncus smiled as he heard that those fighters who remained to defend their communities were being slaughtered at his insistence. Using his father's grief, the last son of Asgurd insisted that their campaign to destroy the Esterbluds would not be held to the warrior code. He told his soldiers, along with the few from Ynyover, that the king would give no mercy. The Aberffraws would loot and destroy all villages, taking the women and children to be their slaves. His warriors knew that all captured lands would be dispensed to those loyal subordinates to be populated by the family bound tribes within Cahmais. Vengeance for King Asgurd meant wiping the kingdom of Esterblud from the memory of Kamin.

After the scout leader had left, the king waved away his attendants. "Our progress is better than I anticipated," the fat man told his breakfast guests. "Even I could not have guessed the slowness of Penhda to respond to our fighters' quick progress. If our weather holds as told by the visions of Satres' Council, I expect we should see the walls of Gramcan late tomorrow."

"You are to be congratulated, my lord. My walk this morning already showed me the trail of enemy heads mounted on pikes lining the road. The screams of women and the cries of children can be heard late into the night," replied the Sacred Overlord. There was no sense of irony in his words from the leader of the priests and temples.

"Hopefully, you still slept well, despite the sounds of war," interjected Lyncus as he shot a knowing glance at the thin man who was taking a drink of wine. The Aberffraw leader enjoyed the discomfort displayed by the man who nearly choked on his drink.

"Ah, I slept quite well, thank you. I believe the hard riding and long hours keeping up with the fighters has been good for my constitution." The Overlord turned to the king. "To change the subject slightly, my lord. Have you thought about my suggestion to have the Majireef Council take over the administration of Gramcan and Eran once you have captured them? The kingdoms of Eernicia and Vulthnal will be very concerned about the power of Cahmais once the Esterbluds are replaced. They might join in an alliance against you."

"Do you really believe they could stop me," asked King Asgurd, his overconfidence evident.

"It would be a way to keep them from interfering with our plans," Lyncus spoke up in defense of the idea. "With the blessing of the Sacred

Overlord and his control of the major ports, I believe the monarchs will be influenced by their merchants and town leaders. They will not interfere as we expand the Aberffraw leadership over lands."

"So you are telling me that the Overlord of Ynyover will provide us cover to finish our mission of destroying the Esterbluds." The fat king leaned in close to Satres. "Now what do you get out of this?"

The Sacred Overlord moved away slightly from the discomfort of such a direct question. "Just a small percentage of the trade and a place for my council to lead the *satgerts* and hakras who reside in the other lands. We can help to control the events within the other kingdoms if we can control the temples."

The king leaned back in his chair, laughing heartily. "No wonder Lyncus holds you in such high regard. It appears you have thought this out. Your diplomatic skills and vision would indeed be useful to our mutual needs. I'll accept your offer." Asgurd stood up with a mug in his hand. "Let's lead our men on to Gramcan so I can remove that so-called king from his throne and place his head upon a pike for all to see."

After a long ride, the main force of the Aberffraw warriors began their descent down the road into a long shallow valley called Awarware. Scouts spotted dust rising in the distance, kicked up by the ossanes of the Esterblud warriors coming to meet the invaders. The Aberffraw and Ynyover fighters began the chatter of speculation and questions among their groups. Would they fight soon? How many of the enemy would they face? By the time they reached the valley floor, the invading warriors could see the rapidly growing Esterblud army assembling in the distance.

Dividing the forming human lines, a small stream ran lazily along the road before splitting the valley. Many generations of farmers left the valley barren of trees, replaced with small farmer fields of *zeam* and *vulgere* dotting the landscape. Within this idyllic gold and green landscape, the fields of Awarware would soon be fertilized by the blood and bodies of many warriors as the enemy lines closed.

King Asgurd pushed his way through the mass of men with Lyncus and Satres trailing behind. The king looked at the smaller force of Esterblud warriors across from him and briefly considered an immediate attack. Lyncus urged his father to send the men forward, volunteering to lead the charge. However, the king shook his head, telling his son they would wait.

"I want the enemy army completely and entirely in front of me to destroy them with one swipe," he explained to his disappointed leaders gathered around him. "Another sunset will get our fleet to Eran. There are not enough warriors to stop us. We will wrap our forces around them and, like a snake, squeeze them until we eat them all at once."

Those leaders among the kings' council saw the potential to inflict a fatal wound upon their eternal enemy were incised by the decision. Several more of the leaders attempted to persuade the king to strike now. But the king issued his order with firm determination. They would rest until morning before they would destroy the Esterbluds. Soon, as the men heard the news spreading down the lines, the push to fight gave way to a smattering of cheers as the men realized they would have more time to eat, drink and, more importantly, to live.

Satres could see that Lyncus was furious at his father for his decision. But the younger man remained quiet as he and Satres followed the king back to a secluded spot along the stream near a huge bluewood tree which nearly covered a small twisted lellowtere tree. It was there that the mass of attendants began to unpack the carts of supplies to maintain King Asgurd's comfort. While they worked to put up the tents and laid out the trappings of comfort, chairs were brought for the leaders where they began to plan for the upcoming battle.

~~~

Urith led the rest of the travelers out of the mountains when the sun neared its zenith as the group had a late start from their camp. Oslaf recovered enough to ride, despite his belly wound which was not as severe as they initially thought. Still, it would take a while to heal, and the long trip would not help ease the pain. Henther rode next to him, keeping a close eye on his movements acting very much like a *kuon* mother watching over her pup. Fedelm and Mivraa trotted on either side of Urith as the road opened up into the grassy highlands. Sitting behind the giant Esterblud was Unis, her hands bound behind her back and her white robe covered in dust and blood. She was quiet, her eyes darting around in anticipation of her eventual rescue. Urith and Mivraa had made it clear to the goddess that she would be free of the gag over her mouth as long as she remained quiet. Urith also made it clear that he would be happy to kill her if she tried using her powers, pointing to the amulet he wore.

The travelers were following the road to Eran, but Urith was focused upon their tribal home of Cilgarran, which lay on the coast just north of the fortress where the king resided. Urith believed that the elders of the Esterblud home village would provide them with food and shelter. He also thought that he and Oslaf could convince them to act as intermediaries with King Penhda, perhaps providing them some protection from his immediate wrath of the king was known to react violently against his prisoners.

"It appears we are sneaking into our lands," Oslaf asked. "Why not go to the king directly?"

The giant Esterblud shook his head. "No, he will know we have arrived soon enough. We have been unjustly accused by the Sacred Overlord and the King of Eernicia. If it were just me, then I would do as you say. However, you and the others are at risk by your association with me. You don't need to lose your heads just for following along my trail. Our tribal elders can protect you when I leave you at Cilgarran. I'll make my way to meet with King Penhda. I'm sure he will listen to reason."

While Fedelm and Mivraa protested, saying they would be willing to risk it, Urith stood by his decision. He made it clear that his plan would be followed. Mivraa seemed to be the one most opposed to the scheme, but she gave no reason for her stand. With no visions to guide them for the moment, Fedelm wondered if Urith's idea of reason ultimately would be his sword and shield. She resigned herself for the long ride to Cilgarran as the giant Esterblud led the way.

As Mivraa rode next to Urith, her mind was focused around an idea she was developing to enter the Sky Realm once more. However, this time, it would be different for she would have the power of the Skool with her. There was an obstacle to her plan. It was Fedelm. Before the Death Bearers, it would have been a simple matter of getting Urith to join her through the gateway. She was sure the warrior she had grown to love would agree with her ideas. However, now she saw his occasional looks at Fedelm. Looks which betrayed his feelings for a human who had little to offer him beyond her visions. Inside the demigoddess resented the warrior failing to defend her from Fedelm's accusations about the trap in Kanhan. The demigoddess grew convinced that the warrior was turning from her despite his displays of affection. She worked on ideas to permanently separate her and the Esterblud warrior from the rest of the group.

On the other side of Urith, Fedelm had her attention on the Sky Realm as well. However, the pretty hakra remained troubled as she tried to think of a way to explain her latest vision from Dughorm. The god's prophet wanted her to lead their group into the Sky Realm. She tried to understand such an impossible task. The realms of the gods were known to be a one-way street where only a spirit could be taken by the gods. Her mind reeled at the thoughts as she looked over at the gleaming metal hand guard on the Clovel Sword, swaying on the warrior's belt. It held a spell from an ancient monster of the underworld which formed the triad of raw power the Esterblud used. A thought came to her, and she suddenly smiled at the revelation that rode next to her. Instead of focusing on the weapons carried by the warrior, she decided the Fates focused upon Urith. He controlled the triad of weapons, and he must be the instrument for breaking through the realms. The hakra tried to recall the myths around Heptarc when he sent the Guardians back through the Great Void. Unfortunately, the tales she knew were few. She could only recall Heptarc and the code of honor. Fedelm decided she had been a fool for not learning more from the Esterblud warriors during the journey. She vowed she would make up for the lost time, suddenly speaking up to ask Urith about the story of Heptarc.

Over the next few sun cycles, the travelers made their way on the road, meeting a few travelers and merchants who updated them about news in the lands. As the Esterbluds wore the colors of the Kings' Geniht, people were more than willing to provide them with food, heathmead, and information. The travelers heard of the invasion from the south, along with news of King Penhda gathering warriors to move against the Aberffraw and Ynyover fighters. The giant Esterblud took it as good news for him and his friends as the king would be unlikely to worry about Urith for the moment, allowing them time to gain the sympathy of his friends within Cilgarran. While not a natural politician, the scarred Esterblud knew the social circles of the king and his advisors.

That evening, they found the best spot for to make camp for the night. Urith and Oslaf were hoping Fedelm's endless supply of questions would stop. Both warriors were running out of stories about Heptarc, along with other tales of the Great Passing. She was apparently thinking about something, but she continued to tell them she was not ready to explain herself yet. "I'm not sure of my last vision," the hakra told them. "That's why I'm asking the questions and looking for answers."

Mivraa took a real interest in the conversation which made Urith happy to see the women talking rather than accusing each other. He could tell by the conversations that something was gnawing at the hakra. He just asked Fedelm to let them know soon. He also told them they were only a short ride from his home village. The warrior grinned at his nephew, reminding him that their family would want to know about Henther. The young man turned red at the words as he smiled at his girlfriend who gave him a blank look. It was evident she had not thought about meeting Oslaf's family.

It was long after dark as the moons fell from the night sky when Urith heard the sound of yelling from the camp. He was taking another pass around the field ensuring no beasts were watching them as part of his patrol that night. The giant Esterblud ran to the camp with his sword in hand expecting the worst. However, the yells were coming from Fedelm and Mivraa, both asleep and wildly thrashing about. Urith immediately suspected Unis bringing his sword to the goddess' neck, but he immediately recognized the fear and confusion in the bound woman's face. Realizing the god was not tormenting the women with her power, he looked over to see Henther was at Fedelm's side trying to wake her with Oslaf struggling out of his bed to help as well. Urith went to Mivraa and tried to help the demigoddess as well, calling out her name. However, both women remained locked in their nightmares, so powerful they seemed to be fighting for their lives. Mivraa was becoming so fierce in her struggles that Urith had difficulty pinning her to the ground. Oslaf came to his side to help hold the woman down, fearful she might suddenly pull her crystal spear hidden inside her cloak.

For her part, Unis saw her opportunity as the humans struggled with their counterparts. She had been steadily loosening the leather that bound her wrists during the journey. Pulling consistently, she was finally able to free her wrists. The goddess carefully watched as the human warriors focused upon the women struggling in their dreams as she slowly found the knot that held the cloth bound around her legs. She struggled with the tight knot for a while before the goddess was able to loosen her legs as well. Unis got on her hands and knees, slowly backing away from the fire with her glowing eyes giving the impression of a large *brokko* looking for its next opportunity to scavenge a kill. However, the goddess decided she would return to the Sky Realm to bring the gods against the humans. She would extract a grim revenge upon their frail bodies and use their spirits to be her slaves in the afterlife.

After a long struggle to keep the two women down and continued yells and pleads to wake up, the women finally opened their eyes. At first, both appeared in a state of shock. Fedelm, in particular, seemed to be affected by the vision for she immediately burst out crying, grabbing Henther as if the woman could somehow protect her from the dream. Mivraa's face was blank at first as if she was still trying to understand, her eyes blinking rapidly, trying to determine if she was asleep or awake. Soon, the demigoddess was aware of her surroundings, and she was yelling at Urith and Oslaf to get off of her.

"What are you doing?" the woman demanded. "How dare you hold me this way." However, when she saw the expression on their faces as they finally released her, she quickly realized something unusual must have happened.

"You and Fedelm were thrashing about like you were in a battle," said Urith. "We didn't want you to pull out your weapon and attack us."

"I'm sorry," she said, her face showing the confusion she felt. "I just saw something I never experienced before. Give me a minute." She sat up, looking around and noticed Fedelm sobbing quietly now. Henther held her, looking at the others with a mix of confusion and heartfelt grief. Urith stood up, sheathed his sword and noticed the empty spot where Unis was sleeping earlier.

"Curse the gods," said the giant warrior, quickly moving to the spot while looking into the night. However, the goddess was out of sight and, with no light of the moons, it would be next to impossible to recapture her. "No way to get her now," the Esterblud kicked at the ground in disgust.

"We can look when the dawn comes," suggested Oslaf as he walked up to his uncle, holding his belly wound which he had reopened during the struggle. Urith put his hand on the young warrior's shoulder, turning them back to the campfire.

"We might stumble upon her. I'll check for her tracks when the light comes," he told his nephew. "Let's look at your wound." Urith looked at Fedelm and Mivraa. "Can you tell us what happened? I've never seen either of you act that way in one of your visions. I'm guessing it was not just a nightmare."

"You're wrong about that," Mivraa shook her head. "It's a nightmare that's going on right now in the fields of Awarware."

~~~

Across the valley that night, the two opposing armies were going about their business of readying for coming slaughter the next morning. Soon, they would charge en mass to butcher their fellow humans using all manner of specialized equipment. But this night was different. As the guards moved around in the darkness, just within sight of the campfire lights, no one heard the slight sounds coming from twisted lellowtere trees which stood behind both lines. The outlines of movement among the brush would occasionally catch a guard's attention, but the night sounds continued, and soon the guard would find other sounds to occupy his attention. When the onslaught came from the underworld hordes, no king or warrior was ready.

In the Cahmais camp, the warriors were sleeping near the campfires or in tents if they were of sufficient peerage and wealth. Led by a devious but skilled warrior, the beorhs took down many of the guards before they could yell out a warning to their comrades, leaving the second wave of monsters to inflict the primary damage upon the camp. Silently, an unholy mix of beorhs, crubas, and *kronogs* fell upon the tents, ripping and tearing through the sleeping warriors. The initial screams of the dying woke the light sleepers, and the campfires that stretched across the valley showed the humans their terrible foes.

Lyncus came out of his tent with his sword in hand and no armor on, unable to believe the scene before him. Two of his attendants were being ripped apart by a pack of *kronogs*. Immediately, the leader of the Aberffraw King's guard tried to organize his men. However, the overwhelming swarm of men and beasts made it nearly impossible. He slammed his sword down on a *kronog* coming at him, causing the monster's arm to fly off into the night. However, the beast continued to come toward the man, before it was finally struck down by his men. Momentarily stunned by his inability to kill the monster, Lyncus stared down briefly at the turtle jaw beast before he gathered himself together and led his men toward the king's tent which was near his own.

As they reached the tent, they could see the bodies of the two personal guards, each missing large parts of their bodies. They heard King Asgurd fighting for his life inside his tent and Lyncus ran through the ripped hole in the tent, trying to help his father against a *kronog*. The king stood in his yellow dressing gown, striking ineffectively at the heavily armored monster. As just myths in tales about the Guardians, the king did not realize the weak spots on the monster. Just as Lyncus impaled the beast in the spine from behind, it swung around its vicious three clawed hands, ripping into the fat belly of the king. The creature fell at the feet of King Asgurd, who held his hands over the large wound, blood pouring through his fingers as his face turned gray. He stared in disbelief at his son who rushed forward to catch the man as he fell forward. By the time, Lyncus gently laid his father upon the ground, the King of Cahmais was dead in his arms.

On the other side of the valley, King Penhda was fighting for his life as well. He gathered those remaining warriors where he could while trying to stop charging groups of beorhs and crubas. The beorhs ran in packs and were focused on picking off individuals who were standing away from their comrades. For those warriors who might survive the onslaught of claws and teeth ripping at their flesh, would be dragged off into the night to be raped and slowly dismembered alive. It was considered by the warriors to be the worst possible death on Kamin.

Still worse for the King of Esterblud were the crubas which were inflicting great damage upon his remaining fighters. With its reptilian head and massive jaws, the monster was capable of inflicting deadly bites through chain mail. Using their long, deadly claws at the end of extra-long arms, the small monsters would move in low against the fighters to strike at the exposed legs of the humans. Once on the ground, the human warrior would be nearly helpless as the crubas would quickly rip into the victim's organs. Amid the screams of dying and confusion, the king directed the line of warriors that gathered around him, and they put up stiff resistance against the monsters who continued to attack them in seemingly endless waves. Brihar, his trusted friend and the leader of the Gramcle tribe, hacked his way through a line of beorhs and joined the king with his remaining warriors.

"We need to retreat to higher ground," yelled Brihar above the screams and battle cries. "We don't have enough men to stop them from surrounding us."

King Penhda's instinctive reaction was against the idea. However, he realized the small man was correct, as usual. He ordered Brihar to cover his retreat, and the king began leading the remainder of warrior up the trail. They were heading to a spot he remembered using earlier the day before to assess the enemy lines along the valley floor. As his men followed him, he yelled at them to gather the torches and seek out any other warriors on their way. The single attendant who still survived came to Penhdas' side with a torch in hand. The young boys' face was bleeding, and he was shivering in the night air as he struggled to hold the large bit of burning wood in front of him. The king laid his bulky arm on the boy's shoulder, telling him he had done well as they moved through the dead bodies of the beasts.

While Brihar backed his men up the trail, fending off the monsters that continued to attack, the man saw a figure moving through dead bodies, oblivious to the screams. The grizzled warrior had to blink his eyes to be sure, but he was convinced that Caruun, the underworld god, stood no more than twenty paces away from the fighting.

The figure was watching the underworld beasts attacking, only cocking his scavenger head as he appeared to take in the carnage around him. The underworld deity looked at the line of warriors trying to hold of the monster while a line of handheld torches revealed a retreating group of Esterblud warriors. The god of the underworld waited, enjoying the wave of beorhs that ran against the tight formation of fighters in front of him. The blood and carnage were soothing music to his ears. Kriell turned and pointed to the line of retreating men. Reppir, standing next to his master, immediately screeched out a call, and beorhs screeched their response. The creatures suddenly stopped their attack, quickly moving the darkness to hunt down the line of retreating Esterbluds and their king.

The sudden stop in the fighting caused Brihar to look around for the monsters in the sudden stillness of the night. When the leader looked back, the creatures were gone, and the only sounds were the cries of the dying and wounded along with the heavy breathing of his men. The warrior suddenly realized that the monsters were heading after his king. He yelled for the men to follow him, and he began running up after King Penhda, following the trail of flickering torchlights.

Carefully walking up the road that led them into the valley of death, Satres could hear the screams of the dying in the night. He moved cautiously from one bush to the next, trying to hide in the shadows. He had seen his attendants and most of the Majireef Council butchered by the underworld beasts when he crawled from under his tent into the dark shadows under a nearby cart. From his vantage point, the Sacred Overlord could see the unarmed religious leaders become easy pickings for the crubas who quickly turned the screaming men into bloody, unrecognizable parts. Working his way through the sparse bushes and trees, the thin man prayed to the gods as he avoided the fighting, unseen despite the fact he was visible in the pale light in his bright red robe. Satres knew no talismans could stop such monsters, and the Overlord carried no weapon but for a ceremonial dagger. But he was determined to escape the bloodbath and return to his Citadel.

Near the road, Satres could make out the dim outlines of the wagons which held the loot from the towns the Aberffraw warriors had pillaged. Sprinting to a hiding place near a tree beside the road, he spotted one wagon with a team of erbas still hooked up. Spooked by the smell of blood in the air, the furry animals pawed at the ground anxiously. The Overlord of Ynys looked around carefully, then ran across the road, holding his robe up with his hands to keep from tripping as he came up behind the cart. Climbing into the back, Satres struggled to remain quiet while he pushed past the baskets filled with assorted pillaged treasures. When the man reached the front of the cart, he carefully pushed his head through a canvas flap which hung over the seat of the vehicle. Seeing no movement, he quietly sat upon the wood seat and took the reins from near the foot rest. Taking one last look around the area, he snapped the reins lightly causing the erbas instinctively to move forward onto the road. He realized that his cart made too much noise with its creaking wheels on the hard packed dirt and the occasional snort of the erbas. However, he was committed, and he hoped the changing color of the sky would bring the sun soon to send the beasts back to the underworld realm.

The cart moved past the destroyed camp of army followers, mostly made up of women and children of warriors and those Esterbluds they enslaved from their village conquests. The horrific slaughter that took place there by the monsters upon the unarmed camp could just be made out in the dim light. Even the calloused overlord tried to look ahead to avoid seeing the torn apart bodies since he was worried the erbas might panic from the strong scent of death. He heard the sound of footsteps coming from the other side of the camp toward him, and he looked up in fright. However, what he saw was a thin, nearly naked woman hobbling along with a cloth-wrapped bundle in her arms. From torn robe she wore, which was almost gone, he could see she was one of the captive Esterbluds. He saw the blood that covered the woman's arm and legs as she painfully tried to climb on while pushing the bundle into the seat of the wagon, desperately whispering for him to help. Satres acted as if he would help, reaching toward her. Suddenly, he used his foot to push the woman off the cart, snapping the reins to get the erbas to speed up. The injured woman fell down, along with the wrapped baby she was trying to give the Sacred Overlord. Satres could feel the cart's back end suddenly rise up and drop as the wheel crushed the woman and child. The thin man in red did not look back as he hurried the slow animals back to Ynyover.

Lyncus looked with hopeful relief at the pale sky behind him as well. He and the few remaining Aberffraw men with him fought off continued onslaughts of underworld beasts, and as suddenly as the monsters had arrived, they disappeared. He hoped that the morning sun would send the monsters back to the underworld as he remembered from the stories of the skalds. Now, he and his men were working their way back to the road leading out of the valley where they would occasionally find small packs of the beasts still roaming. As remaining leader of the warrior army and now king of Cahmais, Lyncus knew he had to save himself and his men. Unable to retrieve the king's body for a proper warriors' funeral, he told his men they would make amends to his spirit when they returned to Cahmais.

The surviving fighters saw a cart moving away from them when they got to the road. Sensing a chance to get out of the area quickly, he sent his men after the wagon. He could not call out, still worried about the beasts that might remain nearby. As all of the survivors began to run after the vehicle in the dim light, Lyncus observed someone trying to get on the cart. Then he saw the thin man driving the wagon. The Aberffraw leader was close enough to see Satres kick the person away as the cart hurried from the area. Soon, the cart went over a bridge, gaining speed and they knew they would not catch it without an ossane. The men found the dead woman in the road, nearly cut in half by the thin wagon wheel, her arms still reaching out for her dying baby lying near her. Even Lyncus showed his disgust, but he was thinking of the coward who just escaped. What the son of Asgurd saw on the ground did not bother the man. Instead, he believed that Satres helped cause the calamity he just went through. The overlord of the priests apparently lacked any knowledge about the attack which just decimated his army. It meant the Majireef Council lacked the vision to see the underworld god's plans. Lyncus knew the gods played the Scared Overlord as a fool, and now his

Aberffraw warriors lay in sacrifice for this stupidity. The Aberffraw recognized the monsters coming from the underworld were a signal of a great evil coming to the human world. He believed they would soon be locked in a battle which could change the allies he, and by extension, his kingdom needed to survive.

Across the valley on a plateau, which overlooked the bloody fields, the dawn saw the last bit of fighting as King Penhda held out with his few warriors from repeated attacks by the underworld creatures. However, a final attack led by Reppir included many other beasts which overwhelmed the fighters. The king and his men fought valiantly, killing many of the monsters to release their spirits from their living death. But the king was no match to the new leader of the underworld hordes on this morning. Reppir and his beorhs horde reached the king last as he tried to fight off a pair of the monsters who pinned him down. The other beast gathered around the still living man to gleefully strip the screaming king warrior of his flesh with their razor sharp claws. When they left, the monsters took parts of the other warrior's bodies for trophies in the underworld.

Brihar led his few men to join their king as fast as they could speed through the unknown terrain at night. On their way, they could hear the fierce battle sounds as they got closer, but the men slowed going up the steep angle of the slope. And as quickly as the sounds of battle reached them, the air suddenly grew quiet, and the remaining warriors stopped, fearing an ambush awaited them. Brihar coaxed his men forward, slowly as the dawn rays broke across the land. Just as the final living Genihts of the king's guard finally reached the plateau, they found the bloody skeleton remains of Penhda minus his head among the scattered remains of his men, most butchered and stripped of their flesh like their king. Dispersed around the human remains were the many bodies of the underworld monsters. The last stand of King Penhda would be a scene that remained etched in the mind of Brihar, his loyal advisor, for the rest of his life.

In the valley below, the god Kriell returned to the underworld realm through the gateway next to the twisted lellowtere tree. Still in the form of Caruun, the god found the form of the humans to be easier for him to move around the realms. Behind him was his new general over the monsters. Reppir had proved his value to the Guardian, and the massive beorh held the swords of the human kings in either hand. Stuck on the

291

tips of each sword were the heads of King Asgurd and King Penhda, which Reppir intended to display next to the throne of his master. At the gateway, they were met by Actita, the Vanth, who came to lead the souls of the massacred into the underworld.

"Bring the spirits of the kings to me," ordered the Guardian, clucking as he spat out the words from the beaked mouth. "I will make sure they do not enjoy the Sky Realm. Instead, they will be placed on my throne of souls. Their misbegotten beliefs will no longer be needed in the new world we are creating."

"You transform them?" asked the Vanth about his new souls.

"We'll see. I'm not sure what I'll do with them yet. I want the other spirits taken down to be used as we see fit. With Mivraa and Wurms no longer helping the Sky Realm gods, their powers will grow weak. No one will oppose you."

"And we go to Sky Realm now," the rat face of Actita twisted into a grimacing smile at the thought.

Kriell disregarded the comment. "When you are finished with your task, you will find the human with the Skool and tell me where he is." The Vanths' master continued into the gateway, returning into the darkness of the underworld realm.

~~~

Urith and his friends were on their ossanes, traveling down the road to Eran that morning. The group was already tired after their unfruitful search for Unis. The Sky Realm goddess escaped. They followed her tracks to a twisted lellowtere tree where she seemed to have escaped back to the Sky Realm. Mivraa had wanted to follow her through the gateway, but Urith and Fedelm were able to convince her that the demigoddess was needed in their quest for the last part of the Skool. While Mivraa was still angry enough to re-enter the realm, she realized she would need the power of the Skool before taking on the remaining gods in the Sky Realm.

After packing and getting on their mounts, they continued their discussions about the nightmare visions of Fedelm and Mivraa as they traveled. Each woman had told them their stories within the bloody dreams in the dead of night. Now they went into more details about the overwhelming slaughter of warriors and residents alike. Fedelm was particularly upset at the horrible defiling and massacres that the beorhs inflicted upon women and children since it was so fresh in her own experience with the beasts. It took a while to coax the words from her, and her trembling voice expressed a sorrow and rage that each traveler felt when she told of what she saw. Urith suppressed an urge to reach out and hold the young woman.

Mivraa's vision was centered more on the death of kings. She was unclear on their names, but her description of one told Urith and Oslaf it must have been Penhda. If she was correct, Urith guessed that at least two kingdoms were without leaders. Such news could cause the lands to become chaotic bloodbaths between tribes within their kingdom, each clawing their way into power. Oslaf mentioned to Urith during their ride that if Penhda were dead, his son would be scrambling to become the new leader. The giant Esterblud agreed, but he told his nephew that the elders of the tribes would have to agree. While Urith had been gone from Esterblud for a while, he knew that no agreement among the tribes would be found without some cost to each tribe. With Penhda gone, a scramble could erupt to gain power.

The travelers were coming upon a fork in the road which led to either the capital city of Eran or to Cilgarran. As they turned onto the path to the Esterbluds' birthplace, they could hear the sound of hoof beats as a large band of fully armed warriors came toward them from the road to Eran. Dressed in elegant green tunics and silver helmets, the line of fighters moved quickly from the shadows of a small grove of trees which concealed them. Urith had no desire to flee, and he knew they stood little chance of fighting their way out against so many unless he used the god's weapon on his back. After the destruction of the Aberffraw troops at Du-Rinell, the warrior was reluctant to use the Skool against honorable combatants. At first, he hoped the fighters might just pass them, but instead they swept around to encircle the travelers. Urith's initial confidence dropped when he recognized the guards' shields as the men surrounded them.

"Urith, I thought I knew you," said the man as he pulled back his helmet to show his face and large crooked teeth when he smiled.

"Good to see you, Wilgam," Urith lied. "You remember my nephew." The Clovel Destroyer nodded his head toward Oslaf, who rode up by his side.

"Of course." The man nodded in acknowledgment as he turned back to Urith. "We heard rumors of you coming on this path. You will go with us to Eran."

"No, my direction lies to the north, back to my village." Urith looked cautiously at the other warriors who appeared very interested in the conversation with the giant man now considered their enemy. Yet, only two had their hands upon their swords, and none had pulled their spears. Urith glanced at Oslaf and Mivraa, who were watching him, wondering what he might do. He smiled with his death grin, and he saw a couple of warriors move their hands to their swords. They knew well his reputation and temper.

"I'm afraid not," Wilgam pulled himself upright in the saddle trying to look taller. He hesitated slightly. "The king has ordered your arrest if you returned to Esterblud."

"And if I don't want to come along to see Penhda, what will you do?" Urith growled. He knew the leader in front of him was of the Gramcle tribe and personally loyal to Penhda. He wanted to see if news of the battle had been received yet.

"Then, we will fight, and some of us will die. In the end, you will be executed as *wafaoil* without a king's pardon. However, we will follow our overlord's command," said Wilgam holding his breath, unsure of what Urith might do.

Suddenly, the giant Esterblud beamed a broad grin on his face. "Then we shall go to see the king." Urith turned his ossane and began moving past the surprised Wilgam. Mivraa and Oslaf glanced at each other before turning their mounts to follow. Henther leaned over to Fedelm, watching Urith gallop away.

"Does he always do the opposite of what you expect?" whispered the woman.

"Most times," Fedelm replied softly, her face remaining serious. "Especially when he has a large audience. I wonder what he's leading us into?"

Wilgam signaled to his men and quickly got up with Urith while the rest of the fighters trailed behind the group. Most of the warriors were focused on the women they were following, with a few sending crude catcalls at the women. This continued until Wilgam gave his men a glare and there was silence but for the rhythmic sound of cloven hoofs on the road. Wilgam told Urith of the king's travel to the south with his warriors. The man seemed eager to tell Urith about the changes within the kingdom since he and Oslaf left on the mission to Ynyover. As they exchanged pleasantries, Urith proudly told the man that his nephew had completed his *sakreta* against underworld monsters and saved a village in Vulthnal. Wilgam looked back at Oslaf, congratulating the warrior, visibly impressed. Urith also noted the man was looking covertly at Fedelm. The looks bothered him, but he dismissed such thoughts as unworthy a fighter.

Continuing on the road as it rose to the top of the bluffs which overlooked the city of Eran and the red fortress that protected the city, much of the conversation had stopped as weariness from their long trip creeped over the group of usurpers. The group crossed the top of the bluffs, and the tall stone spires of the fortress came immediately into view. Getting closer, the barrel-shaped bastions on either side of the gray walls of stone came into view. On the far side, near the coastline, they could see parts of the large city and some of the harbor leading out to the Maflow Sea. They continued along the road which twisted to follow the side of the heavy fortress walls. As Oslaf recalled how the road would lead down to the front of the cliff which ran to the red sand beach, he noticed how his uncle kept talking to the guards around him. Following the path that would lead them to the front of the large gatehouse which overlooked the city and the harbor, it appeared Urith kept diverting the warrior's attention as he pointed out obscure places on their ride. It was something their usually silent friend would never do. Oslaf also noticed the leader of the guard continued to stare at Mivraa, distracted by her familiar looks.

Henther face suddenly brightened and the young woman moved up close to Oslaf and Wilgam. She suddenly took up for Urith as she began asking various questions about the city and the fortress. Urith smiled to himself at her natural ability to pull information with her quick smile and smooth manner. He knew it came from seasons of living by her wits and good looks. It was something he knew that was not easy as a female in this world dominated by warriors. As Henther traveled with them, he had grown impressed because she reminded him of his dead wife, tough, resourceful, with a great tenderness buried deep.

Oslaf grew weary of the attention Henther gave the guards around them as the travelers finally reached the front of the stronghold. The sun reached its zenith when they passed the turn before the massive gates. Oslaf quietly asked Urith what the plan was, but the giant shook his head, turning back to Wilgam.

"So, it appears you might need our help" commented Urith aloud.

"What are you talking about," the leader looked at him suspiciously. "You know that you will be held here until the king returns."

"I don't think you understand," said the giant man as he and Wilgam got off their mounts. "We may know more than you realize. For example, you and your men keep your attention on the lovely women who ride with us. You have failed to notice the sea."

Wilgam turned, and the expression on his face told the others to follow his gaze over the Maflow Sea as well. On the horizon, the group could see the dark forms of many ships nearing the harbor. It was evident that the war between Esterblud and Cahmais had come to Eran. The shouts above them indicated the fortress now saw the danger coming.

"Come with me," said Urith limped close to Wilgam, putting his arm around the man's shoulders as he directed the surprised warrior toward the fortress. "You will need to gather the elders. A plan will be required to stop the invasion that is coming, and I'm betting that Eran is short of warriors since King Penhda went south." Wilgam nodded his agreement with Urith's statement as the realization an invasion dawned on him. His comrades looked at each other wondering what just happened as they followed the two warriors toward the entrance to the fortress. The chaos of war now reached the Esterblud's capital.

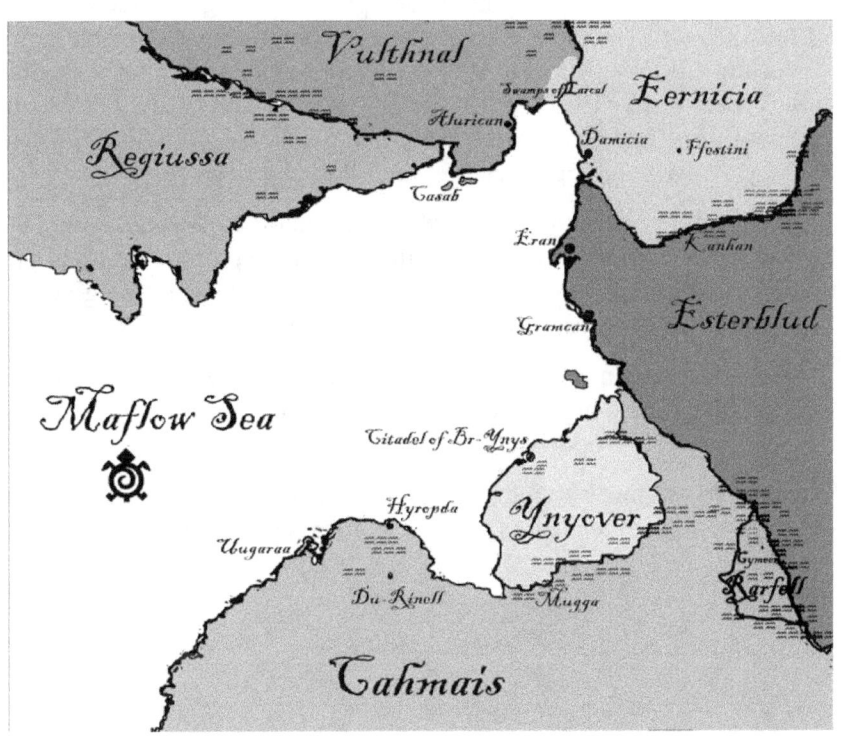

About the Author

Gordon Brewer is the pseudonym for a professional geek, history buff, and full-time dad who took up a challenge from his son to finish his first novel and enter the world of writing. Raised on a farm in Kansas, the author spent nearly five years in the US Navy traveling to 12 different countries during this time. After his discharge, he received his BS degree with majors in History and Political Science.

Over the next twenty years, Gordon focused on the business and IT world. His experiences left him with a need to explore wide-ranging interests in multiple genres, each with historical consideration given to the characters and settings.

Residing in Tennessee, he often uses his family and friends as unfortunate guinea pigs, where they listen to his tales, no matter how poorly conceived they may be.

You can find out more about the author and upcoming books, along with his other works at www.gordonbrewer.com.